THE REALMGATE WARS
WARBEAST

THE REALMGATE WARS

WARBEAST

GAV THORPE

BLACK LIBRARY

A BLACK LIBRARY PUBLICATION

Warbeast first published in 2016.
This edition published in Great Britain in 2017 by
Black Library,
Games Workshop Ltd.,
Willow Road,
Nottingham,
NG7 2WS, UK.

10 9 8 7 6 5 4 3 2 1

Produced by Games Workshop in Nottingham.
Cover illustrations by Peng Bo and Alexandre Chaudret.

A CIP record for this book is available from the British Library.

ISBN 13: 978 1 78496 499 3

See Black Library on the internet at

blacklibrary.com

Find out more about Games Workshop
and the world of Warhammer 40,000 at

games-workshop.com

Printed and bound by CPI Group (UK) Ltd, Croydon, CR0 4YY

From the maelstrom of a sundered world, the
Eight Realms were born. The formless and the divine
exploded into life.

Strange, new worlds appeared in the firmament, each one
gilded with spirits, gods and men. Noblest of the gods was
Sigmar. For years beyond reckoning he illuminated the realms,
wreathed in light and majesty as he carved out his reign. His
strength was the power of thunder. His wisdom was infinite.
Mortal and immortal alike kneeled before his lofty throne.
Great empires rose and, for a while, treachery was banished.
Sigmar claimed the land and sky as his own and ruled over a
glorious age of myth.

But cruelty is tenacious. As had been foreseen, the great
alliance of gods and men tore itself apart. Myth and legend
crumbled into Chaos. Darkness flooded the realms. Torture,
slavery and fear replaced the glory that came before. Sigmar
turned his back on the mortal kingdoms, disgusted by their
fate. He fixed his gaze instead on the remains of the world he
had lost long ago, brooding over its charred core, searching
endlessly for a sign of hope. And then, in the dark heat of
his rage, he caught a glimpse of something magnificent. He
pictured a weapon born of the heavens. A beacon powerful
enough to pierce the endless night. An army hewn from
everything he had lost.

Sigmar set his artisans to work and for long ages they toiled,
striving to harness the power of the stars. As Sigmar's great
work neared completion, he turned back to the realms and saw
that the dominion of Chaos was almost complete. The hour
for vengeance had come. Finally, with lightning blazing across
his brow, he stepped forth to unleash his creations.

The Age of Sigmar had begun.

CHAPTER ONE

A fresh flurry of snow swept across the mountainside, layering onto thick drifts that already half concealed remnants of ancient walls and towers toppled in a distant age. The rusted and fused remains of great gears jutted from the ice, staining the snow the colour of dried blood. The immense barbican that had once housed them was little more than wind-worn boulders scattered across the area. Of the ramparts, buttresses and ravelins that had supported the gatehouse little remained – humps and ridges beneath the snow delineated by heaps and lines of unnaturally regular rocks.

The wind caused tent sides to crack and guy ropes to sing as it keened over an encampment within the comparative shelter of the centuries-old ruins. In the lee of broken stairwells and part-tumbled walls, the nomads huddled close to their fires, wrapped tight in pelts of many different colours and patterns – black bear, the white and grey stripes of snow tigers, exotic carmine and mauve spots against white from slain lyregryphs.

On small spits over glowing charcoal they cooked their meat, slowly turning the skewered flesh while dripping fat caused the embers to sputter and hiss. Cauldrons bubbled over flames, the water within bobbing with pieces of gristle and bone through a greasy slick.

Tonight's was a special feast, despite the weather, for the hunting had been good. Thick haunches and splayed ribs would grace the trenchers of the chief and her favourites, with fresh marrow and small cakes thick with congealed blood, while those less in regard licked their lips in anticipation of liver, shins, feet and fingers.

The cannibals bickered over the other spoils, fighting over metal buckles, tin cups, teeth pulled from the skulls – used as necklaces and for beads in braided hair and beards – while clothes, weapons, boots, jewellery and armour were stacked neatly in piles beneath awnings, awaiting the chieftain, who would award them to those that had fought the best or pleased her in other ways.

A few captives were still alive, roped together to an immense stake outside the large tent of the clan's leader. Naked, they huddled together for what warmth they could find, terrified and numb with shock. There were eight of them, three women and five men, and each bore cuts and bruises from the battle, and rope burns from their chafing bonds at ankle and wrist.

The wind picked up, starting to pull at the tent ropes, flattening the flames of the more exposed fires, throwing sparks and ash into the air. The sky darkened and the arguing and laughter petered out. The Bonekeepers glanced at the heavens and to the tent of their leader, wary of the sudden change. There was good reason why no tribe remained in one place for long, for the mountains of Ursungorod were of ill-temper, always prone to the sudden spasms and constant peregrinations that had laid low the fortress currently sheltering the kin-eaters.

The prisoners started wailing, lifting shrill voices in lament while blue lightning crackled across the unnatural storm gathering above. The children who had been tormenting them fled for the shelter of the tents and the protection of the adults, who in turn rose from the firesides, whispering prayers to *Kronra*, God of the Bloody Feast.

Trailing half-naked suitors, the Gore Maiden emerged from her grand marquee, still clad in red-lacquered leather armour. Hair the colour of raven feathers spilled to her waist from beneath a helm adorned with a crown of bone splinters taken from the body of a goroxen she had slain single-handedly two winters before. She snapped commands, calling for her guards to form around her while others scrambled for spears and shields left close at hand.

The Bonekeeper war party gathered, the strongest at the front, the unblooded behind. Battle and internal politics, as well as long winters of famine, meant none amongst the Bonekeepers lived long enough to become old and infirm.

In a rough half-circle with their chief at its centre, the clan waited. Eight dozen pairs of eyes scoured the gloom, casting their gaze over snow-blanketed stones lit by the flashes of azure above.

A single bolt lanced down, striking the ground no more than a hundred paces in front of the Gore Maiden. All flinched from the brightness and blinked furiously to rid themselves of the after-shadow. When their eyes cleared they saw a single figure, a cerulean statue, standing where the lightning had struck.

It stood half again as tall as the largest warrior of the Bonekeepers, and was clad entirely in gleaming plates in representation of a muscled warrior. A huge guard curved across its left shoulder, the roundel where it met the sculpted breastplate moulded with a sapphire in the design of an upraised hammer that blazed two bolts of lightning from its head. A helm with a snarling visage hid the face beneath a spiked halo-like arc of gold. In the right hand a sword gleamed with moonlight brightness, angular runic shapes lit by their own power along its length. The left held a hammer, its head blazoned with the mark of a twin-tailed comet. From the figure's shoulders hung a slatted cloak, each ribbon tipped by a weight in the shape of a warhammer.

For ten heartbeats nothing stirred save for the snow devils whipped up by the wind. A few of the tribespeople edged forwards, looking to each other for reassurance, grunting in their guttural tongue.

The eyes of the helm blazed into life, filling with a scarlet glow. Magical energy coruscated across the figure's body, crawling up the arms and into the weapons, causing them to shine even brighter with white light. The statue broke into a run, blade and hammer head leaving a trail of silver sparks in its wake.

In a voice edged with a boom of thunder in the skies, the lord of metal let forth a mighty shout. The volume alone was enough to shake all but the hardiest of constitutions, but what stunned the Bonekeepers was that the words were in their own tongue, albeit an ancient dialect.

'The Bear-clad hath returned. The Hard Winter shall end and justice be restored!'

'The storm comes.'

So spoke the sagesayer Radomira. The skies above the great mountains of Ursungorod filled with sinister clouds that flickered with green lightning. Withered hands with nails painted blood-red clutched the twisted wood of her staff, knuckles white with tension. Beneath a hood of coarse black wool, she turned her face up to stare at her krul, the warrior-king of the Ursungoran clans. There were tears in her eyes. 'The omens have not changed. You shall not see the end of it.'

'Ratkin scum,' replied Arka, known as the Bear-clad for the thick black pelt he wore across his immense shoulders. A word came to him, passed down through the many generations that had fought against the plague-rats of the deep. A cursed word that came from the Times Before. 'Pestilentzi.'

He stood nearly a head taller than the men and women of his stratzari, the best warriors from more than two dozen clans. Many had once been clan leaders themselves, of the kort, zakar, hussta, zagir, uztek, kimmeri, ussra, and many others. For this he was also called the Uniter, and the Bear of Hard Winters for other feats, and several other titles across the peaks and valleys of Ursungorod.

The elite of Arka's army waited on the gatehouse, six hundred in number, their armour a mixture of hardened leather and bronze rings, supplemented with bands or roundels of steel for those fortunate enough to have inherited such protection from their forefathers. There were styles from across the mountains – the high-peaked helms and gilded aventails of the valley clans, rounded basinets and dog-faced visors common amongst the scythic clans that had once dominated the caverns of inner Ursungorod, and skullcaps flamboyantly decorated with tassels, crests and beast-visaged emblems from the summit clans of the upper snows. Flags of red and gold, banners of white and blue, and gonfalons of black fluttered and snapped above them in the strengthening wind.

All were set with grim faces turned towards the darkness approaching from the mountain depths – the zienesta abisal, the Shadowgulf. While the coming ratkin horde spread out from scores of tunnels and caves, the air above them seethed with corrupted power, churning and frothing like a maelstrom.

The high walls to either side thronged with three thousand of Arka's spear- and axe-wielding warriors, for the most part guarded against harm by nothing more than layers of leather and wool, and wooden oval shields painted with the rune of their new overlord.

The outer wall of Kurzengor, the settlement itself but a small fragment of the immense city built above and dug below Ursungorod, stood five times the height of a man, and thick enough for chambers within. But it was broken in places, shattered by the constant upheavals that wracked the mountain range, the breaches filled as best as possible with dull brown bricks, mortared stones and thick planks.

It was not ideal, but it was the best place to meet the squealing, shrieking mass of half-man rat-things that boiled up from the tunnels below. The wall itself was nothing, it was the men and women who held it that would decide the course of the battle.

Arka held up his axe, its long haft in one hand, the crescent moon blade glittering in the light of the accursed storm. He lifted his voice above the growing rumble.

'This was the weapon of my mother. She took it from the fist of my father when he fell at Nijholli, already bathed many times in the blood of their enemies. Scores of foes – human, godstainted and ratkin – fell beneath it from my mother's hand. She lived for the battle, but the cowardly vile-rats did not give her the peace of a war-death. Their corruption, their filth, spewed forth on noxious clouds, and plague heralded their attacks. In her bed, choking on lung-rot, every gasping breath an agony, that is how she died.'

He paused, eyes closed as the memory of that sight sank its

claws into his throat, stifling his words. Taking a deep breath, Arka continued.

'Before her final moments, I, a child of eight winters and seven summers, took this axe from her. I bid her farewell, and swore that I would see every one of the rat-filth slain. Every day since, I have cleaved to that oath. Long I have waged that war, and now they are goaded into showing themselves in the full light of day. Today shall live long in the legends of our people.'

Arka spoke the words with passion, but as he looked down at Radomira, who had nurtured him after his mother's death, he shared her sadness – though he could not show it.

'The omens do not give us hopes.' Her words appeared in his thoughts, not passing her lips. 'On the day you were born, the Ursungorod shook and the earth cracked beneath the Skagoldt Ridge to throw up the fires of the deeps. I saw a storm that day, and in its depths comes your ending.'

'You knew as much when you took me as your son,' Arka replied without speech, as he had been able to do with Radomira since that day she appeared at the house of his dead mother and bid him to leave with her. 'You also spoke of great things that will happen this day. Our people will be saved, you said. If that needs my death, so be it.'

'I did not say our people would be saved,' she chided. 'You must pay attention to detail, I have told you before. I said from the events of this day our lands will be freed.'

'It is the same thing,' grumbled Arka.

Accelerating, Arkas gloried in the touch of the frozen ground beneath his feet. The air was crisp and clean in his nostrils, at once so familiar and yet an almost forgotten memory. It instantly brought to mind childhood hunts and stalking the other youths of the Greypelt clan.

Darker recollections encroached, fuelling his long stride. Much had changed, in the lands as well as in his form and knowledge, but still his heart burned with the same furious thirst for vengeance. Sigmar the mighty God-King had furnished him with the means to finally fulfil that oath to his dying mother, gifting him with an immortal reforged body and weapons of celestial power. He was Greypelt no more. His clan loyalties were insignificant compared to the brotherhood ties of a Strike Chamber. All of the old titles were nothing compared to the epithet he had earned from Sigmar himself – Arkas Warbeast.

The kin-eaters were foolishly brave, not knowing the full nature of the warrior that attacked. They saw a solitary figure and perhaps thought to overwhelm him with the first rush of their counter-attack. He pounded up the slope, vaulting toppled stones and bounding across crevasses that had once been tower chambers. Arrows from short bows and stones from slings clattered and cracked harmlessly from his plated body.

'The Lord Sigmar sends this message to all that nestle in the bosom of the Dark Gods,' Arkas roared, his voice carrying like the wind of a storm.

He swept out the trails of his cloak and a flurry of hammer-shaped bolts flew across the gap, slashing golden wounds through the cannibalistic Chaos worshippers. A dozen strides later, he met the first of the kin-eaters' warriors. Arkas' sword flicked out, trailing lightning bolts, its tip parting the depraved barbarian from gut to chin. His hammer smashed the heads from two others. Pig iron blades and studded cudgels clattered ineffectually from his silvered armour.

It was more than the earth underfoot and the air in his lungs – the subtle nature of the Realm of Ghur stirred within him, calling him back to his roots, unleashing the war-beast that had always been part of him. When he had been known as the Bear-clad it had been something of a madness, coming upon him in the heat of combat. As the bloodfever rose he understood now that something more primal was aroused – something in the fabric of the mountains of Ursungorod that ignited inside him.

The leading edge of the storm was no more than a bowshot from the walls. Putridity, foul and yet sweet, carried on the strengthening wind. The rankness of the vile-rats came before them, accompanied by the chittering and squealing of warriors with matted fur and ragged robes.

'There are fewer of them than I expected,' Arka joked. The pestilentzi numbered at least five times that of his host. But in truth he did not think it too many; his warriors were a match for that number, and the walls, though broken, gave them even more advantage. He started to think that perhaps Radomira's dire prophecy was wrong. It was not unknown for her to misinterpret the signs.

A shout from the left brought his attention to the upper end of the valley. There were shapes moving through the rocks of the gorge, the sickly light of the storm glinting from rusted armour and weapons. Men with unkempt locks and filth-crusted beards skulked through broken boulders and stunted trees. Their womenfolk came with them, their hair teased out into untidy braids slicked with human fat.

'The ghoul tribes,' sneered one of Arka's companions, a wiry uzteki called Timur. The one-eyed warrior spat on the stones. 'They are already cursed by the foul powers, and now they have made an alliance with the ratkin.'

'No matter,' Arka replied, though the confidence he had felt

moments earlier was starting to ebb. 'They are hardly better fighters than the scab-rats from below.'

He eyed the storm, which washed over the grand fortifications, bringing with it choking fumes. Men and women on the battered ramparts coughed and retched as foul-tasting smog obscured everything.

'Archers!' Arka bellowed, knowing that the pestilentzi would use the cover of the cloud to advance quickly. He had marked their approach carefully and had expected such a ruse – this was not the first time the ratkin had unleashed the foetid breath of the Horned One. 'Loose to one hundred paces!'

Fifteen hundred bows were lifted and fifteen hundred dark shafts disappeared into the gloom. Eyes stinging, Arka could not mark their flight beyond fifty paces, but the fog could not wholly muffle the shrieks and squeaks of pain a few moments later. The archers reloaded and sent another volley, more ragged than the first, and another.

'Fifty paces!' Arka cried, seeing shadows emerging from the greenish mist. Overhead, the thunder cracked, shaking the ancient city wall to its foundations. Jade lightning crackled down, striking at several points along the rampart, each blast cutting down half a dozen warriors. Another bolt struck just ten paces away, blackening Aslanbek in his cracked armour, molten droplets of bronze spattering those nearby.

'Clear the storm,' Arka snarled at Radomira.

The sagesayer withdrew, her cabal of magicweavers gathering about her, brandishing a variety of rods, staves and wands, the jingle of their amulets and clatter of bone talismans a distraction for a moment.

The ratkin did not come for the gate, but threw the weight of their numbers towards a repaired breach about seventy-five paces to the left of it, where they clearly intended to scale the wall and meet up with the ghoul tribes coming from further along the slope. They brought no ladders or grapples, but simply climbed the wall with thin, clawed fingers, finding easy purchase in the pitted surface of stones laid countless decades before.

The first crash of metal on metal rang out along the rampart. Another immense roll of thunder caused Arka to glance up. It seemed that the tempest was changing, crackles of blue splitting the green, cerulean clouds bubbling through from the midst of the green sky. He did not know what Radomira was doing, but it seemed to be working. The fog that swathed the wall was swirling away in many places, revealing the skittering horde of ratkin approaching below.

Without any need for a command, a storm of javelins and throwing axes descended into the onrushing mass, sending the front-runners tumbling to the bloodied ground to be trodden down by the ratkin that followed.

The din of battle increased, the shouts of both sides and the clash of weapons echoing back from the inner wall some four hundred paces behind Arka. Checking to the left and right, he was reassured to see that his warriors were holding. Axes, swords and spears were relentless in their deadly welcome. Every ratman that made the rampart was met by two or three speartips or blades.

'They use their numbers poorly,' remarked Marta. She pointed with her tulwar, moving the tip along the wall to the right. 'They should draw us out along the entire length, not throw themselves at one place where their mass counts for nothing.'

'Do not expect sound strategy from verminous filth,' replied Ljubo. 'They do not count losses like warriors.'

This last comment stuck in Arka's thoughts. The pestilentzi truly did not care how many died. He had seen twenty perish just to drag down one of his warriors. He stepped up to the wall and looked out, turning his gaze to the left.

The ratmen thrown at the walls were spindly, ragged creatures with bubo-pocked fur, armed with shards of stone, wooden clubs and crude daggers of rusted metal. A terrible choice for a first assault. What was needed was a spearhead of armoured, experienced warriors to create an opening for the masses to later exploit.

There were certainly such fighters in the pestilentzi ranks. He could see them advancing behind the slavish horde, decked in blackened armour, banners and tri-barred icons carried above their more orderly regiments. And then there were the serga-hulla – plague-frenzied verminkind that wore thick robes and shrieked disturbing chants. They hurled themselves fearlessly at their foes. Either would make better siege breakers than the scum being tossed up against the walls.

Tossed up against the walls...

He leaned out further to look down at the ground at the base of the great bastion. Already hundreds of dead ratmen were piling up.

'They are using the bodies of the dead for ramps!' he cried out. 'Fetch oil and brands, we must turn them into pyres!'

While this order was passed along the wall, a new wave of pestilentzi reached the defences, thrusting through the milling crowds of slaves. They were bigger, darker furred, with swords, halberds and shields. Arrows and sling bullets met the next assault but made little injury to the numbers of the foe.

Arka was about to order part of his guard to move down to the wall to form a mobile reserve when he felt a shift in the wind. He spluttered and others around him coughed and retched as a noisome reek blew along the wall.

'What sorcerous...' The words drifted away when Arka spied the answer to his question.

The ranks of the elite vermin were parting, the filthy ratkin throwing themselves to their knees and stomachs in obeisance. Through the gap advanced a monstrous figure, more terrifying even than the bekevic that haunted the mountain meres and could swallow a warrior whole.

A frightened muttering broke out through the stratzari. Warriors who had faced battle dozens of times whispered curses and flexed sweating palms on their weapons. Arka felt his mouth dry as he watched the approach of the creature.

CHAPTER TWO

Incensed, driven along the teetering line of insanity between abject terror and suicidal desperation, the kin-eaters tried to drag down the Stormcast Eternal. Crudely forged blades shattered on his armour, and broken fingernails caked in blood scrabbled at his plate. He bulled his way through, crushing bodies underfoot and slamming his foes aside with sweeps of his arms.

Arkas had once been a man of flesh and blood. Now he was something far greater, fashioned by the spirit of Sigmar and armed by the great duardin god Grungni. Reborn, reforged, remade in an ideal – hope and nobility, courage unsurpassed, strength tempered by humility.

But here, now, on the slopes of Mount Vazdir, where he had seen his people fall to the filth of the Pestilens skaven, he was simply death incarnate. His runeblade and hammer had been created in the great foundries of the smith-god, made from purest sigmarite, but in his mind he bore an old crescent-headed axe given to him by his mother. In spirit if not in any physical sense, the weapon lived on.

'Know this, servants of darkness! Your end has come! The Light of Sigmar falls upon Ursungorod and by his beacon shall the warriors of the storm be guided to his foes.'

Enemy blades shattered at the touch of his sword, leather armour and crude mail no guard against the weight of his lightning-wreathed hammer. In the Gladitorium of Sigmaron, Arka Bear-clad had finished his transition to Arkas Warbeast, Stormcast Eternal, herald of Sigmar's wrath. It was not until now that he fully appreciated the changes wrought upon him by his Reforging. The kin-eaters fell to his sword and hammer like wheat before the reaper, leaving a dismembered trail in his wake as he cut and smashed his way towards their leader.

Not only in prowess had he been altered. The magical energy of the Mortal Realms, the essence of Ghur that sustained the Realm of Beasts, flowed around him, suffusing the landscape. He saw it escape the bodies of his foes as they fell, returning to the great flow of the wild and untamed world. He felt it in his body too, as he had once felt the enlightening power of Azyr open his mind to the full truth of the universe.

Arkas had desired revenge, but the sensation of justice fulfilled as he cleaved apart another handful of foes was unlike any feeling he had encountered. It was a redemptive force, payment for the agony of his Reforging, the reward for enduring endless trials and hardships to become a Storm-cast Eternal.

He realised less than a score of heartbeats had passed since he had been hurled down to Ursungorod by the power of Sigmar, yet three dozen enemies already lay dead behind him. The kin-eaters' mistress looked on with an expression of joy, not fear, and he stared into her dark eyes and saw only the madness of Chaos. In her the spirit of Khorne the Blood God was strong. Arkas could smell the taint on her as strongly as the metallic scent of blood leaking from his slain foes.

Drawing a wickedly serrated tulwar, the Gore Maiden leapt to counter-attack, hurdling the headless corpse of one of her followers as he fell away from Arkas' swinging blade. She was as fast as his Stormcast companions, the tip of her sword cutting across the curve of a moulded pectoral. The blade appeared to steam with the power of Khorne, leaving a molten welt on the breast of Arkas' armour.

Stunned for a moment, he stepped back, raising his hammer to ward away the next slashing attack. The sigmarite rang cleanly at the impact of the Gore Maiden's tulwar, sparks of power erupting from its head. Another blow sped towards his arm and Arkas turned quickly, allowing it to fall just past his shoulder.

He kicked, his armoured boot connecting with the midriff of the Khornate champion, breaking ribs and throwing her a dozen strides across the snow. She rolled through a flurry of white, coming to her feet with a grimace just in time to block Arkas' descending blade with her own.

'Your bloody master cannot aid you against the righteousness of Sigmar,' Arkas spat, knocking aside the Gore Maiden's weapon with the haft of his hammer.

The Stormcast Eternal felt blows clanging against his back and helm, but all of his attention was directed on the Gore Maiden. He pressed his advantage, swinging his hammer towards her head. As she jumped aside, the tip of his blade met her neck, parting flesh and spine without pause.

Seeing their chief decapitated robbed the kin-eaters of their remaining courage. The cannibals fled as he turned, some abandoning their weapons to speed their flight down the mountainside. They dashed left and right, splitting up, too many for Arkas to chase them all down.

The Stormcast Eternal lifted his hammer above his head, pointing to the skies where the Tempest of Sigmar still churned in cerulean glory.

'To me, warriors of Sigmaron! Celestial Vindicators, our moment is upon us! Heed the call of your Lord-Celestant, my Warbeasts!'

There was a little likeness of a rat in the monster's features, but it walked five times the height of the Chaos vermin, its head surrounded by a mane of curling, twisted horns. Its tail, longer than the beast was tall, was like a barbed whip tipped with metallic blades. Overlapping plates of serrated oil-black armour covered a ragged tunic of dun and pink-grey flesh, and a faceted helm of the same unnatural metal protected its skull and cheeks. A thick belt of cracked hide girded its waist and a huge book was bound there by a corroded chain, a smog-like cloud slipping from the fluttering pages.

In taloned hands it gripped a spear, the head splitting into four curved tines that sparked with magical energy. The air thrashed around the monster and the ground blistered under its tread, as if its simple presence offended the earth and sky.

'Verminlord! Daemon of the Horned One!'

Arka heard the gasp and glanced over his shoulder in time to see Radomira collapsing. Blood ran from her eyes and ears, and her attendants looked on helplessly, ashen-faced, quivering with fear.

The verminlord thrust its spear towards the ramparts and a bolt of green energy struck the stones, sending up jagged chunks and charred corpses. The ratkin flowed forwards, their screeches deafening. Another bolt of magic slashed through the defenders to

Arka's left, turning armour to rusted flakes and the flesh within to rotten meat.

Arka saw again the face of his mother, withered before its time, claw-like hands grasping at the sweat-soaked bedding. Coughing wracked her body. In the horror of that moment, Arka knew that the creature stalking towards the gates was the same that had unleashed the pestilence on Ursungorod and ripped his mother's life away.

He levelled his axe at the creature in silent challenge. It looked up at him with glowing green eyes and bared sharp fangs in what might have been a smile.

A rolling blast of thunder drew Arka's gaze up for a moment. Blue lightning crawled across the bottom of the storm clouds, like nothing he had seen before. The stones beneath his booted feet shivered as the verminlord unleashed a blast of power at the gates, turning wood to mouldering splinters.

The lightning lanced down, hitting Arka's upraised axe, earthing through his arm and down his spine.

He thought himself dead in that instant, but the feeling of energy that ran through him grew rather than weakening. He felt himself lifted, ascending towards the heavens. His body dissolved into energy, a bolt of power erupting upwards.

With a last conscious thought, he saw the ratkin swarming over the walls of Kurzengor and knew he had failed his people.

From the head of Arkas' hammer, a beam of blue light leapt up to the skies, its signal carrying beyond the Mortal Realms to Sigmaron. An instant later, a crackle of storm energy lanced down. The two crashed together and a tempest of lightning bolts flared, raining down around the Stormcast. Where each blast touched the ground, the snow melted and the earth beneath charred. Each blinding flash left behind another giant warrior clad in turquoise armour, until a company of the greatest warriors stood before him.

Two lightning strikes flanked Arkas to the left and right, each just a few paces from him. On his left appeared a warrior bearing aloft a golden standard in the shape of crossed hammers, wreathed in parchments adorned with the blessings of Sigmar in Azyrite script.

'Dolmetis, my Knight-Vexillor, raise the standard and proclaim these lands the domains of Sigmar, God-King!'

On the right his Knight-Heraldor materialised, bearing a long clarion from which hung a pennant in the colours of Arkas' Exemplar Chamber.

'Doridun, sound forth the challenge so that all will know that Sigmar's rule has returned to Ursungorod!'

The Knight-Heraldor lifted the instrument and let forth a single peal, its note matched by a thunderous crash from the heavens that echoed across the mountain valley. As the last reverberations died away, Dolmetis approached his Lord-Celestant, casting glances at the mutilated remains of the kin-eaters that lay scattered across the blood-stained snow.

'I thought we were to attack as a chamber, Lord Arkas?'

The Lord-Celestant laughed and pointed to the fleeing Chaos war party.

'I left some for you! Doridun, signal the pursuit. Leave none alive!'

CHAPTER THREE

'Such a sight to stir the blood,' said Theuderis Silverhand, speaking as much to himself as to his steed. He patted the scaled neck of his dracoth, Tyrathrax.

The sight to which he referred was a display of unparalleled martial glory. Retinue after retinue of the Silverhands Warrior Chamber marched forth from the realmgate. The portal had been opened on the Plateau of Omens in the Celestial Realm, and led to the Capricious Wilds, an untamed region within the Realm of Beasts. In a few strides, Sigmar's army had crossed the cosmic gulf. The portal itself was formed of two jutting pilasters of gleaming rock, their surfaces etched with runic devices each as tall as a man. They rose from opposite sides of a canyon, which was scored like an axe wound across the mountains. Arcs of energy blazed between them and flared into the dark sky, lighting the white armour of Theuderis' host.

They issued forth in ordered ranks, every precise step crashing against the grey mountain stone. Brotherhood after brotherhood they came, bearing blades and bows and axes charged with Azyric energy that filled the air with a cerulean light.

Flights of Knights-Azyros raced into the glowering sky, each warrior carried on lightning wings and bearing with them lanterns that shone with the light of Sigmar's ire. Behind them rose Knights-Venator and soaring Prosecutors, their celestial arrows and javelins like sparks against the stormhead, a flock of star-eagles swirling around them in the mystical vortices and thermals of the pulsing realmgate.

Drilled beyond mortal discipline, the Stormcast Eternals of the Silverhands Chamber moved like the pieces of an intricate, perfect machine. Ranks and files slid effortlessly together, expanded and reformed to negotiate the broken terrain, rapidly forming a line in echelon across the mouth of the broad defile. The conclaves formed, their arrangement an abstraction of a fortress. Swift, sky-borne Angelos Conclaves acted as the outer defences, the insurmountable warriors of the Paladin Conclaves forming a living barbican behind them. This 'gatehouse' was flanked by the walls of the Redeemer Conclaves, a solid bulwark of gleaming hammers and azure shields. Theuderis Silverhand and his sub-commanders kept company with the Justicar Conclaves as a central keep from which reserves could pour forth to exploit any weakness or counter any enemy advantage.

The Lord-Celestant did not need to utter a single command. The entire manoeuvre had been set in motion before he had led the vanguard though the gate. Each Stormcast Eternal knew his exact place, the Strike Chamber a single entity far more than it was a collection of individual warriors.

When the several hundred warriors were assembled, Theuderis raised a hand and the army advanced as one, sweeping onto the barren ground of the Capricious Wilds in an unbroken line, while Sigmar's heralds swooped above.

From just below the iron-grey clouds, Theuderic had a magnificent view of his knights' final charge. His hippadon, Sasyran, dipped a wing at his spoken command, plunging them back towards the battle garlanded by streamers of the reptilian beast's steaming breath. On silvery styllions the knights of the Glittering Breaches thundered into the serpent-bannered ranks of the alter-folk. Detonations marked the impacts of a thousand thunderlances, each flaming spark tearing apart a follower of the Fallen Gods. The styllions, flesh and bone magically bonded with the finest engines of the auromancers, crashed through the alter-folk, crushing them beneath flailing hooves and tearing at them with iron-sheathed fangs.

A battery of falconet heavy gonnes let fly another barrage, incendiary ammunition destroying a motley band of vulpus riders trying to outflank the jezzailers holding the right. Theuderic's personal grenadiers supported the charge of the knights, their magically wrought explosives detonating with purple-and-white fire amongst the barbarian foe.

The hippadon exhaled orange flame as king and mount fell upon the fleeing remnants of the enemy chieftain's entourage. Skin blistered and fur garb blazed while Theuderic struck left and right with his slender blade.

The enemy were broken, the last of their strength desperately assembled, and now purged on the fields of the Iron Dunes. Theuderic lifted a fist and from his armoured gauntlet a blaze of white pierced the spring air, signalling the general pursuit.

No more than half a mile from the realmgate stood a citadel raised from the dark rock itself, not a single seam or join on its forbidding surface. The blazon of Sigmar flew from a dozen poles along the walls. It was not large – barely the size of a tower of Castle Lyonaster of old – but it was far more potent than size alone would suggest. At the approach of the Knights Excelsior Strike Chamber, a horn sounded three notes from the castle and bronze gates opened to release a column of figures in white plate.

Theuderis urged Tyrathrax on and the dracoth broke into a run, claws striking sparks from the exposed rock, heading towards Lord-Castellant Neros Stormfather, who led the garrison force. Coming closer, the Lord-Celestant saw damage on the armour of the other Stormcast Eternals. He brandished his blade in salute to the efforts of Sigmar's warriors.

'Well met, Lord Stormfather,' he called out when Tyrathrax came to a halt beside the Lord-Castellant. 'I see that you have been kept in useful engagement.'

'We have that, Lord Silverhand,' said Neros, clasping his halberd to his chest in a gesture of respect. 'But not for seven days have the degenerates attempted to regain the gate. I do believe they might have learnt the lesson taught by our weapons.'

'Or they bide their time awaiting a moment of laxity,' warned Theuderis.

'They shall wait in vain. The Silverhands are always vigilant.' Neros looked past Theuderis, to where the host was wheeling en masse, heading towards the hills above which the crimson glow of sunrise was creeping. 'I judge from the direction of the march that the Capricious Wilds are not the final objective.'

'No.' Theuderis followed his gaze. 'Securing this realmgate was only the first stage, Neros. I march for the lands of Ursungorod.'

'The Mountains of the Bears – I have heard of them. Home to vile Chaos filth and skaven, and where the lands themselves rebel against the touch of the Dark Powers. No easy task.'

'Sigmar did not elevate us to undertake easy tasks, Neros.'

'He did not, but enough grains of sand can bury even the greatest monument. Another realmgate? It always is.'

'Of course,' Theuderis answered with a nod. 'An important one. Buried beneath a mountain, no less, and surrounded by skaven. When we take the Ursungorod realmgate it will bring us to the Vaults of the Spring Moon, within striking distance of the Lifegate. Others are moving into position for the other great realmgates that lead to the Allpoints. We are the fist of Sigmar God-King, tightening around cursed Archaon. So our immortal lord demands.'

'Blood-hungry hordes above, vile ratmen below. I hope your sword-arm is fresh, my lord. That is a long wound to cleave.'

'We are not alone in the endeavour.' Theuderis leaned forwards and dropped his voice. 'The first piercing blow has already been made. The Warbeasts have been cast directly into central Ursungorod as a breaching force. They will draw the enemy to them for a time and allow us to cross into the mountains without hindrance.'

'The Warbeasts? Lord Arkas? I have heard of them.' Neros looked away, letting his halberds swing down to his side. 'You best hurry.'

'You think they will be overrun before we reach them?' Theuderis was surprised that the Lord-Castellant showed such little faith in his fellow Stormcasts.

'I think they will have torn a bloody path to the realmgate before you can catch up!'

Theuderis sheathed his sword and shook his head. He lifted a hand in farewell to Neros and turned Tyrathrax back towards his army. He signalled for his Knight-Vexillor, Voltaran, who broke from the other members of the command echelon, carrying the lightning strike icon of the chamber. While he waited, Theuderis eyed the mountains that lined the far horizon, stretching like a jagged barrier. Lit by the new dawn, a wall of cloud obscured the mountain peaks, roiling with a life of their own.

'We must be prepared,' he said to Tyrathrax. 'And focused. Nothing shall stop us seizing the realmgate. Nothing.'

Voltaran fell in beside his Lord-Celestant.

'A change of orders, Voltaran.' Theuderis looked again at the distant mountains. 'Double-pace. I want to reach Ursungorod by dawn.'

'As you command, Lord Silverhand.'

By the time the sky was bronzed by the approaching dusk, not a single alter-warrior was left alive in the Glittering Breaches.

Ten times a thousand glowing torches lined the road back to Castle Lyonaster. A thousand banners from a hundred lands and more were lit by their pale light, each borne by a champion of the realm. Behind the colour bearers, the regiments of the Reforged Kingdoms stood in solid ranks, weapons lifted in salute to their lord.

Demigonnes and other great machines of war stood sentinel between the companies of cavalry and infantry, the weaponcasters and forge wizards who created them standing proudly with the crews. Overhead, flights of pteragryphs and hippadons seeded the skies with explosions and ribbons of colour from censers and maces empowered by the light of Chamon.

Theuderic dismounted before the gate of Castle Lyonaster, having ridden the length of the triumph to acknowledge his followers. Once it had been a simple keep and curtain wall, erected by Theuderic's ancestors to hold against the hordes of the alter-folk. Like other castles across the Glittering Breaches, it had become a focal point of the resistance against the demented armies from the Iron Wastes. Generation after generation, supplied by springs and mines, walled orchards and fields, Lyonaster weathered every assault and siege laid upon it by the likes of Turkhar Nex's draconic hosts, the Silvered Horde and the half-dead shambling legions of Ghorgorondoth the Tumourfiend.

To call it a gate was not wholly accurate. It was nothing less than an outer citadel, made of five towers in pentagon formation, each capable of housing a company of five hundred soldiers. Passing into the central courtyard, Theuderic crossed the gilded sigil carved into the flagstones, so large it took him five paces to cross it. He felt the shimmer of Chamonic energy flicker through his armour as he passed into the Auric Shield, the true strength of Castle Lyonaster.

Seven forefathers, seven Dukes of the Breaches, had held court here, but for Theuderic it had not been enough. He had seen the toll it had taken on friends and family, a lifetime lived close to walls, ever fearfully watching the horizon. Children grew up with a haunted look and parents quelled any adventurous spirit and curiosity with grim tales of the savages and nightmare armies that lay just a few days' march away.

On ascending to the Marble Throne, Theuderic had declared it not enough to hold their lands against invasion. Lyonaster had to expand if it was going to thrive. The first marcher forts had been built the following year. Neighbouring dukes sent emissaries, complaining of encroachment into their lands – lands that were for the most part overrun with rogues, monsters and wild thaumic automatons from the Great Unleashing, but their lands all the same. Rather than argue with these messengers, Theuderic sent them back to their masters and mistresses with gifts of metal from the mines, of plans and engineering secrets that had been kept in the vaults of Lyonaster since its first founding. Artificers and auromancers were escorted at great expense to the other keeps, to advise on how to improve their defences, taking with them designs for demigonnes and enchantments for flameswords and other wonders.

The others started to call Theuderic 'Forge-lord', delighting in the double-meaning of the title. When the terrible wrath-drake Ankalaonos descended upon the realm of Princess Swanachild, Theuderic himself rode out with his knights and jezzailers to bring down the bronze-scaled beast. By example he led the other rulers, always ready to defend their lands, never requiring any oath in return but receiving promises of fealty nevertheless.

Lyonaster grew along with the dominions of its lord, and its population swelled along with its defences, to the point that it now rivalled the old cities of Tyren and Colbertine, before they had been swallowed by the expansion of the Iron Wastes.

Theuderic reached a flight of steps and ascended them two at a time. Gaining the rampart, his arch-warden Carloman awaited him. Decked in robes of red threaded with gold, platinum and steel, the auromancer shimmered as he bowed, his steel skullcap reflecting the ruddy twilight. Straightening, Carloman smiled, his expression twisting the burns and scars of many an alchemical mishap.

'Magnificent, my king, simply magnificent,' said Carloman. His voice was a staccato whisper, which some took for constant agitation but was actually the result of damage to his vocal cords from inhaling the wrong sort of fumes during an experiment. 'A wondrous day to live for.'

'And credit all to you and your brethren, Carloman. If not for your skills, the strength of Lyonaster would have been outmatched by the fury and number of our enemies.'

A walkway of shining steel marked with many runes linked the towers, cunningly wrought so that its outer fence created an overhang from which jezzailers could pour bullets down onto *a foe through murder holes. The metal rang to the tread of the king, almost drowning out Carloman's next words.*

'A weapon needs be wielded, my king,' he said humbly, bowing once more and allowing his liege to move on alone to greet the next group.

Standing back from the battlement, his wife Ermenberga and their two daughters waited with broad smiles. Theuderic kissed Ermenberga on the cheek and knelt to carefully embrace his children, wary of the unyielding nature of the plate that covered almost every part of him. He stood, laying a hand on the head of each child.

'It is done!' declared his wife, her smile bright in the gleam of his magic armour. 'The war is over!'

'Is it true, papa?' asked the youngest, Peneranda.

'The alter-folk have been slain,' he told them, the words bringing home the scale of the victory he had won. He stroked the child's cheek. 'I started this campaign before you were born, little one, but now the lands are free of their taint.'

'Does that mean we'll have more time to play?' said Clothild, older by three years.

'We will,' he assured her, standing up. 'Though ruling the Glittering Breaches will not be without its tasks. Now that the foe has been driven out, I must work to keep the unity of the Reforged Kingdoms. But if the serpents of the Iron Wastes cannot keep me from my daughters, the arguments of princes shall not either.'

He heard chanting – his name – and Ermenberga waved him towards the parapet.

'Your subjects await you,' she said, eyes moist with joy. She patted her stomach meaningfully, 'and soon you will have other news to brighten their spirits further. I think it is a boy...'

Theuderic was struck dumb, his thoughts whirling. He pulled himself up onto the rampart edge. His army, led by princes and dukes and war leaders of many other castles and citadels, erupted into even greater noise, such that Theuderic almost didn't hear the rumbling of thunder above.

He looked up and saw that the darkening sky was filling with ominous clouds. Fearing some last treachery of the alter-folk, Theuderic glanced back at his family.

With his name still ringing in his ears, and the loving expressions of his wife and children etched into his mind, Theuderic juddered as a bolt scythed through his body without warning.

In a moment, all that he knew, the wide plains and jagged hills of the Glittering Breaches, dropped beneath him. The great keeps and fortresses of his lands became specks of gold and silver before they too were lost, and in a moment the blur of the Auric Shield of Lyonaster disappeared from view.

He thought for a moment that he had been swallowed by a star, suffused with light and heat.

And then he was no more.

Watching his adjutant turn away, Theuderis considered his command. Every warrior had been selected by Sigmar himself, chosen from across the Mortal Realms to be the best fighters in history. His own feats had marked him out for leadership, but each and every Stormcast Eternal had a similar story of heroism and defiance to tell. There was not one amongst them that would take a step back in the face of the enemy, or flinch from the battle ahead. These were concerns for leaders of mortal soldiers.

Yet for all that, the Strike Chamber of the Silverhands was untested in war. The training fields of Sigmaron and the orchestrated battles of the Gladitorium were tests, nothing more. Theuderis did not fear death, for he would be remade if he fell, just as would all who followed him. There was a price for immortality, he had heard, but the greater loss would be the pang of failure. Though Neros Stormfather's comment had been light-hearted, it had cast a doubt in Theuderis' thoughts – the Silverhands were ready to be tempered in battle, but what of the Warbeast and his warriors? More than skill, bravery and fury were required to overcome the foes ahead.

In his former life, Theuderis had never known defeat. The Silverhand was not about to commence his eternal service to Sigmar with anything less than total victory.

CHAPTER FOUR

Much had changed, though much had stayed the same. Arkas found the spot where he had been standing when Sigmar had ascended him to the Celestial Realm. Not only was he able to pick the place from the general layout of the collapsed fortifications, he could feel an imprint on the world from where he had been plucked for a new existence. The bolt of Sigmar that had taken him, the same cosmic energy that had deposited him earlier that day, left an indelible mark in the fabric of Ursungorod.

'How long?' he whispered as he looked at the tumbled ruin of what had once been Kurzengor.

'Did you say something, Lord Arkas?' asked Dolmetis, a few paces behind his lord.

'When I last stood upon these stones they were mounted on each other as a great gatehouse,' he told his companion. 'I suppose they were knocked down by the sorceries of the foes that came that day, but it is the passage of time that has buried them. How long would you say, Dolmetis, would it take for the land to claim back its own?'

'Centuries, Lord Arkas, as judged in the Realm of Heavens. Perhaps half a dozen or more.' He stepped closer. 'It is only a mortal measure, my lord. The past is of no consequence, only the future holds the hope of change. Many of the God-King's host were taken from their realms in even more distant times.'

'A good point, Dolmetis.' He stamped a booted foot on the hard block beneath him. Blue sparks flew. 'These walls were old even when I held them, set down in a time long past, along with the rest of the city below Ursungorod.'

'The Shadowgulf?'

'The lowest parts are called that. We thought they were the tomb of those that hollowed Ursungorod. I know better now. Gnaw-burrows of the skaven, bleeding the realms together, spreading canker into the depths of this place and the neighbouring regions.'

'That is where we are heading?'

'In time. We do not simply thrust our hands into the vermin nest. The clans of the Ursungorod I knew are no more – the hand of Chaos stretched far across these lands and despoiled the souls of its people. We will purge this taint and secure our route to the realmgate. Theuderis the Silverhand marches from the dusk to rendezvous for our attack and we shall crush the followers of Chaos between us like a fist closing. The battle will wet our blades and whet our wrath for the true war below.'

Doridun had been close at hand too and now stepped forward. His clarion was slung across his back and he held a blade slicked with blood.

'And where will we find these enemies, lord?' He sounded eager.

'Everywhere,' Arkas replied with a chuckle. He turned and pointed up the mountainside, to where the slopes disappeared into dark clouds. 'But there is somewhere else we must go first.'

The Lord-Celestant raised his hammer thrice and from the gloomy skies a spark of light dropped in response, quickly resolving into the shape of Hastor, his Knight-Venator. On blazing sapphire wings he descended, the long curve of his realmhunter's bow in hand. He landed as softly as a feather and held out his free arm. A blur of colour streaked across the pale mountainside and a few moments later Hastor's star-eagle settled on his wrist, resplendent with yellow and red plumage.

'Hastor, take the Prosecutors and scout me a route to the summit. You will find an old outpost there, I hope, of duardin style. Do not enter, simply return to me with the news if it still stands.'

'There are duardin in Ursungorod, my lord?' Dolmetis looked up the slope as if he might see one of Grungni's stocky descendants. 'I did not know.'

'No cause for excitement, they were driven out by the skaven before I was born. Another… person makes her lair in their old workings though, and she will have invaluable intelligence about the Pestilens and the corrupted tribes.' He looked at Hastor. 'On no account are you to enter the tower. The Queen of the Peak may be a useful ally, but she will certainly be a foe if you come upon her unannounced.'

'How are we to announce our presence, my lord?' asked Hastor.

'Leave that to me. Though I am reforged, I still have a few tricks from the old times.'

Hastor nodded and tossed his star-eagle into the air, leaping effortlessly after it a moment later. His shrill cry cut across the wind and the Knight-Venator's twenty Prosecutors rose up to meet him, the pale spines of their Azyr-crafted wings shimmering.

'Dolmetis, you will remain here with a small rearguard. Take Martox and his Decimators, and half the Retributors. Doridun, call the rest of the chamber to column. We have a long climb ahead of us.'

CHAPTER FIVE

The march across the foothills passed without incident. The peaks rose abruptly ahead of Theuderis' army, delineating the boundary between the Capricious Wilds and Ursungorod. As the Lord-Celestant had commanded, the host had started ascending the lower slopes before the light of the rising sun fell upon their backs. They advanced without pause, covering the ground with giant strides, as relentless as the pistons of a duardin engine.

The formation changed organically to match the variations in terrain, the different elements repositioning as they passed along defiles or spread out across valley floors. By mid-morning the sun was hidden behind the clouds again, its wan light barely penetrating the deep gorges and ravines.

At times they were hemmed in by vertiginous cliff faces of solid ice, chasms barely wide enough for the Stormcasts to walk three abreast. Inside the frozen walls could be seen the dim shapes of carcasses from gigantic beasts and the bones of monsters consumed in aeons past. More disturbing were the shark-like apparitions that lived within the solid ice scavenging on these remains, half-seen creatures with long fangs and dagger-spined fins.

Amongst the blue-needled trees, they would hear the tinkling of metal and come across great oak-like arboreal giants with bark of iron and leaves of bronze. The column found itself negotiating winding trails that seemed to shift as they passed, the trees moving imperceptibly, subtly closing off routes and opening others, directing their progress towards dark ravines and coursing rivers that fumed like boiling blood.

They passed much evidence of the ancient human and duardin strongholds that had once dominated these lands. All was worn and broken by countless years, but from the back of Tyrathrax here and there Theuderis spied a rune-etched column or some carved face of a deity long consumed by the ravaging Chaos Gods. In places, the tribes had tried to rebuild parts of the mountains-spanning dead city, leaving ramshackle walls and circular encampments of piled stone. Symbols of the Dark Powers were daubed on these hovels and there was other evidence of depraved practices.

'I thought the Realms of Beasts would be teeming with life,' remarked Voltaran. 'Yet all I hear is the wind and tread of boots. Not a bird cry or snuffle or growl.'

Theuderis had noticed the silence too and developed a theory.

'It is our presence that stills them. We carry with us the light of Sigmar, the power celestial. Long they have nestled in the crux of the Dark Gods' embrace – they are suffused with its corruption.' He gazed about at the tumbled rocks and spiny trees that littered the slope around them. 'Trust nothing here, no matter how fair-seeming. All has been touched by Chaos.'

'You think nothing has survived of what once was?'

'There is no purity to be found in this forsaken realm, Voltaran. When it has been purified, when we have seized the realmgates and wrested the Allpoints from accursed Archaon, the beauty of the untrammelled wilderness will blossom again and those untouched by the darkness will live here in peace.'

'That is a very long time yet, Lord-Celestant. The work has only just begun.'

'Yet longer has the Lord Sigmar planned this return. In an age the Mortal Realms fell. Not overnight will they be restored to goodness. Be comforted that each region we purge, each realmgate we seize, brings that blessed state closer.'

'In the God-King's name.'

'For eternity may he reign.'

They continued on for some time, the landscape growing ever more barren and contorted as they progressed. The slopes were gouged with great welts that wept ruddy blood-like tar and the Prosecutors scouted far and wide to find the best route through the maze of pits, ruins and chasms that blocked the army's route. At times Theuderis was forced to dismount to allow his dracoth to negotiate a steep climb, and just after noon he and many others were virtually on their hands and knees, pulling themselves up the near-vertical wall of a canyon. Tyrathrax scrambled up behind, panting hard, her claws scratching against the unforgiving rock.

Theuderis dragged himself over the lip of the cliff, joining the several dozen Stormcast Eternals of the vanguard who were already there. A sudden wild cawing and a mad flapping of wings announced the rise of a panicked flock of huge crows, each with a wingspan that rivalled a star-eagle's. Other birds were wildly trilling and shrieking, taking to the skies in haste, predators and prey fleeing together.

The ground trembled.

Theuderis launched himself back towards the cliff edge, skidding along the brown grass with outstretched arms. The clifftop bucked even as he reached the edge. He looked down and saw Tyrathrax looking back at him, her pale blue eyes staring out of the slits in her gilded chamfron. To either side the ascending Stormcast Eternals doubled their efforts, heaving themselves between footholds, cracks and small ledges.

'Jump!' the Lord Celestant roared, digging the fingers of his left hand deep into the dirt and throwing out his right.

The dracoth bunched its muscles and leapt even as the face of the cliff sheared away.

Theuderis snatched a horn as it passed close to his hand, pulling with all of his strength to wrap his arm around the neck of his faithful mount. Tyrathrax's claws gouged furrows in the disintegrating stone. The Lord-Celestant powered to his feet, dragging the dracoth with him in a welter of rock shards and clumps of mud.

'Stay back from the edge!' he bellowed over the cracking and groaning of tortured earth, as warriors of the vanguard moved to aid their companions on the cliff. There was nothing they could do and more would be lost.

Theuderis staggered away, pulling Tyrathrax after him, the ground rising and falling violently under his feet. Twice he fell to his knees and he let go of the dracoth to look back. The cliff was still tumbling away, breaking apart in boulders and sheets as the strata split, the edge moving closer and closer. It settled just a few strides away.

A few of the Stormcasts made it to safety. Armour cracked and buckled as they clambered through the deluge of rock. Beyond them the landslide was lit by detonations of power, glimmers of lightning as Theuderis' warriors were crushed and pummelled, their physical remains summoned back to

Azyr by Sigmar's magic, there to be forged anew. The gleams from many who perished were swallowed by the burgeoning cloud of dust and grit that billowed up from the gorge. A last convulsion threw the surviving Stormcast Eternals to the ground. Theuderis' legs buckled beneath him as the clifftop briefly dropped away and then sharply rose up to meet him like a bucking steed.

The shaking subsided. Commanding Tyrathrax to stay, Theuderis pushed himself to his feet and made his way carefully to the slew of broken rock that now descended into the valley. The shattered bodies of wounded Stormcasts were strewn amongst the grey and brown. The quake had lasted no more than a dozen heartbeats but had done as much damage as any enemy attack.

After the deafening tumult, the quiet was profound. It was quickly broken as the Stormcasts still alive called out, some shouting for aid, other voices coming from the Primes as they tallied who remained and who had been taken. The raucous cries of the circling birds echoed along the ravine to join the hiss of streaming dirt, the creak of settling stone and the last resounding thuds of rocks bouncing further down the defile.

Theuderis clambered down into the anarchy of piled boulders and broken tree trunks, scanning the debris. Movement above drew his attention to the descending flights of Prosecutors, the Knights-Venator gesticulating to the carnage below.

'Back!' roared Theuderis, waving his hand to attract their attention. 'Back to your posts! If the enemy come upon us in this parlous state we are ruined. Keep vigilant!'

The flying warriors acknowledged his command and ascended, wings thrumming with celestial power, spreading out to form a watchful cordon. Theuderis joined his warriors, lifting the rocks and hurling them away with superhuman strength to unearth the Stormcasts trapped beneath. He pulled away a boulder to reveal a Retributor, his starsoul mace still tightly gripped in his hands. Blood seeped from a gouge across his chest, but he turned his head to look at the Lord-Celestant.

'It will take more than a mountain falling on me to keep me from the fight, my lord.'

'Elegias?'

The Retributor nodded.

'I saw Vortemon Azyr-drawn. You are Retributor-Prime now. Lead well.'

'I am honoured,' replied Elegias, grasping Theuderis' proffered arm to haul himself out of the rubble. Others were also emerging from the crush, the hardened sigmarite of their armour bearing scuffs, dents and cracks inflicted by the earthquake's fury.

Some were not so fortunate. Theuderis levered aside a boulder almost as large as the warrior beneath, freeing a Judicator named Sementor. His arm had been ripped off by the churning rocks and his boltstorm crossbow lay off to the side, mangled amongst the stones. The side of his helm had been caved in, too, jagged edges cutting deep to the bone of the exposed skull, a single blue eye revealed.

'I cannot fight on, my lord,' said Sementor. 'I shall be no burden to the Silverhands. Sigmar calls me.'

'And he will remember your sacrifice,' Theuderis said quietly, drawing his runeblade to place the point between Sementor's cuirass and his helm. 'We shall meet again on the far side of the forge.'

He leaned his weight onto the weapon, pushing it deep. The Judicator's body crackled and vanished, leaving the faintest aftertrail of blue heading skywards from the point where he had lain.

They worked their way down to the rock-littered canyon floor. As they descended, the survivors grew fewer and fewer – those at the bottom had faced the full weight of the cliff coming down upon them. Theuderis lifted clear another of his companions, the Knight-Heraldor Attaxes Darkbane. The plates of his armour seemed mostly undamaged; only the weight of the rocks pinning him down had necessitated assistance. Nodding his thanks, Attaxes retrieved his slender clarion.

'I thought…' The Knight-Heraldor's voice trailed off as he turned his head to look past Theuderis.

Casting his gaze about, the Lord-Celestant saw that many of the others had stopped their labours and were also staring back up the slope. He turned to see what had caught their attention.

The stones of the rockfall had parted into two main flows, leaving an uneven expanse of the grey cliff between them. At first Theuderis could see nothing, just jags of rock and striations. And then, tilting his head slightly, the image came to him, the shadows and light resolving into a picture. It was unmistakable – the cliff had formed the face of a gigantic roaring bear, with sharp promontories of rock for fangs, and exposed clay beds casting a red hue within the open mouth.

'What do you suppose that is?' said Attaxes.

'Proof of this land's corruption,' replied Theuderis. He said nothing more, but it seemed more than coincidence that the earthquake had struck at the most damaging moment.

He called out to the others to free their remaining companions and did the same himself. When the last of the buried Stormcasts had been dragged from the toppled boulders, the army ascended once again, though Theuderis remained behind for some time, staring at the cliff face. The sun had moved and the image was no longer there, and had not his companions also seen the apparition he would have dismissed it as a hallucination brought on by the sudden stress of the earthquake.

A rasping bark from Tyrathrax drew his attention away, to where his sub-commanders awaited him at the top of the rock pile. Suppressing his unease, Theuderis pulled himself over the rocks and joined them, glad to put the depressing episode behind him. His Knight-Vexillor, Knight-Heraldor and the most senior of the Knights-Azyros, Samat, attended to him.

'Our strength is much diminished, my lord,' reported Voltaran. 'Nearly half of the Paladin Conclaves were lost, and a third of our remaining warriors.'

'We press on regardless,' commanded Theuderis. 'Sigmar shall see fit to return them to us when needed. Let us not turn an unfortunate incident into a disaster. The Warbeasts are depending upon us to make rendezvous in three days, and we will make the meeting point in two. Samat, spread the search groups further ahead. Find me the swiftest route to the inland region.'

'As you will it, Lord Silverhand,' replied the Knight-Azyros.

'If I might make a suggestion, my lord,' Voltaran said quietly. Theuderis nodded. 'Overground is proving troublesome. Perhaps there is an alternative. The ruins of the subterranean city of the duardin are said to stretch far into Ursungorod.'

'We would lose my warriors' mobility,' said Samat.

'And there is no reason to believe the underground passages have survived in any fit state,' said Theuderis. 'Also, I would have the skaven remain unaware of our presence for as long as possible. Delving into their underground domain would be sure to announce our arrival, but overground we might yet continue a day or two unnoticed by them.'

'If Arkas and his Warbeasts draw their eye, we might even be upon them before they know it,' said Attaxes.

'I am certain Arkas is making quite a disturbance,' replied Theuderis.

CHAPTER SIX

During the ascent of Mount Vazdir, the air grew thinner and colder, until the breath of the Warbeasts followed them like a mountain fog. But the snows held and, except for the ever-present dark clouds, the skies were clear for the Prosecutors to lead the way. At first they had reported a steep climb marked by treacherous ridges and thick forest, but the way proved less than formidable. The dense thickets of trees appeared to open up before the Stormcasts and the winding trails seen by the scouts resolved into broader paths, as though the mountain itself wished to speed them on their way.

Arkas led from the front. There were some Lord-Celestants who preferred the distance of command, placing themselves in the main body so that they might act and observe more dispassionately. He had heard as much regarding Theuderis Silverhand. Arkas considered himself a more *intuitive* leader in battle. Just as one had to look into the eye of a foe to judge their character and intent, so he had to be in the forefront of the clash of arms to know, to *feel,* the best course of action to take.

'I am sure we saw those trees before,' remarked Dolmetis, indicating a stand of immense pines ahead of them. 'Are we sure Hastor is not entertaining himself at our expense?'

'I forgive your ignorance, so perhaps Hastor will forgive your distrust,' replied Arkas. 'Those are spectral pines – the leaves are bluer than the mountain firs we saw earlier. And the ways of Ursungorod are not always straight. It might seem but a javelin's throw to your destination, but a defile separates you that cannot be crossed but at the expense of half a day's march.'

'Or the opposite,' Dolmetis said quietly. 'I feel that we are not being welcomed so much as lured...'

Arkas stopped, sensing a ripple of energy flowing through the roots of Ursungorod. He held up a hand to halt the army. A heartbeat later he felt the ground shiver. Some snow fell from the tree branches and slid across drifts, but nothing more serious. In moments the tremor had passed.

His mortal experiences meant that, despite the intervening age, he could feel Ursungorod as closely now as when he had been the Bear-clad. The perturbations in the Ghurite energy told him that the quake had been to the west – from where Theuderis approached. He hoped his fellow Lord-Celestant had weathered the incident well.

More days than not witnessed a quake in Ursungorod. It had made it impossible to launch an attack on the skaven lairs, as entrances opened and closed with every earth movement. This time would be different – he had an army capable of breaching the underdeeps and even the Shadowgulf itself. He would strike like a dagger into their heart.

A flit of shadows heralded the arrival of a quintet of Prosecutors.

Their Prime, Venian, landed in front of Arkas while the others kept station on humming wings.

'My lord,' he began, dropping to a knee to deliver the report. 'Knight Hastor dispatched us. A foe lies between us and the ruin we seek. Five hundred strong, at least, garbed for war. We did not reveal ourselves and Hastor awaits your command.'

'Where?'

'A still lake, frozen in a bowl-shaped valley. Even the rivers and falls are ice. We saw a town of tents and more solid structures arrayed the slopes.'

'I know this place,' Arkas said. 'Icemere. You saw the enemy?'

'Briefly, my lord,' replied Venian. 'Many were well armoured, not like the scum we chased down earlier. The encampment looked more settled also. There were several burnt-out pyres and totemic poles raised in the centre, and a charnel stench – sacrifices no doubt. We approached stealthily and heard the growl of hounds and caught glimpses of larger beasts.'

'What were they doing? Where exactly is the camp?'

'The route to the tower passes onto a sharp ridge, but we could see no further than that. It was the opinion of Knight Hastor that they were deliberately blocking the approach. It is far too high and inhospitable for them to have remained there for any other reason.'

'They have good reason,' said Arkas. 'The Queen of the Peak is a powerful oracle and many seek her wisdom. They might hope to keep her visions to themselves or just ambush and murder those who would consult with the Queen.'

'Do you have orders for Knight Hastor, my lord?'

'They will find their next guests harder to handle, be sure of that.' Arkas loosened his runeblade in its sheath. 'Heed my command for Knight Hastor. We must secure the safety of the Queen of the Peak. I will lead an attack on the main camp. The

Angelos Conclave has two missions once the attack is under-way. Part of your force must hold the ridge to ensure none of the enemy can reach the Queen's tower. You must personally locate the tower and ensure there are no foes in the surrounding area. Kill any that are, but do not enter under any circumstances. Allow nobody to pass into the tower until I arrive.'

'What if the Queen of the Peak should emerge?' asked Venian.

'She cannot leave the tower,' Arkas said. He knelt and used a finger to mark a symbol in the snow. 'Mark this sigil and pass it on to Hastor. There is a gate-arch carved with duardin reliefs. He will know the presence of the Queen beyond it. He is to leave this, my rune, at the threshold, but is not to pass in.' He closed his fist. 'We will advance at haste. Make your move when Doridun signals the attack.'

'Understood, Lord-Celestant.' The Prosecutor-Prime stood up and lifted a crackling javelin as a salute. Turning gracefully, he sprang into the air, taking his warriors with him.

'Dolmetis!'

The Knight-Vexillor hurried to attend his commander.

'Form the army for attack. Trident formation, Judicator vanguards.'

'It shall be done, my lord.'

Arkas set off again along the faint trail through the snow, trusting his Knight-Vexillor and the Primes to implement his command without delay. He knew the Icemere well and was surprised that it had changed so little over the many centuries. It had to be the influence of the Queen of the Peak. In a land wracked by constant upheaval, she was stasis personified.

With their Lord-Celestant setting a relentless pace, the Storm-cast army soon came upon a band of thick forest, beyond which lay the Icemere. As Arkas had ordered, the host broke into three detachments, the general leading the central tine while Dolmetis and Doridun commanded the others. Forming the points of the trident, Arkas' thirty Judicators advanced just ahead of the main columns, their various bows and crossbows well suited to taking down any patrols or sentries set by the foes.

Arkas' force was small but formidable, its warriors elite even amongst the Strike Chambers of the Celestial Vindicators. He could sense the anticipation for battle in his host, infusing the ever-present aura of Ghur with a predatory hunger. The skirmish with the Bonekeepers had been a simple execution. True battle awaited.

They had not long passed under the shadowy eaves of the woods when one of the Judicator-Primes returned to report to Arkas. He led the Lord-Celestant to where his retinue were waiting amongst the trees, a broad clearing visible ahead of them. The ruined stones of a road passed directly into the pale sunlight.

'There are watchers in the trees, my lord,' said the Judicator-Prime, indicating half-seen shapes in the branches of the pines to either side of the track. From what Arkas could see, the sentries did not appear human – he caught glimpses of grey flesh and leathery wings.

'Harpies?'

'I don't believe so, my lord. Something else, but we cannot see them well enough to say.'

Arkas looked more closely, crouching next to the trunk of a huge mountain pine. As he laid his hand upon its bark to steady himself he felt a tremor through his fingers. Glancing at the tree, he saw knotholes blinking, and within, green eyes looking back at him. He recoiled to his feet, seeing other eyes opening on the

trees around him. Turning his attention to the trail ahead he saw
that the 'beasts' in the trees were in fact twists of branch and leaf,
forming humanoid shapes.

The dark bark of the tree he had leaned against started to
split, the splinters of wood forming a maw. A low moan issued
from this hole.

'The trees are tainted,' he snarled to his companions. 'The
trees are the sentries!'

The warning groans were getting louder and the branches
were swaying, their rustling alarm rippling outwards.

'If we cannot be stealthy, speed and shock will do. The Icemere is only three hundred paces more from the break of the
trees,' said Arkas.

He looked back to see the warriors of his command picking
their way through the woods, their turquoise armour catching
rays of weak light and then plunged into shade as the wind moved
through the canopy above. He could hear the snap of twigs and
thud of heavy boots even through the muffle of old leaves and
mulch. 'I do not think Sigmar was concerned with us sneaking
around when he bid Grungni to forge our armour as he did...'

Looking through the trees, he spied the other Judicators,
their Primes looking to him for some sign of what to do. He
raised his hand as a sign for all to halt and then looked for
his Knight-Heraldor. Doridun was at the head of his column
a hundred or so paces away to the left. With two simple gestures, he passed on the command to sound the charge and
then turned back to the Judicator-Prime.

'Move now and kill all that you can. We shall pass through
you. Guard our backs.'

'Kill what, my lord?'

'The trees! Burn them!'

'As you will it, my lord.' The Judicator-Prime moved his hand as though pulling a string on his bow, a lightning bolt appearing in place of where an arrow would be on a mortal weapon. The sparkle of others doing the same lit the trees. A heartbeat later the bolts flashed across the clearing, searing into the treetops.

Like candles, the trees lit with flame, sap crackling, needle-swathed branches thrashing as blue fire leapt from one to the next. The moaning became a higher pitched keening as another volley of enchanted missiles streaked into the arboreal watchers.

The peal of Doridun's clarion reached Arkas' ears and he launched into a sprint, hammer in one hand, runeblade in the other. From all along the treeline the Stormcast Eternals burst forth, thundering into the cloud-shrouded sunlight, the flicker of the Judicators' lightning bolts catching on their armour as they ploughed through drifts of snow on the uneven ground.

Arkas surged ahead with his Retributors close at hand, their lightning hammers at the ready. Glaive-wielding Protectors followed Doridun and Dolmetis to either side. Made of unalloyed sigmarite, their thick armour was no encumbrance as they raced across the clearing.

Shouts from ahead warned that the enemy knew that something was amiss, but there was no chance they could know the nature of the foe about to fall upon them. Soon brash horns and drums called them to arms.

The clearing widened out as they neared the banks of the Icemere. Its surface was mirror-smooth, reflecting the tall trees around its edge and the grey sky above, stretching to the horizon to the left, where Arkas knew it became a frozen waterfall. To the right it was bordered by the stumps of the duardin walls that had dammed it in ages past. The enormous piles of a bridge still rose from the ice.

The Chaos tribe had spread across the banks and part of the lake opposite where the road had once run down the perimeter of the water. The scene was just as it had been described by Venian, with tents of all sizes arranged haphazardly on the snow-covered shore and frozen tarn, interspersed with bivouacs and more permanent structures of wood, hide and bone. Drifts of smoke rose from the fires of the previous night and five mighty pillars had been erected in a circle at the centre, held in place by thick rope cables.

Arkas could see the bold shapes carved into the wooden totems and recognised four of them immediately as interpretations of the Chaos Gods – Khorne, Nurgle, Tzeentch and Slaanesh. The fifth caused him some surprise, a rendition of a horned figure crouched upon a spiralling tower of skulls and bones covered with swarming vermin. The Great Horned Rat.

Why was the fifth member of the despotic pantheon, the skaven god, being worshipped by an Ursungoran tribe?

Chaos worshippers boiled out of their tents and rough hovels, leaving Arkas no time to ponder this question. Though they could not have expected to face a Strike Chamber of Stormcasts, the Chaos followers were well prepared to attack at short notice, and judging by the trophies and human remains that adorned their altar-pyres and totems, they had gained considerable success doing so.

Horsemen erupted from the woods, bringing with them baying packs of hounds. Riders, steeds and mastiffs all showed signs of Chaos mutations – horns, scales, sting-tipped tails, fiery eyes and burning manes, along with myriad other deformities. Rather than attack directly, the riders and their hunting packs circled to the right, along the lake shore, using their speed to outflank the oncoming Stormcast Eternals.

Marauders in mail and leather armour formed quickly into

war-groups ahead of Arkas' charge, at least two hundred of them clustered beneath tattered banners and standards made of bone and sinew. Here again there was skaven influence, triskele symbols similar to those of the Pestilens among the runes of the Blood God, Lord of Decay, Changer of Ways and Pleasure Prince. Brandishing spears and axes, the Chaos thugs jeered and hollered abuse. They crashed their weapons on wooden shields daubed with thick blood, taunting the Stormcasts and defying their own fear.

Warriors in a mix of heavier plate, gilded fishscale and banded laminar jogged into position to the left, facing the onrushing column led by Doridun. Many sported crab-like claws, tentacles, tusks and immense fangs, some of them bursting from their armour in places with unnatural muscles and tumorous growths, several easily as big as the Stormcast warriors pounding towards the lake.

Holding out his hammer, Arkas redirected the charge, acting as a pivot for the entire formation. The Warbeasts responded immediately, wheeling left towards the most dangerous foes. Arkas and Doridun speared into the heavy infantry while Dolmetis and his retinue of Protectors and Decimators redirected their assault towards the marauders in the centre. They would trust to the Judicators behind to waylay the cavalry encircling the oncoming host. Overhead, the glitter of artificial wings showed the progress of the Prosecutors as they headed over the lake towards the ridge beyond, their arcane missiles scything down the shrieking harpies that had escaped the initial attack.

Running down the sloping shore, Arkas caught a glimpse of the larger beasts reported by the Prosecutors. They might have been men once, or perhaps bears, it was hard to say. They lumbered forwards on their hind legs, a handful of moaning, snarling creatures covered in dark fur, chained together at the neck by thick iron links. Like the warriors, they bore signs of gross mutation, their flesh in places thick with pale chitin plates and pustules, while metal rivets had been driven into their bodies to make a kind of studded armour. Whipping pseudo-limbs thrashed back and forth, each lined with vicious barbs.

For all that the Chaos tribe was organised and experienced, it had never faced attackers like the Warbeasts. Armoured in sigmarite, the Stormcast Eternals cared little for the damage the enemy weapons might deal. Arkas applied the same principle to his strategies, training and drilling his warriors to drive into the thick of the enemy army, to seek out as one the toughest foe, just as he had singled out the Gore Maiden when he had first arrived. They had but one concern – to bloodily rip the heart from the opposition, destroying their best warriors and most fearsome beasts first. The Judicators and Prosecutors were well equipped to finish off those that remained.

So it was that Arkas was the first to fall upon the enemy, hammer and sword at the ready. Halberd blades and jagged maces rose to meet him as he leapt.

'Death to the unclean!' he roared, smashing into the Chaos warriors' ranks, his weapons trailing twin tails of gore like Sigmar's comet, celestial energy exploding through the ranks of the foe at his impact.

He crushed one beneath his weight as he landed, rings of mail scattering when the Chaos follower's ribcage exploded. Crouching, Arkas smashed his hammer through the legs of three more, greaves and armour no defence against the sweeping blow. As he straightened, his blade carved a diagonal furrow across a pair of full-plated foes who were still drawing back their enormous maces.

Two heartbeats more, three more foes sliced and crushed.

The Retributors crashed into the foes pressing around Arkas, their hammers unleashing a blazing storm of lightning that split open armoured plates and charred the warriors within. Starsoul maces cracked like thunder, their touch bursting apart the bodies of the Chaos-tainted. At the centre of this celestial tempest the Warbeast struck the head from a foe with his runeblade, his hammer slamming into the chest of another.

'Spare none!' he roared, though his followers needed no such instruction. Driven by a hate aeons in the making, finally given true release in battle, the Stormcasts of the Celestial Vindicators let free their vengeance in a bloody outpouring of rage.

A fighter as tall as Arkas loomed out of the blood-spray, a jagged sickle-like blade in each hand, slabs of thick steel painted black covering his flesh. He wore no helm, and a reptilian third eye protruding from his forehead fixed the Lord-Celestant with an inhuman gaze, the regular orbs a glossy, sightless white beneath. Lips wrinkled back, revealing teeth like glass shards in bloodless gums, and a bulging black tongue.

'Spawn of corruption!'

Arkas' runeblade crashed against the Chaos champion's upraised arm, red sparks flying as Chaos sigils burned in the hexed metal. The shock of the impact sent a tremor up Arkas' arm and he stepped back, flexing his numbed fingers around the hilt of his sword. The Chaos champion let out a gurgling laugh and hacked at the Lord-Celestant, both weapons aimed for his throat.

Arkas raised his hammer in time to catch one blade on its haft, the sickle's edge skittering over his gauntleted hand and leaving a furrow through the sigmarite. The other passed over his rising runeblade and struck him just above the left eye, whipping his head back.

Snarling, Arkas swung his hammer at his opponent's midriff,

but the blow fell short and was turned aside by a timely parry. The Chaos champion's defence left him open, however, and the Lord-Celestant's boot crashed into the man-beast's chest, driving him from his feet.

The Retributors needed no urging and fell upon the toppled champion with hammers and maces, pounding incessantly upon his armour until the heads of their weapons glowed white with power and the runes of his plate burned yellow. The champion rolled to all fours, trying to escape the deluge of blows, but a starsoul mace cracked against his skull with an electric detonation. Bone and blood flew and the champion slumped, his collapse only drawing an even more incensed assault from the raging Stormcasts.

Arkas slashed and hammered his way into the press around his companions, slaughtering the Chaos warriors who sought to fall upon his Retributors as they finished off the champion. He cared not who dealt the final blow – it was only pride that led champions to seek to best each other in single combat.

Bursting free from the tangled mass of corpses and wounded, Arkas had just enough time to see Dolmetis' warriors carving apart the last of the marauders before the gigantic mutant beasts were upon him, snarling, ropes of stinking saliva flowing from their enormous maws.

A tentacle-limb wrapped itself about his wrist as he drew back his hammer to strike the first blow. He hacked at the pseudopod with his sword, parting it on the second attempt. By then, the brutish monster was upon him, bowling him over with its immense mass. Sword-arm pinned beneath the creature's foreleg and his hammer equally trapped, Arkas head-butted the beast, splintering dagger-like fangs.

Claws raked and gouged at his pauldrons and cuirass, slivers of sigmarite falling like curled thread as another brute joined the attack. He felt blood trickling down his shoulder, the first wound his flesh had known since passing through the pain of Sigmar's forge. The shock sent a surge of energy through him, firing him with a strength unknown before.

Bellowing, Arkas threw off the hellish beast atop him, rising to his feet. His hammer slammed into the face of the second, snapping horns, tusks and skull, pulping the brain within. Heaving aside its dying bulk, he threw himself at the monster that had trapped him. It howled and launched itself in a counter-attack. Ignoring the tentacles flailing at his face, Arkas speared his sword into the brute's mouth, following the blade in with his whole arm. Blade and fist punched out through the back of the creature's bony head. Bracing a foot against the slumping corpse's shoulder, he dragged his arm free, tearing the head away like a macabre bracelet before he threw it aside.

Doridun's combined assault with Arkas had torn through the Chaos warriors' flank as they had been forced to turn towards the Lord-Celestant. The Knight-Heraldor and his warriors battered and cleaved at the last remaining foes while Arkas turned his attention to Dolmetis' progress.

The Protectors slashed a bloody path through the barbaric tribesmen. They swept their glaives in arcs that left their foes dismembered and bisected, the marauders' numbers counting for little against the far superior weapons, physique and armour of the Stormcast Eternals. Beyond the Protectors, a spearhead of Decimators encircled the survivors, led by Dolmetis. Their thunderaxes streaked bolts of energy from the corpses of their slain foes, the ice underfoot lit by the fury of the war-storm.

The carnage lasted for a little while longer as Hastor and his winged Stormcasts ran down the hounds and horsemen that had attempted to circle, and others fell upon the Chaos followers breaking for safety towards the far end of the lake, heading for the ridge leading to the Queen of the Peak's lair. Not one survived to reach the shore, incinerated by heavenly shafts and javelins, pierced on the tines of the Prosecutors' tridents.

The ice was cracked in places, amongst the red wash of freezing blood and the scattered remnants of limbs and bodies. Arkas noticed a few of the Stormcasts gazing down at the sheer surface, concerned.

'No need to fear for your footing,' he declared to them, stamping a heavy boot. 'The Icemere is sustained by the magic of the Queen of the Peak. All year round it could take our weight.'

'Who is this queen?' asked Diocletus, one of the Protectors-Prime. 'Such sorcery is surely Chaos-born.'

'Not so,' snapped Arkas. 'Do you think I would seek her aid if that were the case? No, her power comes from the strength of Ghur, the pure wildness of Ursungorod rendered into magic. The legends claimed she was a goddess in the World Before, but I cannot say that is true. She is powerful, certainly, but a goddess? All that matters is she will know me.'

'I did not mean any insubordination, my lord,' Diocletus said, offering a bow in apology, the long blade of his glaive dipped in submission. 'I sought knowledge. I do not understand why we need the assistance of... a witch.'

'When I last fought for these lands I had nearly all of the clans at my side and it was not enough. The grip of Chaos is tight and the pollution of the skaven runs far. I would talk to the Queen of the Peak and find out the extent of the power of both.'

'She can be trusted, Lord-Celestant?'

'She will not break a bargain struck,' replied Arkas. 'I will pay the price she names and she will tell all.'

While Arkas had been speaking, the other Primes had started their post-battle practices, arranging for the bodies of the tainted to be dragged into piles ready to be consumed by cleansing fire. Here and there were mottled patches of ice, the surface crazily scarred by the detonations of those Stormcasts who had been physically overwhelmed and called back to the Celestial Realm. Half a dozen, no more – though Arkas would have preferred it to have been fewer still.

Searches were conducted throughout the camp, all possessions and artefacts added to the pyres. As a Decimator walked past with an armful of rags and trinkets, Arkas called out to him.

'Wait, Philodus!' The Lord-Celestant pulled out a necklace fashioned from small, sharp teeth and sinew. The pendant was a large fang inscribed with a symbol similar to the triskele icons the barbarians had carried. 'This is a Pestilens amulet. Where did you find it?'

The Stormcast indicated a hut of crude planks and untreated hide.

'There are all kinds of gewgaws and baubles,' he said. 'Everywhere.'

'Forget the pyres!' bellowed Arkas, tossing the amulet away. 'Burn it all where it stands! If these cretins were in league with the skaven, who can say what foulness of the Great Horned Rat lurks in their camp. Purge it all, now!'

The Primes rushed to obey his command and moments later arcs of holy lightning flashed across the camp, setting pale flames in the tents and hovels. More celestial blasts incinerated the scattered bodies, the cleansing fires burning a scintillating blue. Arkas stalked through the flames, pointing out bodies and heaps of belongings that had been missed. The surface of the melting ice shimmered while azure smoke poured into the sky.

Only when all was ablaze did Arkas order his warriors onwards to seize the approaches to the ridge taken by the

Prosecutors. It seemed as though the clouds descended at their approach, swathing the ridgeline in a thick mist. Ice crystals crackled across their armour. Where the mountains had ushered Arkas on, it felt as though the Queen of the Peak sought to dissuade him.

'We saw more warriors out on the ridge,' Venian reported, when Arkas reached the slope. 'It was your command not to proceed any further.'

'They are of no consequence,' Arkas assured them. 'Hastor holds the far end, does he not? Decimators, to me!'

The Paladins answered to his call, forming up behind Arkas in a dense block, their thunderaxes held ready. Dolmetis and Doridun approached.

'What orders, my lord?' asked the Knight-Heraldor.

'You shall remain in command of the rearguard here, Doridun. None are to advance further without explicit command, and nothing is to pass.'

'As you command.'

'Decimators, you will follow at fifteen paces. You will approach no closer without specific order, no matter what occurs.'

The Decimators signalled their understanding with silently raised axes.

'What am I to do?' asked Dolmetis.

'If needed, you will turn and run,' Arkas said. 'As fast as you can, back to Doridun. From there you will lead the army to the rendezvous with Theuderis.'

'That is... comforting?' said Dolmetis, staring into the swirling mists. 'What exactly is waiting for us?'

Arkas said nothing, but set off up the ridge into the whiteness.

CHAPTER SEVEN

The first night fell upon the mountains of Ursungorod, the sky alive with unsettling lights and ribbons of magic that lit the heavy clouds from within. The snow came again, silently filling in the footprints of the host, erasing the evidence of their passage. Theuderis and the Silverhands pressed on through the building storm, limbs as tireless as when they had first breached the realmgate into the Capricious Wilds. The Knights-Azyros and other airborne warriors of the Angelos Conclave had been forced to land by the growing snows and wind, and so Samat marched at the side of his Lord-Celestant. He held a great lantern, a celestial beacon that gleamed with Azyrite fire, penetrating the darkness with its white glare. Along the column, the other four Knights-Azyros lit the way for their Stormcast comrades, sparks of brightness against the dark backdrop of the mountainside.

'There is a certain beauty to it,' said the Knight-Azyros, casting his gaze to the illuminations of the heavens.

'Glamours of Chaos,' said the Lord-Celestant. He snorted and shook his head. 'The air itself is thick with the corruption of the Dark Powers. See how it rebels against the presence of Sigmar's truthbringers and forces you to the ground.'

'You think there is more to this storm than mountain climate, Lord Silverhand?'

'I am certain of it. Since we crossed into Ursungorod I have felt its enmity. We are strangers in this land, bearers of Sigmar's grace. We are not wanted here.' Theuderis noticed Samat glance at him. 'Do you not sense it also? There is a presence here, hiding in the shadows, spying on us, stalking us.'

'The skaven, perhaps?'

'No, though their stain is close at hand. One of their lairs is nearby, but it is not the skaven presence that I feel. It is Ursungorod itself, I am sure of it.'

'A daemon, maybe?'

'That may be it, Samat,' said Theuderis. Tyrathrax shook her head, dislodging the snow gathering on her chamfron. 'Yes, something nascent, like a daemon trying to break into the realm through Ursungorod.'

'A curse on this storm that blinds us to the way ahead and shields our foes.'

Theuderis said nothing and they continued on in silence for some time. It was well past midnight when the snows faltered and the clouds started to break apart, revealing a purple-tinged sky. Shooting stars streaked yellow trails while two red crescent moons stared down from past the mountain peaks.

'Shall we ascend?' asked Samat, loosening his starblade with his free hand.

'Not yet.'

Theuderis could see blocky shapes jutting from the slopes ahead. More duardin ruins. As the vanguard approached the broken remnants, they slowed their march, stopping to examine the collapsed towers and fallen walls. The Lord-Celestant urged his dracoth into a run, swiftly covering the ground along the trail forged through the snows by the conclaves ahead.

'Keep moving!' he bellowed as he came upon the first warriors of the vanguard. 'We can afford no delays.'

'My lord, look at this,' called out one of the Liberator-Primes, pointing to a leaning column not far from the path. There were faces in the stone.

'Just old duardin carvings,' Theuderis snapped, but on riding closer the cause of his warriors' curiosity became obvious. Though once the designs had been of stout bearded faces beneath crested helms, they had been subtly changed, looking now more like bears, cats and dogs.

In the flickering lighting of the celestial beacons it looked as though the faces were alive. Then a monstrously fanged wolf-shead on an arch keystone not far away opened its mouth and Theuderis heard a howl. He started in shock as Tyrathrax lurched away, hissing and spitting.

'Sigmar's wrath!' exclaimed the Lord-Celestant, clearly seeing the wolf curl back its lips with a snarl that echoed through the ruins. He could feel magic seeping up from the ground, the weathered masonry contorted under its influence. Theuderis drew his sword, its blade silver in the flow of magic. 'Hold ground! Angelos aloft! Paladins secure!'

The Strike Chamber moved as a single entity, blue and white shining in the light of the Knights-Azyros' lamps as they led the Prosecutors skywards. The Liberators and Judicators of the Redeemer Conclave fell in towards the ruins where Theuderis waited, while the Paladins – retinues of Decimators, Retributors and Protectors – formed a solid outer wall of hammers, glaives and axes.

The snarls, barks and growls of animals intensified as more and more of the ruins sprang into unnatural life. To Theuderis it seemed as though massive claws scraped on stone and he spun in the saddle, whipping his sword around. There was nothing but for the glaring faces in the tumbled stones. His dracoth paced left and right, unnerved, snow falling from her scales.

'Hold steady!' Theuderis called, the words helping to calm his mood as much as that of his fighters. 'Scour the dark!'

With the celestial beacons shining their light from above, the Stormcast Eternals stood ready, eyeing every shadow, hole and broken doorway around them. Voltaran moved up beside his lord, bringing with him a regiment of Judicators armed with shockbolt bows. The fire of their projectiles made the darkness and light dance all the more crazily. Theuderis did his best to pierce the night with his inhuman gaze, but could see nothing except his own warriors.

He forced his breathing to slow and relaxed his grip on the hilt of his sword. Slowly the Ghurite energy seeped back down into the earth and the stones returned to their inert state, the grimacing faces of duardin ancestor heroes and lesser godlings returning where feral visages had leered before.

Even when all seemed to have returned to normal – whatever passed for normal in these Sigmar-cursed mountains – Theuderis did not stand down his force. He waited, reassuring Tyrathrax with pats on the shoulder, until Samat descended, his beacon lamp bathing the ruins with its comforting light.

'No foes in the sky or on the land,' reported the Knight-Azyros, hovering a few paces from his lord. 'As for what passes below… Our eyes cannot see there.'

'Very well,' said Theuderis. He suppressed a sigh of relief, unwilling to betray to his companion how tense he had become. The Lord-Celestant stared at the ruins for a few moments more, daring them to change again. Nothing happened and he raised his voice. 'Form column! Divine Fury formation. Advance with all haste.'

The ruins shuddered to the thunder of marching boots and the scrape of armour. Conclaves of Stormcast Eternals seamlessly filed and split, arranging themselves without delay or hesitation, the lines and ranks almost mesmerising in their efficiency. Watching the conjoining retinues settled Theuderis. His army in motion was a thing of pleasure to witness, a single beast of sigmarite and reforged flesh that answered to his command as quickly as his dracoth.

He waved them onwards, urging Tyrathrax forwards with a single word, glad to quit the ruins. When they were well clear, and heading back down into a cleft between two vertiginous peaks, he turned to look back. The first smudge of the coming dawn lit the sky and for an instant it seemed that two broken gateways formed eyes glaring at him.

'Onwards,' he told the dracoth and she moved into a smooth run, taking him towards the head of the column. 'In the name of the God-King, we will strip the Chaos from these lands. We shall wash it clean with the blood of the corrupted.'

CHAPTER EIGHT

The vast chamber reverberated with the scurrying of thousands of clawed feet on bare rock, an incessant scratching that gnawed away at the soul even as the skaven gnawed at the underbelly of the mountains. The skittering of the slaves drowned out the click of picks and hammers, obliterated the crack of overseers' whips and masked the tormented shrieks and squeaks.

A living tide of mangy furred bodies seethed across the cavern floor, ebbing and flowing down side tunnels, across rickety bridges that spanned bottomless chasms, along ladders and scaffolds built from the bodies and bones of their predecessors. Lash marks competed with buboes and sores on their suppurating hides, cankered limbs forced into agonising service while cataract-pale eyes gazed blindly in the green light of the warp-lamps. Boulders and baskets of smaller rocks passed across the slave carpet, hewn down from the walls by rusted tools and bare hands, to be passed out into the great spoil heaps that littered the surface of the Whiteworld Above.

The air was thick with turgid swirls of emerald smoke from hundreds of incense braziers, the fumes causing the slaves to constantly hack and cough while its warpstone essence fuelled near-dead limbs with unnatural stamina. The musk of the downtrodden mass was equally cloying and foul, as was the rank aroma of the splashing filth underfoot.

A gong sounded, a single strike that echoed long through the undercity. Almost as one the slave mass looked up, their chittering quieting to a hushed dread, the sighted and the sightless turning towards the source of the noise. The black-furred overseers stayed their barbed whips for the moment, sniffing the air, agitated, pink tails twitching.

Squeals of pain and panic swiftly silenced announced the arrival of the priests' black-furred bodyguards. Even burlier than the slave-masters, clad in robes and coifs of corroded mail, mercenary spitevermin battered and chopped a path through the packed slaves. A ripple spread through the downtrodden horde as the spitevermin trampled the mangled corpses of those that had no room to evade the bloody advance. Terror spread like a bow wave before the armoured skaven. Slaves squealed and bit and clawed, tearing at each other to escape the unforgiving cudgels and blades.

As the press started to thicken more and more, the overseers were forced to wield their whips again, lashing out with snarled fury. Some fled before it was too late, others were buried under the weight of the slaves pushing away from the incoming procession. The musk of fear and scent of blood was overpowering, driving the slaves into an increasingly panicked orgy of ear-splitting shrieks and feral violence.

Behind the spitevermin came the first of the plague monks, clutching long staves from which hung warpcloud-spilling censers. The censers glowed with sorcerous power, the mutating effect of the warpstone plain to see in the cadaverous faces and blistered skin of the wielders. Their eyes glowed in the darkness, spittle flecking lips and fur and falling in drooling ribbons to the ground.

After the censer bearers came the procession proper, rank after rank of skaven robed in tattered green and black and red, their cowls and hoods half-hiding faces marked with pox scars and weeping sores. Their garments were stained, held together by fraying rope belts, and covered in a thin layer of shed fur and flakes of skin. They clutched foetid blades and woe-staves in fingers tipped with cracked nails.

With them came chanting. A sonorous, repetitive dirge filled the tunnels, stirring the warp-fog like the breath of an almighty beast. It was accompanied by the slow beat of heavy drums and the clatter of bone rattles. The gong boomed again at the moment the procession entered the vast chamber, its ominous note silencing the tumult for a moment.

The plague monks issued forth into their cathedral like pus filling a boil, dominating the space created by the spitevermin. They parted to create a path towards the object of the slaves' labours, now revealed.

It was an arch. At least, it had been an arch at some time in the distant past. Of duardin construction, it stood five times the height of the spitevermin, broad enough to enter ten abreast. It leaned off-kilter, filled with blocks of rubble etched with duardin runes, brought down when the hall beyond had collapsed. The supporting columns were carved with angular, bearded faces that glowered down on the interlopers, the shadows caused by the flickering lamps making the eyes appear to stare around the room with distaste. The lintel stone, a single immense slab of carnelian-speckled granite, was covered in gilded script that glowed with a light not of the warp-lanterns.

A single figure swathed in voluminous black shrouds appeared at the tunnel mouth, his scabrous muzzle protruding from the patched hood. The plague monks turned and bowed their heads. Baring their fangs, the spitevermin glowered and snarled until the slaves threw themselves to their knees and bellies, grovelling and whining the name of their master.

'Poxmaster Felk…'

With him came his plague priests, six robed attendants bedecked in amulets and fetishes of the Great Horned Rat. Battered copper and tin censers hung from their belts, dribbling more warpfume. Each bore a staff taller than them, tipped with a triangular device of bones surrounding a hunk of raw black warpstone. The air churned around these staves, their corrupting magic like a faint green fire. Felk's rod was even larger and more impressive, a bifurcated branch with the skulls of five humans bound to it with rotted twine and rusted chain. Their eyes were nuggets of warpstone and their jawbones wired in such a way that they chattered madly with each stride that took him across the cavern. His priests followed a few steps behind, their gazes constantly shifting with nervous energy.

Felk stopped before the huge gate, under which a small gap had been dug. It was just large enough for him to step into had he desired, like a postern gate formed where two blocks of stone butted against each other at a sharp angle.

Instead of darkness, the hole glowed with an inner light, the same as that which lit the golden runes of the lintel. Felk's lips curled back in pleasure, revealing shards of broken teeth and black gums.

'Yes-yes!' he crowed, turning to his companions. 'See-see? Divinations were right-right. Duardin gate! Not just city, realm-burrowing tunnelway. No more begging, no more playing nice to Clan Nekrit for Poxmaster Felk and esteemed acolytes of Withering Canker.'

'We spray musk on the tolls of Warlord Shrilk!' exclaimed Priest Festik.

'Our own gate-gate!' laughed Priest Chittir.

'Where does it lead-lead?' Priest Kirrik asked as he took a step closer to the portal.

Felk gestured to one of the nearby spitevermin and then to the slave cowering at the warrior's feet.

'Send it through,' the Poxmaster commanded.

The spitevermin heaved up the squalling slave in one hand and dragged it up the ramp of stone and bodies leading to the gate. The slave twisted and made one last lunge for freedom, but was too weak from its exertions. Its eyes fixed on Felk with a last panicked glare. The spitevermin heaved the protesting skaven into the flickering light of the gap.

Felk saw the slave for a moment, silhouetted against the golden glow. A heartbeat later the shadow dissolved, accompanied by a drawn out screeching that suddenly stopped.

'Nowhere yet,' said Felk, turning away. Somewhere in the Realm of Life, that much the Poxmaster knew. It mattered not. A realmgate would give him access, the power to move far more swiftly than the gnaw-ways allowed. 'More dig-dig, whole gate must be open.'

He signalled to his troupe to turn around and follow him back to the upper chambers. As they left, the spitevermin withdrew, leaving the surviving overseers to lash the slaves back into action.

The route back to the main skaven city took them through a mixture of gnawed burrows and duardin-delved corridors and halls. There was filth everywhere, including half-eaten carcasses of animals and slaves, though anything of use had been stripped from the bodies. In the larger halls, where once duar-din lords had held court over their followers, nests crowded around the walls, ramshackle conglomerations of stones, mud, sticks, furs, bones and other materials.

Felk knew his city well and could navigate its byways and tunnels by smell alone in the places there were no luminous fungi or warp-lamps to light the way. Fresher draughts of air from the Whiteworld Above signalled their arrival at the upper-most level, dug from the ruins of a human city. The ground had swallowed the buildings whole in times past, though most had collapsed, scattered into a litter of broken pieces of once brightly coloured temple domes and age-worn bricks.

The Great Shrine, centre of Felk's domain, had been raised out of the combined duardin and human detritus. Built onto the remains of a palatial complex of buildings and towers, it resembled a gigantic termite mound more than anything. Packed earth, broken duardin mortar, human-crafted bricks, all had been thrown together for floor after floor. Haphazard bridges, walkways and stairs circled its girth, held together by frayed rope and rotting sinew. In many places it was shored up with ramshackle buttresses, cracks and slides in its surface caused by the frequent tremors. It looked as though it might collapse with the smallest shudder of the earth, but in reality was solidly built within and had withstood some of the fierc-est quakes since Felk's predecessors had erected it.

From chimneys and smokeholes issued a dozen columns of fumes, ranging from thick black smoke to misty green vapours. The effluence of the plague furnaces within spilled down pipes and rusted gutters, a spew of noxious liquids that pooled and spattered across the splintered remains of royal chambers and courtly cloisters.

At the summit stood a towering framework of rotted timbers

and chain, from which hung the great gong of the Withering Canker. Lit from above by weak sunlight coming through a great crack in the roof of the cavern, at first it looked to be made of simple copper stained by verdigris, but the surface shimmered with something like oil. On a rope-bound arm next to it was a warpstone-headed hammer. A network of wheels, belts and tackle descended into the Great Shrine to a capstan where three hundred slaves waited for the command to work the hammer.

The approach to the Great Shrine was joined by smaller temples that housed the plague monks, and a warren-like mess of barracks that held the spitevermin regiments. A causeway zigzagged up from the huddled abodes, joining with a stained arch that might have once been the vault of an immense cathedral, but was now the last bridge to the gate of Felk's inner domain.

The gate was made of overlapping planks and boards nailed and bolted together, reinforced by bars of untreated tree trunks and rusting rivets. It hung on two tusks that formed the entry arch, each higher than the duardin gate in the depths.

Felk started his ascent, dismissing his plague monks with a waved claw, though his priests and bodyguard remained close at hand. As he passed under the shadow of a broken human tower he felt a presence beside him that had not been there a moment earlier.

He suppressed a squeal, turning his fear to anger.

'You approach unannounced, Eshin lackey,' he snarled at the black-clad scout who had materialised at his left hand. The gutter runner cocked an emerald eye towards him, showing no fear or apology. The spitevermin belatedly dashed forwards but Felk stayed their attack with a sneer and a dismissive gesture.

'Come, quick-quick!' whispered the assassin-scout. 'Very important news. Come see!'

'Tell me,' said Felk. 'What news?'

Thriss, the agent Felk had hired from Clan Darkclaw, glanced warily at the nearby plague priests and shook his head.

'Come see. Alone.'

'Not mad,' snapped Felk, fearing duplicity. 'Tell me!'

The assassin's tail twitched twice, the blade attached to its end glinting. He shook his head again.

'Must see for self. Not let others see yet. *Big problem.*' These last words were delivered *sotto voce*, so vehemently that Felk stopped in his tracks, every nerve taut. He had never heard the gutter runner speak in such a way.

'Prepare for dismal feast,' Felk commanded his underlings, affecting an imperious stature to glare at them. 'I return soon.'

Before any of them could offer complaint or question, Felk directed Thriss to lead the way with a quick glance. The spitevermin split at their approach, uncertain what to do. Their fangleader, a hulking one-eyed blackfur called Skarth, moved to block his master's route, the tip of his halberd moving towards Thriss.

'What orders, Poxmaster?' His one good eye fixed on the assassin, the words issued as though he were chewing a gristly remnant of a victim. Foaming saliva wetted balding fur. 'We spill blood-blood?'

'Not now, fangleader.' Felk considered Thriss' short but worrying report. 'Soon-soon. Very soon. Guard Great Shrine ready for dismal feast. None but priests to enter.'

With a last surly glare at Thriss, Skarth moved aside, bringing up his wickedly bladed halberd. Felk hurried past, his thoughts a sudden whirl. It was enough to balance the contesting loyalties and usefulness of his own priests and monks, without worrying about developing rivalries between Thriss and his hired elites from the Savage Fang. The success at the realmgate and the dismal feast he had ordered in celebration were fast becoming overshadowed in his mind.

He made no complaint when Thriss set a brisk pace, leading the Poxmaster down through the barracks and into the widespread skaven dwellings beyond.

Along tunnels and alleys they sped, Felk feeling more and more out of his element with every step. Much of the city was deserted, its inhabitants hunting and scavenging in the Whiteworld Above during the last sunlight – the skaven disliked the sun, but knew better than to venture at night when all manner of monstrous beasts and birds searched for prey on the mountain slopes. The twilight of dawn and dusk was their domain.

They travelled for some time, leaving behind the dropping-strewn streets and passageways, coming into a poorly explored part of the duardin ruins that had only recently been uncovered by a quake.

'Must climb,' said Thriss, stopping beside a crack opened in the side of a broad, smooth-hewn tunnel. Without another word he disappeared into the fissure, claws scraping on rock.

It had been some time since Felk had needed to perform such physical activity. He tightened his rope belt and tucked in the hem of his robe to free his legs. Wedging his staff into a safe crevice, he started the ascent, finding easy purchase in the jagged break.

To his relief the climb did not last long, the split rock chimney taking them to a columned gallery somewhere in the mountainside. Clambering over the edge, Felk found himself on a neatly tiled floor, the colour faded but a duardin design just about visible in the dusk glow. The long balcony stretched for dozens of paces to the left and right, archways in both directions blocked by debris or overgrown by roots from trees in the soil above.

Thriss was at the edge, looking down over the low stone balustrade.

'There!' He pointed to the right, jabbing a claw repeatedly at something below. 'There-there! Quick-quick!'

Felk approached cautiously, not wishing to give Thriss the opportunity to throw him over the edge if that was his intent. Staying far out of reach, he risked a glance into the valley below.

At first he was not sure what he could see. Something shone in the light of the setting sun, a ribbon of white winding along the valley floor. He thought it was a river at first, but as his eyes adjusted he saw that there was a column of figures picking their way between the rocks and broken remnants of duardin architecture.

From this height it was hard to make out details, but Felk could see that the armoured warriors were gigantic, almost as large as the rat ogres of the Moulder clans. They bore unsheathed weapons and many had broad shields decorated with a design: a stylised golden star with a long tail.

'What-what is it?' snapped Thriss. 'Not tribes. Not human.'

'Not human,' Felk murmured, caught between intrigue and dread. They might have been warriors of Chaos, but he saw no mark or icon that indicated which power they served.

'Back-back!'

Thriss threw himself at Felk, snatching hold of the Pox-master's robe to drag him away from the edge of the gallery. Felk thrashed from the assassin's grip in time to see more of the giants swooping past on shining wings. He slithered back across the tiles, worming his way into the dark shadows where Thriss had already taken shelter.

Eyes wide, teeth bared, they watched in trembling silence while five of the winged soldiers peeled away, wheeling through the sky towards the gallery. It seemed as though their leader looked directly at him, the red eyes of the masked helm blank and pitiless. A moment later the strange warriors changed trajectory, descending out of sight.

'Bad-bad,' he said. They were so close to unearthing the realmgate. The imminence of that victory, a few timely decapitations by Skarth and a couple of accidents engineered by Thriss had stayed off the worst of his underlings' latest efforts to grab power, but an outside threat could provoke a coup more dangerous than the daily infighting of skaven politics. 'Bad-bad. Bad-bad.'

Thriss had earned his warpstone payment twice over. Felk turned to say as much to the agent, only to find the assassin had already fled back down the crack.

Alone and exposed on the balcony, the Poxmaster quickly followed.

CHAPTER NINE

The crunch of the snow sounded impossibly loud. The creak of armour was an assault on Arkas' senses. The blustering wind skirled and hooted in fantastical melodies, every gust carving swirls in the snow. He could hear breathing, fast and heaving, distorted by a helm. He had thought it was Dolmetis, but realised it was his own. He fixed his eyes ahead, seeing vague silhouettes through the blizzard that had descended moments after they had started up the ridgeline. Even vision made perfect by the artifice of Sigmar could not penetrate the white veil ahead.

With every stride he expected the ground to give way and he knew he should proceed with more caution, but his blood was still fired from the fight with the Chaos warriors. The spirit of Ursungorod, the magic-infused air, drove him on as much as memories of the oath he had sworn.

The wind surged for a moment, clearing away the fog, and then stillness enveloped the ridge. He heard Dolmetis take in a sharp breath as the darker shadows materialised into the shapes of men, women and beasts. Like Arkas, the Knight-Vexillor already had his sword in hand, but the Lord-Celestant caught a glimpse of the blade as Dolmetis drew it up in readiness.

'Calm yourself,' Arkas said quietly. 'These foes are beyond our wrath.'

As they neared the figures Arkas could see what he had already suspected – each was clad in a faceted sheath of translucent ice. Like blue-tinted glass it covered them, a layer of frozen water no thicker than his finger. There were fighters in the garb of the Ursungoran tribes, most with expressions forever locked in fear or pain, eyes wide and glittering with crystals, the spittle on their tongues like air bubbles. Amongst them were men and women showing various signs of Chaos mutation – extra limbs, lizard-scaled skin, cat-like eyes, a profusion of horns, tusks and fangs.

There were snow tigers and cave bears too, and larger beasts also warped by Chaos – manticores, hippogryphs, hydras and others, towering twice as tall as the Stormcast Eternals, some even larger still. A squid-like bekevic had been drawn from its watery home, or forced out by some mortal hand. A few of the monsters still carried riders clad in armour of Chaotic origin, made of bone or whorled with strange devices, or etched with runes that continued to shift and writhe even within the ice bonds.

'What bizarre display have we discovered?' whispered Dolmetis. The muttering of the Decimators sounded dully from further back.

'Touch nothing,' Arkas reminded them, stepping around a frozen hound skulking close to the ground, its legs buried in the snow, ears back as it whimpered at something unseen ahead. 'These are the trophies of the Queen of the Peak. Disturb them and we risk joining their ranks.'

He stopped when he realised Dolmetis was no longer at his shoulder. Arkas turned in time to see the Knight-Vexillor approaching a statue-like woman, her hands upraised as if to protect her face, locks flowing from beneath a tall helm like a frozen waterfall.

'What enchantment slew them?' asked Dolmetis, slowly circling the female warrior. 'Why did she kill them?'

Arkas stepped up next to the standard bearer as he completed his circuit and stopped in front of the woman, bent slightly to peer into her face.

'Why do you assume they are dead?' asked Arkas. He could imagine Dolmetis' look of surprise inside his helm as he twisted sharply to look at his lord.

'They live? Inside this frost-born casing?'

'So legend speaks,' replied Arkas. 'For a time, at least, until the Queen of the Peak grows weary of their company, or forgives them, or otherwise releases them from torment.'

'There have been survivors?'

Arkas shook his head.

'You misunderstand me, Dolmetis.' He pointed to the woman's chest. The ice was darker, denser in the slight hollow her breasts formed in the mail shirt. 'She spares them further suffering by lancing an icicle through their hearts. The bodies remain.'

'I do not think it is wise to risk this venture.' Dolmetis straightened and looked back along the ridge towards the Icemere, though it was far from view. 'Let us lead the army to the rendezvous and begin the attack on the skaven. We have no need of this hag's aid.'

'I think we do,' said Arkas, stepping away a few paces. He

indicated something further ahead, gesturing for Dolmetis to look.

The Knight-Vexillor adjusted his position to see what Arkas intended. Two dozen paces ahead, just within the retreating bank of fog, stood the unmistakable shape of a skaven. Three, in fact, huddled close together, hunched over, their rags stiff in a breeze that no longer blew, their serrated daggers held in frozen hands and prehensile tails.

Arkas set forth with long strides, Dolmetis following after the briefest hesitation. On closer inspection they found that the skaven were clad in brown and black, the garb of thieves and silent killers, their ratty faces wrapped with dark bandages. Something greenish-black shimmered on the edges of their weapons.

'Weeping blades,' said Dolmetis. 'Assassins. They meant harm to the Queen of the Peak.'

'There is another skaven, over there,' said Arkas. He pointed at a frozen vermin figure cowled in thick robes, a staff in its hands. 'They tried to send an emissary and when that failed they dispatched would-be killers. When that also failed, they had the approaches barred by their tame tribesmen. I think that none have approached in many years, decades or perhaps centuries even.'

'The Queen of the Peak is probably mad with loneliness too? Any other good news, Lord-Celestant?'

Arkas grinned inside his helm and pointed with his hammer. A much larger shadow rose from the ridge, curving away to the left. It looked like a bridge composed of a single arc, though its far end was lost in the mists. Something moved above, coming closer.

'We draw close to our goal,' said Arkas. 'And here comes Hastor to accompany us on the last stretch.'

The Lord-Celestant spoke truthfully and the flying shape quickly resolved into the Knight-Venator, gliding down towards the ridge with vortices of snow trailing from his shimmering wings. He landed a short distance away and met Arkas halfway.

'You seem unsettled, Hastor,' said Arkas, feeling a wash of agitation from the commander of his Angelos Conclave. 'I hope you did not pass the gate as I commanded.'

'In truth, my lord, only a direct command to step over the threshold would have forced me beneath that arch,' confessed the Knight-Venator. He turned his attention to Dolmetis. 'I trust all went well on the lake.'

'Righteous bloodshed is its own reward,' replied the Knight-Vexillor. 'I find myself on more uncertain ground at the moment.'

'The way ahead is free of foes?' said Arkas, cutting across Hastor's next words. 'None approached the tower?'

'None dared try.' Hastor indicated the sharp slopes to either side of the ridge. 'A few attempted to negotiate the snows below, but the storm took them.'

'We shall push on.'

The going was quicker from then on. The mists parted before them, revealing more and more of the frozen statues as the ridge widened to a plateau from which rose the bridge Arkas had seen. Like before, the Queen of the Peak's victims were a mix of human, Chaos-tainted, skaven and beast. The ice covering betrayed the greater age of many of them, frosted, chipped and cracked in places, though the screaming, terrified faces within showed no sign of decay.

The bridge itself was of duardin construction, perfectly fitted and mortared stones creating a span ten paces wide with a low parapet at each edge. Though the skills of the old duardin mason and engineers had been magnificent, it was the enchantment of the Queen of the Peak that had protected the bridge from the decline that had ruined the rest of Ursungorod's ancient cityscape – the snow did not settle here, but a thin veneer of ice covered every intricately carved block and thread of mortar.

Arkas did not ascend immediately, but led his Stormcast companions beneath the bridge, to the crumbling edge of the plateau. The mountain dropped down into a sheer chasm, the forests below just a dark smear against white, the glittering ribbon of a frozen river even further away. The fog continued to roll back, revealing the gorge. It was over five hundred paces wide, the far side a jagged face of black rock and pale ice.

'It was not like this when last I came here,' said Arkas, turning his gaze to the left, towards the bridge. 'This chasm was but a javelin's cast across, the duardin bridge crossing over the ruins of the outer castle.'

'What use is a fortress that has a bridge over its wall?' asked Dolmetis. 'An enemy could march in and besiege the keep with ease.'

'The bridge was not built in time of war,' replied Arkas. 'It linked the duardin lands to those of my forefathers, when Sigmar first drove the taint from Ursungorod and peace prevailed for a time. The bridge was marked by powerful duardin runework. I think that it would collapse at their command if needed, taking any attackers to their deaths and sealing the castle.'

'The remains of the outer wall and gates, such as they are, are down there,' said Hastor, pointing into the abyss. 'I descended earlier. The far side of the cliff is marked by old passages and halls, revealed in cross-section as if a blade had cut through them.'

'What of the tower?' Arkas' question was answered not by the

Knight-Venator but by a swirl of wind that revealed the furthest extent of the sky-bridge. The stocky design of the ruins unveiled by the retreating cloud was obviously of duardin making, but the central tower was taller and more elegant, topped by an onion-shaped dome that still sparkled with red and gold.

'Remarkable...' breathed Dolmetis.

'Indeed it is,' replied Hastor.

Arkas looked on in stunned wonder.

The bridge descended as it had always done, to a sturdy four-towered barbican in front of the Queen of the Peak's abode. The tumbled remnants of the duardin fort lay about on broken cobbles and flagged courtyards. In turn, the tower and ruins stood upon a great hunk of frozen rock, held only by the bridge itself, the vastness of the chasm dropping away below the inverted cone of the foundations so that it seemed to hang in the air. Openings that were the remnants of duardin vaults and storerooms broke the outside of the edifice, squared caves and smooth-hewn ledges.

'The duardin runes you spoke of, my lord,' said Dolmetis. 'You think they might still work?'

'I think they were activated long ago but nullified by the power of the queen,' replied Arkas. He looked at the Knight-Vexillor and shrugged. 'Should she wish to deposit us into the gorge, she has only to release her icy grip. Bridge and castle would drop as surely as a stone from your fist.'

'But she would plummet also,' said Hastor, 'without the bridge to hold her tower. There is little danger.'

'Says the knight with the wings,' Dolmetis said sourly.

'Time is passing,' Arkas said, turning back to the bridge. 'I will return to the army before night falls if possible. I will proceed alone.'

The Knight-Vexillor and Knight-Venator accepted this order

without comment and moved to join the Decimators that had formed a defensive ring around the approach to the bridge. Arkas started his ascent.

The climb was not steep but the slippery surface of the bridge forced him to proceed with a little more caution than normal – the duardin-height wall to each side did not even reach to his waist and would have been little barrier against a fall.

At the apex of the arc he stopped to survey the mountains that had once been his home. The peaks seemed so familiar – he could remember the names of them all – but it was more than geography that made Ursungorod, and the indefinable spirit that suffused the land had been changed. Near the roof of the world, far from the rivers and forests that were the foundation of the peaks, the traces of magic that rose this high were thinned, like the air. Away from the near-overwhelming rush of power he had felt on his first return, he could taste the change, the telltale foulness of Chaos pervading everything.

Could it have even entered into the mind of the Queen of the Peak? She had been an ally at best for Arka Bear-clad, never a friend – giving support only in return for something. The Chaos Gods had become all-powerful in the centuries of Sigmar's enforced exile to the Celestial Realm and over the turn of the years the queen might have succumbed to their threats and temptations.

With more uncertain thoughts in mind, he started down the far side of the bridge, heading towards the half-ruined fortress that hung impossibly over the valley. The stones soon gave way to timeworn paving, which led a short distance to the shadow of the gatehouse looming over the road. The wall to either side had long since been toppled, by time and assault, even as it had been in Arkas' life as a mortal.

Of the gate itself nothing remained either. Even so, there was a barrier, a shimmer of energy between the massive bastions that flanked the road, a haze that obscured the tower beyond. Moving off the path towards the ruins of the wall, Arkas could see a line of thick frost that encircled the keep as surely as any curtain wall. His keen eyes picked out the shine of bones and skulls trapped within the ice beyond the boundary circumscribed by the ancient stones.

'Though you might not know me by sight, know me by heart,' he announced, using the dead tongue of his homeland rather than the language of Azyr. The words seemed heavy and crude after so long conversing in the speech of the immortals. 'I am Stormcast, a warrior of Sigmar, God-King from the world-that-was. Arkas I am called, though I am known to my lord and companions as the Warbeast. The Bear-clad I was before Sigmar took me, Arka the Uniter, the Bear of Hard Winters. By another name you knew me, and you alone, written with this rune by your hand.'

Laying down his weapons, Arkas knelt before the portal.

'"Saviour", you told me it meant when last I was here. The Fang of Freedom you called me. I am here to deliver on my promise, though it has been long in the reckoning.'

Silence followed, even the wind stilled while the Queen of the Peak considered his pledge. Arkas gripped his hammer and sword, stood up and waited. Nothing happened.

A test, he thought, looking at the shimmering curtain just a pace away. Beyond that he could see the wide, low steps leading up to the arched doors of the tower itself. One step, one stride would take him into the domain of the Queen.

An act of courage? No. His courage had never been doubted, by any that knew him.

An act of trust.

He stepped into the veil.

CHAPTER TEN

The sky was blue above, the air sharp, cold and invigorating. The sun was low in the sky, a winter sun devoid of warmth but reassuring all the same. Frost crackled under Arkas' tread, his boots leaving clear imprints in the thin layer that covered the flagstones leading to the tower.

Exactly as it had been hundreds of years earlier when the Bear-clad had made his last journey along this road.

It's a gate, he realised.

The barbican was a realmgate of sorts, the Queen of the Peak's domain a pocket enclave, a self-contained magical plateau shifted slightly aside from Ursungorod and the Realm of Beasts. The Bear-clad would not have understood such a thing, the concept of the Mortal Realms layered and entwined about each other as alien to his mind as the idea that he might one day become an immortal war leader clad in armour forged from metal mined in the heart of a dead world.

The grand doors at the top of the steps were open, the flickering light of brands glowing from within. He ascended the stairs four at a stride, covering the ground quickly. He paused for a heartbeat at the entrance. Like everything else, a veneer of snow and ice lay like a patina on the stone and wood. The sigils and images carved into the doors glittered in the light of the brands – faces of bears, suns with beneficent smiles, and stylised lightning bolts that reminded him of the magnificent city of Sigmaron.

It was exactly as he remembered. *Exactly*. Like a dream being re-enacted. It was impossible, of course, a trick of this mind. Even so, as he stepped into the light of the braziers and torches within, he could not shake the feeling that he was doing more than following in his footsteps.

The entrance hall was lavishly decorated, a thick red carpet running the length of the chamber. Archways curtained with velvet of the same colour broke the walls to either side. Both fabrics were threaded with gold in a repeating design of flame-like waves interspersed with triangular mountains and simple star-like suns.

But all was frozen still, every bend in the cloth, every flame in the sconces caught in a moment of time. The silence was all-consuming, muffling his step, swallowing the scrape and creak of his armour.

The only movement was Arkas. Leaving a trail of vapour from shallow breaths he advanced along the hall, as he had done before. He knew nothing of what lay beyond the curtains and dared not speculate.

Something caught his attention and he looked down, surprised to see a single trail of footprints leading towards the stair. His stride was much longer now, his body magnified by the Reforging upon the Anvil of the Apotheosis. Yet when he glanced back, he saw only that single set of tracks. He could even see the pattern of the hobnails in his old boots.

The stair inside, ascending from left to right, was more like that of a rampart, narrow enough for two men to hold back an army. Arkas covered the distance to the next floor in moments and then from there, ignoring the wooden doors to the left and right, walked along a short landing to a spiral staircase that he knew took him to the domed chamber at the top of the tower.

He had to duck to fit his massive frame through the door at the top, and stepped into a circular hall roughly thirty paces across. The door closed behind him with the faint click of a lock.

The ice coated the inside of the dome, with facets and edges forming crystal faces at odd angles to each other. Arkas saw his reflection three dozen times over, turquoise and gold refracted and contorted all around. He stepped into the centre of the chamber, the images splintering and reforming.

Hammer held to one side, runeblade sheathed at his hip, Arkas waited in silence. He looked up and saw his helm mask glaring back at him from between the dark wooden vaults of the ceiling, eyeholes suffused with a glow of celestial energy. It was reassuring to know that, even here in the heart of the icy palace, the link to Azyr was strong. Should anything happen, should his body perish, he would be called back to Sigmaron, there to be recast and remoulded.

Immortality, though not without a price.

A breeze drifted across the circular hall, the slightest gust that barely stirred his cloak. It brought with it the queen's voice, soft but hostile.

'Who claims the name of Arka Bear-clad?' she demanded. To the right a reflection of Arkas was replaced by a vague outline of a middle-aged woman clad in white robes edged with fur, her silvery hair hanging long and straight about her shoulders. Her eyes were a piercing blue, shards of ice given sapphire life. 'Reveal yourself!'

'I am Arka,' he replied. He lifted away the mask that hid his face. He almost started at his reflection, having forgotten the changes that had been wrought by the artifice of Sigmar. His beard and hair were short, never requiring to be shorn again, his eyes sunken and dark. Three scars ran across his face, one from each eye to the ears and another down the centre of his forehead.

'What have they done to you, my champion?' A sigh wafted through the chamber, perhaps of pity, or sadness. Another reflection shifted, revealing a matronly figure in the depths of the ice, bundled in a black shawl with a hood over her head.

'They made me strong,' Arkas replied.

He turned his head to face this new image. Other mirrored figures fractured and reformed on the edge of his sight. He caught glimpses of different people, though when he looked directly at them he saw only his own ravaged face. His mother, his father, Radomira, the sculpted masks of his warriors, even the bearded, noble visage of the God-King himself.

A third manifestation of the Queen of the Peak appeared, almost directly in front of Arkas. She was young, clad in white-enamelled armour chased with silver and sapphires. It was no ceremonial suit, and neither was the blade in her hand a weapon for parades. A warrior-queen, her face enclosed within the cheek guards of a helm with a white horsehair crest, eyes boring into Arkas.

'Oathbreaker! Deserter! Traitor! You abandoned your people.' Her voice dropped to a plaintive whisper. 'You abandoned me.'

'Never, my Queen of the Peak,' Arkas replied. As he addressed the latest apparition he could see himself as he had been in an ice mirror to his right – a full beard and head of hair, a nose broken more times than he could remember, glowering eyes beneath bushy brows. For an instant he forgot that he was Stormcast as the memory of his past life was given form in this place. 'I was taken. I would not have willed it, but I have returned to fulfil my oath.'

'Your oath?' This was from the first Queen, imperious and distant. 'Your oath to your mother or your promise to me?'

'Both.'

'Yet it was not in your power to do either.'

Her words bit as deeply as an axe blow. The memory of his ascension to the Celestial Realm welled up inside him, bursting free from deep behind the walls raised by Grungni's craft.

'I tried,' said Arka. The frustration and sadness that had overpowered him in that moment surged through him. He fought through the bleakness, a snarl escaping gritted teeth. 'The Bear-clad is dead, but the Warbeast will deliver where he failed.'

Quiet followed, his words ringing around the chamber and in his ears. The images of the queen moved of their own accord, coming together into one reflection, an amalgam of all three – stately, armoured and motherly all at the same time.

'You know that which I desire more than anything,' said the queen. 'Do you renew your pledge to deliver it?'

'It shall be done,' said Arkas. He replaced his mask and the likenesses all became that of the Lord-Celestant again, his mind of a single purpose. 'There is something you must do for me first.'

'No,' said the Queen of the Peak. 'The pact was sealed long ago, and I have fulfilled my part.'

'You did not,' insisted Arkas.

'I gave you the winds and the snows to command, as you demanded.'

'A power I never had the chance to unleash.'

'Of no consequence. The fault of your *god-king,* not mine.'

Arkas turned on his heel and took a step towards the door. He stopped as he felt a chill seep up through his foot. Glancing down, he saw tendrils of ice crystals snaking up over his boot and onto his leg.

'I am here to grant us both a fresh chance,' he said. 'Answer my questions and I will deliver on what I promised.'

'I will not let you betray me again!'

The cold branches crept further up his leg and fresh veins of frost started to encase the other. His breath formed a thick fog. The plates of his armour paled with a thin coating of ice.

'I am your last and only chance for freedom,' Arkas said. 'Aid me and you serve the God-King, who shall be handsome in his favours. Or strike me down with frost-spite and remain here in your prison forever.'

Arkas felt his heart thudding, every pulse a drumbeat in his chest, the rush of blood a surge of noise in his ears. Had he judged her wrong?

A rime crept over his face, fogging his vision, crawling along the channels of his scars. He could feel a current stirring inside, the Anvil of the Apotheosis beckoning to his spirit while death stole along his nerves.

He could no longer feel his legs, his hands were leaden weights, a coil of ice binding his fingers to the haft of his hammer. In a dozen reflections he saw himself as he should be, a withered, frost-bound corpse.

The fate Sigmar had spared him, he realised with a shock.

'You will... be free...' he gasped, his breath forming crystals on the inside of his mask.

He heard the faintest whisper, barely audible over the thunder of his own heartbeat.

'Sleep.'

'I cannot,' Arkas managed, each word a triumph of will against the freezing of his muscles.

'Beloved descendant.'

Arkas swallowed, the motion painful, as though swallowing a stone. He closed his eyes, frost thickening on the lashes.

With a shudder, he took in a great final lungful of chilling air and the magic of the queen's breath flowed into him.

CHAPTER ELEVEN

Descending into the valley, Theuderis' host had left the worst of the snows and storms behind. The wind was strong, bending tall firs and pines, whipping the great branches back and forth to dust the marching Stormcasts with falling snow. Roots slithered like serpents underfoot, opportunistically snaring feet and ankles. Even the stones and boulders rebelled at the presence of the Stormcasts, forming frowning faces and leering eyes as they passed, rolling to trip and hinder the step of Sigmar's chosen, the larger rocks toppling down banks and hills in lumbering attempts to crush the invaders.

Tyrathrax padded quietly across the whiteness, her harness and armour jingling. The creak and tromp of the Stormcast Eternals advancing between the trees were the only other sounds. The lack of birdsong and small animals still disturbed Theuderis, but he allowed himself a moment of reverie as he contemplated his surrounds.

'It has a certain grandeur, I give it that,' Theuderis said to his dracoth. 'A fallen glory, you might say. When the taint has been cleansed it will be beautiful again.'

The trees formed an almost unbroken canopy and except for the odd beam breaking through a gap caused by the wind, Theuderis had not seen the sun since they had entered, not long after dawn. The white-and-blue of his warriors was muted in the gloom, swallowed by the green and brown shadows.

A shaft of light sprang into being a short way ahead – not the soft gold of the mountain sun but a paler glow Theuderis recognised immediately as the gleam of a celestial beacon. Samat descended slowly through a break in the leaves, coming to rest a few paces ahead of the Lord-Celestant. The Knight-Azyros' wings furled with a last glint of colour as the two met.

'There is no sign of the road we saw yesterday, Lord Silverhand.' Samat turned to look along the line of advance. 'It has been... swallowed. The forest is vast. We shall not see the sky before midday tomorrow if we continue in this direction. A wide river bounds the forest half a day to the south. We saw no ford or bridge and the current is strong.'

'North?'

'The slopes rise steeply but we would break the treeline before dusk. The ground is broken by shoulders of rock and more ruined settlements. The snow is heaped on the higher slopes, and I fear avalanches would be a constant threat, needing only the slightest tremor to bring a storm of ice and rock upon us. The land has not taken kindly to our presence – who can say what other threats it harbours.'

The memory of the collapsing cliff flashed through Theuderis' mind – warriors engulfed by a tide of earth and stone, bright flashes of lightning as so many Stormcasts were called back to Sigmaron.

'We continue through the forest. Though it is hostile, it does not appear to pose too great a danger,' said the Lord-Celestant.

Samat hesitated before bowing his head in acknowledgement.

'Speak your mind.'

'There is still the option of the city beneath,' said the Knight-Azyros. 'The duardin ruins we have seen stand atop vast delvings. I expressed my doubts before, but I must say that I am of a mind that the route below might prove the swifter.'

'The swiftest road is by no means the surest,' replied Theuderis. 'We have been fortunate to have eluded the attention of the skaven thus far. Doubtless Arkas and his Warbeasts have stirred their nest. It serves no purpose for the moment to draw their eye to us.'

'We cannot know how the Celestial Vindicators fare, my lord,' argued Samat. 'They could be sorely beset and every delay threatens the success of our mission.'

'It is the task to which Sigmar appointed them,' said Theuderis, crossing his arms. 'We cannot judge from afar whose need is greater, ours or Arkas'. If we hasten and run into peril, what succour can we provide?

'It is for your wisdom that you are Lord-Celestant,' admitted Samat, bowing further, 'and through your words is spoken Sigmar's will. As you command, we obey.'

'Do not chastise yourself, Samat.' Theuderis reached out a hand and beckoned for the Knight-Azyros to approach closer. 'I would not have my officers close their lips and minds. The advice was given in good temper, and I accept it. Yet my own mind is set upon its path for the moment and I would see it run the course for a while longer.'

Before Samat could reply, a noise silenced him. It was a distant horn blast, far shriller than the clarions of the Knights-Heraldor. Tyrathrax snarled and the Stormcasts threading through the trees stopped where they were, instinctively raising their weapons.

Answering notes came from ahead and behind. Theuderis twisted in his saddle to peer through the trees but could see nothing. He turned back to issue an order to Samat but the Knight-Azyros had already taken flight. Nothing could be seen through the branches and leaves above.

Tyrathrax sensed her master's agitation and snarled, tail lashing back and forth like an angry snake.

Theuderis heard a cry, the metallic shout of one of his warriors. He could not make out the words or direction in the press of trees. Some of the nearest Stormcast Eternals started out into the woods, calling to each other to find the source of the disturbance.

'Stand fast!' he roared, dragging free his tempestos hammer. 'Form a perimeter, castellation line!'

The horns sounded again, louder and closer, coming from all around it seemed, yet still Theuderis could see nothing and no report came from his men. The Stormcasts did their best to reform the marching column into a defensive line, but the closeness and thickness of the trees meant that they could stand no more than four or five abreast in many places. The Primes strode back and forth, tightening the shield walls of the Liberators, moving the Judicators into gaps in the line from where Azyr-forged bows and crossbows would be able to mark an incoming foe.

Theuderis headed back to the rearguard as a third chorus of strident horns sounded out of the gloom beneath the trees. Tyrathrax's claws gouged great divots of mud and leaves as she ran, spraying wet mulch and ice behind. Low branches whipped at Theuderis' helm and pauldrons as he crashed through them, needles and splintered wood falling in his wake. Armour clattered as a troop of Protectors sprinted alongside, their Prime urging them into position with short, sharp commands.

'Trajos, what can you see?' Theuderis called out to the Judicator-Prime in charge of the Justicar Conclave that formed the foundation of the rearguard force. Hefting his thunderbolt crossbow, the Judicator-Prime glanced back at his commander.

'Nothing, Lord Silverhand. Just trees and snow.'

'They must be almost upon us,' warned Theuderis as he stared up and down the slope trying to discern any movement in the shadows. 'Those horns were close at hand.'

Snapping wood above drew their attention to the canopy. A white-armoured figured crashed through the branches, his wings scattering iridescent metal feathers, bloody droplets streaming from a great rent across his breastplate. A heartbeat later another Prosecutor plunged down from above, his left arm missing. Both hit the ground like meteors, throwing up explosions of dead plant matter and dirt.

'Hold ground!' Theuderis bellowed as several Justicars broke the line to move towards the wounded flyers. 'Trajos, control your men.'

The Judicator-Prime snapped reprimands while Tyrathrax moved out of the column at Theuderis' urging. He saw the one-armed Prosecutor push to his feet, using his hammer as a prop. The other crackled with celestial power and disappeared, succumbing to the wound he had suffered.

'A manticore, my lord!' gasped the Prosecutor. 'And a griffon also!'

A shout drew Theuderis' attention back along the host, towards the main body of troops. Flares of power seared between the trees as a regiment of Judicators unleashed the missiles of their skybolt and shockbolt bows. From his position,

Theuderis could see nothing of their targets, but amongst the crackle of celestial energy he heard feral snarls and howls.

Even as his mind raced to accept this development, a darkness passed over him, accompanied by thrashing in the treetops. A short distance away a tree snapped and into view tumbled an immense beast. It had the body of a giant black-and-white striped cat and an eagle's head, its red-and-black feathered wings tattered and bloody. Its beak was locked around the right arm of a Prosecutor-Prime, his hammer still in his grip.

The Prime repeatedly smashed his fist into the creature's eye as the two flailed into the mulch, while its front claws raked back and forth across his ivory cuirass. With a supreme effort, the Stormcast hauled himself onto the back of the beast as it struggled to straighten, still raining blows against its feathered skull.

A nearby retinue of Decimators leapt into the attack, hewing at the downed monster with thunderaxes as though it were a fallen tree, every blow throwing up a fountain of thick blood.

Shouts and monstrous howling betrayed the airborne battle continuing out of sight above, but Theuderis had no time to consider this – their attackers had revealed themselves, charging along and down the slope from out of the shade.

Beastmen, hundreds of them. Most had goat-like features with curling horns, as tall as a normal man, crude axes, swords and clubs in hand. They carried wooden shields fixed with hardened hide, onto which triangular symbols and circular devices had been painted. Some were almost as big as a Stormcast, using both hands to wield their axes and mauls, their horns twisting like helms about their faces.

Before them rushed a swarm of smaller creatures, some no bigger than waist-high to Theuderis, the largest no taller than his midriff. They wielded stone-tipped spears and hide bucklers, brutish faces snarling, leather-skinned with stubby horns and chins sporting tufts of ungainly thick hair.

'Target the gors,' the Lord-Celestant commanded Trajos. 'Leave the ungors to me.'

The Judicator-Prime gestured for the wounded Prosecutor to retreat into the sanctuary behind the retinue, his Stormcasts parting neatly to let him pass and then reforming. Tyrathrax bounded towards the enemy as a fusillade of celestial energy flared through the trees, over the heads of the smaller onrushing ungors and into the foes beyond. Explosions of cosmic power lit the forest, every detonation accompanied by the shrieks and bellows of dying beastmen.

Theuderis rode on, trusting to the impeccable aim of his warriors as another salvo of fire and lightning scythed past to wreak more bloody ruin through the mobs of charging Chaos-tainted. Scant moments from crashing head-on into the oncoming tide of ungors, the Lord-Celestant glanced around and truly saw the extent of the enemy they faced. The forest teemed with beastmen of all sizes and varieties, their banners and shields bearing the marks and icons of dozens of different tribes and champions, their sigils and ornaments showing worship to all of the Chaos pantheon, with many skavenesque symbols amongst them.

Even as Tyrathrax leapt into the throng of smaller beastmen, fangs and claws mauling and slashing, Theuderis realised that a greater power had forged the unholy alliance of beastmen warbands and clans that now assailed his host. Only a creature with immense influence could command such a force; only the most lucrative promises and dire threats were capable of overwhelming the natural antipathy and infighting of so many warp-tainted creatures. A daemon perhaps, or a Champion of Chaos not yet revealed.

He laid about with his tempestos hammer, every strike oblite-rating an ungor with a blast of celestial force. He and Tyrathrax continued to plough through the small beastmen, their spears shattering and splintering on sigmarite plates, shields hewn asunder by dagger-like claws and teeth, or crushed and smashed aside with every swing of Theuderis' hammer.

Like a swimmer surfacing, dracoth and rider burst through the throng of the ungors, taking a moment to pause and eval-uate the progress of the battle. Immense bull-headed creatures, equine mutants and other types of beastmen joined the fray, lowing and snarling and screaming in the dark tongue of Chaos. They fell upon the vanguard first, but solid lines of Liberators with shields locked weathered the initial storm and now they counter-attacked with warblades and ham-mers, their Primes surging forwards with devastating sweeps of two-handed weapons.

The manticore had been forced down through the canopy, its ruddy fur marked with many wounds, leathery wings bro-ken and ragged. Its bizarre human-leonine face was a picture of rage, its deafening howls and roars audible over the crash of weapons and war-shouts of the Silverhands. A ring of Retribu-tors formed around the beast, ensorcelled hammers and maces pounding like Grungni himself at the Forge of Ages, protected from attack by rapid volleys of missiles from nearby Judicators that cut down any beast that came within fifty paces.

The centre had been spared any meaningful assault so far, but the Stormcasts arranged in retinues of alternating melee and missile troops knew better than to break formation yet. If the van or rear was overwhelmed it would be to the core of the army their Stormcast companions would retreat. Like the keep of a castle, the Redeemer Conclaves were the underlying strength of the army, the fulcrum of strategy and refuge in need.

Movement rippling through the branches above drew Theuderis' eye before he could check how the rearguard fared. More ungors scampered monkey-like through the boughs, thinking themselves safe from the ire of the Lord-Celestant.

Tyrathrax reared at his simple command, roaring forth a tempest of magical bolts from her maw. The storm ignited the cones, wood and leaves, setting fire in fur and flesh. Shrieking and gibbering, the ungors dropped to the forest floor, to be met by the dracoth and rider pouncing forwards with tireless fury.

Two dozen more foes had been slain when Theuderis redirected his attention back to the line. Voltaran had moved back with some of the Judicators to pour more lightning-fuelled bolts into the horde, carpeting the ground with the bodies of the dead. Yet it seemed for all the ire of the Stormcasts, the numbers of the beastmen were greater, and they were driven on by some power more potent than their horrendous losses.

Tyrathrax snarled, her claws sticking in the mire of bodies underfoot, the corpses sliding and splitting beneath her tread as she laboured towards fresh foes. She spat lightning again, frustrated that she could not rend with her claws, turning another handful of ungors to ashen clouds. Bunching her muscles, the dracoth leapt free of the bloody morass and found firmer ground, sensing Theuderis' desire to return to the line.

CHAPTER TWELVE

When he opened his eyes, Arkas could see all of Ursungorod. It took him a moment to accept it, so vast and unnatural was the view. Every sheet of ice was an eye, every snowflake an ear, every icicle a fingertip.

See, hear and feel as I see, hear and feel. Seek what you must.

His presence stretched the length and breadth of the mountains, the power dizzying. He focused, drawing the vision within him, seeing the tower from the outside, as though standing on the broken curtain wall. He turned his mind's eye and flowed effortlessly back across the bridge, sparing barely a glance for Hastor, Dolmetis and the Decimators at the far end.

He allowed his consciousness to fracture like a splitting ice flow, part of him zooming to watch over the Stormcasts still holding position on the Icemere, the rest of him skating to and fro through the wilds, leaping from snow-laden branches to drifts to frozen puddles in the blink of an eye. He scrambled across rockfalls of skull-shaped stones and slid along stone arches with icicle fangs. In the waters of Ursungorod's hundreds of rivers he splashed through rapids between dagger-pinnacles and across impossible waterfalls that flowed up the slopes. He felt the eternal presence of the trees, slumbering in places, alive and predatory in others.

Arkas felt the tread of many feet as though on his skin. Concentrating, he saw different tribes, some in camp, others following the herds or enemies, raiding and fighting, sacrificing their own and their foes to the Chaos Gods. Pyres burned bright, blades gleamed with blood, voices were raised in guttural chants in praise of unholy powers.

Down he delved, following the cracks and chasms, into the lairs of the skaven, though he could not penetrate deeply. Even so, he recoiled at their teeming thousands, overwhelmed by the slithering, skittering touch of them, their greasy, furred bodies rubbing against him, pulsing and pushing like corrupted blood through veins, claws eternally scratching, teeth biting.

Repulsed, he almost withdrew, but as he did so Arkas saw something that pulled his thoughts away from the creeping touch of the rat-filth. He witnessed hooded figures buying slaves and mutated beasts from human warlords, paying in warpstone tokens and laying on blessings of the Great Horned Rat.

It seemed impossible that humans would worship the rat-god.

There are those who follow other powers, but when you fell and the last resistance ended, it was the Lord of Thirteen Dooms that stretched out the furthest to seize what was lost. To escape the disease they swore their souls to the rat-masters, allowed to keep the lands above in return for their obedience and service to those below.

There was a daemon, he recalled, a monstrosity that had filled him with dread. Arka Bear-clad had heard of such a thing only in the darkest legends, but Arkas Warbeast knew well the verminlords of the Great Horned Rat. Brought forth from the gnaw-wounds between realms, the rat daemons were incarnations of death and pestilence. It was this vile monster, a Corruptor, that had unleashed the plague winds that had slain his mother and later destroyed his army after his ascension.

Skixakoth.

It has a name?

An ancient evil from the world-that-was, given form once more.

Arkas tried to delve deeper, pushing as far as he could into the unforgiving bedrock, but he met a wall of resistance. No matter how hard he tried he could not penetrate the depths he knew to be there – the Shadowgulf.

Even my power does not extend so far. Another rules there.

Arkas felt the darkness pulse, a wave of hostility forcing him to retreat, suddenly wary of discovery. As he withdrew, he sensed another knot of power, a whorl of Ghurite energy that drew him in as a whirlpool might snare a boat. Rather than resist, Arkas allowed himself to drift upon the flow until he found the source.

It was a realmgate, half excavated by the skaven from the duardin undercity. At the moment of discovery he realised that this was his goal, the objective Sigmar had set for the Warbeasts and Silverhands. He had assumed the realmgate was active, but now he understood why the God-King had dispatched his Strike Chamber with such swiftness. The skaven were on the verge of opening the portal between realms, and once they did so they would have another route into the Realm of Life where Alarielle and her sylvaneth armies were sorely beset. A portal into Therdonia would bring the skaven perilously close to the Lifegate. Taking the gate of Ursungorod would not only hasten the Stormcast assault on Archaon at the Allpoints, it would stave off a potentially devastating skaven invasion into Ghryan.

I have shown you that which you desired to see.

Arkas' thoughts moved quickly to his ally, Theuderis of the Knights Excelsior. Even as his mind turned to his fellow Lord-Celestant, his awareness shifted, racing away from the skaven caverns and into the peaks once more. In a few moments he felt the heavy footfalls of white-and-blue warriors, at their head a lordly figure on the back of a red-scaled dracoth. Above them burned the celestial light, shining down from the lanterns of Sigmar's Knights-Azyros. Its touch filled him with a sense of belonging and ease.

Even as he luxuriated in Sigmar's reflected glory, Arkas felt something marring the light, a darkness close at hand. In the ground beneath Theuderis' warriors, a coming together of evils. Diving down, seeking the source, Arkas chanced upon a chamber lit only by luminescent fungi. A skaven clad in black conversed with a goat-headed creature with twisting horns that wore thick layers of tanned human skin as a robe and cloak. Their intent was clear – they plotted against the army of Theuderis.

An ambush. Arkas had to warn the Silverhand somehow.

What you have seen is but a shadow, a mirror of the past. Events are already in motion.

Dark woods spread out across the advance of the Knights Excelsior and in the shadows beneath the boughs gathered a throng of beastmen and Chaos-warped monsters. The immense trees shielded them from the eyes of the Prosecutors flying overhead. Theuderis was already marching straight into the trap.

There had to be some way to reach Theuderis. If through the magic he could see the Lord-Celestant, perhaps he could communicate with him? Arkas felt resistance from the queen.

That was not our bargain, Bear-clad.

The freezing became an agony, lancing through Arkas' thoughts, blood snapping, marrow cracking.

Remember your oaths!

CHAPTER THIRTEEN

A sudden darkness warned Theuderis an instant before a monstrous beast hurtled through the trees close at hand, descending in a welter of snarling and broken branches. He barely had time to register it as another griffon attacked, black like a dreadful blend of raven and panther, eyes aflame with Chaos magic. On its back clung a knight armoured in bronzed plate and links, a sigil of the Dark Gods burning with yellow fire upon the blade of his axe.

Griffon and dracoth collided, the winged monster bowling over the mount of the Lord-Celestant. Theuderis released his hold and rolled with the motion of Tyrathrax, throwing himself clear of her as she turned onto her back, claws raking at the underside of the griffon even as its beak skittered and screeched across the armour protecting the dracoth's throat.

The Chaos champion's axe blade bit into the back of Theuderis' shoulder as the Stormcast came to his feet. Powered by vile sorcery, the edge of the blade parted sigmarite and flesh down to the bone. Theuderis threw out an arm in reflex, the head of his tempestos hammer crashing against the flank of the griffon, snapping bones and pulverising flesh.

Spitting and snarling, Tyrathrax struggled free of the griffon's clawed grip, lightning crackling along her fangs. Theuderis sprang forwards, using the back of the dracoth as a launch point to hurl himself at the Chaos champion. Taken unawares by this tactic, the griffon's rider could do nothing as Theuderis' hammer connected with the side of his helm. Arcs of power erupted from the Stormcast's weapon and the champion's head caved in, skull splintered and neck snapped by the force of the blow.

Wound gushing from its flank, the griffon was not yet ready to die. Battering Theuderis aside with a wing, the monster charged Tyrathrax once more, beak closing around the dracoth's foreleg with a sickening snap of bones. Tyrathrax snarled in pain. Lightning flared from her mouth and crackled across the sable hide of the griffon, leaving burning welts in the flesh.

Theuderis swung his hammer in both hands, bringing the head around in a long arc to connect with the shoulder of the griffon where leg and wing met the body. Bone shattered beneath pulsing flesh, forcing an unearthly scream from the beast. The blow lifted and toppled the griffon to its side, a wing buckling and snapping beneath as its heavy body rolled onto the blood-pooled dirt. Tyrathrax was on the wounded monster in a heartbeat, chewing into the exposed flesh until her head disappeared, tearing out entrails with swipes of her claws.

Gore-slicked scales shining in the cerulean light of Theuderis' hammer, the dracoth ripped herself free of the twitching corpse, ribbons of tissue hanging from her jaws. She limped to her master, feeling now the wound caused by the griffon's assault. It was obvious she would not be able to bear Theuderis' weight.

The larger gors and bestigors that had been following their smaller cousins stalked closer, perhaps thinking the wounded creature would be easier prey. Theuderis turned a glance back to his army and saw half of the centre had now broken away to reinforce the rearguard, where hulking beast-brutes, thrashing, formless spawn and nameless foul creatures were throwing themselves at the Liberators and Judicators.

Tyrathrax was not Stormcast, she would not be reforged but returned to the stars to be reborn as a child of the cosmic serpent, Dracothion. He did not know whether they would be reunited. Yet for all the tenderness Theuderis felt for his mount, who had bonded with him on the arduous Trail of Starwalking and deigned to carry him since, his duty lay with his warriors.

He laid a hand on her neck and she understood his intent without words. The dracoth turned towards the approaching beastmen and hissed a challenge, standing over the body of the griffon as though she defended a prize or nest.

Theuderis turned his back on her and broke into a run, carving into the ungors that ebbed and flowed around the Stormcasts like a sea breaking on rocks. The righteous fire was tinged with a bitter feeling as he set upon his deformed foes. Grief powered his arm more than vengeance. The Lord-Celestant battered his way back to the line, crushing smaller beastmen beneath his boots as he opened a path with devastating sweeps of his hammer.

Two Decimators stepped forwards to meet him, parting to allow him past while their gleaming axes smashed aside a flurry of ungors hurling themselves at their commander's back. As fluidly as they had counter-attacked they fell back into place, their comrades' blades rising and falling in unison to carve apart the next wave of foes.

Theuderis sought out Voltaran and found his Knight-Vexillor commanding the opposite side of the line, facing down the slope of the mountain. Swift centigors rode back and forth just a dozen paces away, hurling axes and javelins while they laughed and cursed in their barbarous tongue. The missiles were of little threat, but the Liberators were pinned in place by the attacks, unable to move to support their brothers beset by fiercer foes while the centigors threatened a charge.

'Their leader is dead, their spirit will break soon,' Theuderis assured his officer. 'Stand fast for the moment.'

'I fear otherwise, my lord,' replied Voltaran. He gestured down the mountain. 'We have not yet seen the worst of it.'

Further down the slope Theuderis could see a group of figures, horned heads visible beneath the cowls of their robes, staffs hung with grisly baubles and runes made of sinew and bone.

'Shamans,' snarled the Lord-Celestant.

'They summon fresh forces,' Voltaran added.

The lower slope was filling with all manner of mutated creatures – hounds and wolves with mutated spines and misshapen heads, slug-like, tentacled abominations and gangling monstrosities with snapping jaws and blade-like limbs. Baying and howling broke out, accompanied by whining and mewling from the Chaos spawn.

The forest started to shudder, shedding leaves and snow. A trunk snapped as a gigantic figure pushed through the press of trees, its heavy tread setting the other boughs shaking. Several times the height of a Stormcast Eternal, the gargant heaved and shouldered its way forwards, tree limbs snapping, gigantic feet sinking into the soft mulch and earth. It was clad in a crude jerkin and trousers of patchwork furs and hide, its engorged belly testing the rope-like stitching. A roughly shaped and poorly welded helm wobbled on its head, while pieces of ancient plate and broken shields tied with belts and scavenged horse harnesses made for vambraces and gorget. In its hand it trailed several long staves spliced together, cart or chariot axles perhaps, three axeheads wedged into the length to make a fearsome polearm.

There were more beastmen coming, following the packs of dogs – ungors with short bows that scampered up into the trees and bestigors clad in thick mail hauberks and coifs. In the sunlight from the gap in the trees made by the giant, Theuderis estimated another two or three hundred goat-headed fiends. Other creatures prowled the shadows, eyes glinting, their growls and snarls audible even at this distance.

A glance over his shoulder confirmed to the Lord-Celestant that his Knights Excelsior were still holding against the attack from above. The outer line had been pushed back, forcing the Judicators behind their companions in the retinues of Decimators, Protectors and Liberators battling with the beastmen. Trajos was doing his best to stem the flow of attackers trying to encircle the line but time and numbers were against him.

'Enough!' snapped Theuderis. 'Attaxes, report to me!'

The call for the Knight-Heraldor went along the line but it was a while before Attaxes appeared, running down the mountainside from the fighting at the head of the column. His armour was dented and scratched in several places but he had no obvious wounds.

'We cannot hold like this,' Theuderis said. Looking from Attaxes to Voltaran. 'We must attack.'

'As you command,' the Stormcast Eternals chorused.

'What battle formation, my lord?' asked Attaxes, readying his clarion.

'Divine Vengeance, Jaws of the Dracoth drill,' Theuderis replied. 'Signal the storm of wrath to Samat.'

The bray-shamans were ordering their latest wave of attackers up the slope as Attaxes lifted his instrument and let out a series of peals and blasts, ascending and descending sharply. He repeated them twice, but the army was already in motion before he had started the third.

The Silverhands collapsed together, the vanguard and rearguard falling back towards the main body, each retinue withdrawing a few paces while its neighbours held off the beasts, and then in turn they fell back and others continued the defence. Even as the Stormcasts settled their line, retinues of Liberators, shields locked, advanced into the brunt of the fighting, weathering the storm of missiles, blades and mauls to push forwards again on the flanks, while the centre continued to withdraw to form a 'v' of retinues into which the beastmen were guided.

The Prosecutors descended through the canopy, a hail of mystical javelins scything down dozens of gors and bestigors. Samat and several other Knights-Azyros led a charge against the bull-beasts and other large foes still assailing the left flank, the light of the celestial beacons burning bright beneath the leaves. The energy of Azyr rippled along the hammers, grandaxes and grandblades of the winged Stormcasts as they fell upon their foes, circling to attack with a whirlwind of crushing and slashing blows.

To counter the threat from the lower force, Theuderis moved his Judicators to cover the approaches, their celestial missiles bursting forth once more against these fresh targets.

'Clear the ground,' Theuderis told Trajos. 'Hinder their advance and leave them no sanctuary.'

Trajos passed the order to the other Primes and the next salvoes sliced not through flesh but wood, felling trees across the line of advance. Another fusillade from skybolt bows and thunderbolt crossbows set branches ablaze, forcing the creeping ungors to the ground. Here they were targeted by the Judicators carrying shockbolt bows, every crackling arrow that hit causing a chain of lightning to leap from one beastman to the next, slaying several score of foes in a few volleys.

Fresh torrents of fire continued to shred and rip through the forests, leaving a blackened, smoking swathe of destruction littered with burning and charred corpses.

The 'Jaw of the Dracoth' was starting to close on the beastmen, the two flanks of Liberators pushing hard towards each other, not using their hammers or blades, but simply presenting two walls of white-and-blue sigmarite that the beastmen could not pierce or break.

Theuderis joined the attack as dozens of Decimators and Retributors became the fangs of the dracoth, sallying forth between the ranks of the Liberators, who parted briefly to let them through. Axes cleaved flesh, hammers pulverised bone, the dead and dying beastmen wreathed with crackling remnants of celestial force.

The beastmen, even the more disciplined bestigors, were ferocious but unskilled. Theuderis abandoned any finesse and waded into his foes with his hammer swinging in wide arcs, scornful of any attack that might be directed at him. Leaving trails of blood and blue fire, his tempestos hammer swept aside every enemy before him. To his left and right the other Stormcasts were advancing over a carpet of beastmen dead, their weapons spitting and hissing with vengeful energies.

Behind them the Judicators were falling back once more as the gargant and other large monsters crashed towards their line. The beastmen were clearly content to allow these enormous creatures to lead the charge, loitering close behind to dash in and pounce on the Stormcasts once they were engaged.

'Samat!' Theuderis smashed his hammer through another three beastmen and pointed it towards the approaching monster. 'The gargant!'

The Knight-Azyros saluted with his starblade and leapt into the air, disappearing through the branches in a heartbeat. A bullgor charged at Theuderis, horns lowered, distracting the Lord-Celestant for a moment. He crushed the monster's bull head with a single blow and rolled over the body as it ploughed into the dirt. Theuderis came to his feet and looked back in time to see Samat's descent.

It seemed at first as though a thunderbolt had struck the giant creature, but the flash of light resolved into Samat, blade in two hands, his lantern on his belt, wings stretched to the full as he swooped head first towards the ground. At the last moment the Knight-Azyros spun feet-down, landing smoothly a few paces from the gargant.

Samat took a step backwards and looked up, the gigantic figure framed by two trees blazing with pale blue fire. It twitched and then parted, two halves neatly slewing away from each other down a cut from the top of its head to its groin. Samat leapt to avoid the wave of blood and offal that spilled out. Pieces of bisected vertebrae and ribcage washed across the ground beneath him.

A great cry of woe went up from the beastmen as their enormous ally degenerated into a fleshy, shapeless mass. Caught in the vice of the advancing Stormcast retinues, many of them turned and fled, but the Prosecutors fell upon them in moments. They flitted between the trees, summoning celestial power to cast javelins into the routing gors and ungors while their companions hunted them down with their hammers, sweeping and wheeling through the boles to shatter spines and pulp heads.

Even so, it was no easy task to overcome the remaining foes. The bray-shamans grunted and barked at their underlings, forcing them into a fresh assault while the Stormcasts were still occupied driving through the remains of the first wave. Chaotic energies churning around their horned heads, raised fists and staff tips glowing with infernal magic, the shamans themselves joined the fray, escorted by scores of heavily armoured bestigors that advanced like a solid wall of fur, metal and horns.

And there were still several hulking mutants shambling closer, their skins pocked with sores, vestigial limbs waggling like cilia, plates of bone and chitin sliding and scraping. The centigors had abandoned their taunting attacks when the Stormcasts had withdrawn but now they returned, their broad-headed spears tilted ready for the charge. The yammering of the hounds intensified, carried through the crackle of flames up to the Stormcasts with the grunts and snorts of boar-like creatures and the coughing barks and low bellows of the beastmen.

'For Sigmar!' Theuderis raised his hammer above his head as he issued the shout. The echoing cry from his warriors rolled along the mountainside like thunder, shaking the ground. While the Decimators and Retributors of his Paladin Conclave continued to wreak bloody mayhem upon the last of the gors and ungors, the Lord-Celestant rallied the Redeemer Conclave's Liberators and Protectors. 'We are the God-King's knights of vengeance. Our weapons are his wrath, his faith our armour. We are the righteous death, born for battle, created to kill. Hold back no ire and harbour no mercy. Death to the unclean!'

CHAPTER FOURTEEN

Arkas opened his eyes and found himself standing on the far side of the barbican, outside the demesne of the Queen of the Peak. He harboured the idea of returning but stopped himself from passing back through, aware that he had pushed his previous relationship as far as possible.

He broke into a run, remembering the attack about to unfold. As he powered up the bridge he thrust his hammer thrice into the air.

'Hastor!' he bellowed as he reached the top of the bridge. 'Attend to your lord!'

In a flash of colour the Knight-Venator rose, trailing particles of ice. Arkas called out his orders as he skidded to a stop in a spray of snow. Hastor signalled his understanding.

'Speed towards the dawn and seek them in the forests of the southern valleys,' said Arkas. 'Fly as swift as Sigmar's scorn!'

The Knight-Venator made no comment and raised no question, but simply dipped a wing to wheel away, a flash of rainbow colours and gold that soon disappeared into the clouds that were closing in on the mountain once more.

Dolmetis started to climb from the base of the bridge, his hasty steps betraying his concern. Arkas turned to look back at the queen's tower. Her presence was everywhere, and in every icy sparkle and frosty glimmer he felt her gaze upon him. Had she played him false, out of spite showing him the peril of Theuderis when it was too late to act? Had she known what would happen on the walls of Kurzengor when Skixakoth had issued forth from the deeps to sweep away mankind's last reign over Ursungorod?

Despite his doubts, Arkas could not ignore a simple principle – an oath was an oath. It was not his place to judge the Queen of the Peak but to measure himself by the standards of his spirit.

He lowered to a knee, head bowed, hammer in both hands with the brow of his mask against the haft.

'God-King, my Lord Sigmar, Protector of the Faithful, Shield of Mankind, I beg leave of you for a boon.' Arkas could hear Dolmetis' rapid steps approaching and spoke quickly. 'Grant peace to the Queen of the Peak, and forgive any wrong she has done in worlds past and ages forgotten. Through her I have received wisdom and guidance, in this life and in the other, and she has earned freedom from the curse laid upon her. Reward her loyal service and free her.'

'Free whom, my lord?' asked Dolmetis, catching his commander's last words. 'And whence does Hastor speed?'

'The Queen of the Peak has provided and I must pay her price or be dishonoured. It is in the hands of Sigmar Almighty.'

'You think he would set her free?'

'I do,' said Arkas, looking skywards. The clouds were turning dark, edged with a cerulean gleam. 'It was he that imprisoned her, after all.'

Dolmetis said nothing and looked up as well. Streaks of power lashed across the bulging mass of the thunderhead forming over the gorge. As when he felt the touch of the celestial beacons of the Knights-Azyros, so now Arkas bathed in the presence of his master and creator.

With a thunderclap that shook the bridge and caused flocks of birds to launch from the forests far below, a single bolt of light flashed down and struck the top of the tower's dome. Ice exploded like glass splinters, showering down into the chasm beneath. A blast of wind howled, swirling up from the gorge around the two Stormcast Eternals. Arkas thought he heard a whispered farewell.

The last reverberations of the thunderstrike echoed away.

The cocoon of ice that had encased the fortress and the queen's tower started to shear away, crumbling into sparkling fog.

'That is freedom?' asked Dolmetis.

'Oblivion,' said Arkas. 'All that she has craved for countless lifetimes of men. I swore once to end her existence, and now Lord Sigmar has delivered on my promise.'

'Perhaps you might have invoked the power of our God-King whilst on solid ground,' suggested Dolmetis, pointing his warhammer at the rents and cracks spreading up the far end of the bridge. As the enchantment failed the whole of the duardin stronghold plummeted into the valley, foundations and vaults and barbican as one, a deluge of stones and mortar following it.

The two warriors broke into a run as the bridge collapsed, pounding down the span just a few paces ahead of the falling masonry. Making a last leap for safety, they threw themselves over the edge of the parapet, falling towards the ledge beneath.

Both landed heavily in a fountain of snow while chunks of stone rained down, glancing from their armour. Arkas pulled himself back to his feet and looked down into the gorge where the fallen castle had ploughed a massive furrow into the trees far below.

'Perhaps I should have thought that through,' he admitted.

'I forgive you, my lord,' said Dolmetis. 'I am sure the warriors we left stationed on the Icemere will be equally understanding. When they dry out.'

CHAPTER FIFTEEN

Theuderis seized a beastman by the throat as it swung a hatchet at his head. The axeblade glanced ineffectually from the side of his helm. He snapped its neck and used the corpse to swat away an ungor that was trying to ram a dagger into the back of his knee.

'Attaxes, let us up the tempo of this dance. Signal stormfall. Voltaran! It is time to bring the hammerstrike.'

As the rising notes passed along the line, the Stormcast Eternals battling the horde of gors broke from the fight, retreating from the enemy with swifts steps. Stunned, the beastmen scrambled away or milled about, unsure whether to retreat or attack. Behind the melee ranks, the Judicators did likewise, falling back before the oncoming rush of monsters and bestigors. Their Primes shouting out swift commands, the two lines passed through each other and turned, smoothly swapping positions.

Now the bray-shamans attacked, and a horde of beastmen

and spawn found itself hurtling towards a bristling line of hammers, axes and glaives, shimmering with celestial heat. The Judicators unleashed their projectiles into the gors and ungors fleeing up the mountain, scything them down in a hail of crackling bolts and eruptions.

In the midst of this, Voltaran held aloft his icon.

'Lord of the Celestial Realm, heed our call,' the Knight-Vexillor shouted. 'God-King, saviour, avenger, let free your wrath upon these cursed beasts!'

The gilded lightning strikes that tipped his standard started to glow, turning from shining gold to a bright, pale blue. A fierce wind swirled upwards, ripping trees bodily from the ground and hurling them into the sky. Above, stormclouds boiled into existence, dark and low, seething with celestial energy. The beastmen and their leaders cowered beneath this display of divine might.

Attaxes let forth a refrain from his clarion. The noise rose in volume, swiftly becoming a deafening call to arms. It reached a crescendo and crashed like thunder, a shockwave of power exploding from the Stormcast. The wall of sound sped out, churning mud, cadavers, splintered trees and ice. When it hit the beastmen it lifted them from their feet and skewered them with broken branches. The wind hurled the survivors into each other, tossed them into tree trunks and sent the ragdoll carcasses spinning and skidding across the rough earth.

Just as the peal of thunder dissipated, the storm cloud burst into violent life, raining down strike after strike, every bolt centred on a mutated Chaos creature. Dozens of blasts fell in a matter of a few heartbeats, blinding in their intensity. Celestial power crawled across the ground like a tide of serpents, writhing up the shattered trunks of the trees and coiling tentacle-fashion around the legs of Chaos spawn as if to drag them down.

Theuderis strode into the fire and bolts with his Paladins at his back and flung out his hammer, casting it into the air in a looping arc. It thudded into the ground not far from the bray-shamans, who were berating their bestigors, trying to restore some semblance of control after the fury of the storm.

'Let the hammer of kings strike!' the Lord-Celestant bellowed, drawing his runesword, the pommel and blade etched with symbols that were the bane of Chaos. His thrown hammer shook with a life of its own, sending out sparks and fronds of blue lightning that fizzed across the ground.

The Stormcast Eternals advanced. Another blaze of power erupted above. The strikes did not lance towards the foe, but this time were met by streaks of energy leaping out from Theuderis' hammer.

Where they touched, a Stormcast Eternal appeared, fresh and ready for battle, Liberators bearing great axes and swords, or short warblades and shields.

Flash after flash, the tempest grew in magnitude with every heartbeat until the smoke-shrouded clearing reaped by the Stormcasts was bathed in blue light and filled with giant soldiers. An entire Redeemer Conclave burst into existence in the midst of the foe, reserves from the Celestial Realm that Theuderis had been waiting for the right moment to summon.

At their heart the cloud descended for a moment, a funnel of darkness and lightning touching down with a crack of thunder. Another Stormcast Eternal materialised in its heart. His armour was black, and wrought into the plates were bones that glowed with celestial energy. His helm-mask was fashioned in the shape of a skull, its eyes gleaming with a cold red light.

In one hand the Stormcast Eternal bore a massive hammer,

a silver thunderbolt trailing from its head. In the other hand he bore a huge staff, not unlike the standards of the Knights-Vexillor. Its head was no icon of the Silverhands, but an open sarcophagus. The bones within were bound with shroud and corpse-tatters, its dead eye sockets filled with the same scarlet energy as the bearer.

Lord-Relictor Glavius, lodestone of the power celestial, guardian and champion of the Silverhands.

Still wreathed in the last vapours of his summoning, Glavius lifted his hammer high. The head started to glow, channelling cosmic energy from the raging storm above until it shone like a star. The Lord-Relictor thrust the hammer towards the beast-men and lightning leapt across the gap, slicing through their depleted ranks.

'Glory to the God-King!' Theuderis roared.

The Silverhands charged.

CHAPTER SIXTEEN

The Stormcast Eternals thrust as a white spear into the dark innards of the beastmen army. Wherever they struck, the creatures of Chaos fell. The freshly arrived Redeemer Conclave formed the point of the spear, already in the midst of the enemy. They drove onwards through gors and bestigors, those armed with grandhammers and grandblades at the forefront, hewing into the enemy with their double-handed weapons. After them came the Liberators with warblades and sigmarite shields, guarding the flanks and backs of their brethren in the vanguard, cutting down any that survived their assault. Lord-Relictor Glavius walked in their midst, urging them on to the greatest effort, blanketing them in the energies of the Celestial Realm.

On their heels advanced Stormcast Eternals with paired warhammers or dual-warblades, spreading out from the incision made by the assault formation, widening the breach for Theuderis and his warriors to exploit.

Hound packs, mutated wolves and centigors tried to evade the oncoming attack, peeling away from the blasted clearing into the thicker woods to the left. Samat and the other Knights-Azyros followed them, darting between the trees with inhuman speed and skill, the rest of the Angelos Conclave following swiftly behind.

Theuderis did not look back, trusting to the Judicators to finish off any threat from the rear. As he ran he pointed his sword towards the cabal of bray-shamans.

'Pierce the heart and the body will die,' he commanded.

Out of desperation more than bravery the beastmen were rallying against the attack. Several score of bestigors had survived the tempestuous assault of celestial energy. Snarling and bleating, they held their ground between the oncoming Stormcasts and their masters, presenting a thicket of spears, axes and shields. Several bullgors that had fled from the earlier counter-attack returned from the darkness, bloody with wounds but still formidable. A few mindless spawn and writhing mutants flopped and scampered along the periphery, hauling bloated carcasses towards the gleaming ranks of the Stormcasts, smaller creatures chittering and shrieking, leaping and gambolling through the burning trunks and felled trees.

Theuderis felt the air around him changing, the ground underfoot shifting. At first he feared another earthquake, but he soon realised that the sensation was something far more supernatural.

The bray-shamans were summoning the power of Ghur, dredging it from the deepest earth and draining it from the trees. The magical energy coiled like a trapped serpent, the corruption of Chaos bubbling through its loops, polluting and blackening where it spread. The trees surrounding the fire-ravaged clearing started to sway with violent life, their bark blistering with sores that spat hissing gobbets of acidic sap while grasping root appendages thrust from the mulch-covered earth to snare and trip.

The ground became boggier, sucking at Theuderis' feet as he reached the bullgors. Almost losing his footing, he brought up his runeblade just in time to meet the downward arc of an axehead the size of his breastplate. The metal of the bullgor's weapon shattered against the sigmarite of the Lord-Celestant's. Shards of iron slashed into the enormous beastman's flesh and pinged from the Stormcast's armour. Grunting in surprise, the bullgor stepped back, but not far enough to elude the tip of Theuderis' blade, which found the creature's throat a moment later.

Dragging his boot free from the mud, drenched in the congealing blood of the brutish monster, Theuderis pressed on. His Paladins to either side laid into the bestigors, bullheads and Chaos spawn heedless of the poor ground underfoot, overcoming the worsening conditions with raw strength.

Across the furious din of battle, the Lord-Celestant heard a disturbing, ululating cry. It emanated from the bray-shamans, and echoed back in strange ways from the surrounding trees. Increasing in pitch and intensity, the call stirred up the polluted Ghurite energy frothing around the beast army, sending it soaring into the sky like a fountain. Here it met Sigmar's Tempest, and began pushing back the celestial clouds to disperse across the forest.

Theuderis had no idea what this spell boded, but he was determined to win victory before the consequences made themselves apparent. His force had joined with the Liberators of Glavius, dividing the beast army into two almost equal parts. To the eyes of the beastmen, it must have seemed as though the Stormcasts had allowed themselves to be surrounded. Grunting and roaring orders, the gors and bray-shamans sent all of their forces into the attack.

Above the throng of hairy, deformed bodies flew tattered and patched banners, and grim standards of bone and wood. Held aloft by the fiercest warriors of the assembled warherds, these standards became the focal points of the attack, leading the beasts directly to Theuderis' host. Every ungor, gor and bestigor threw itself at the Stormcasts, trying to break the line of ivory and blue. Though there was little guile to the attack, the feral intensity of the Chaos-born beasts threatened breakthroughs at several points. Though not classic strategists, the leaders of the beast-herds could sense areas of weakness and threw themselves into the fighting with ferocious bellows. The battlefield shook with the crash of weapons and shouts from both sides, bestial howls competing with the sonorous war-chants of the Silverhands.

'Blade of the Triumphant, Purifier formation,' Theuderis told Attaxes, judging that the moment had arrived to deliver the killing blow.

The Knight-Heraldor's trumpet signalled clean and clear through the cacophony of war. Hearing its command, the Silverhands acted as one. Paladins and Redeemer Conclaves moved through each other, while the Judicators guarding the rear fell back to join the rest of the army. All the while fending off the savage assault of the beastmen, the Knights Excelsior formed into a kind of wheel, with the Judicator Conclaves as the hub and the other Stormcasts spearing out like axle-blades, each two rows of warriors back to back.

The wheel started to rotate, the Stormcast Eternals keeping in perfect step whether moving forwards or backwards. Missiles and lightning bolts flared from the centre while the Stormcasts cut down everything before them. With warriors in front and behind, the beastmen were thrown into anarchy once more, unsure where to direct their attacks. Unable to simply hold position against the relentlessly advancing 'spokes', the beastmen were either pushed to the centre where they fell to the missile fire, caught by the swords, glaives and hammers of the Silverhands, or forced to try to break free.

The Stormcasts' formation slowly moved across the clearing, pace by pace. The warriors stepped over and past burning logs and piles of dead beastmen, weapons still swinging, the whole army functioning as a single perfect machine.

A raucous screech from above drew Theuderis' gaze away from the righteous carnage. His eye was drawn immediately to the large shape swooping down through the break in the celestial storm. Tendrils of Ghurite energy trailed from its leathery wings and sword-long claws. Evidently the magical call of the bray-shamans had attracted it from its hunting ground further up the slopes. More winged shapes in the distance betrayed the approach of other creatures that had also heard the summoning cry.

'Manticores!' he shouted, heart sinking. His warriors were in no position to defend themselves from an aerial attack, but to change formation now, in the heart of the enemy's force, would be equally disastrous. He glanced at Attaxes. 'Signal for the Angelos, now!'

Attaxes had raised his clarion but before a single note had been sounded a light streaked across the sky. Theuderis' eyes adjusted to see a winged figure in armour of turquoise, a rainbow-coloured bird at its shoulder, a golden bow in hand.

Even as Attaxes sounded the alarm, the newcomer's wings flared with a thunderous crack that could be heard on the ground, bringing him to an instant halt. He loosed a single bolt from his weapon. The missile blazed across the sky, a comet trailing white and blue fire.

The star-fated arrow struck the descending manticore full in the chest, becoming an inferno of colours that engulfed the monster with licking flames. The diving beast was quickly consumed by the fireball, thrashing and howling in pain as it disappeared from view and crashed into the forest some distance away.

Samat and the rest of the Angelos Conclave raced from the trees, abandoning their pursuit at Attaxes' signal. The newly arrived Knight-Venator met with the Knight-Azyros and a moment later was directed groundwards while the Knights-Azyros and Prosecutors turned to face the following monsters.

Theuderis' made his way back along the line of Paladins, allowing himself to be absorbed by the Judicators at the centre. There was a space two dozen paces across in the heart of their formation and into this gap dropped the Knight-Venator.

The Stormcast's appearance confirmed Theuderis' guess – a warrior of the Celestial Vindicators, doubtless a Warbeast despatched by Arkas. The Lord-Celestant feared the worst, unsure what the warrior's appearance foreshadowed, and spoke before any introduction was made.

'How fares your master? Do the Warbeasts still fight on?'

'To the best of my knowledge, Lord Silverhand,' the Knight-Venator replied, taken aback by the demanding tone of the Lord-Celestant. 'He fares better than you, I would wager.'

'What purpose brings you here, Warbeast?' Theuderis had little time for jest, and this was certainly no occasion for levity. 'You distract me from the course of battle.'

'I am Hastor, Knight-Venator of the Lord Warbeast,' the other Stormcast said formerly, giving a slight bow as he furled his wings. His star-eagle settled on a nearby bestigor corpse and started plucking at its exposed innards. 'I bear a warning from my lord.'

'A warning?' Theuderis wondered what further strife could befall his host. Since arriving in Ursungorod they had been beset by misfortunate and enemies at every step.

'Yes, Lord Silverhand. Lord Arkas wishes you to know that the skaven have stirred a great alliance of beasts against us and they are setting ready for ambush in the forests.' He looked around and shrugged. 'I apologise for the untimely nature of this news...'

Theuderis was about to deliver a rebuke but stayed his tongue. This was his first encounter with his new allies and it would bode poorly for the relationship if he started it with chastisement. He had to accept that the warning had been sent in earnest, and that Hastor was simply attending to his duty as he had been commanded. Hastor was forthright in his manner, but the Celestial Vindicators, and the Warbeasts in particular, had a reputation for less-than-perfect discipline. He chose his reply carefully, mindful that his words and deeds might soon be reported back to Arkas and his warriors.

'Thank you, Hastor. Though your skills as herald are lacking, your warrior-craft is not. You dealt with that manticore in admirable fashion.' He purposefully turned to survey the ongoing battle. As they spoke, the two warriors moved along with the Judicators, unconsciously keeping station with the whole formation. 'I regret that I cannot offer you a reply to Lord Arkas at the moment. My attention is keenly needed elsewhere.'

'As is my bow,' said Hastor, glancing to the flights of warriors closing on the griffons, manticores and other monstrous creatures aloft. 'My lord's other message will wait a while, I'm certain. With your permission, Lord Silverhand?'

'Knight-Azyros Samat is Angelos-Prime,' said Theuderis. 'I am grateful for your bow, Hastor.'

The Knight-Venator said nothing else and sprang into the air. A whistle summoned his star-eagle to follow and in a matter of moments they were another colourful blur amongst the many soaring across the cloudy vault of the sky.

Theuderis lifted his sword, the runes flashing with renewed celestial energy. The Judicators parted at his approach, allowing him to rejoin the fight.

'No beast lives past nightfall!' he declared, hacking his way towards the bray-shamans with renewed intent. 'Sigmar God-King expects nothing less.'

CHAPTER SEVENTEEN

The Black River had always been named for its dark waters, not just murky but as black as pitch. Even after many lifetimes, its inky depths were unchanged. It bubbled and frothed between dozens of jutting pillars that had once held aloft the roofs of a great palace, the walls and floor also long since consumed by the torrent. The blackness of the water was deceiving, obscuring the speed with which it moved – too fast even for a Stormcast to forge across. The Celestial Vindicators were thus forced to follow the old road that ran beside it – though it was not so much a road as the remains of an old mosaic-covered floor that had been thrown up by the convulsions of Ursungorod, laid out before Arkas like a carpet set before an arriving dignitary. The broken tiles were slick with river mud and water plants, but made for surer footing than the sheer ice that stretched for miles to either side as they approached the central uplands.

From ahead a shape descended quickly. Arkas recognised Venian, his Prosecutor-Prime.

'A stranger approaches, my lord.' There was something odd in Venian's tone, as if this event was more worrying to the Prosecutor-Prime than the coming of a flight of dragons.

'A stranger? A very particular choice of word,' replied Arkas.

'I can think of no other.' The flying warrior landed next to his Lord-Celestant and fell into step with him as they continued along the path. 'A woman of the tribes. Armed with bow and spear, and armoured in scale, wearing a cloak of white fur.'

'And how does she "approach", Venian? What do you mean?'

'She crosses the snow drifts ahead, directly towards us.'

'And she saw you?'

'She raised a fist in salute, my lord.'

Arkas pondered this for a few strides.

'Alone, you say? Are you sure?'

'The ice field ahead is expansive, my lord, and devoid of much cover,' Venian said, his tone slightly clipped with indignation.

'She bore no marks of the Dark Gods? No mutation or symbols?'

'I would have reported such, my lord,' said the Prosecutor-Prime, growing increasingly vexed by his commander's questions. 'Unless she possesses unprecedented and hidden mystical abilities, I do not think she is a threat.'

'That's what confuses me,' admitted Arkas. He shook his head. 'I resigned myself to the fact that my people were no more, slain or fallen to Chaos worship. Now you tell me that a woman approaches, unmarked by the Dark Gods, which suggests that there are yet some that still resist the skaven and their allies. Your report stirs hope where I had none. Its loss would be a fresh wound.'

'It seems your hope is not misplaced, my lord. Her trail across the snow was simple to follow for a while, though it petered out eventually. She has been heading directly towards us for the better part of a day. She is seeking us out, I wager my reputation on it. How she can know of us or where we travel I cannot say.'

Arkas looked up and gestured with his hammer. Across the river there were dark specks moving over the clouds – crows and other carrion eaters. They had been growing in number since the Celestial Vindicators had descended to the lower slopes, having quickly learnt that the Stormcasts would provide ample pickings.

'In my days as a mortal there were those that could speak with the birds and the beasts.' He thought of Radomira, a reader of bird sign, and remembered the times she would have a raven or hawk or finch upon her wrist, woman and bird cawing and chirping intently to each other. 'If there were survivors of the alliance, if their descendants still strive for freedom, such secrets might still be known.'

'Not only by potential allies,' said Venian. 'Such spies could serve our enemies also, my lord.'

'I have been counting on it,' said Arkas. 'Do not forget our part in this campaign. We are the rod that attracts the lightning. We will stir the Chaos followers and skaven from their camps and holes and bring them to us, so that Theuderis and his Knights Excelsior can lay the vengeance of Sigmar down upon them with their arrival. We shall be the bait that draws the serpent's strike, the Silverhands the blade that severs its head.'

The path veered away from the bank, moving around a block of stone mounted on the bank of the river. On its worn surface could still be seen faint markings – duardin runes worn nearly smooth by the elements. Even so, Arkas could read them, running his fingers over the faint indentations.

'A mile marker,' he said aloud. 'A day's marching to another duardin city, though long ago it was swallowed by the glacier we called *meshka kozia*. The Bear's Pelt. The city lies beneath the ice field you have just come back from.'

'It has been swallowed deep then, my lord,' said Venian. 'We saw no sign of tower, gate or wall.'

A thought occurred to Arkas and he turned, his gaze seeking out his Knight-Vexillor. Dolmetis followed a hundred paces behind with a guard of Decimators and Retributors. Seeing that his lord required him, the standard bearer hurried forwards, his icon gripped in both hands.

'A new command to the chamber, Dolmetis,' said Arkas, as soon as the Knight-Vexillor was within earshot. 'We leave the river and head across the ice field.'

'Towards the stranger?' asked Venian.

'Of course. I'm sure she has something important to tell us. We shan't make her labour longer than necessary.' Arkas leaned closer, placing a hand on the shoulder of the Prosecutor-Prime. 'You assured me she was no threat, yes? You staked your reputation on it. Let us see what that is worth.'

CHAPTER EIGHTEEN

The dark cavern stank of human sweat and fear. Felk breathed in deeply, whiskers trembling with delight. The captives huddled naked in their rope bonds, most kneeling or sitting, some lying down from weakness. There were four hundred in total, eyes wide with fear, shaking with cold and hunger. The Pox-master rubbed spindly hands together as he paced back and forth, examining his prizes.

'Good-good meat,' said Felk, addressing nobody in particular. 'Good tribute, yes-yes. Great Horned Rat touched you, yes-yes. Honoured, to become the flesh of the Great Witherer. Dismal feast will be grand, grander than all before. Gaze of the Great Horned Rat be upon the Withering Canker. Felk will rise, yes-yes, rise past all, even Skixakoth. Not to fat rotting god will life-woods fall. To the children of the Horned Rat, to the Clans Pestilens, to the Withering Canker. Plague and pox and pustule, yes-yes, the flesh of the life-queen will crawl with gifts of Pestilens.'

The cluster of pale faces stared up at him in horror as the prisoners recoiled from his presence, shifting like a single organism to avoid being in the Poxmaster's vicinity as he stalked back and forth, staff clacking on the stone floor. In the light of the warp-lamps, their skin seemed so white, so smooth and pale, and their eyes, glistening with tears, were almost good enough to pluck out and swallow right there.

Felk fought back against the urge.

'Not for now. For dismal feast, yes-yes.' He stopped and leaned on his staff, peering down at the captives, broken claws tapping an arrhythmic tattoo on the twisted wood. He inspected the closest specimens, finding on each one some mark of the Great Horned Rat – a wart or cluster of boils, a suppurating lesion or weeping sore, cataract or rash.

'Chosen, yes-yes. You will be punished. Great Horned One has taken blessing from you, bad-bad man-things. Roast and boil and spitted, for the dismal feast your bones broken, such crispy skin, flesh purged of evil and devoured for Blessed Plague of Plagues.'

Drool flowed as Felk imagined the eating pits filled with the meat of his sacrifices. One of the captives started to moan and others broke into sobs, their despair a virus that spread quickly through the craven mass until all were crying and groaning. Some wailed with lament, clawing at their hair and skin.

'Stop-stop!' snapped Felk, claws and tail shaking violently.

The temptation was too much, he had to turn away. Skarth, whose spitevermin ringed the cave, approached a few steps. He said nothing but jerked his head towards the entrance to the chamber. Thriss lurked in the shadows, hands wringing close to his chest.

The gutter runner's demeanour punctured Felk's good mood, concern sweeping away his anticipation of the dismal feast. With an irritated wave Felk commanded Thriss to enter.

The gutter runner sidled up to his employer, head held low, tail limp. The Poxmaster had never seen Thriss so subordinate and he instantly suspected trickery.

'Stay-stay there,' Felk snapped, prodding the gutter runner with his staff to force him back several paces. Thriss complied without resistance, heightening Felk's suspicion.

'Bad-bad news, legendary Poxmaster,' began Thriss, head bobbing in deference. 'Makargas. The Beast-caller... '

'Yes-yes? Demanding higher price? Treachery?'

'Is dead-dead.'

Felk shrugged. 'Not problem for us.'

'All beasts dead. Metal giants kill-kill Makargas and all beasts.'

The Poxmaster thought he had misheard for a moment.

'Beast army dead? All dead?'

Thriss nodded and bared yellowing fangs. He shifted from one foot to the other and back, unable to hold still any longer.

'Metal giants bring magic and fire. Much-much magic.' His voice dropped to a whisper. '*Star magic*, power of storm and sun!'

This news sent a fresh shudder of fear through Felk. He had heard tales – many of them from Thriss, it was true – regarding a new foe that had been seen throughout the many realms. They were carried on a dire storm, relentless and merciless. Several clans had been wiped out and terrified survivors of others had fled back to the Blight City with stories of indestructible armies and warriors that rode lightning.

'Is true-true?' Felk's gaze flicked around the room, from Thriss to the slaves to Skarth and back again, suddenly wary of everything. 'Very bad-bad for us.'

'For you...' Thriss corrected him. The Eshin agent took another step back as though physical distance would spare him any consequences of their association.

'Us-us!' hissed Felk. He crooked a finger towards Skarth, beckoning him closer. Thriss sidestepped at the larger skaven's approach, the gutter runner's hands hovering close to the dagger hilts jutting from his belt. 'Fangleader, what is our contract, my will-will?'

'Power to the Withered Canker. Foes slain.' The fangleader looked pointedly at Thriss. 'Revenge in death.'

'What about gate?' said the gutter runner, eyes narrowing.

'Metal giants come for gate, must be true-true,' said Felk. 'Not chance we find gate and star-born army comes to White-world Above. Dig-dig faster. More slaves. Pay warpstone to man-things, beast-things, all-things. Kill-kill metal giants first.'

'What if star army comes here?' said Thriss.

'We fight,' replied Skarth.

It took all of Felk's self-control not to release a squirt of musk at the thought. The moment passed and he looked at the slave-sacrifices. His resolved hardened and his grip on his staff tightened.

'Too close-close to fail. Gate is ours! Glory to the Withered Canker! Must be ready for fight. For war.' He waved a staff towards the slaves. 'Dismal feast not wait! Tonight we honour Great Horned Rat with offerings. Prepare the meat.'

As Felk departed, Thriss following a few steps behind, Skarth signalled to his spitevermin. The ring of warriors readied their rust-spotted weapons and closed on the humans.

CHAPTER NINETEEN

Though the shadows were long, the Knights Excelsior were equal to Theuderis' demand. After the crash and shrill clamour of battle, the forested slopes fell to deathly silence, only the crackle of flames to break the stillness.

Theuderis walked amongst the dead – the corpses of foes, of course. A number of his Stormcasts had been undone, overpowered by hulking Chaos brutes or outnumbered and dragged down. They had been taken back to the Celestial Realm to be reforged again. It was a strange experience, to survey the carnage of the fighting and yet not know the true cost he had paid until his Primes reported.

'I am not altogether sure that I like it,' he told Attaxes, who had been at his shoulder since the arrival of Glavius' conclave.

'Like what, my lord?'

'The emptiness.'

'There is plenty to see,' said Attaxes, stepping over the remains of a centigor, its head cleaved to the chin. He pointedly turned over the body of another, its hind legs flopping where they had been mangled by a hammer blow. 'Much to be happy about.'

'Do you not find it unsettling, Attaxes? When you were mortal, before you ascended, you were a general, yes?'

'A Sinistran Legation Commandant, in the Westering Marshes, in the Realm of Shadows. Is that important?'

'And you walked many battlefields as we do now.'

'Thirty-eight battles I fought, thirty-seven I won before the poisoned wind of the skaven nearly took me and Sigmar ascended my spirit.'

'Were you never moved by the bodies of those that had fallen under your command? Did their loss mean nothing?'

'It meant everything. On their shades I swore each time to bring vengeance for their sacrifice.'

'Exactly! How do we remember the lost if they are not truly gone? I have lost many warriors today, but they are not dead. What does that mean?'

'It is not for us to count the cost any longer.' This came from Theuderis' left, where Lord-Relictor Glavius approached, his war-plate as bloodied as his lord's. The icon he held was dormant now, as was the hammer in his fist. The bones of his reliquary seemed just that – dead bones strapped into a metal coffin.

'But there is a cost,' Theuderis replied.

'Only to them,' said Glavius, pointing with his hammer at the hundreds of dead beastmen. 'That is the only tally of merit. When the enemy are all dead, the battle is won, not before. That is why the Lord Sigmar takes the fallen from us. Their loss should not trouble your thoughts, until your thoughts cannot be troubled any longer.'

'You wield the power celestial,' said Attaxes. 'What do you know of the Reforging? Truly?'

'No more than you,' Glavius admitted with a reluctant shake of the head. 'When a Stormcast passes beyond the veil of the mortal and back to the Celestial Realm, he passes from my sight also. If the God-King chooses to pass a little of his blessing through me on occasion, that is all I can hope for. To kill or heal, two equally potent powers, yet neither the greater over the other.'

A shout from one of the Liberators drew their attention. The Stormcast Eternal stood near a pile of ungor bodies, which were heaped like a curving wall. Theuderis realised it was the spot where he had left Tyrathrax and hurried over.

'What is it?'

The Liberator gestured in reply, indicating the dracoth half buried under the bodies, the remains of a small beastman still clamped in her jaws, scales slick with their vile blood. The sight was difficult, a reminder that perhaps it was better not to see the remains of one's companions. He knelt down and held out a hand to stroke the beast's gore-covered neck, aware of the shadows of Attaxes and Glavius falling over him.

Tyrathrax twitched, an eye opening to stare at Theuderis.

'She lives...' He stood up, as stunned as though dealt a blow. 'She slew many and their corpses hid her from vengeful foes.'

'Only just,' said Glavius, pushing aside the mound of corpses with a booted foot. This exposed the cuts and gashes along the flanks of the dracoth, her hide rent in many places, armour broken and buckled. 'I feel the celestial power leeching from her. The darkness of death beckons her spirit back to the stars.'

Theuderis stood up, eyes still on Tyrathrax. 'Can you save her?'

Glavius looked between lord and dracoth several times, though whether doubtful of his ability or duty was unclear.

Glavius planted the haft of his icon in the pile of dead,

spearing it through the corpses into the ground. He reached out and a star of celestial energy appeared in his fist, the energy leaking through his fingers in golden rays.

'Stand back,' he warned them before kneeling beside the quivering form of Tyrathrax. He looked back at Theuderis. 'She has but moments left. I make no promises.'

'There are no guarantees in matters of life and death,' the Lord-Celestant replied.

Nodding, Glavius returned his attention to the dracoth. He laid a hand on the side of her head, whispering calming words, and placed the sphere of shining energy upon her exposed chest, nestling it into a wound just above the heart.

'Almighty God-King, father of war, guider of the lost. Send forth your power to this loyal servant that I might bring your light to others. All that fall in your name are worthy of your mercy and your blessing. Unto the anvil as metal, unto the battle remade.'

Glavius stood and grabbed his hammer in both hands. Theuderis could not stop a reflexive step forwards as the Lord-Relictor swung with all of his might. The hammer crashed into the spark of celestial power. A thrust of lightning crashed down from above. The impact sent Glavius staggering back and the resultant explosion engulfed the nearby Stormcasts, blinding them for several heartbeats.

When Theuderis' vision cleared he could see tendrils of energy crawling across the body of the dracoth, sparking in her eyes, flaring from exposed fangs. It moved like a living thing, like a flame along paper, but where it touched it did not destroy but remade. Bones healed, flesh knitted, scales regrew. Plates of armour straightened, rents in the sigmarite flattened and joined together.

With a growl, the dracoth rolled to her feet. The globe of

celestial power fell to the ground, much dimmed. Glavius picked it up, turning it this way and that as though examining the mote of power for damage.

'Welcome back,' said Theuderis, as Tyrathrax pushed herself up, shaking free dried blood and dead scales with a toss of her head. 'There is still much fighting to be done.'

The dracoth gave an appreciative growl and lowered to the ground, inviting Theuderis to climb into the saddle upon her back. Her tail whipped in excitement.

'My lord?'

Theuderis turned before he mounted to see the Knight-Venator Hastor descending. The Lord-Celestant raised an arm to beckon him.

'You had another message from your lord,' said Theuderis.

'I did, and he bade me repeat it exactly.' The knight paused for a breath before receiving a nod to continue. 'I have entreated the aid of... a local power. The skaven are unearthing the realmgate in the depths of Ursungorod. They are close to activating it. Hastor bears warning of an ambush, but I fear he will be too late. I trust you will survive, and no matter what manner of force you lead afterwards you must make all haste to the rendezvous. We have no time to spare.'

'What power does your lord speak of?'

'Power?' Hastor understood Theuderis' meaning after some thought. 'Ah, I see. She is a sorceress, the Queen of the Peak. Or was.'

'Was a sorceress? What do you mean?'

'I do not know the whole tale, Lord Silverhand. She has dwelt in Ursungorod since Arkas' mortal life. She was an ally of my commander when he was known as Arka Bear-clad.'

'What manner of aid did she give? What sorcery?'

'I do not know, Lord Silverhand.' The Knight-Venator

shrugged. 'Lord Arkas sent me soon after and none but he passed into her tower. I believe he received a warning of the attack, amongst other information.'

'What do you know of a realmgate beneath Ursungorod?'

'Nothing, Lord Silverhand. I left my commander at the tower of the Queen of the Peak as his army made camp on a frozen lake called Icemere. What has happened since, what my lord saw, is beyond my sight.'

'Of course,' said Theuderis. 'What were your orders once this message had been delivered?'

'Unfortunately, Lord Silverhand, in his haste I believe Lord Arkas overlooked that necessity. I am, for the moment, at your service. Do you wish me to return to the Warbeasts?'

Theuderis thought about this as he pulled himself up onto Tyrathrax's back. The dracoth growled contentedly under the familiar weight.

'Remain with Knight Samat and his Angelos Conclave for the time being. I will compose a reply to the Warbeast for you to take.'

Hastor accepted this judgement with a slight bow. He waited in silence for a few heartbeats longer.

'You may go.'

'I am obliged, Lord Silverhand,' the Celestial Vindicator replied with a further bow. His star-eagle had been sitting in the branch of a burnt-out tree above. It let out a long screech and swooped down, reaching its master just as his wings snapped into streamers of light and lifted him skywards.

'These Warbeasts are strange warriors,' said Attaxes. 'They stand on ceremony yet I hear they are also ill-disciplined and swift-tempered.'

'I do not like this talk of native sorceresses,' Theuderis told the Knight-Heraldor and Glavius. 'Ursungorod has been under the yoke of Chaos for centuries, the taint runs deep. There is no power here that is good, save the power of Sigmar that we bring with us.'

'I am sure that Lord Arkas is beyond any corruption,' Glavius said quickly, misunderstanding Theuderis' meaning.

'Of course, he is Stormcast,' the Lord-Celestant replied. 'His heart and spirit I do not doubt. His wit and wisdom, on the other hand, might be all too easily swayed by the wrong notions. The God-King knows best his own strategy, but I would not have sent a commander as unpredictable as the Warbeast back to his home realm. We have only a single purpose here, the liberation of the realmgate.'

'Yes, my lord,' said Attaxes. 'All other considerations are secondary.'

'There are no other considerations.' Theuderis leaned closer to Glavius. 'Speak with Samat, have him discuss with Hastor the surest route to the rendezvous. And get him to find out all he can about the Warbeast and this sorceress from the Knight-Venator. I do not like mysteries. I expect a full account by nightfall.'

'Yes, my lord, as you will it.' The Lord-Relictor bowed and withdrew to the other Knights Excelsior.

'I overheard the Warbeast's message, my lord,' said Attaxes. 'He seemed insistent that we proceed with haste.'

'Indeed. Form column, Javelin formation, ready to depart at my command.'

The Knight-Heraldor had his clarion lifted even as he turned away. Soon the notes of the command call pealed across the devastated forest. Theuderis watched as his retinues fell into line, five files wide, with the Justicars at the tip, the other Stormcast taking the inner places behind their missile weapons. It was a fragile formation, able to move at speed and negotiate rough terrain with ease, but it left his army strung out over some distance.

Looking at the ground scattered with hundreds of beastmen corpses and the carcasses of manticores, griffons, gargants and Chaos spawn, he knew the risk of another attack was minimal.

'Judgement awaits!' he cried. At a tap from his heels, Tyrathrax broke into a run, taking him to the head of the column. He galloped on. 'Swift justice!'

The Stormcast Eternals broke into a run as Theuderis continued into the forest, their long strides covering the ground with speed.

CHAPTER TWENTY

Even surrounded by Prosecutors circling like hungry eagles, their hammers and javelins burning with celestial light, the woman looked remarkably calm. She was older than Arkas had expected, nearly sixty he would have guessed, though she held herself straight and showed no infirmity. The tribal elder, for such she had to be in the estimation of the Lord-Celestant, was short even for a mortal, no taller than his hammer was long. The bow in her hand was of bone and wood, recurved in the style of the ussra valley riders of the north, though the sword in her other hand was straight and double-edged in the manner of the kimmeri warriors from the ice caves above the Bear's Pelt. Her cloak was from a black-and-grey ice bear, trimmed and tied with leather thongs. The fangs of her necklace were delicately carved with lettering, distorted over many years from the forms that Arka had used, but still readable.

'Whose names do you wear?' he asked in the old language, pointing to the inscribed teeth. 'Your mothers'?'

She started, eyes showing surprise for the first time since the huge warriors had marched into view across the flat stretch of ice that became the Bear's Pelt glacier. The stranger had stopped and waited for them, weapons bared but held at her sides. Arkas had recognised it not as an act of defence or aggression but one of trust – a tribal custom that declared 'Here I am, I hide nothing'.

'You speak as we?' she said as she recovered from the shock. Her speech was oddly inflected but not so different from the tongue the Bear-clad had shared with the other tribes. She glanced down at her necklace. 'Yes, mothers and mothers' sisters.'

The woman had been staring at Arkas since he had approached, her brown eyes soft in colour but unflinching. Now she looked away to glance at the other Stormcasts before returning her stare to the Lord-Celestant.

'You are the warriors of the tempest.' It was a statement, not a question. 'Soldiers of the heavens.'

'We are...' Arkas struggled to find the terms that would explain how they had been mortals once but had now been made into something deadlier. 'We are tempest-born, servants of Sigmar the God-King. We were men once.'

He lifted away his mask to show the flesh beneath. The woman smiled and nodded.

'Yes, I see that the birds spoke the truth,' she said with an assured nod. 'I am Katiya Gospor and I have been waiting for you since I was a child.'

'How can that be?' He replaced his mask, the chill breeze on bare, ravaged flesh making him feel exposed without it.

'Of tempest-warriors I know nothing. But I have had dreams for many years. Of a bearded king who once ruled. Others did not listen – they said I was touched to believe the legends were anything but stories. But I knew. I knew. Arka the Uniter would return.'

Stunned, Arkas said nothing. Katiya lowered herself to the flat ice and offered her weapons up to the Lord-Celestant.

'I knew,' she said again, eyes brimming with emotion. 'Your army awaits, Bear-clad. I have summoned them for you.'

'Army?' Arkas stepped forwards and motioned for Katiya to stand. 'What army?'

Katiya winked then and raised her fingers to her lips. She let out a piercing whistle that drifted into silence across the emptiness of the ice field. For several heartbeats nothing happened. Then, two hundred paces to the left the ice shifted. It looked as though a boulder rolled aside and suddenly half a dozen men emerged from nowhere, clad in leathers and plate, wielding swords and oval shields. Five more rose up from a mound a little behind them.

The retinues of Stormcasts rearranged themselves instantly, the thud of boots on hard ice and scrape of armour plates the only noise as they executed drill and manoeuvres practised a thousand times in the arena of the Gladitorium. The giant warriors seamlessly moved to form a cordon of weapons between the newcomers and Katiya. An aurora of celestial power from bared blades and cracking hammers shimmered over the host and cast hard shadows across the ice.

Everywhere Arkas looked more men and women seemed to materialise from the ice field. Most were dressed in grey, pale blue and white, with furs and patterned hides that made them seem as much animal as human.

Turning about he guessed that two hundred had revealed themselves already and more were still appearing, rising up from crevasses and cracks, climbing out of openings cut into the ice itself. Twenty heartbeats passed and Katiya's army numbered at least a thousand, springing into existence like snow devils.

'Venian?' Arkas called out. 'I would have words!'

CHAPTER
TWENTY-ONE

'They ran,' explained Katiya as she led Arkas between two shoulders of rock. Doridun flanked the Lord-Celestant on the other side, the Protector-Prime, Diocletus, following close with his retinue. 'They thought you dead, struck down by the sorcery of the daemon-lord. Faced with such power and the unending numbers of the ratkin, the defenders of Kurzengor fled.'

An undercut formed the start of a tunnel that ran steeply into the ice, the pale walls indistinguishable from the rest of the glacier. Led by other guides, the rest of the Warbeasts descended into the hidden settlement – Katiya had been swift and insistent with her demands that the giant warriors did not remain on the surface to attract hostile attention.

'They would have died, had they remained,' said Arkas.

'The stories tell of how they flung down their shields and threw off mail coats to speed away,' the Ursungoran elder replied. 'Some, the cursed ones, turned on their own and cut them down.'

'They hoped to find alliance with the skaven by slaying their allies?'

'They were already agents of the rat-filth,' spat Katiya. She looked up at Arkas. 'Traitors that would strike from within the walls. The legends speak for some time on how they are accursed for eternity and the Uniter would return to revenge himself upon them in many unpleasant ways.'

'I thought every one of them my brother or sister,' murmured Arkas. 'We had spilt and given blood together, shared ale and meat at the fires. It was for nothing?'

Katiya did not reply. She stopped as the tunnel widened, pulled back the hood of her fur coat and had a brief conversation with a young, broad-shouldered warrior waiting for her. He nodded and dashed off into the cavern.

Stepping across the threshold, Arkas suddenly understood how it was that Katiya's 'army' had survived and been able to appear so swiftly. The glacier was riddled with passages and tunnels, dug from bare ice but shored up with duardin-hewn stone. The ceiling of the hall into which he stepped was so low he could almost touch it, but the hollow was easily three hundred paces across, the floor of the open space paved with cracked flagstones. He counted eight more archways leading off, as well as several sets of steps winding further beneath the ice field. Lines of Ursungorans and Stormcasts were emerging from these other tunnels.

'Amazing,' said Doridun. 'A lifetime's work.'

'What did he say?' asked Katiya. Arkas explained.

'Nineteen,' she said. 'Nineteen generations have carved the City of Ice until today.'

'Nearly four centuries,' Arkas told his Knight-Heraldor. 'It is not so long as I thought since Sigmar took me. Ursungorod has not aged lightly in my absence.'

'Time is a cruel companion,' replied Doridun. 'For mortals.'

'What language do you speak?' asked Katiya, watching the exchange with wide eyes.

'It is the language of the celestial sphere, of the God-King and his immortals.'

'It is like thunder and music at the same time!' Her brow furrowed. 'And loud!'

'It is a tongue for battle, to be heard over the crash of metal and the dying cries of our foes,' said Arkas, making an effort to speak softly. 'Our chambers in Sigmaron are vast, so I suppose we do quite a lot of shouting. Just how far does this city stretch?'

'For nearly the length and breadth of the Bear's Pelt,' Katiya said, her back straightening and chest swelling with pride. 'As grand as the duardin city that came before.'

They crossed the chamber while Arkas' warriors gathered in their brotherhoods, looking in astonishment at their surroundings. The native warriors drew back from the armoured giants, their expressions displaying disbelief, fear and hope in equal measure.

'How have you not been discovered? The Pestilentzi must know you are here.'

'The city is known but we are few enough that we hide when the cursed tribes come. We know the City of Ice and its ways, and we kill those that trespass. A few we allow back to the surface to spread tales of the snow-killers of the ice. The rat-filth do not come and we do not disturb them.' She smiled with grim determination. 'Until now, of course. Now we disturb them much.'

'Are there more of you?' he asked, looking at the hundreds of men and women crowding into the chamber, faces expectant yet wary. Quite a few had seen as many years as Katiya, and there were few young faces amongst the throng.

'Some patrols and sentries that keep guard, maybe another hundred,' Katiya told him. His heart sank a little and she must have noticed.

'Each is worth ten cursed ones and twenty rat-filth!' she said.

'I am sure of it,' said Arkas. He had been equally sure of it on the walls of Kurzengor. He directed his next words to Doridun, keeping his tone even so as not to betray further disappointment to Katiya. 'Twelve hundred fighters at most. I had hoped to liberate many more to add numbers to our cause but that is not going to be the case. Send word to Venian, he has a chance to redeem himself. Tell him to seek out Hastor and Theuderis. He will guide them to this place, not the agreed rendezvous. Our foes will surely have marked our progress here. It would be wrong to abandon these people now.'

'If we depart they will come, my lord,' said Doridun, looking along the lines of Ursungorans. 'They have the manner of people that have run and hidden for long enough. They may not be many but they seem capable. They will certainly engage the foe for some time.'

'Here, on their own territory, defending their homes they may be powerful.' Arkas took a deep breath. 'We must venture into the depths of the skaven tunnels and there will be only victory or death, no retreats and ambushes. These are the last of the true people of Ursungorod. The uncorrupted. We came to liberate them, not spend their lives to shield ourselves.'

'You misunderstand–' Doridun began but Arkas cut him off with a sharp gesture.

'No, Knight-Heraldor,' he said sternly, 'you misunderstand your commander. Ursungorod will be freed and its true people will repopulate these mountains. Look at them – their strength is diminishing with each generation. If I asked, each would lay down their life – but I cannot ask. Katiya thinks I will lead them to some new age of glory. I cannot lead them into battle and do that at the same time.'

Doridun stepped back and glanced away, towards the other Stormcasts.

'I will send Venian on his mission, my lord,' the Knight-Heraldor said stiffly. It was clear he had more to say but was holding his tongue. 'Do you have orders for the rest of the chamber?'

'We hold here for the moment,' Arkas replied. When he said nothing further, Doridun nodded and left. Switching back to the Ursungoran language, Arkas addressed Katiya. 'When Ursungorod is free, from here its people will rise. Show me your city.'

CHAPTER
TWENTY-TWO

What the free Ursungorans had built was remarkable, when so many other civilizations had risen and fallen during the turning of the ages. Even if they had not been his people, to Arkas the Ursungorans would still have been as precious as diamonds found in the filthy mire of Chaos. Katiya guided Arkas through barrack-chambers, along tunnels lined with deadfall traps and pits that could waylay pursuers. Cunningly balanced tip-doors and hatches allowed the defenders to redirect the path of an attacking force, built using ancient duardin door mechanisms engineered beyond anything Katiya's people were capable of.

'What about food? Forging metal? Clothes?' the Lord-Celestant asked when she brought him into a living chamber. It was squared with duardin stone slabs but the floor and ceiling were naked ice, with columns formed from thick icicles. Fur mattresses and pillows were scattered in small groups where families slept, and rough planks were used as shelves for a small assortment of jugs, pots and trinkets. The chamber was uninhabited for the moment, sparse and cold, but Arkas could remember far less comfortable and homely abodes from when his people had roamed the mountains, following the herds and avoiding the skaven and Chaos attacks.

'We do not live all of the time in the city,' explained Katiya. 'Much of the time we hunt and trap in the forests above the Bear's Pelt. We take what metal we can from our enemies, like-wise other tools and weapons. There are high pastures where we farm goats, though they are often raided by wolves and worse.'

She crossed the chamber and crouched beside a bedroll. Unfurling it, she revealed two long knives, wickedly sharp.

'We carry weapons at all times, and even asleep it is our law that we are armed.'

'A law I created,' said Arkas, smiling inside his helm.

'Indeed, and many more laws that have kept us safe.' She turned her eyes away, embarrassed by her own awe, and rolled up the bedding again. 'In the wild no group more than twenty gathers. We run when we can, and if we are attacked we fight only until we can run. Each third-moon we return to the City of Ice to exchange news, trade what we have scavenged and hunted, tend to the wounded and deposit the dead.'

'Deposit?' The low ceiling of the chamber made it hard for Arkas to follow her, and he was forced to walk in a stoop. 'What do you mean?'

'Many of the cursed tribes are corpse-eaters, and they will take the dead as happily as the living. And the skaven use corpses to fuel their plague winds and poxes. We try to leave no bodies. There are several shafts, run holes that go to the bottom of the glacier. Bodies go into those, into the purity of the ice, returned to Ursungorod.'

'Very sensible,' Arkas told her. She blushed and moved into

a side tunnel. He squeezed his bulk through the opening after her, helm scraping shards from the icy roof. 'No danger of manticores down here.'

'That is another advantage,' Katiya said, her wrinkles deepening as she smiled.

'Are you their leader? Their queen?'

Katiya did not answer, but led him along a curving corridor that sloped gently upwards, slats of stones providing surer footing. The tunnel stopped and became a near-vertical shaft going up and down, metal rungs driven into the bare ice. When she shimmied up, Arkas inspected the ladder closely, dubious about its potential to hold his considerable weight. He saw that each rung had once been a blade, the edges blunted, ends turned to right angles.

Arkas tugged at one and it started to come away in his grip. Thrusting the rung back, he looked up into the shaft. It was about ten times his height, wide enough for him to fit comfortably. Turning his back to the ladder he rammed his gauntleted fingers into the ice, driving them deep enough to get a handhold. Pulling himself up, he bent his leg and repeatedly drove a boot through the wall until it could take his weight. Gathering confidence, he hauled himself up with increasing speed, leaving a trail of indentations.

'I hope this is worth the effort,' he said, clambering over the lip of the top.

There was no need for Katiya to speak – what he discovered at the top was answer enough.

They stood in a triangular tower made of reclaimed duardin masonry, tall enough for Arkas to stand. Three broad, shallow windows showed a view out over the ice fields in every direction. They were at a considerable elevation, much higher than where Katiya had been waiting for the Stormcasts. Two

Ursungorans sat on ledges by each window, another couple sat in one corner, their bone dice clattering on the hard floor.

Moving to a window, Arkas saw banked snow packed around the tower to obscure its shape. From a distance it would be impossible to spot against the whiteness of the ice field. Yet from such a vantage point they could see far across the Bear's Pelt. Arkas' keen eyes picked out other humps and mounds, and the telltale slits of dark windows that would have gone unnoticed had he not been looking for them.

'Watch towers,' he said.

'Also escape routes,' Katiya added, pointing to a wooden trap-door in the ceiling, linked to a counterweight by a thick chain. 'We can also ambush from here, in many places across the ice field. As you know.'

'Impressive,' Arkas said. He was about to turn away when something caught his eye. It was a smudge of darkness, barely visible, beyond one of the other watch-mounds. He had noticed a pile of logs and small red-coloured blocks in one corner. 'Do you light beacon fires?'

'Yes, that is how we send a message of an attack.' Katiya moved up beside him just as flames licked into view from the summit of the intervening tower. 'Cursed ones! They are coming along the Black River.'

'They followed us,' Arkas said. 'We should investigate, find out how many.'

'No need,' Katiya told him. She pointed out of the windows and he saw a trio of ravens heading out from another tower, one of the birds coming towards them.

When it was close, Katiya gave a shrill whistle, much like the one that had summoned her army. The raven dropped down to the window and settled upon the ledge. Chirping and bobbing her head, Katiya held out a hand. Arkas could feel the power of

Ghur wreathing around her, the magic responding to her call. The raven croaked and pecked at the sill, bobbing in agitation.

Katiya drew back sharply and Arkas read shock on her face. She turned to look at him, horrified.

'What is it,' Arkas demanded. 'How many?'

'Many,' Katiya mumbled. She said nothing for a few moments, before some semblance of comprehension surfaced. The elder flicked a look at the bird and then back to Arkas. 'She said she could not count so many. More cursed ones than there are trees in the forest.'

CHAPTER TWENTY-THREE

It took some time for Arkas to traverse the city for a look at the incoming army. Whole areas were inaccessible to him and his warriors due simply to their size. Many of the watch-mounds were equally impassable, and when he eventually found his route towards the river curtailed again he was forced to speak with Katiya.

'I must take my warriors above ground,' he told her. 'I have to see the nature of what we face.'

'It is not our way,' Katiya insisted, a saying she had used several times in the fraught journey across the City of Ice. 'We do not allow them to see our numbers or place.'

'They will not see you at all. My Stormcasts will face this threat and you will remain in the tunnels.'

'You do not understand, you cannot face an army like this. You are too few.'

'We are Stormcast Eternals, forged by Sigmar in the celestial fires of the heavenly sphere. Into us is poured the wisdom and skill of the Six Smiths. We are armoured with sigmarite, the undying strength of the God-King made real. Our weapons are the breaking storm of vengeance. There is *no foe* we cannot face.'

'An army greater than the trees of the forest!' Katiya was on the verge of tears. To her it seemed her hopes had been raised and cruelly dashed in the passing of an afternoon. 'How can you prevail against so many cursed ones?'

'I do not place much trust in the counting of ravens,' Arkas replied, his temper fraying. 'I will lead my warriors back to the surface even if I have to call a storm and blast a hole through the ice!'

Shocked at the thought, Katiya was torn between two minds. He could see the uncertainty written on her face where there had been such conviction. Arkas crouched, resting his hammer across his thighs. He spoke softly, as a father might to a distraught daughter.

'We will prevail. Across Ghur, across all of the Mortal Realms, the armies of the Stormhosts have struck back against the darkness of destruction and Chaos. Where we bring the light of Sigmar, evil cannot stand. We have come to Ursungorod to liberate you. The nightmare is coming to an end.' He laid a hand gently on her quivering arm. 'Trust me. Trust yourself. You saw the return of Arka Bear-clad, and I have come. Together we will deliver our people from the horror and tyranny of the Chaos Gods.'

Katiya sighed, looking tired and old. She wrapped an arm around his massive limb and laid her cheek upon the armour.

'It is warm,' she murmured. 'I thought it would be cold.'

'The power of our forging still burns within us,' Arkas explained.

He waited for some time, allowing her to hold his arm, drawing strength from his presence.

'I need you, Katiya,' he told her. She looked up, confused.

'But you are the Bear-clad, Arka the Uniter. All of our people are yours to command.'

'To command, yes, but not to lead. You are their leader. When we have delivered Ursungorod I cannot remain. I am Stormcast, beholden to the will of Sigmar. It is not our fate to make homes and have family. It is to you we must look for the building of a new future, and others like you that cling to resistance and freedom across the Mortal Realms. I need you to lead your people and I will command mine.'

Nodding, she released her grip and stepped back. Her eyes were moist but her jaw was set with determination.

'I have to prepare,' she told him.

She gestured to one of the Ursungorans close at hand. The denizens of the City of Ice had been gathering in their war-packs, ready for the defence of their homes. The man she signalled was rangy, his face stubbled with blond hair. He wore a full hauberk of mail and a breastplate; he carried a tall helm under his arm, and a long-hafted axe was strapped to his back. He might have been one of Arka's stratzari in a different age.

'This is Ajfor, one of my grandsons,' Katiya said. 'Ajfor, show the Uniter to the north sally tunnels by the Chasm of Sighs. He wishes to see the army coming from the Black River.'

'It is my honour,' said Ajfor, eyes fixed widely on Arkas. Eventually he dragged his gaze away. He picked up a pack and a silver-headed spear, and indicated for Arkas to follow him through one of the archways.

'I must assemble my warriors first,' Arkas told Katiya.

'It would be better if you went alone,' she replied. 'Secrecy is still our best defence. Our only defence, truthfully. If the cursed ones cannot find the entrances to the City of Ice, they cannot attack.'

Arkas considered this and could not fault the logic, or the

proof that the Ursungorans had survived when countless others had not, though part of him was reluctant. His unease formed into something more solid.

'I cannot defend the City of Ice if I do not know the field of battle. I need a map, so that I can see where to place my warriors, where we can manoeuvre and counter-attack.'

'There are no maps,' Katiya said, brow knotting. She tapped the side of her head. 'All that we need to know is kept here. It cannot be stolen, cannot be lost or looted from here. We do not allow ourselves to be taken alive. Only those that grew up in the City of Ice know its ways.'

'Then I cannot fight underground,' Arkas said.

'I will give you guides,' said Katiya. 'They know the routes, the ambushes and escapes.'

'That will not work,' Arkas said with a shake of his head. 'There are passages where my warriors cannot fight but your tactics do not allow for that. We are too large for this tunnel-fight. Your people are put at risk if they must stay with us, and the enemy will use the narrow ways against us. If I cannot see a map, I cannot make a plan.'

A resolution started to form in Arkas' thoughts, coalescing from various threads of doubt and questions about the City of Ice.

'You have it wrong, Katiya,' he declared. 'You cannot have me thinking like an Ursungoran, I am a commander of the Stormcasts. The Chaos corrupted do not come here for you, they seek my army. I shall give it to them, on the surface where we can fight in the open. We are not a guerrilla force, to hit and run from shadows. It is for this purpose we came to Ursungorod, to be the flame that lights the beacon of fresh hope. We will not skulk in tunnels and caves and expect you to fight the battle for us.'

'There are far too many for us to fight,' said Katiya, fearful at the thought. 'Skulking and hiding has seen us survive for long years, Uniter.'

'My words were not meant as an insult,' Arkas replied quickly. He lowered to one knee and leaned close so that she could see his intent in his eyes. 'What you have achieved is incredible, Katiya. Almost miraculous. That is why we must do this my way. Our coming is to liberate you, not doom you. It would dishonour the sacrifice of all those that came before if I allowed the darkness to consume what you have protected for so long. We will fight on the surface and we will kill many, many of the cursed ones. If it is our fate to fall in that fight, so be it. We are Stormcasts, we will be reforged.'

He did not think of the price of Reforging. The memory of becoming a Stormcast, of passing under the hammers of the Six Smiths, was vague but full of pain. Every time a Stormcast was remade, they lost a piece of themselves, and Sigmar too gave up a fragment of his power. The God-King had diminished himself to create his armies, and this crusade would be the one that brought victory or defeat, conquest or oblivion. There would be no retreat to Azyr next time, no quiet centuries to build and prepare. The Stormcasts were heralds of the final war that would decide the fate of all, mortals and gods alike.

'You *must* continue to survive,' he told Katiya. 'If we fail to turn the tide you will still have the City of Ice to protect you. You must hold on. My companions from the Knights Excelsior are being led here. Theuderis Silverhand commands them, a host ten times the size of mine. It was for this reason we are here, to bring forth the poison of Chaos and destroy it.'

Katiya said nothing, conflicted. It was Ajfor who replied.

'We will show you the way,' he said. 'A place where a few can stand against the many.'

'The Teeth of the Bear,' said Katiya, looking to her grand-son and receiving a nod. She smiled. 'If there is anywhere this flood of foes can be dammed, it is there.'

'I know it,' said Arkas. 'A defile along which the Black River flows, steep-sided and narrow.'

'It is not as it was in your day,' said Katiya, as Arkas stood and replaced his mask. 'The land does not stand still. But you will see for yourself.'

Ajfor moved away to several more men and women and spoke to them, pointing at Arkas and then continuing for a short while longer. He turned back to the Lord-Celestant.

'With your permission, Uniter, we would bring you to the Teeth of the Bear by several routes. My cousins will take your warriors by the secret paths.'

'Tell them the Warbeast commands it,' said Arkas. He repeated the phrase in the celestial tongue and had the guides practise the words. 'Speak thus and they will know it comes from me.'

The Ursungorans said their farewells and disappeared into the white-and-grey tunnels. Ajfor directed a look to Arkas, a silent inquiry.

'One moment,' said the Lord-Celestant. He led Katiya to one side and spoke softly. 'I see where you draw your strength. It is a long bloodline, but the power of Radomira flows in your veins still. Am I right?'

'I am one of her daughters over many generations,' said Katiya.

'Then know this, Katiya Gospor, daughter of Radomira, child of Ursungorod. Your ancestor raised me as her own when my mother died. She said she saw omens that I would save my people. The storm claimed me, as she knew it would, and she stood beside me even though she knew that day would end in death and misery. Today know that the circle has turned, the night becomes day and light returns to Ursungorod. Your dreams of salvation are her memory returned, her hope reborn. Whatever happens, never abandon hope, never submit to the darkness.'

'Death first,' Katiya said hoarsely, throat tight with emotion. She stroked his armoured arm, child-like next to the giant but as motherly as Radomira ever was. 'Go. Fight. Free our people.'

CHAPTER
TWENTY-FOUR

The Black River was narrow and fierce here, still fresh from the highlands, strengthened by the meltwater of the Bear's Pelt. It frothed and rushed over jagged rocks, between the walls of a valley that were almost vertical. The defile did not run straight, but jagged back and forth around sharp bends, in places becoming waterfalls, in others slowing slightly into broader pools.

The way was impassable but for the remains of a duardin road that led down to the ruins Arkas had seen before meeting Katiya. Made of seemingly imperishable stone, the dark grey ribbon ran alongside the Black River, sometimes crossing over it on steep arches, in other places heaping up on thick piles to run across the surface of the cliffs and the clifftops themselves. The river itself was not in full flood, for when it was even the road was barred. Had it been the short spring, the host of the cursed ones would have been forced across the snow fields and exposed to the bitter winds and blizzards, not to mention the hidden chasms and ambushes of the Ursungorans. They had learnt to tread warily across the Bear's Pelt, and so they approached through the Bear's Teeth, sure of the ground beneath their feet and confident in their numbers.

The Bear's Teeth had been, in Arkas' mortal time, a pair of high rock pillars that flanked the river at its narrowest point – black columns each nearly a quarter of a mile high. Making his way towards them, Arkas saw that the landscape had changed, as Katiya had warned. The river now spread into a deep pool half a mile across, and more rock pinnacles speared from the black depths at its edge, curving towards each other to form a boundary of immense rock fangs, leaving the original Bear's Teeth as monstrous canines.

The lake was not impassable though, for a maze of boulders and walkways stood proud of the water, slick but broad enough for the Stormcasts to use them as stepping stones and bridges if needed.

'They were not here before,' gasped Ajfor, pointing to the wetted boulders. He looked in amazement at Arkas. 'The lands form to your command, Uniter!'

Even as he watched, Arkas saw another rock push forth in a welter of bubbles, capping the end of a bridge-like spur. Rocky steps led down from the cliff-like banks to the waters.

'So it seems,' he grunted, unsure of this revelation. Ursungorod had always been erratic, but this behaviour reminded him of the touch of Chaos. Could he trust the land enough to cross the lake?

From the clifftops, Arkas could see further down the river. As he had suspected, the arithmetic of crows and hawks left something to be desired – the Chaos army numbered several thousands, but no more than ten thousand. Even so, it was a formidable sight, a snake of black and red and leather-brown, of silver and bronze mail that snaked for some distance along the canyon below.

Pennants stitched with vile symbols fluttered above the host, alongside wooden placards burnt with runes or daubed in blood with symbols of Chaos and the Pestilens. The tramp of their feet was louder even than the roaring of the Black River, echoed and amplified by the defile walls. Harsh laughter, the baying of mutant hounds and monstrous bellows of lumbering, blood-coloured khorgoraths added to the din.

'So many,' whispered Ajfor, his hand shielding his eyes against the low sun. He crouched behind a pillar of rock jutting from the cliff edge, a little way ahead of Arkas who stood in the column's heavy shadow. 'They usually fight each other, raid and steal from their camps. They blood and burn each other in sacrifice! Why have they become allies?'

'I don't know,' said Arkas. 'I don't know what the skaven have offered them, or what threats demanded this loyalty.'

It was a lie. The Warbeast knew exactly what had finally brought the tribes together, for it was the same thing he had exploited to become the Uniter. Fear. The skaven perhaps had instigated the union, and fuelled it with promises and payments, but it was fear that welded it together. The Stormcasts and news of their victories had moved swiftly through the mountains, doubtless made all the speedier by verminous messengers. One by one, the tribes of Chaos could be crushed, but together...

As Arka Bear-clad, he had sent the same message to free men and women, warning of the danger of the skaven in the deeps. The rewards for alliance coupled with the dangers of isolation meant that when a few clans had joined, the rest saw more benefit in friendship than enmity.

The tribes of Chaos were afraid of the Stormcasts, and had been promised the City of Ice. Their rivalries and hostility put to one side for a time, now was an opportunity to take that which they had desired for an age – to rid themselves of the thorn that had worried them for so many generations. Slay the Stormcasts and sweep into the City of Ice to kill the free people. And the skaven could happily trust that once their foes had been destroyed, the tribes would quickly fall back to old ways, fighting each other over the spoils.

'See how they still march as tribes and warbands?' he said to Ajfor. He could see where the different factions kept to themselves, each a distinct section of the whole, fault lines that could be exploited. 'They are uncoordinated, and will fight piecemeal. They have no commander, just competing warlords. Some will try to let the others take the brunt of the fighting, some will be eager to earn themselves glory in the eyes of the Dark Gods.'

'That does not lessen their number, Uniter,' said Ajfor. 'There are still many to kill.'

Arkas took a deep breath, still eyeing the approaching army. He let free some of the celestial energy inside his immortal body, his warhammer and runeblade flaring in his fists. He looked at Ajfor and smiled, though the Ursungoran could not see it.

'Not too many.'

CHAPTER TWENTY-FIVE

The crackle of thirteen vast firepits and the smoke from their flames filled the immense cavern of the undercity. The fires fizzed and popped with multicoloured light as wood, hide and warp-saturated flesh burned.

By the dim light of the fires, the huge structure of the Great Shrine loomed over the proceedings. The hammer of the great gong was pulled back, ready to strike and pronounce the beginning of the festivities. From every rickety balcony and pole hung banners of human skin and slave hide, decorated with the symbol of the Withered Canker, the thrice-slashed claw mark of Felk himself.

A hundred slaves laboured at the enormous turnspits erected over the pits, roasting the flesh of the diseased captives. Limbs and ribcages were pierced on the raw wooden stakes, while in mighty cauldrons tended by a further army of ragged slaves, organs and fat bubbled away, stirred by Felk's watchful plague priests.

A barricade had been erected around the new enclosure, piled from brick and stone taken from the excavation of the realmgate, and supplemented with mouldy planks and boxes, tattered sacks stuffed with sand and gravel, and sheets of crudely flattened brass and bronze. Skarth and his spitevermin patrolled the perimeter, hissing and snapping at any that approached, hurling stones and darts at those that did not heed those warnings.

The floor of the cavern was layered with deep filth from many years of occupation. Through the accreted effluent of the undercity, trenches had been dug, waist-high to the slaves that had carved them from hardened excreta and filth. The trenches were arranged in an angled circle, with branches and offshoots running off at strange angles – the rune of the Great Horned Rat, the name of the Great Witherer, given shape.

The bottom of the trenches had been lined with the bodies of those that had dug them, the corpses so fresh that the blood was still drying in the wounds from the spitevermins' halberds. From the banks of the trenches, plague monks poured out libations from cracked pottery urns and amphorae. The line of skaven passed dented golden goblets, stained porcelain vases, tin cups, glazed pots, silvered jugs and crystal pitchers all the way back from the skewed gates of the Great Shrine. Filled from the festering pits beneath the shrine, every receptacle brimmed with noxious fluid gathered over many years, faintly glowing with power from the warp deposits at the Great Shrine's heart.

The plague monks breathed deep of the fumes that emanated from the frothing brew of corruption. Their tails twitched with excitement, eyes saucer-like with narcotic delirium, chattering and squeaking without words as they laboured to fill the trenches.

Felk prowled at the centre of it all, alternating between triumphant hand-rubbing and nervous twitches as his thoughts and moods shifted from his excitement about the feast to his concerns over the metal giants.

A shape ghosted out of the fire-shadows and resolved into Thriss, a splintered human thighbone in his claws. There were scratches on the bone, written in a code unknown to the gutter runner. Felk could smell rotting leaves and sensed the dissipating aura of Ghryan, the Realm of Life. He took the bone and quickly read the inscription. It was a simple statement explaining that it was not known where in the Realm of Life Felk's portal would open, but assuring him that his agents would be prepared when it happened.

'And other thing? The skull-skull?' Felk demanded, beckoning with impatient claws. 'Have it, yes-yes?'

From beneath the folds of his cloak, Thriss produced a skull, yellowed and much cracked. A prominent break pierced one temple. Felk could smell the dried blood ingrained in the bone. The holes had been stoppered with fatty-smelling wax. The skull was slender in the jaw, high in the cheeks, with a pronounced forehead and shallow brow. The head of an aelf. Not just any head. It had been taken from its owner by none other than Felk's master, the verminlord Skixakoth.

Felk shook the artefact and was satisfied by the dull rattle of something within.

'It is still inside, yes-yes? The Tooth of Skixakoth?'

'Yes-yes,' snapped the gutter runner. 'As promised. Clan Darkclaw never fails.'

Felk cocked an eye at this ludicrous claim, but chose not to list the numerous times both Thriss and his Eshin companions had been total failures. The Poxmaster was too excited by his new acquisition.

'Life-life and death-death,' he crowed, stroking a claw across the top of the skull. He sniffed, taking in the heady scent of depraved magic, the raw Chaos of the verminlord fang still trapped in the skull. 'Much magic! Power of Great Witherer itself! Yes-yes, glorious feast tonight.'

'What is it for?' asked Thriss, eyeing the skull with a dubious look. 'What does it do-do?'

'Is talisman,' said Felk, voice dropping to a conspiratorial whisper. He clutched the skull to his ear as if listening. 'Is key to the gnaw-ways. Is symbol of Skixakoth. Is many things. Is greatest channel, opening, window to highest and lowest places.'

'Channel where?' Thriss' eyes darted in all directions as though he expected some portal to open immediately. Felk hissed with irritation.

'To burrows of the gods, to Great Horned Rat!' he spat. 'When dismal feast is done, we speak to Great Witherer and with blessing take all Whiteworld Above.'

'What of metal giants? Humans not stop them.'

'No-no, but metal giants come too late. Trap set.' Felk lifted the skull in triumph and then, realising all of the plague monks could see it, snatched it back and hid it in a ragged fold of his robe. 'Great Horned Rat will destroy metal giants. Felk will rule all Whiteworld Above. Open the gate, we will, and Withered Canker will destroy sylvaneth. All bow to Felk's power!'

Thriss muttered something.

'What say?' demanded Felk. 'Say-say again!'

'Praise mighty Poxmaster Felk,' Thriss intoned flatly. 'Great leader of Withered Canker.'

Felk eyed the Eshin agent for a time, until thoughts of the dismal feast distracted him back to a more pleasing topic. The plague monks had filled the ditches, tossing the broken pots and jugs into the noisome soup. At a gesture from Felk, the plague priests started a low chant, uttering praises to the Great Horned Rat, invocations of pestilence and decay. The lower ranks took up the hymnal, swaying forwards and back, left and right, caught in drug-fuelled throes of elation.

Stalking between the undulating lines of robed skaven, Felk raised his staff, signalling to the slave-masters at the firepits. Whips cracked and voices were raised in command, ordering the slaves into action. Teams of bent-backed skaven lifted up the great skewers and pots and brought them across to the site of the feast, eyes rolling in fear, pink tails lashing.

Trenchers of rough-beaten brass and iron had been set up in long rows, forming a triangle around Felk. While the chanting of the plague monks grew louder and louder, the slaves bore their loads to the trenchers. Using broken, filthy claws, they tore away hunks of meat, corroded bonesaws severing thighs, shinbones and ribs, immense ladles filling the trenchers with thick, greasy stew.

Their tasks complete, the slaves cowered together, fearful of their masters' goads. Felk walked amongst them, staff and empty hand upraised.

'No fear-fear!' he told the quivering mass of poxy fur and scabbed skin. 'Tonight is dismal feast. Slaves no more! Eat-eat! Strong you will be, blessed by the Great Witherer.'

The slaves eyed him with suspicion, glancing nervously at the trenchers and then back to the Poxmaster.

'Eat!' Felk snarled, grabbing the closest slave by a ragged ear, pulling it towards the food. 'Fill bellies!'

Starvation won over distrust and the skavenslaves broke en masse to the trenchers, gorging themselves on the roasted and boiled meat. They squabbled and snapped, raked their claws across each other's muzzles and bit the tails of their neighbours in their desperation.

While the slaves feasted, the plague monks turned, chanting still, lining the sigil of the Great Horned Rat. Felk's priests disappeared into the gloom and emerged with thirteen bound humans. They were stripped to the skin, revealing lesions and boils, open sores and ruddy clusters of buboes. They were the most diseased, the greatest tribute to the power of the Great Witherer. Gibbering and sobbing they stared in horror at their hellish surrounds, recoiling from the frenzy of gluttony and depravity as they witnessed the fate of their former companions.

Unresisting, the humans were pushed to the ground, forced to kneel facing each other, Felk at the centre of the circle. The Poxmaster licked the air to taste their abhorrence. It was sweet nectar.

The activity at the trenchers was slowing, the slaves sated, staggering and groaning with bloated bellies. The plague monks continued their dirge, the rhythm starting to quicken, staves rising and falling to thud softly on the packed detritus that covered the ground. Faster, harder came the beat, and through it Felk could sense the magic of Ghur shifting, responding to the ritual.

The monks panted, gasping for air but unable to stop the liturgy. Possessed by the rising spirit of the Great Horned One, they continued to pound with their staves, the rhythm becoming more ragged, the chant discordant.

Felk was mesmerised by the chorus of mewling captives, moaning slaves, shrieking monks and thundering staff beats. He slowly turned on the spot, marvelling at the way the sound changed as he spun, the acoustics of the massive cavern twisting, rebounding and changing the music of the Horned Rat.

Arms still held high, he closed his eyes, his natural paranoia dropping away for an instant to allow him a moment of pure intoxication. He felt his heart juddering in his chest, could smell the musk and sweat and the taint of warpstone.

The sensation passed and he opened his eyes, wobbling to a dizzy stop. His vision swam for a while longer, the faces of his priests blurring in and out of focus, sometimes leering jealously, other times concerned and fearful.

'Great Witherer!' Felk declared, regaining his equilibrium. 'Horned One of Decay! Felk offers you Whiteworld Above. Grant me this boon, grant me bounty, and Felk gifts all lands to your praise. Bless Poxmaster Felk, bless Withered Canker in your name. Felk beseeches Great Horned One, hear our prayers, hear laments of your victims! Plague we are. Pox and infection we spread. In your name, for your praise. We are Pestilens. Harbingers of the Doom of Worlds. Gnawers of vitality. Swift bringers of your filthy blessings.'

Felk pointed his staff at the human captives, who recoiled as if struck.

Their depressed moaning turned into wailing and crying.

'See these offerings! Most foul, most touched by your divine hand. Back to the Great Horned One we send them.' Felk skittered over to the prisoners and grabbed the hair of the nearest, dragging her head back. His thin tongue licked along her neck, leaving a trail of thick saliva in the crusted dirt, blood and pus. 'Feast as we have feasted! Eat-eat, mighty lord of the thirteen plagues.'

Felk stepped back as his plague monks set about messily sacrificing the captives to their horned deity.

Now was the time. Now was the moment of his glorious triumph.

Felk snatched out the skull taken from the lair of Skixakoth. The daemonic fang within was rattling and bouncing of its own accord. The green glow of warp energy seeped through the wax and cracks, bathing Felk in its light.

The Poxmaster dashed the skull against the ground, releasing the power of the verminlord's tooth.

CHAPTER TWENTY-SIX

Green lightning arced with violent snaps, leaping from the broken skull to the corpses of the sacrifices. The bodies jumped and jittered as though given fresh life. Limbs spasmed, chests heaved, eyes darted to and fro while twitching, bloodied fingers grasped at open wounds and shattered bones. Engulfed by the torrent of power, the cadavers rose to their feet, listless puppets sustained only by malicious magic.

Warp energy surrounded the sacrifices with an aura of sickly roiling magical fumes, like the vapours that rose from the sigil of the Horned Rat carved around the feast. The air grew thick with power, clinging to Felk's claws and teeth, matting his fur. The noxious liquid in the mark of the Great Witherer started to bubble and boil of its own accord.

Still the magic grew in strength. It pooled into the engorged slaves, who were now lying in torpid piles beside the trenches. It filled them with unnatural vitality. They staggered to their feet with jerky movements and started to writhe and dance, distended bellies swinging, emaciated limbs shuddering and twisting.

His thoughts becoming a feverish blur, Felk heard a snap behind him and spun around in time to see the first slave collapsing, his weak bones unable to sustain him. A wet slapping noise heralded the gut of another splitting, its distended organs spilling out in a welter of undigested food and blood. The magic of the Horned One animated them still, set them flapping and cavorting across the uneven floor while more slaves burst, collapsed and broke under the magical assault.

Beside Felk the human corpses withered. The magical lightning sapped them of blood, fat and flesh. It turned their bones to dust, their blood to vapour, leaving only empty skin hanging in the air.

The fang of Skixakoth, as big as Felk's outstretched claw from thumb to little finger, rose into the air, slowly rotating, held aloft by a miasma of jade warp energy. The fang stopped at about head height and righted itself, hanging down as though in an upper jaw. The fog started to coalesce into something more solid. Around the tooth a huge rat-like face crowned by thirteen horns shifted in and out of the mist.

Felk threw himself to the ground, averting his gaze. From the corner of his eye he saw his priests doing likewise. Some of the plague monks were not so swift. Their agonised shrieks cut across the thunderous pulsing that now filled the chamber, as they looked upon the visage of the Great Horned One and were sent mad. Wet mewling followed as they clawed out their eyes and gouged their flesh, trying to rid themselves of the sight, trying to free themselves from the gnawing that worried at their souls.

SPEAK.

The voice of the skaven god was not heard, it was felt. It was a rumbling in the rocks, a reverberation in the gut, a noise in the back of the head, a hissing in the ears. The scratching of ten thousand claws on the bones. The rasp of innumerable teeth, gnawing, gnawing, gnawing. The Poxmaster felt blood dribble from his ears and nose, but kept his face pressed into the dirt.

'Poxmaster Felk, most devoted of the Horned Rat's servants.'

FELK? WHY DO YOU SUMMON ME?

'Offer Whiteworld Above to you, mightiest of mighty, potent deliverer of plague and distress. Grant me boon, hear Felk's plea. A realmgate we have. Victory over sylvaneth. Death of life, pox unbound.'

THIS I SEE. FOR A LIFETIME YOU HAVE PROMISED WHITEWORLD ABOVE.

'Yes-yes, but patient Felk has been. Good priest, loyal-loyal servant. Let humans kill and fight, look for realmgate. Now-now it is ours. Yours! Realmgate yours, great herald of oblivion, master of the thirteen deadly ways. Metal giants come-come. Much slaughter. Celebration not certain. Victory unclear. Beseech you, conjurer of abyssal torment, thirteen-times blessed lord of the realms. Grant power. Grant magic. Much-much power.'

IT SHALL BE.

Felk was snatched up by an invisible claw, lifted bodily into the air above his minions. He clutched his staff tightly to his chest, clenching every muscle to stop his musk glands betraying his terror. Tendrils of power flickered around him, caressing his fur to make it stand on end and sparking from his exposed teeth.

He looked down and saw the blazing rune of the Great Horned One, the lines of plague monks duplicating it within, the corpses of the slaves spattered in replica of that awful, awesome sigil.

KNOW MY POWER. FAIL ME NOT.

The gong of the Great Shrine tolled, louder than ever before, the shockwave of noise rolling out across the feast, tossing bodies into the air, passing on to flatten the walls of the spite-vermin, toppling the hovels and ramshackle streets beyond. On and on it seemed to echo until Felk's world was nothing but his claws digging into the wood of his staff and the dreadful ring of the Horned Rat's declaration shuddering through his whole body.

In the silence that followed he thought he was falling. Falling so far he had to have passed into a great chasm, dropping into the gap between realms, disappearing along the gnawholes of the skaven and into the lair of the Great Witherer.

Felk saw the fang of the verminlord hanging in the air before him, glinting cruelly in the light. His hand reached out, not of his volition, clawed fingers opening to grasp the cursed tooth. He did not resist, knowing that it was the will of his god. His arm shaking, he held the tooth before him like a dagger.

Everything was darkness, but for the light from that jagged tooth. Felk moved his arm to expose his chest, his robes parting with their own life to bare his furred flesh.

With a hiss, he dragged the tooth closer, plunging it into his heart.

Pain engulfed Felk. Pain of every pox, every plague, every disease unleashed by the pestilent lords combined. He felt their power spreading from the wound, infecting him with their potency, the virulent energy rippling along arteries and veins, infusing organs with eternal power, the energy of Chaos itself.

In a blast of ecstatic fusion he was joined with the Great Horned One. His minds were filled with blistering images, of the gnaw-tunnels between worlds, stretching into the past and future, coiling through infinities, an impossible maze that burrowed through and under every mortal thing. And further still, into the Realm of Chaos, undermining the dominions of the four great powers.

The scurrying, gnawing, endlessly teeming mass of skaven thrived in the under-empire, enslaving, scavenging, growing in numbers beyond counting, ready to burst forth across all of the realms.

And there – a glimpse of realm-burrows working towards the bastions of Azyr, locked for so long by the will of the human god-king. An army of golden warriors bringing fire and death to the followers of Chaos. The metal giants, the soldiers of Sigmar.

For some it was the end. The last war that would see the worlds of mortals destroyed. Not for the Children of the Horned Rat. Death brought opportunity. Famine and plague, the companions of war, were ever ripe ground for the disciples of the Great Witherer.

Felk opened his eyes. A shadow loomed over him and he held a hand up, reflexively squealing in panic.

'Poxmaster?'

The blur resolved into Skarth's face. He bared his teeth, halberd held at the ready. A slight movement allowed Felk to see the ring of plague priests around him, concerned more by the blade of his fangleader than the state of their master's health. Some looked openly disappointed at his recovery.

Felk sat up, fingers unconsciously questing for the reassuring feel of his staff, seeking the familiar cracked wood.

He remembered a last image, of the collapsing under-empire, of the dominions of the Great Horned One imploding back into him. Felk recalled the surge of power, and his staff exploding into threads and splinters.

It was his badge of office, his weapon and the channel for his power. He felt naked without it.

He stood up, staying close to Skarth. The priests and the spite-vermin forming a cordon against the plague monks beyond let out a communal hiss of surprise. Skarth took a step back, lips curling back over dark gums.

Where Felk's robe had fallen open, his chest was in plain view. The roots of Skixakoth's fang could be seen just over his heart, protruding slightly from suppurating flesh. Threads of corruption pulsed like a web from the wound, spreading from the tooth across Felk's chest and abdomen. He lifted a claw, allowing the voluminous sleeve to roll back, revealing corded tendrils of warp power gently gleaming beneath the skin. His nails were long and sharp as he flexed his fingers.

He pulled his robe closed and rose to his full height – a little taller than before, he thought, though perhaps he had always stooped without realising. The power of the Horned Rat's bless-ing was evident not just in the visible signs. Felk could feel the energy flowing through him, spiralling and weaving through his body, suffusing his organs with putrid vitality.

'Come-come, brothers.' He gestured for his priests to gather closer. 'Disciples of Felk, chosen of the Great Horned Rat. Bear witness to our master's divine will.'

Cautiously, the plague priests approached, clutching their staves and knives, casting glances at each other.

'Time has come,' declared Felk. 'Wrong we are, poor wor-shippers, selfish rat-rats! War we make. War good.' He clenched his fists. Warp power dribbled from between his fingers like smoke. 'Not fight with fist. Not fight with sword or halberd. We the masters of disease! Not conquer Whiteworld Above. Destroy it! All life, all humans, all giant men of Sigmar! My ruin-bringers, my plague-heralds, my warp-fiends, bear wit-ness! Corpse-mountain we build. Plague furnaces we make. Wind of annihilation blows. Death-death, all things dead!

When realmgate opens, tide of death unleashed. Much work to be done. Felk decrees, you obey.'

Cowed by this grand oratory and the halo of power wreathing their leader, the plague priests bowed and fell to their knees, faces hidden inside their hoods.

'Praise Felk,' cried the Poxmaster. 'Lord of the Withered Canker, Slayer of the Whiteworld Above.'

'Praise Felk,' they intoned.

CHAPTER TWENTY-SEVEN

Not only had the Black River dammed itself to aid Arkas, it had steepened its banks downriver, swallowing the makeshift road beneath jagged rocks and mudslides. Some of the Chaos clans were not content to funnel up the gorge and attempted to scale the shallower sides of the defile to reach the wide expanse of the Bear's Pelt. Arkas took this as the sign to announce the presence of his warriors.

Having crossed the stone bridges on the lake to set their ambush along both sides, Judicators lined the precipice edges to welcome the climbing warriors with volleys of shockbolts and skybolts. Burning from the touch of the celestial missiles, an avalanche of corpses fell back into the defile, causing panic amongst the packed tribal warriors below. Those not caught under their falling companions responded with angry shouts and a surge that sent many splashing into the river, scrapping with each other to forge their way to the easier ascent further along.

At a word from Arkas, his Prosecutors swept into the gorge,

speeding along the twisting ravine and unleashing more heavenly arrows into the throng. Scattered projectiles leapt up to meet them but were poorly aimed and of little threat to the armoured fliers. Trolls and larger beasts hurled rocks and fistfuls of smaller stone, bellowing impotently at the tormentors soaring out of reach.

'Arrows alone will not slay them all,' said Ajfor, who had remained with Arkas to act as a messenger if needed. He pointed to the narrowest part of the ravine, where sharp, ice-covered rocks thrust like gigantic fangs. They glittered in the weak sun, the striations of red stone inside like trails of dried blood. 'That is the best place to defend.'

'The Jaws,' said Arkas. 'A good choice if I was going to pick somewhere to make a last stand.'

'What do you intend, Uniter? We cannot hold them on the open ice.'

'I don't intend to hold them anywhere.' Arkas beckoned to Doridun. 'Prepare to signal the attack. We'll push down the river and cut down anyone stupid enough not to run.'

The Knight-Heraldor nodded and relayed the order to Dolmetis, who carried the command to the nearest Primes. The Warbeasts moved closer to the edge of the ravine, ready to start their descent.

'Attack?' Ajfor's eyes were so wide they seemed to bulge out of his head.

'We are the storm of Sigmar's wrath, the Celestial Vindicators, the Warbeasts,' Arkas said with a grin. 'We do not wait for battle to come to us, we seek it out.'

At his word, the Strike Chamber started the climb. Reaching the pebble-strewn bottom, where ice covered the small stones, the Warbeasts quickly assembled into their retinues, rallying on their Primes. The canyon turned to the left, masking them from view for the moment, though the Chaos warriors leading the attack could not have failed to see them disappearing from the clifftop.

'Full charge, no mercy,' Arkas barked to his Stormcasts. 'Kill the foe in front, leave the foe to the left and right to your companions. We fight together, we win together.'

A guttural roar signalled the assent and readiness of the Warbeasts.

'Come on then,' laughed Arkas.

They reached full speed before the enemy came into view, pounding across the blue ice and splashing through the frothing water. Rounding the bend, Arkas saw that the foremost Chaos tribe were also moving swiftly.

Well-armed and armoured warriors led them, advancing at a trot, gathered beneath a banner of bone and stretched skin inked in gore with the symbol of the Blood God, Khorne. Some had bare heads, their faces heavily scarred and pierced, while others wore helms with curving bull's horns fitted like tusks and tipped with jagged iron shards. Each bore two heavy hammers or maces, their gauntlets were spiked at the knuckles, and they wore metal bracers on their forearms.

Issuing bloody challenges, the Chaos warriors broke into a sprint, heedless of the threat posed by the Stormcasts, relishing the opportunity to slay the most powerful foes. The Warbeasts continued on at the same relentless pace, a wall of sigmarite that left a trail of shimmering celestial power on the rocks and dancing across the rapids.

The crash of the two forces rang down the canyon. The bodily impact of the Stormcasts sent many of the Chaos warriors hurtling and tumbling, while sweeps of starsoul maces and stormstrike glaives sent hewn corpses spinning into the reddening spume of the river.

Pushed on by the weight of their comrades behind, the leading edge of the Warbeasts rumbled down the gorge. Arkas, running along the left bank, cleaved a path with warhammer and runeblade, as Dolmetis and Doridun formed the point of the attack on the opposite side of the river.

The Prosecutors returned from their raking attacks further downstream and poured their missiles into the tribesmen just a dozen yards ahead of the Stormcast assault. One in three Chaos followers fell beneath the aerial onslaught, the survivors disorientated and split, easy prey for the rampaging Warbeasts.

The steep sides of the ravine left little room for manoeuvre – or escape. The more cowardly tribesmen found themselves trapped against the unforgiving rocks, cut down as they fled, crushed against the boulders by hammers and maces forged in the heavenly foundries of Sigmaron.

Preceded by the volleys from above, the Celestial Vindicators swept all before them, only the occasional flash of blue light showing where an unfortunate Stormcast had fallen to a lucky blow or an aggregation of many wounds. A corona of azure light moved before them like a bow wave, flickers of lightning from skybolts and shockbolts detonating in the depths. Ruined flesh and armour carpeted the defile in their wake, and the Black River ran crimson.

'Easy now,' bellowed Arkas as the gorge widened. They had pushed on perhaps a thousand paces, and here the river was slower, the sides of the defile not as steep. Warhounds and cavalry skirted the flanks, holding back for the moment, but waiting for the Stormcasts to over-extend and give them room around the flanks.

'Hold fast!' Arkas ordered.

The notes of the command rang out from Doridun's clarion and the Strike Chamber stopped in a heartbeat, extending outwards as far as possible, the end of the line bowing slightly to present no space through which the enemy might slip.

'Enough glory for each of us, my lord,' said Martox. The Decimator-Prime stood a little way to Arkas' left, his thunder-axe over one shoulder as he surveyed the mountain hordes.

Though his tone was light, Martox's observation was correct. Two thousand at least had fallen already, but Arkas watched a sea of warriors still coming up the river. Freed from the strikes of the Prosecutors, several tribes, each a few hundred warriors strong, had started the ascent to the ice field again.

The nearest tribal groups pulled back, taking advantage of the sudden halt in the attack. Over their heads, Arkas could see larger monsters being brought to the fore – skull-faced khorgoraths with bulging bodies and flailing bone-tentacles, Chaos-twisted spawn that defied category and description, and other mutant monstrosities covered in scale and fur and sharp spines. More heavily armoured warriors shouldered their way through the barbarian marauders, line-breakers determined to make a breach in the Stormcast wall. Behind them came plate-armoured warriors on the backs of huge destriers covered by caparisons of bronze mail, fire burning in the eyes of their daemonically blessed steeds.

War altars dedicated to the Dark Powers were carried forwards on the backs of scaled beasts or held aloft by chained slaves blinded and whip-scarred. Arcane magic spilled from these unholy totems, polluting the draughts of Ghurite energy that flowed with the Black River. Cockatrices and chimerae from the deep forests were goaded forwards by hooded beast-handlers. All the myriad forces of the Chaos Gods were arrayed against the Warbeasts, the river valley thick with their numbers.

'At least it's stopped snowing,' Martox continued.

Laughing, Arkas looked up. The clouds were there, grey and pregnant with a fresh blizzard, but for the moment Martox was right.

The Lord-Celestant saw something against the gloom, small at first but swiftly approaching. As it came closer he could make out that it was a bird, quite large, with multicoloured wings.

Smiling, Arkas raised his sword and flexed his grip on his warhammer.

'Charge!' he roared.

The sky glittered, a coruscating backdrop of magic that made stark the descending silhouettes of angels. The Angelos Conclave of the Silverhands fell with swift fury on the dark legions, first clearing the ravine walls of foes before raking missiles into the Chaos tribesmen. A few dozen tainted warriors managed to clamber to safety on the glacier, only to be met by Hastor and Venian, who were quickly joined by the rest of Arkas' Prosecutors.

The army of Theuderis arrayed on the heights above the river, a line of ivory and blue that stretched far, the air above crackling with latent celestial energy. The Silverhand himself sat astride his dracoth, which reared in salute to the Warbeasts, lightning forking from its mouth. Knights-Vexillor and Knights-Heraldor held the line for a moment, awaiting the command of their lord.

Theuderis swung down his blade and the clarions blared. Icons aloft, the Knights-Vexillor led the attack. Lightning churned along the defile, leaping in chains through the warriors in the river, charring fleshing and melting armour.

Wrath incarnate, the Knights Excelsior fell upon the Chaos host with a single refrain echoing down the gorge.

'For the glory of Sigmar!'

CHAPTER
TWENTY-EIGHT

The first charge of the Knights Excelsior broke the will of the Chaos tribes. Pressed into the confines of the Black River those at the front could do little but fight desperately, but even their greatest warriors were no match for the spear of Theuderis and his Paladin Conclave leading the charge. Those further down-river saw the thousands of ivory-and-blue giants and fled at the sight, all bargains with the skaven, all alliances and dreams of possessing the City of Ice, overwhelmed by the spectacle of Sigmar's wrath given form.

Arkas and his Warbeasts met the monstrous khorgoraths, gargants and mutants head-on, relishing the challenge of fighting such warped beasts. The waters of the Black River frothed with unnatural blood and ichor, and the ravine sparked with flares of celestial energy as Stormcasts were torn apart or crushed, but the Celestial Vindicators were irrepressible.

Scoured and blinded by the purging light of the celestial beacons held aloft by the Knights-Azyros, the barbarians called prayers to their twisted gods, beseeching the Dark Powers to save them, even as the warriors of Sigmar slew with abandon. None were answered.

While Arkas and his warriors were a rampaging beast, slaughtering at will as they forged down the river, the Silver-hands were a devastating, unstoppable storm that swallowed everything with a machine-like relentlessness and left nothing but corpses in its wake. The black waters reflected the fire of the heavenly realm and seemed to burn with it as the followers of Chaos were consumed.

The killing went on until mid-afternoon, spilling from the river onto an expanse of the Bear's Pelt, where thousands more tainted natives were cut down where they fled – slashed, crushed and pierced by the celestial weapons of Sigmar's host.

Arkas did not weary of it, but ran out of foes. Hastor came to him bearing greeting from Theuderis and he bade his Knight-Venator to return the compliment and lead the Lord-Celestant to Ajfor so that he might be brought into the City of Ice.

In the depths of the city, in a chamber of reclaimed duardin stone and carved ice lit only by a small, guttering oil lamp, Theuderis evaluated his companions. Arkas Warbeast looked like any other Stormcast Lord-Celestant, though his armour showed far less wear and damage than Theuderis' own. He crouched, arms on thighs, speaking with the woman, Katiya. She was not what the Lord-Celestant had been expecting when the Warbeast had offered to broker a meeting with the leader of the free Ursungorans.

She was small, though not frail, skin weathered by constant exposure to the harsh elements. She wore only rudimentary armour, but bore a sword, bow and quiver with the ease of a lifetime's experience. She spoke softly to Arkas in their shared language. For all that elders were objects of respect and receptacles of wisdom, it was hard for Theuderis to believe this woman was a war-leader. Her voice would never rise above the din of battle. She could not be at the heart of the fighting, leading by example.

Katiya looked at him, and he almost flinched from her grey stare, ashamed of his thoughts. He suddenly understood, recognising in that glance the hardness of a castle wall, the strength of forged sigmarite. She returned her attention to the Warbeast, her words coming swifter and more forcefully.

'What are you discussing?' Theuderis asked.

Katiya stopped and frowned at the interruption in annoyance, or perhaps simply in incomprehension.

'If we are to debate strategy I would be involved, Lord Arkas.'

'I'm sorry, Lord Silverhand,' the Warbeast replied. 'The City of Ice was not dug with warriors of our stature in mind.'

'It is of no consequence, we will not be remaining here,' said Theuderis. 'Your message said that the skaven are on the brink of activating the realmgate. We must stop them before that happens.'

'We will,' said Arkas, 'but first we must ensure my people are safe.'

'The Chaos army has been scattered,' said Theuderis, troubled by Arkas' use of the phrase, 'my people'. It betrayed his split loyalties, but there was no purpose in raising the matter there and then. Doing so would only foster division and suspicion. Better to offer support to his ally. 'Dead skaven are no threat. The sooner we destroy them, the safer for all of Ursungorod.'

'The cursed ones will return,' argued the Warbeast. He cast a glance at Katiya and stood up. 'As for the skaven, we have seen nothing of them since we arrived. They could be preparing an attack, hoping to exploit the damage done by their human puppets.'

'If that is the case, I suggest our original strategy remains the best course. Divert the skaven, lure them from their lair, and I will strike into the heart of their domain and seize the realmgate. Faced with two armies of Stormcasts, the skaven will pay little mind to the few survivors hiding here.'

Arkas considered this until Katiya spoke. The two exchanged heated words, accompanied by small but insistent gestures, Katiya jabbing a finger at Arkas and pointing away, the Lord-Celestant making halting motions with upraised hands.

'She wants to fight,' said Theuderis, guessing Katiya's intent, picking up on some of the words already familiar to him. 'You should let them.'

Arkas approached and spoke quietly, concerned that Katiya might take something from their tone even though she could not know the meaning of his words.

'We go into a battle that even our Stormcasts cannot imagine. For centuries the skaven have dominated here, multiplying unchallenged, strengthening their defences. I do not expect many of us to see victory. We cannot take the Ursungorans into that.'

Theuderis took a breath and a pace back, uncomfortable with Arkas' closeness. He looked around the chamber, nothing more than a space created in the glacier. There were no furnishings, no belongings save the pack and bedroll that leaned against the wall behind Katiya.

'They have been wanting to fight for generations,' said the Knight Excelsior. 'But they have clung to a different ideal. To survive. That so many of them are still here is testament to the success of that strategy, but it cannot last. We have heard the tales from other chambers, other Stormhosts that have been into the Mortal Realms. Many lands are completely lost, others have but a handful of people not swayed or enslaved by the Dark Powers.'

'Every reason why we cannot risk them,' Arkas said sharply. He clenched his fists. 'This is our war, we must fight it for them.'

'They are an army, of sorts. They have proven themselves capable. For what reason have they clung to existence if not for the day when they can strike back at their oppressors, to fight for the freedom they crave? It is clear they venerate you – I saw their looks when we entered their city. As you say, we need every warrior we can muster.'

Arkas shook his head and did not reply. Katiya barked something at him and he turned away. She grabbed at his arm as Arkas strode towards the arch of ice leading from the chamber, but he pulled from her grasp, the hammer weights that adorned his cloak clattering against each other.

'Wait!' Theuderis dashed after Arkas and laid a hand on his shoulder. 'We are n–'

Arkas rounded on the Knight Excelsior, seizing him by the breastplate and thrusting him against the wall. Ice chipped under the impact, Theuderis' head jarring back in his helm.

'We are done talking!' growled the Warbeast. 'We stay until daybreak to ensure the Chaos tribes do not return and then we set out for the undercity. That is the plan.'

Theuderis said nothing. Arkas released his grip and stalked away, leaving the Knight Excelsior to exchange a look with Katiya. She sighed, took up her pack and moved to follow Arkas. Theuderis stepped in front of her, holding up a hand.

'Do you understand me?' he said, approximating the Ursungoran tongue. He turned to Katiya.

She looked in surprise at his words. 'You understand me?'

'Mostly,' Theuderis said. 'Enough for the moment. All human

language can be found in the tongue of the immortals. Your accent, your dialect is strange but brief study has revealed its workings to me. Another gift of the God-King.'

'This is powerful sorcery, lord,' she said, still looking at him with shock. Her manner settled and she glanced away. 'It is good that we can speak without the Uniter.'

'His heart is sore at the moment,' Theuderis replied. He did not wish to speak ill of his companion, despite his misgivings, and it was important that Katiya trusted him as much as she did Ursungorod's 'saviour'. 'What has he told you of us, the Stormcasts, and our mission here?'

'He is the Uniter, he has come to lead us to victory over the cursed ones and the rat-filth.'

'We are warriors of Sigmar, the God-King. We come from Azyr, the Realm of Heavens, where he rules. The Stormcasts are waging a war to free all of the Mortal Realms from the corruption of Chaos.'

'I do not understand. Sigmar is a myth. What are these Mortal Realms? Lands beyond Ursungorod?'

'In a sense. It would take me a long time to explain and you might still not understand. Sigmar is a myth, that is true, but that does not make him any less real.' Theuderis felt pride as he spoke. 'He is the master of the Uniter. As Arka Bear-clad brought together the tribes of Ursungorod, Sigmar will unite the Mortal Realms and the scattered gods. There are many worlds and places, all of them overrun by the darkness of Chaos and the forces of destruction, save for the sanctuary of Sigmaron and Azyr. Many people are looking for new lands to live in, lands where they can be free from Chaos and death. A land like Ursungorod, once we have rid it of the Chaos tribes and the skaven, could be such a sanctuary.'

'You are powerful warriors, but you are so few,' said Katiya.

'How can you hope to destroy all of the ratkin and the cursed ones?'

'We come on the storm of Sigmar, sent by his divine will, but there is also another way to travel between the planes of existence. Realmgates, we call them. The skaven have one. We will seize it from them and our allies will use it to reinforce us. This is a war, not a battle, Katiya. We will not win in the next day or the next ten days. I do not know what Arkas has promised you, but you must fight on for a while longer.'

Katiya looked downhearted but rallied quickly, entwining and releasing her fingers as she considered her next words.

'There are others coming? People like us, not warriors like you?'

'Yes, in time. Not just humans. Duardin, aelf and others. The free peoples, allied under the eyes of their gods. We will forge a new civilisation here.'

'We are not part of the plan, are we? Arkas thinks we can stay, but he is wrong.'

'I make no promises. I do not know how long this war will last. We have been reforged, made immortal. We cannot die, but we are no longer alive like you.' He paused, not sure whether he should say what he had to, but Katiya deserved the truth. 'It is unlikely you will live to see peace, Katiya. Your children, perhaps. Perhaps not. For all that Arkas protests, he will not make this decision for you. He is a servant of Sigmar, not Ursungorod, and I will remind him of that.'

'My sons and daughter are already dead,' Katiya replied, looking away. 'My grandchildren have known nothing but hardship and fear. But we do not want to be safe, we want to be free. We will stay, we will fight.'

Theuderis nodded.

Ursungorod had constantly defied expectation and eluded

definition since he had arrived, and continued to do so. Of all the battles and dangers he had prepared for, a confrontation with the Warbeast was not one.

CHAPTER TWENTY-NINE

The ice tunnels swallowed Arkas, deadening the distant sounds, surrounding him with their isolating whiteness. He found a small side chamber, perhaps occasionally used as a guard-room or storehouse, perhaps of no purpose at all. There was no stone, just the ice carved by pick and chisel. He ran a hand over the wall, trying to calm himself. His fingers picked out every indentation, every gouge and striation.

Hard, unforgiving labour had dug the City of Ice. Genera-tions of Ursungorans had chosen to cling to an ideal of freedom and defiance rather than accept the dominion of Chaos. It was tempting to claim some credit for that. The Bear-clad, the Uniter, had shown their ancestors that it was possible to fight. But that was false praise. He had learnt to defy the Chaos Gods and the rat-filth from his parents, and they from theirs. His had been the most successful resistance, but not the first. Now he had the chance to make Katiya's people the last to know what it was like to be afraid for their lives every day, to never settle for fear of discovery, to hide and make themselves small. They had exchanged one form of slavery for another, had become captives to their dread.

Was it worth it? His finger followed a channel at about chest height, ice crystals falling from the tip as he dragged it along the crack. Someone had stood where he stood, an Ursungoran, and had hewn at this wall. What had they been thinking? What did they think they were digging for? Was it just instinct, burrowing like an animal, or had the digger thought of loftier goals, of a future where they would not have to dig any longer?

All the time he had spent in Sigmaron, he had been honing his skills, becoming accustomed to his new body, a new way of war; coming to terms with the pain of Reforging, turning it into something meaningful, a sacrifice in exchange for the strength to fight back.

Hardest of all had been remembering those he had left – those he had been snatched from. Sigmar had reached out and plucked him from the battlefield. His saviour? Very likely. Arka Bear-clad would not have run that day. He would have fought and died, and with him the other free tribes would have perished too.

But he didn't feel saved, or blessed, or righteous.

He felt the spirit of Ursungorod, the background ebb of Ghurite energy that flowed around him, and welcomed its touch. After that first moment of awareness on Mount Vazdir he had tried to fight it, to keep back the lure of the savage, bestial heart that still beat in his chest.

It called to him, begged him to be free.

It was impossible to resist. Returning to Ursungorod was not an opportunity, it was a punishment – a reminder of what he had failed to do in life. He had only to think of his ally, the

Silverhand. He was just as well known among the Stormcasts.
A king, a conqueror, and a unifier just like Arka Bear-clad. But
he had saved his people. Sigmar had ascended the Silverhand
in triumph, not defeat.

Arkas smashed a fist into the wall. Splinters scattered and
a crack ran across the pale ice. He drove his other hand into
the ice, again and again, feeling the power of Ghurite energy
lapping at his armour, its feral howl in his ears urging him on.

He gritted his teeth, fists hammering like pistons, sigmarite gauntlets buckling under the impacts. Arkas started to feel
something, the first pangs of pain in his hands. It was not
enough. Blow after blow he rained onto the wall, each strike
sending a cascade of ice shards falling. When he felt the bite
of breaking metal on his knuckles it only drove him on into a
greater fury, desperate for some release.

Snarling and growling, panting between blows, Arkas' started
to slow his assault. He snorted, throwing one last strike, driving
all of his might down his arm and through his fist, punching
elbow-deep into the ice.

He leaned his head forwards, the chill of the ice wall seeping through his helm, cooling his anger. Arkas laid his other
hand against the wall, fingers splayed, their tips seeking the
undulations and cuts.

Generations of labour. Clinging to an ideal he had embodied.

Not survival. The Bear-clad had not fought for survival, he
had fought for victory. Arkas knew that he could not have won.
Every rational part of him recognised that his alliance had been
doomed, that he could not have been victorious. The logic of
the God-King's intervention was clear. Arkas was here, now,
to deliver on his oath, given the means to do so by Sigmar. A
longer view. A godly perspective.

Straightening, Arkas inhaled, enjoying the coldness in his

lungs. His first breath had been of this chill air. It was as much a part of him as anything else.

The rage was a memory now, no longer a living part of him, exorcised through his bloodied hands, returned to the well of Ghurite power from which it had come.

He knew what he had to do. It would not be easy. He had to find Katiya and tell her to prepare to leave. For good or ill, the Ursungorans would hide no more.

As he came to this conclusion something pricked his attention. A sound, much muffled by the distance and tunnels. Shouts.

Screams.

Arkas exploded with celestial energy, his fists remaking themselves as he drew forth his weapons.

He ran.

CHAPTER THIRTY

Theuderis was not sure what was happening. The Ursungorans were calling out in their tongue. Amongst the panicked bellows and shrieks there was one word again and again, but he could not fathom its meaning.

He raced after Katiya, who had set off like a coursed hare, gathering a trail of Ursungorans as she went. More followed behind the Lord-Celestant. Despite the tumult, everyone seemed to know what was happening, enacting a well-rehearsed drill in which youths snatched up infants and the able-bodied readied their weapons.

They passed into one of the larger chambers, not far from the surface. Several hundred Ursungorans were coming and going. Katiya grabbed some of them, speaking quickly.

'Is it an attack?' Theuderis demanded.

Katiya paid him no attention. She snapped off orders, pointing, directing, speaking with quiet assurance to some. Theuderis did not wish to interfere, but set forth to look for more Stormcasts.

A Celestial Vindicator burst into view ahead, blazing with celestial energy. He had a warhammer and runeblade, and his hammer-tipped cloak was blazing with light.

'Arkas!'

The Warbeast turned, surprised.

'What is it?' demanded Theuderis. 'Have the Chaos tribes returned already?'

'No.' The Warbeast shook his head.

'What are they saying? What does that word mean?'

Arkas hefted his weapons and looked at Theuderis.

'Vermintide.'

Across the dead of the battle they swarmed. Up from the Black River, down from the forested slopes, emerging from every crack and crevasse in the ice field. A living carpet of fur and fangs and glinting eyes. Many were simple rats, bodies slicked with grease and blood from the corpses, each no bigger than a fist. But there were thousands of them. Tens of thousands. Others were far larger – warp-mutants as big as dogs, collared with rusted iron, naked tails as long as broadswords. Some were scaled, some naked but for protrusions of bone, some even skinless with visible muscle and flesh and strands of rope-like sinew.

From across Ursungorod they had come, white as snow, grey as ash, black as pitch. The air was filled with the nerve-jangling scratch of claws on ice and armour, the slither of dark bodies over flesh and the rustling of cloth, the chittering and squealing – a nightmare orchestration.

The wave moved as one, possessed by the singular will of the Great Horned Rat, directed by the malevolence of Poxmaster Felk. As an undulating mass, the swarm welled up from the ravine of the Bear's Fangs and slithered across the glacier from the valley walls. The rats burst out onto the snowfield, surging like a storm front.

With them came a sorcerous mist. It streamed from hex-laden bodies like green smoke, a trail of pestilent vapour flowing from fanged mouths, heavy with foul enchantment.

A band of Ursungorans had been burning the dead of the battle. They were taken in a few heartbeats, vanishing into the ravenous swarm with barely a shriek. The lookouts had just enough time to shout warnings before the dark wave was scampering up tower-mounds and into window slits, pouring down open sally ports like filthy water. Beacon fires stayed unlit, bells and horns unsounded. The guards screamed, the only alarm calls they could muster before they were overwhelmed by biting, clawing horror.

Into the tunnels washed the deluge of rats, pooling and bursting in waves, overrunning everything. Some of the Ursungorans tried to run, others fought. Neither were successful; whether dragged down from behind or with weapons in their hands, it made no difference. Armour was no defence against a foe that was dozens of slashing claws, scores of gnawing fangs. Flailing and shouting, flesh turned to bloody ribbons, they fell.

Such was the scene that confronted Arkas as he and Theuderis burst into one of the great chambers, dozens of Stormcasts converging from different directions. The massive warriors waded into the vermin, laying about with maces, swords and hammers. Dozens of the foul creatures died with every sweep of the enchanted weapons but there were dozens more to take their place. Against the armour of Sigmar's chosen, claws and fangs were small threats, but in turn the Stormcasts could not slay enough. Their greatest weapons, tempest-wreathed javelin, crossbow and bow, were useless against such a heaving mass, the warriors unable to unleash their full power for fear of harming the few Ursungorans that continued to battle vainly in the midst of the vermintide.

'Knights-Azyros! Samat!' Theuderis forged waist-deep through the leaping, snarling rats, carving a furrow through them with metronomic swings of his celestial hammer. 'Glavius!'

No specific order was needed. The Silverhands' warriors knew exactly what was required. The Lord-Relictor plunged into the morass of vermin, spearing a gigantic rat with the haft of his morbid icon. Planting the mortuary standard, Glavius thrust out his hammer towards the swarm. His divine icon shimmered with the power celestial. Forks of lightning crawled down his arm and across his body to spear from his out-thrust weapon. Where they struck, bursts of blue fire erupted, incinerating the vermin a score at a time.

Samat and his fellow Knights-Azyros could not take flight, but that was not their intent. Flanking Theuderis, they strode through the snapping, hissing rats, oblivious to their scratching and biting. Holding aloft their celestial beacons, they called in unison for the power of the God-King to smite their foes.

The blast of Azyrite light that filled the chamber blinded even Arkas, who had left mounds of dead rats as tall as himself in his wake. Blinking clear his vision, he saw hundreds of smouldering rodent corpses littering the chamber floor. Closer to the ring of Knights-Azyros, the corpses were ash mounds, and at their feet nothing was left but dark grease stains on the stone flags.

The respite was momentary. More and more rats were streaming down the tunnels and passageways. Arkas turned, seeking Katiya. She stood at one of the corridor entrances shepherding the last children away while her followers hacked and slashed at the few rats that had survived the tempest of celestial energy.

'Go!' he shouted at her. 'Run!'

She looked as if she would argue. Her eyes moved past him and widened in horror. The fresh wave of vermin was more monstrous than the first, a clawing, squealing pile of hound-sized rodents with curling ram's horns, barbed tails and dagger-claws, spreading like oil across water. Thick clouds of filthy breath followed them, stinging eyes and burning throats. The handful of Ursungorans that had been saved by the celestial beacons were overwhelmed by the noxious vapours, hacking up blood, eyes and noses weeping thick pus while buboes blistered like burns on their exposed skin.

Katiya turned and ran, taking her people with her, leaving Arkas and the other two dozen Stormcasts alone with the plague rats.

'Seal the chamber!' bellowed Theuderis, moving to block the exit by which Katiya's group had fled.

Arkas broke left, crushing bodies underfoot, using his fists as much as his weapons to smash his way through the swarm while feral rodents hurled themselves at him with hisses and snarls. He swept his cloak round in a long arc, unleashing a wave of Azyr-born hammers that crackled and spat with lightning as they smashed a furrow through the vermin throng.

The others, an eclectic mix of Judicators, Knights-Azyros, Decimators and Liberators, pushed towards the tunnels like men wading through heavy surf, battering and slashing against the living tide. Decimators brought down their starsoul maces in mighty two-handed swings, unleashing thunderous explosions that scattered the giant rats by the score. Judicators loosed missile after missile into the heaving mass, their quivers never emptied, firing as swiftly as they could summon the celestial energy for each projectile.

A gigantic rodent leapt for Arkas' neck. He caught it in mid-air with the flat of his blade, snapping its spine, its lifeless

GAV THORPE

body splashing against the wall to leave a red smear across the ice. So thick were the bodies underfoot that he almost tripped, bogged down as though crossing a mountain fen.

The miasma of sickness cloyed in his throat and nostrils, acidic and dry. His reforged body was strengthened against even the harshest warp-taint, but his eyes streamed and his lungs burned all the same.

The Lord-Relictor, Glavius, raised his storm-wreathed icon, incanting a benediction of Sigmar. The bones within his sarcophagus-icon gleamed with power. Where the light touched the vapours they burned with white fire. The wave of cleansing power coruscated through the air in a ragged ring around Glavius.

Eventually the incoming tide stopped, the seemingly inexhaustible swarm ending as suddenly as it had arrived. It was little comfort, for Arkas knew that they had faced only a fraction of the vermintide. His sword slashed through another handful of beasts and a final volley from the Judicators scoured the chamber of the remaining rodents.

'We must hunt down the rest,' said Theuderis.

'We have to evacuate the Ursungorans,' Arkas replied, waving a hand through the last wisps of plague-fog that lingered. 'Nowhere is safe below ground while this pestilent smog remains.'

Theuderis nodded and snapped out orders to his warriors. The few Celestial Vindicators looked to Arkas for command.

'With me,' he said, stepping towards the passage where Katiya had left. 'Move speedily, kill swiftly. Time is the greater enemy now.'

CHAPTER
THIRTY-ONE

Clouds obscured the stars and moons, blanketing the Bear's Pelt in utter darkness. A pale blue light flickered in the forests on the western slopes of the valley, casting long shadows from the trees. The beacons of the Knights-Azyros lit the way for the dozens of scattered groups of Stormcasts and Ursungorans as they picked their way across the treacherous ice, heading towards the sanctuary promised by that holy light.

Three times Arkas made the journey from the City of Ice to the growing encampment on the slope, each time heading back into the chill catacombs to search for Katiya, each time finding pockets of terrified, shocked Ursungorans to lead to safety but no news of their leader.

Flights of Prosecutors circled and criss-crossed overhead, their wings a faint trail of iridescence against the gloom. Cordons of Liberators and Protectors guarded the approaches through the trees, wary of rats, skaven and the Chaos-tainted.

Knowing that he could wander the City of Ice all night and

never find Katiya, Arkas resigned himself to a patient wait until morning. He sought out Theuderis, and found the Silverhand at the heart of the camp marshalling what resources were to hand. Trees had been felled to create wind breaks and the few belongings that had been snatched from the icy depths were passed to those in most need. Pale-faced children huddled in blankets and cloaks close to the fires banked up by their guardians, watching, mesmerised, as the stars of the celestial beacons passed back and forth overhead. In numb shock, they found comfort in the divine light of Sigmar shining down from between the boughs.

There was little enough food, but some stores had been saved and the Ursungorans' best hunters had quickly checked their closest pits and snares and brought back several hares, deer and foxes. Hastor had insisted on leading Arkas' Judicators on a hunt and had returned with three enormous mountain boars, their flesh seared by the blasts of celestial missiles. The Ursungorans were still butchering the huge carcasses ready for cooking.

Seeing Arkas approach, Theuderis dismissed his companions. His dracoth prowled the shadows at the perimeter of the camp, eyed warily by the Ursungorans as it sniffed and snorted in the darkness.

'I can think of no surer guardian,' said Theuderis, following Arkas' gaze and line of thought. 'Tyrathrax's senses are far superior to even the patrols of our winged companions.'

'I do not doubt it,' said Arkas. He fell silent, tongue tied by awkwardness. He felt a fool for putting his hands on another Stormcast, but could not find the right words.

'We are fortunate that the skaven did not seek to exploit their attack further,' said Theuderis after a long silence. 'Had they been waiting on the surface we would have been easy targets to bring down.'

'Luck had no part in it,' Arkas said, bitter memories stirring. 'They kill from afar rather than risk their scrawny necks.'

'Perhaps. It signals a change in the skaven's plans, whatever their motivation.'

'I have spoken to some of the Ursungorans. Neither in memory nor in their oldest stories has anything like this happened before. Our arrival has stirred the ratkin. They are trying to keep us from their lair so that they can concentrate on unearthing the realmgate. They will not be drawn forth, you can be sure of that.'

'Even so, why have the skaven not tried anything like this before? What are they hoping to achieve now that we are here?'

Arkas thought about this but had no quick answers.

'They are afraid. Desperate. Cowards to the last, but lashing out any way they can. Do not look for more ambition than cruel spite in these creatures. What they cannot dominate they kill.'

'You are right.' Theuderis tilted his head, deep in thought. 'And perhaps in that you have found the solution. We stand at a confluence of events and must trust that the Lord Sigmar did not send us to Ursungorod at this time by whim. The preparation for the assault on the Allpoints gains momentum, the battle for the Realm of Life is pitched to full fury, and the skaven discover a realmgate that leads close to the Lifegate, hidden for... centuries, maybe millennia?'

'Kill or be killed,' said Arkas. He started to pace. Movement assisted the flow of thought. Light from the growing fires gleamed on his armour, countless scratches marring the surface. With a thought he let a surge of celestial energy sparkle across the surface, turning the plates back to unblemished turquoise while blood and crusted gore fell away in a shower of dried flakes. 'When I fought the skaven they were led by a verminlord, a Corruptor named Skixakoth. By description I think this creature is among the daemonkin that assault the sylvaneth in the Vaults of the Spring Moon.'

'How did you come by this knowledge?' The question was asked in a neutral tone – too flat for Arkas' liking, clearly masking more than curiosity.

'Does it matter?' He regretted his snapped reply immediately. It looked like evasion, which hinted at guilt. Arkas sighed. 'I learnt this from the Queen of the Peak. It was her power that granted me the visions of the undercity of the skaven, and the realmgate.'

'You have seen its location? Could you take us there?'

Arkas nodded. 'That is my intent.' He hesitated again, clawing for words that were uncomfortable to say. 'I would welcome your opinion, Silverhand. In matters of strategy. I am the Warbeast, I'm sure you know my reputation as well as any other. I can seize the realmgate, I am sure of it. But I need your help to hold it.'

'We are allies, are we not?'

'We are.' Arkas swallowed hard. 'And in the spirit of alliance I want to say I'm sorry. I'm sorry that I laid hands upon you.'

'Worse has been done in the Gladitorium.'

'No, it should never have happened. I... This place, Ursungorod, affects me. I am a child of these lands, more than in flesh, in spirit. Sigmar took me, made me a being of the Celestial Sphere, but he cannot remove that shard of Ghur that is in my heart.'

'I cannot say that I understand,' said Theuderis. 'It is obviously something more than simply returning to the place of your birth, but it is not an experience I have shared.'

Arkas looked at the Knight Excelsior for some time. Theuderis was unsure what the purpose was for such scrutiny.

'Ask me what you want,' he said. 'I will answer truthfully to the best of my ability. There will be no secrets between us.'

'Why do you care?' said the Warbeast.

'Care about what?'

'All of this,' said Arkas, waving a hand towards the Ursungorans, the camp, the forest, the mountains beyond. He turned slowly, looking up to where the light of celestial beacons flickered. 'Why do you fight for Sigmar?'

The question surprised Theuderis. It took him a few moments to articulate his reply.

'For the same reason as you. To save my people. To ensure that mankind has a future free from the tyranny and wrath of uncaring darkness.'

'But you had saved your people, when Sigmar took you. The Glittering Breaches, your castles and armies, were safe.'

'At that time. If I have learnt anything in Sigmaron it is that the threat of the Chaos Gods waxes and wanes. For a time they were held back by the God-King and his allies, but that did not last. We are where we are. Sigmar took me because I protected my lands, fostered cooperation rather than war, built as well as conquered. I would repay that honour.'

'Honour?' Theuderis could hear the grin in Arkas' voice. 'You think honour will help us in this place?'

'I think that I believe in two principles. My honour and my duty, and they are entwined. I cannot say that Ursungorod holds any particular relevance for me. I would feel the same wherever Sigmar despatched me.'

'Even to the Glittering Breaches?'

Theuderis had no answer for that. He did not like theoretical situations and questions.

'I have a special regard for that place, but it is not my home.'

The Knight Excelsior started towards the perimeter, put on

edge by Arkas' attitude. The older Ursungoran children were digging in the mulch and dirt, creating a ditch and rampart between the trees. It was hard work on the frozen ground, and only a few paces had been erected. Theuderis did not see the point in any defensive sense, but it kept them engaged and made the Ursungorans feel they were doing something useful.

'How can you say it is not your home?' Arkas kept at his shoulder, speaking quietly but insistently.

'The worlds turn, places change. Castle Lyonaster might be a great city or it might be nothing more than the duardin and human ruins that make up the bones of Ursungorod. My family are dead. The people I served and who served me are dead. The Glittering Breaches I knew no longer exist.'

Movement in the darkness further into the trees drew his eye, but it was only a trio of Ursungoran hunters prowling the shadows on patrol. Like the entrenchment, it was of little purpose when Stormcast Prosecutors, Knights-Venator and Knights-Azyros kept an immortal watch above. Theuderis' warriors would know of any threat long before the natives.

'You do not know?' said Arkas, shocked. 'How the war fares in the Glittering Breaches?'

'No Stormcasts have yet been sent.'

'It is possible to find out what is happening in the realms beyond Azyr. Lord Sigmar could tell you...'

'I do not wish to know!' snapped Theuderis. He kept his next rebuke in check, snatching in a breath instead. When his temper had cooled a little, he continued with quiet words. 'I know you, Warbeast. Hungry for revenge, needing to punish those that wronged you. I cannot blame you, but I do not sympathise. You harbour a doubt, the thought that if you had stayed that perhaps your people would have prevailed?'

'It is unlikely, I know, but...'

'But nothing! I had won, Warbeast!' Theuderis turned on his companion, taut with aggravation. He kept his voice low, conscious of the Stormcasts and Ursungorans close at hand. 'I had ensured peace for a generation, for my family and my people, after a life of war and death. My wife was bearing my third child.' Theuderis leaned close, his helm almost touching Arkas'. 'Do not think that I gave up nothing! But the sacrifice was worth it. They lived long and happy lives and my children sired many descendants who continue to protect Castle Lyonaster to this day.'

He did not say out loud the alternatives that crowded his thoughts in the dark moments. Ursungorod was proof enough of what had beset the Mortal Realms during the long age of Chaos. The bare truth was that the Glittering Breaches would be no different to the rest of Chamon, overrun or at least besieged by the followers of the Chaos Gods. His great victory had been a blink, a momentary respite in the great turn of history.

The real lesson he had learnt as a Lord-Celestant was that all victories were fleeting, until the last one.

The Knight Excelsior turned and marched away, shoulders stiff. He thought for a moment that Arkas would follow, but was grateful when he heard the other Lord-Celestant calling for his Knight-Heraldor and Knight-Vexillor.

He strode out past the perimeter and into the fluctuating shadows away from the campfires, fists tight, teeth gritted. He already regretted his outburst. It was a display of weakness he should have avoided. Whether Arkas was deliberately baiting him, it was impossible to say, but the effect was the same. Maybe the wildness of Ursungorod was affecting him too.

The pad of large feet on frosted leaves caused him to turn. Tyrathrax emerged into the fronds of pale blue light, drawn by her master's unease. She came up alongside Theuderis, close enough for him to lay a hand on her armoured shoulder. Her presence was reassuring, anchoring him back to his purpose.

Being paired with the Warbeast taxed the Knight Excelsior's patience. Raised to admire the perfection of interlocking functions, the beauty of military drill and expertise, the wild nature of Arkas and his Strike Chamber concerned Theuderis.

'It is not our part to guess the ways of the God-King,' said Theuderis. 'Which is fortunate, for I am baffled that he would set me beside the Warbeast. I cannot help but feel it is some kind of test. Perhaps the Lord Sigmar wishes to know if I am strong enough to return to the Glittering Breaches and whatever waits for me there.'

Tyrathrax said nothing, which was why Theuderis considered her the best of all possible companions.

CHAPTER THIRTY-TWO

The fires had guttered down to embers and the Ursungorans were nothing more than shapeless lumps of shadow in bedrolls and blankets, huddled close to each other and the remnants of the fires. Dawn had arrived on the far side of Ursungorod, but had not yet reached the valley of the Bear's Pelt. The air was freezing, and mist curled from the breath of the Stormcasts as they stood watch. The Warbeast sat atop a broad log, his back to the fires, gazing out into the shadowed forest.

The Ursungorans might have been driven from their city, but they were at home in the wilds too. Just as when Arkas had been a warrior of the Greypelt, the people of the mountains were nomads by necessity and long tradition, and had brought with them everything they needed. They lived lightly, able to hunt and trap on the move, sharing kinship with the wilderness that went beyond familiarity. They were part of Ursungorod, steeped in the magic of Ghur, their collective instincts honed by a lifetime of wariness and bitter experience.

It had been a long night and the morning bode little better. A few more refugees from the City of Ice had arrived, but there was still no sign of Katiya. Accounts conflicted. Some had her safe and well in the southern tunnels, others thought they saw her turn to fight the tide of rats, protecting the young ones she had taken with her. A few thought they had seen her on the ice field, tirelessly rallying survivors in the darkness. None could say they had seen her fall, but Arkas held little hope to see her.

Theuderis had been absent also, gone into the woods since his sharp words with Arkas. The Silverhands made no remark about their missing leader, but minded themselves and their duties with quiet diligence. For their part, the Warbeasts prowled the camp and surrounding woods like guard hounds confined within a wall.

To ease communication, Arkas had spent some time instructing the Knights Excelsior in the language of Ursungorod, refining what they had already learnt so that they could talk with the Ursungorans and also understand the battle-tongue of the Warbeasts. Being able to address the natives, and understand them in return, eased the mood somewhat.

A glint of celestial light betrayed the descent of Hastor. He had spent the night scouring the Bear's Pelt for survivors and foes. He landed effortlessly, as though newly forged, with no sign of fatigue in his gait or voice.

'A rough time,' said Hastor, gauging his commander's mood. He looked around at the sleeping Ursungorans. 'Four hundred, I would say. There will be others still below the ice.'

'Four hundred and thirty-six,' replied Arkas. 'Three hundred and eight of fighting age and ability. Half those that woke yesterday dawn.'

'When they have rested, we will search the city for others,' said the Knight-Venator. 'I have crossed the opposite slopes but if they are choosing to hide, which would be wise, even I would not find them.' Hastor glanced up, about to say something further, but remained silent.

'You would prefer someone to light your way?' said Arkas, following Hastor's gaze to the slowly circling Knights-Azyros. 'They are not my warriors to command.'

'The Silverhand has chosen an inconvenient time to go exploring. When dawn arrives we must be ready with a plan.'

'We do not need Theuderis for that.' Arkas straightened his back and stretched out his long legs. 'You are right, we search the City of Ice for other survivors. One day, that is all.'

Hastor's lightning wings crackled into nothing to allow him to sit next to his lord. He clasped his hands together, resting his arms on his knees. He did not look at Arkas, but at the Knights Excelsior standing like statues at the edge of the encampment.

'I do not think Theuderis will agree.' The Knight-Venator paused for just a heartbeat, and then continued. 'He might be right not to.'

'The realmgate,' Arkas said with a nod and a sigh. 'I know.'

'What will we do?'

Activity off to the left drew the Warbeast's attention before he could reply. Theuderis had returned and his officers were moving across the camp to attend to him. Dismounting, the Silverhand approached with his retinue.

Arkas felt others behind him and glanced round to see that Doridun and Dolmetis were at his back as though summoned. How much of his conversation with Hastor they had overheard he did not know but he was grateful for their timely arrival.

'A nice ride, Lord Silverhand?' Hastor asked as Theuderis stopped in front of Arkas.

'Hush your tongue, knight,' the Warbeast growled. Hastor stood and stepped away, head bowed in apology. Arkas rose and folded his arms. 'I hope you spent your time in the wood productively.'

'I did,' replied Theuderis. 'And with Samat's aid I have located the entrances by which we will attack the skaven city.'

'You have?' Arkas looked at the Knight-Azyros. 'I did not realise you knew the mountains so well already.'

'The vermintide trail was not difficult to follow even at night, and the skaven here have grown arrogant. Their spoil and spoor is evident everywhere.' Samat glanced at Theuderis and received a nod of assent. 'There is a large cavern on the other side of this mountain, across a ridge to the south-east.'

'I know it,' said Arkas. 'Flanked by the remains of two human towers?'

'That is the one.'

'We cannot attack there,' Arkas said with a shake of his head. 'The skaven use it easily enough but there is a chasm not more than three hundred paces into the warren. They will cut the bridges and topple the crossings the moment we enter.'

'I see,' said Theuderis. 'And the gorge west of there, an out-flow of an underground river.'

'The Ratway it was called. Obvious, but possible.' Arkas flexed his fingers around an imaginary sword hilt, remembering when he had last been there. 'I tried that before, but was baulked on the surface. However, I did not have Storm-cast Eternals to lead back then. But it would not be enough, there are too many other ways for the skaven to get out and come in behind.'

'Do you have a better plan?' said Attaxes, stepping forwards. 'If you know these mountains so well, find us a way to attack the skaven.'

'I already have,' said Arkas, keeping his gaze locked on Theuderis. 'But you knew that, yes?'

'Our success cannot rely wholly on your survival, Warbeast.' The Silverhand shrugged. 'Or your mood.'

Arkas laughed, slapping a hand to his chest.

'My mood? Yes, my infamous temperament!' He turned to his knights, put a foot up on the log, a hand resting on his knee. 'Headstrong, that's me. Incautious, they say. Rash, perhaps. What do we say?'

'Swift and deadly,' the Warbeast officers replied in unison.

'Swift and deadly...' Arkas returned his attention to Theuderis. 'I understand. As hard as it is for you to share command, it is the same for me. Do you want to know my plan? Do you think I would keep it secret, bargaining with my knowledge for time to search the glacier for Ursungorans?'

'It had occurred to me,' Theuderis admitted. 'It seems we know each other well enough.'

'We do, Silverhand. We do. Which is why I want you to lead us.'

'What?' Hastor stepped forwards, shaking his head.

'I do not understand,' admitted Theuderis. 'Are you placing yourself under my command?'

'I am,' said Arkas. He drew his warhammer. The celestial weapon shone in the pre-dawn gloom, bathing them all with pale blue light. He offered it to Theuderis, a gesture of fealty. 'You are the general, the king. You are the strategist. I am a brute. Cleverer than most, but still a brute in my heart. Guide my hand and it will smite our foes.'

Theuderis had no response at first. He looked at the assembled Celestial Vindicators, his expression hidden behind his mask, eyes cloaked in the shadow of his helm. He nodded.

'I accept. And I apologise for doubting you. Perhaps, despite prior experience, we might actually possess sufficient wisdom between us.'

CHAPTER
THIRTY-THREE

While dawn brightened the forest, the Lord-Celestants planned. Arkas told Theuderis everything he knew of the skaven tunnels, though long centuries would have changed much. However, the more he recalled the vision he had received from the Queen of the Peak, the more certain he was that he could find the realmgate.

While plans were discussed, the Ursungorans started to wake. Arkas became aware of their coughs and gentle moans in the background. He paid the noise little heed until he heard his name tersely called. It was a young man, twenty years perhaps, nervously wringing his deer hide hat in his hand. There was fear written across his face and his glance kept moving back to a group of Ursungorans a short distance away. They were crowded around a blanketed figure, concerned. Several War-beasts interposed themselves, stopping the approaching native.

'A moment, by your leave,' Arkas said to Theuderis and received a nod in reply. He approached the Ursungoran, waving his warriors aside. 'What is your name? What is wrong?'

'Mika, our Uniter. I am Mika.' He flopped a hand towards the others. 'My brother. Elder brother. He is sick.'

'Sick?' A cold feeling crept into the pit of Arkas' stomach as he strode over to the group. One of them was still in his bedroll. He could hear the man's wheezing breaths, each touched by wetness in his lungs. There were scabs at the corners of his mouth and in his nostrils. 'How long?'

'He was well when we ate last night,' said an old man swathed in a thick shawl. His spindly fingers teased at some loose threads in its weave. 'Bortis had quite the appetite.'

Bortis was awake, but only just. His eyes were yellowy, pupils little more than pinpricks staring without sight up into the trees. He kept swallowing hard, each time a wince creasing the skin at the corner of his eyes. The Warbeast crouched to examine him more closely. The Ursungoran's gums were bleeding, his tongue swollen.

'Show me his arms,' Arkas commanded, trying to keep the concern from his voice.

They complied, rolling back the tattered sleeve of Bortis' coat. The veins stood out like wire beneath his pale skin. His fingers twitched spasmodically, the brittle nails split and cracking.

'Wait here. Light a fire to keep him warm,' Arkas said, rising to his feet.

They looked up at him, hope and desperation etched into their faces. Arkas was thankful they could see nothing of his expression, nor his doubtlessly ashen skin. They did not ask if Bortis was going to be all right, and for that Arkas was also grateful, because he could not lie to them.

Returning to Theuderis, he gestured for the Silverhand to meet him. Exchanging a last few words with Attaxes, the Lord-Celestant approached.

'Plague,' Arkas said before Theuderis could ask what was wrong. 'Skaven-pox of some kind.'

'How many?' Theuderis asked, looking past Arkas' shoulder and then turning towards the rest of the camp.

The Warbeast felt dead inside as he replied. It was better that way, to feel nothing. The alternative was too hard to contemplate.

'All of them, perhaps. If it came from the rat-fog in the tunnels...'

'Quarantine? Purging?'

'There'll be no purge! These people have seen every horror of war, plague and famine. That is the fact of life in Ursungorod. They can deal with it.' He cast a glance behind to confirm what he suspected. 'As for quarantine... See how the other groups do not approach. They already know what is happening. They are not strangers to this.'

'Everybody has been exposed.'

Arkas sighed heavily. 'Yes. Those that weren't infected during the attack have been nearby ever since. There might be a few families, maybe some that escaped but haven't made it to the camp yet.'

Neither of them said anything for a while. Arkas was too familiar with the scenario. He had seen how this devastating turn of events unfolded before, whole clans wiped out. As the Uniter he had razed villages to the ground to rid them of the Pestilens-taint.

'We keep watch, keep the camp safe, that is all we can do,' said Arkas.

'We cannot afford distractions. We still have to finalise the plan for the assault on the realmgate.'

'We do,' said the Warbeast, dragging his eyes away from Bortis and his family. He focused on Theuderis, but the effort of maintaining an air of control and calm was almost too much.

'Do not worry about leaving guards here, Silverhand. When we attack, the skaven will have more to deal with than they have ever feared. We cannot protect the Ursungorans against this latest wrong. We can avenge them.'

'I understand that you want to strike back at the skaven to punish them for this,' said the Knight Excelsior. 'In time we will wipe them from the face of the mountains. We will purge the bowels of Ursungorod of every skaven and Chaos-tainted soul to be found.'

'Aye, as it will be in all of the Mortal Realms when we drive Archaon from the All-gates.'

Theuderis laid his hand on Arkas' arm, a placating gesture.

'But not today. Not this battle.'

'I don't understand what you mean.' Arkas tried to pull his arm away but Theuderis' grip tightened and his tone was insistent.

'We fight for the realmgate. We will seize the realmgate and guard it for as long as we must. As instructed by Sigmar himself, when the gate is ours Glavius will call for my Lord-Castellants to arrive with the rest of the Strike Chamber. When *all* is secure, when the realmgate is opened and ready for the attack on the Lifegate, the cleansing will begin.'

'I swore an oath, many times, to destroy the skaven and free Ursungorod from their clutches,' Arkas said, prising himself from Theuderis' grip. 'You do not need to lecture me on how that will be done, Silverhand.'

'Very well.' Theuderis stepped away and looked around the camp. 'Make whatever provisions you need to deal with this... situation. I want to march at noon.'

'I'll find you soon enough,' Arkas assured him.

He turned away. Hastor and the others officers moved to approach but he waved them back without a word.

His warhammer seemed heavy in his grasp as he walked out into the woods, a sign of his inner burden.

He could leave it, throw it away, dispense with the burden. To do so invited a very dangerous train of thought. The hammer was a badge, the symbol of the God-King. It was Sigmar's authority. It was also Arkas' duty, which was why it weighed so heavily at the moment.

The Warbeast looked back through the trees. The sun had not yet penetrated the canopy and only the light of celestial beacons shone through the camp. By the pale blue glow he could see the Stormcasts moving back and forth, the deadly warriors utterly unable to combat the threat growing in heart of the encampment. The Ursungorans were rousing in greater numbers, awakening to the news of infection and plague. Mothers and fathers would have to look at their children and know that these could be their last days together.

Suddenly his armour felt constricting, his helm a prison. Gasping, Arkas tore off the mask and threw it aside. He gulped down the fresh, cold air, the sudden chill stinging his eyes, tingling his scarred skin.

He felt the faintest of shudders beneath his feet. A fine mist of snow fell from the needled branches overhead. He barely noticed it, his mind going back to the camp and the horror that would unfold there.

It was good that they would leave, that the attack would take him far away into the bowels of the skaven lair, out of sight of the spreading sickness.

Guilt welled up at that thought. The feeling of abandoning his people again forced him to take in another stuttering lungful of mountain air.

Another tremor shook the mountain, strong enough to sway the trees this time. Arkas staggered over to a nearby trunk and leaned his free hand against the rough bark, trying to draw reassurance from its solidity, its unyielding nature.

He could feel the rush of Ghurite energy streaming from the roots and into the trunk and branches, spreading into the air like a fog. Not just the roots of the tree, the roots of the mountain, the depths of Ursungorod itself. The endless deeps of the Shadowgulf. It was in him too, connecting him to the land, to the wild places above and below the ground.

Pain scored up through his bones, the like of which he had not felt since being reforged. His fingers dug knuckle-deep into the tree as he fought back against the agony that suddenly coursed through him.

He remembered the meaning of that pain, what it heralded. He stumbled away, tearing a fistful of wood as he went. Arkas flung away his hammer. He fell to his knees, eyes wide, teeth bared like an animal. The ground shook constantly now, dusting him with falling snow and pine needles.

'No,' he snarled.

He thought that he had been freed of the bear's gift-curse when Sigmar had altered his body upon the Anvil of the Apotheosis. He was Stormcast, a lord of the Celestial Vindicators. His spirit belonged to another.

Perhaps he was wrong. His sigmarite-fused fleshed rebelled against the influx of Ghurite energy. Celestial power and savage, aeons-old magic confronted each other, like a pack of wolves howling at the distant moon.

On all fours, Arkas shuddered and the mountain shuddered with him. Through the rushing of blood in his ears he heard the shouts of the Ursungorans and the bellowed commands of Stormcast Eternals. The words were meaningless sounds, drowned out by the thunderous heartbeat that threatened to burst his chest.

He could not resist the pain any longer, could no longer fight the surge of energy trying to break his bones and reshape his flesh.

Staggering to his feet, Arkas seized the closest tree. Celestial magic and beast power came together. Lightning flashed across his armour and the glow of savage power lit his eyes. He ripped up the tree, roots tearing the frozen earth.

He wanted to roar, to howl, to free the savage noise building in his head. In the small part of his mind that was still his, Arkas knew he could not. It was his will, his choice whether he embraced or rejected the beast trying to possess him.

The tree exploded into burning shards, showering him with ash and sharp splinters.

Arkas stood with fists clenched in front of him.

'I am a Stormcast of Sigmar,' he hissed between gritted teeth.

Warbeast, a voice whispered, but its power was dissipating, its hold on him broken by his assertion of fealty to the God-King.

He stood with head bowed, eyes closed, fists at his side, and waited for the quaking to subside. When all was still again he sought out his mask and fitted it to his helm. The click of it snapping into place was an affirmation of who he was and why he lived.

And he also knew exactly how to defeat the skaven.

Arkas Warbeast, Lord-Celestant of the Celestial Vindicators, strode over to his hammer and snatched it from a pool of melting snow. He turned back to the camp, filled with renewed purpose.

CHAPTER THIRTY-FOUR

The morning passed quickly. After the distraction of the earthquake – which was disruptive but caused no serious damage – Theuderis spent most of it in deep conversation with Arkas. The Warbeast was filled with a vigour that enthused Theuderis. His short sojourn into the woods had proven very productive and the strategy they devised on his return gave the Knight Excelsior fresh hope. For the first time since he had crossed into the Realm of Beasts, Theuderis felt that he was moving in the right direction, after the many setbacks that had waylaid him previously.

In the main camp there were many more showing symptoms of the virulent infection. The first, the man called Bortis, was still alive, but only just. It was unlikely he would see nightfall. The sores, the watery breath and facial bleeding varied in severity from victim to victim, showing no favour to age or gender, but it was only a matter of time for those who had been caught by the pernicious attack. Theuderis took some heart that nearly half of the Ursungorans so far seemed unaffected, a few family groups that had not encountered the plague rats free from the taint thus far.

With a plan settled between them, Theuderis and Arkas sent word for their officers to make ready for a war council. Theuderis heard Glavius mention his name in passing and joined the Lord-Relictor where he was crouched in front of three dozen Ursungorans, more than half of them no older than ten years. He had removed his mask, revealing brown eyes that were warm and comforting, in marked contrast to his demeanour as Lord-Relictor.

'Here he comes, the Lord Silverhand!' Glavius declared. The children smiled, their joy somewhat incongruous given the morbid ornamentation of their entertainer. 'King of the Glittering Breaches! Master of Castle Lyonaster! Lord-Celestant of the Knights Excelsior!'

'What was your castle like, Lord Theuderis?' asked a young woman, her infant swaddled close to her breast. Theuderis could see the child was pale, and there were flakes of dried blood on its chin. He looked at the mother's face, suddenly lost for words.

'Was it as large as the fortress at Raven Gorge?'

'I do not know this fortress,' Theuderis admitted. 'I cannot make a comparison.'

'It's as tall as a mountain, and made of black bricks from the world-that-was,' a little boy cheerfully informed him. 'It used to have a whole tribe of ogors what lived there, but the rat-men killed them all before I was borned.'

'There were no ogors at Castle Lyonaster, though we had to fight off armies of orruks several times.'

Theuderis looked at the families, their expectant faces streaked with dirt and blood, huddled in cloaks and blankets.

So different from the citizens of the Glittering Breaches in appearance – so pale and thin and scared. But inside they were the same. They wanted the same thing, to live in peace, to raise their children and die of happy old age.

He lowered to one knee, still avoiding looking at the sickening child.

'Does he have a name?'

'Ljubo,' the mother replied. 'After his father and grandfather. They were fine trackers and huntsmen.'

'A very good name,' said Arkas, coming up beside Glavius. 'I fought beside Krul Ljubo of the hussta, a very clever warrior and excellent marksman. If you are of his blood then I know where your ancestors' cunning and woodscraft comes from.'

The woman smiled up at Arkas and Theuderis used the moment to rise, desperate to return to more certain ground, such as the discussion of lines of advance and flank protection. He could not get involved with these people. He could not pick favourites, it was not his place. They were all worth saving or none of them, just as those that served the Chaos Gods could not be pitied or saved, simply exterminated.

'Are we ready, Lord Arkas?' he asked, his tone stiff with formality, uncomfortable with the feelings stirred by his encounter with the Ursungorans. Why had he not kept his distance? Like battle, such things were best directed from afar.

'Is everything well, Silverhand?' Arkas asked quietly.

'It will be noon in a short while,' he replied. 'We need to commence the final council.'

'We cannot begin until Hastor and your Knights-Azyros have returned,' said the Warbeast. Along with patrols on foot and Theuderis' aerial forces, they had been scouring the glacier and the valley for signs of survivors. 'I took the liberty of dispatching one of your Knights-Venator to summon them.'

'He has flown swiftly,' said Theuderis, pointing towards the sky above the Bear's Pelt. A flight of Arkas' Prosecutors descended at speed.

'Wait,' Arkas said as Theuderis moved towards where the other officers waited. 'That is not Hastor.'

The Prosecutors dipped out of view briefly, disappearing behind the trees. It was not long before one of them reappeared, speeding towards the camp on azure wings. He landed a few paces from Arkas and bowed to his lord and then to Theuderis.

'Venian, what tidings?' asked the Warbeast.

'Ursungorans, my lord, in the woods.' The Prosecutor-Prime turned and pointed back the way he had come. 'My retinue escorts them. Several score more, I would say. We did not see them on the ice.'

'There are a few routes from the glacier directly into caves in the valley walls,' said Theuderis. 'Some of my warriors found concealed entrances on the lower slope.'

'They will be here shortly, my lord,' said Venian. 'I do not know if they carry the skaven taint. Shall we let them approach?'

'Several score?' said Arkas. 'More than a hundred, would you say?'

'Yes, Lord Arkas. At least that many, from what I observed.'

'Katiya will be with them,' Arkas told Theuderis. 'There is no other reason for so many to be in the same place.'

'A leap of logic,' warned the Knight Excelsior. 'Do not surrender to false hope.'

'Maybe not logic. Call it instinct, if you must. Katiya is with them, I am sure of it. We cannot hold the council yet. I will go with Venian to meet this group and decide where best to direct them.'

'I think your Prosecutor-Prime is able to deal with...' Theuderis fell quiet, understanding Arkas' intent. 'Very well, Lord

Arkas. See if Katiya is with them, but return swiftly. Our march will be difficult and dangerous, and we need to be across the mountain before dusk.'

'This won't take long,' Arkas assured him. His voice had dropped to a murmur.

When Arkas had departed, Glavius rose from where he had been entertaining the Ursungorans. Theuderis saw his eyes scanning the camp as he approached, though alert for what threat he could not tell.

'You have a gift with words,' said Theuderis. 'And a way with infants I find at odds with your calling in Sigmar's host.'

'You are not the only Stormcast who was a father before being called to the Stormhosts, my lord,' replied Glavius. 'When I was mortal I was a bard-blade of the Wraithlands. We fought with words as much as weapons. In the Realm of Death a rite can be more dangerous than a sword or axe.' He glanced at the Ursungorans. 'They hide it well, but they are all afraid, child and adult alike. This is skaven-plague. Chaos-tainted.'

'Indeed.'

Glavius fixed his helm back in place, concealing his features behind the grim skull-mask of his rank once more.

'We have to purge them all,' said the Lord-Relictor.

CHAPTER
THIRTY-FIVE

The walk down through the trees was the hardest Arkas had ever taken. It seemed to last longer than the forced march across Ursungorod. Despite Theuderis' doubts, the Warbeast was certain of what he would find at the end. The gathering of so many refugees in one place had to be the work of Katiya, and he had seen her close to the fighting, close to the skaven-spawned plague mist.

Leaving deep footprints in the thawing mulch he headed straight downhill, his heart as heavy as his tread. As much as he wanted to avoid confronting the reality that awaited him, it was unavoidable, and delaying simply allowed his doubts to nag at him for longer.

It was obvious that Theuderis thought him blindly optimistic, but the Silverhand did not understand the mind of an Ursungoran, even one that had been reforged. Arkas hoped, in his soul, that he could fix the ills of the world, and he hoped that he could bring peace and prosperity to his lands and people.

It was this hope that had sent him on the path to become the Uniter. Without hope he would have given up, crawled under the blankets with his dying mother. Without hope he would not have stood upon the broken walls in defiance of the skaven horde, despite the dire prediction of Radomira.

But it was not a hope that all would simply be made well. It was not a hope that everything would get better without pain and suffering, without sacrifice and effort. It was, he thought, simply a hope that the hardship served a purpose, that there was always a goal worth striving for. His hope for an end to the misery of Ursungorod did not preclude acceptance that the misery existed and had to be endured.

So he did not hope for anything as his long strides took him down the mountainside. He did not dread the coming reality either, because dread was just another form of denial. The survivors in the camp embodied this characteristic, accepting the reality of the plague without fear or favour, hoping that some might slip from its grasp, accepting the likelihood that most would not.

Venian flew down through a gap in the trees ahead and waited for the Lord-Celestant to reach him.

'Another two hundred paces, my lord,' said the Prosecutor-Prime, pointing. Between the trees Arkas could see figures in the distance, barely visible in the forest shadows.

'Very well. Return to your retinue and take them back to the camp. We are mustering for the march. Knight Hastor will have your orders shortly.'

'We are abandoning the search of the Bear's Pelt, my lord?' Venian looked up. 'It is not long since the sunrise reached the valley.'

'We have more pressing duties, Venian,' Arkas told him, with conviction. 'There is little point in rounding up a few more survivors if doing so grants victory to the skaven. We have a realmgate to take.'

'Of course, my lord, I did not mean to disagree.'

Arkas said nothing else, dismissing the Prosecutor-Prime with a flick of the head. The Warbeast watched the approaching refugees, able to pick out their pale faces now, a picket of armed men and women leading the way, ever wary. Knots of others followed a few dozen paces behind.

The hunters saw Arkas and gravitated towards him, their expressions a peculiar mix of relief and anxiety. It was obvious they were pleased to see the Uniter, but their glances back towards the other Ursungorans told him without any words exactly what he needed to know.

He spied Ajfor amongst the rearguard. He beckoned and Katiya's grandson approached quickly. There was a cut across his left eye, the infected wound weeping blood and less wholesome fluid. His eye was a black orb, his skin jaundiced.

'Where is she?' Arkas asked softly.

Ajfor looked back, scanning the other survivors. He pointed away to the left, at the largest following group.

'She is...' He choked on the words.

'I know,' Arkas said, laying a hand as gently as he could on the young man's shoulder. He nodded uphill. 'There is a camp not far away. Most are also afflicted. But there are fires and some shelter.'

Nodding, Ajfor broke away and continued upwards without looking back, the other hunters drifting after him with solemn looks at the Lord-Celestant, perhaps having overheard his conversation, perhaps simply guessing what had passed between them.

The Ursungorans parted as Arkas strode through the trees, all but making a path for him to find Katiya. She was being dragged on a bier of lashed wood, hide and rope. Some around her were also showing signs of infection but were strong enough still to walk, while many others were on stretchers, some with their faces covered, their bedrolls already shrouds.

Her hand fluttered from beneath a deer pelt blanket at his approach. Her wrinkled face was almost devoid of colour and her left eye was crusted shut with scabbed pustules.

'Uniter...' she said. Her voice was firm, though she was forced to take in a ragged breath after. Arkas winced as he heard the bubbling in her lungs. The bearers set down the bier and stepped away, granting them a little privacy.

'Katiya.' He knelt beside her and saw, perhaps properly for the first time, her thinning hair, the curve of cheek and jaw, the line of her nose. 'You look like Radomira.'

'Yes,' she replied. Another rattle of inhalation. 'A daughter in every generation. Her bloodline is strong.'

Arkas could not shake the sensation of familiarity, beyond simply recognising Katiya. Seeing her lying on the makeshift bed brought back such strong memories.

'Do not give in to grief,' wheezed Katiya, sensing what he was thinking even though his face was hidden.

'No,' he promised, nodding slowly. 'Never grief.'

Still he could not fight back the hurt, the sense of injustice swelling inside at the sight of her so forlorn and weak. Perhaps it was simply the context, but Arkas could not ignore the resemblance, not just to Radomira but also to his mother.

'It is time to tell... you something.' Katiya coughed as she sat up. Arkas helped her, providing an arm for her to lever herself upright. He could smell the infection on her rank breath. 'It is about your mother. About... Radomira and your... bloodline.'

'The past is the past,' said Arkas, echoing the traditional Ursungoran saying.

'It is.' Katiya did not smile but there was softness in her good eye. Sympathy, perhaps. The look was so uncannily like his mother's last expression. Insight flashed.

'Radomira... She was a relation?'

Katiya nodded.

'My grandmother?'

'No...' More coughing prevented Katiya from continuing but Arkas already knew what she was going to say. He barely whispered the words.

'My mother. She was my real mother.'

Katiya nodded through the spasms, her grip weak on his arm.

'Then who...?'

'Your sister,' Katiya managed. She took several deep breaths and recovered a little. 'Older by fifteen years. The man that was bonded with her acted as your father. You were... unexpected arrival. Radomira was sworn sagesayer, sundered from family, forbidden liaisons with... outsiders. Old, old past childbearing... it was thought.'

'I see,' said Arkas, though he was not sure he did. He understood, intellectually, what Katiya was saying. What it meant, on the other hand, eluded him. 'That is why her thoughts were so close to mine.'

Katiya simply nodded, her strength exhausted by the brief confession.

'But when my... my mother and father died, I was their only child.'

Katiya nodded again. 'Radomira had no more children either. But you did.' Katiya looked away, suddenly ashamed. 'You bedded women, yes? Your children... they were hidden from you... by your mother. To protect you. To allow you to lead all without favour.'

'You said the bloodline was strong.' Arkas turned her face towards him. She frowned. 'What did you mean? The touch of Ghur? The beast-gift?'

'In some, yes,' Katiya told him. 'The men, a few of them. For the women... The sagesight. The Ghur-tongue.'

'And what of my real father?'

'Nobody knows for certain.'

'Why are you telling me this, why now?'

'The truth.' Katiya lay back, folding her hands to her chest. Her eye fluttered closed. 'What you fight for.'

And there it was again, that startling, heart-stopping resemblance to his mother's – to his sister's deathbed. Radomira had lied to him for years, and even when he had been inside her thoughts she had kept this secret from him.

'Was it part of her vision?' he demanded, but Katiya did not answer.

Arkas' heart trembled as he moved his head closer. He could not feel or hear her breath, but he saw the weakest of pulses in her neck. She held on, but only just. The conversation had sapped much of her remaining strength, taking an effort of will just to speak.

'She needs rest,' said one of the nearby women. The others came back as he rose to his feet. Arkas could see the family likeness, nieces and nephews, cousins, siblings perhaps. How many were his descendants? How many had really survived that day on Kurzengor? Not just his people by culture. His descendents, his blood.

'Look after her,' he told them, though it did not need to be said.

He gave a last look at his daughter by nearly a score of generations and turned away. He started the long climb back to the camp, knowing that he would not look upon her face again.

CHAPTER THIRTY-SIX

Thick black smoke choked the sky, but though the twilight was obscured by the fumes, the light of many flames provided ample illumination for the marching Stormcasts. Their armour glinted in the gleam from the six fiery peaks of the Skagoldt Ridge, lit by bubbling lava flows and burning rivers that split and conjoined in a ruddy maze.

The ground was as black as the air, the hard volcanic rock strewn with ash. The column of Stormcasts navigated through a mesmerising labyrinth of pore-like tunnels, jagged spires and bulbous columns. In places the floor was ribbed and undulated, broken by clefts that could trap feet and break ankles. Fumaroles belched forth constant sprays of lava and vapour. Seemingly solid plateaus proved treacherously unstable, shaking and splitting to reveal themselves as skins across pools and lakes of semi-liquid rock. Sheets of fire and pillars of flame burned from naked rock, and ash-devils swept through, driven by no natural wind. Lizards the size of dogs with pelts of coals and ember eyes scuttled over the dark rocks.

Everything shimmered in the heat haze – heat so incredible only Stormcasts could withstand its sapping effects. Arkas laboured with heavy breaths, his reforged skin slicked with sweat, but the hardship was nothing – any advance along the ridge known once as the Bear's Spine would have been impossible for his mortal army.

The ruddy, flickering light played tricks with the bizarre landscape, creating shadow-giants and threatening simulacra. Combined with the oppressive heat, and the knowledge that they were marching into battle against an untold number of skaven, the jarring volcanic wasteland subdued the spirits of the Celestial Vindicators and Knights Excelsior.

In the red-and-black sky, flitting through the wreath of smog, the Prosecutors, Knights-Venator and Knights-Azyros swooped and rose on the hot air from jagged thermal vents and winding lava trails. Theuderis had sent them ahead as scouts but no sooner had the Stormcasts started up the Skagoldt Ridge than Samat returned with news that almost nothing could be seen from the air, the cloud was so thick and low. Even so, they stayed aloft, ready to respond swiftly to any threat.

Theuderis' Judicators, led by the Prime called Trajos, scoured the land ahead searching for the best route through the meandering streams of lava and gaping chasms. Several times the army was forced to stop and turn back, retracing its steps until a way ahead was found. On occasion they scaled steep cliffs of dark rock and scrambled down tumbled slides of scree and obsidian shards. In places their route took them along crystal-lined gorges, the walls sparkling and faceted, in places sprouting prismatic growths as large as the Stormcast warriors.

Pillar-like intrusions rose far above their heads, a mixture of dark, pitted crags and smooth, white columns.

The sun had set, as best could be judged, by the time the army crested the top of the ridge. From this vantage point, rare breaks in the fumes allowed them to briefly look down into the valley on the far side. In places the drop was precipitous, layer after layer of volcanic expulsion and magma extrusion forming a dense network of canyons and bridges.

Their goal was on the far side, the flank of the central peak of Ursungorod, from whose vertiginous slopes long-dead humans and duardin had delved and built the great city of Kurzengor. Beneath lay the bulk of the skaven lair, nestled in the ruins of the massive conurbation.

'A volatile place,' remarked Doridun.

'My... My mother told me that the ridge first split asunder and spewed its fire on the day I was born,' Arkas replied. He looked at the cratered peaks around them. 'Its fury has not abated since.'

'What was that?' asked Dolmetis, marching on the other side of Arkas.

'Did you see something?'

'I thought so.' The Knight-Vexillor pointed to a sharp spur of rock that overhung the trail ahead. 'On the top there.'

Arkas looked but there was nothing to be seen.

'My eyes are tired,' Dolmetis admitted, 'and filled with grime and soot. But I would swear I saw a figure on the rock.'

'Impossible,' said Doridun. 'Nothing could live in this place.'

'Nothing mortal,' Arkas corrected him, scanning the surrounds with renewed interest. 'If we can survive here... The Chaos powers have more than mortal followers.'

He weighed up whether to call a halt. In his years as the Bear-clad few had ventured to this part of the mountains and none had returned after anything but a cursory investigation. He had learned, as a Stormcast, of places where the realms sometimes bled together – overlaps between the planes. Often these were near hidden or damaged realmgates, the mystical energy of the cosmos mixing together in unpredictable ways.

Though there was no reason to suspect anything other than volcanic activity shaped the Skagoldt Ridge, Arkas had stopped taking evidence at face value a long time ago. He had never seen Aqshy, the Realm of Fire, with his own eyes, but something rang true in the descriptions of those that had returned from the war there.

'Move on,' he said. 'We need to be in position to attack mid-morning.'

They carried on in silence for some way, negotiating the rough terrain without complaint. Arkas' thoughts were focused on the battle that waited at the end of the punishing march. As with the entire endeavour in Ursungorod, his was the bolder, more dangerous mission. Guided by the memory of his vision from the Queen of the Peak, he would lead the Celestial Vindicators directly for the realmgate. It was imperative that the skaven were prevented from opening it.

While the Warbeasts lanced into the heart of the undercity, paying no heed to any foes save those directly in their path, the Silverhands would advance in a more systematic fashion. Their strength divided between attacking the Warbeasts and defending against Theuderis' assault, the skaven would succeed at neither. It was a simple but effective stratagem, and victory was further assured by the unexpected route of the attack.

A long clarion call broke through Arkas' thoughts. The Silverhands swiftly changed formation, forming defensive clusters where they were, as allowed by the intervening terrain. Attaxes, the Knight-Heraldor, sounded another signal and the white-and-blue Stormcasts adjusted their ranks, skilfully moving together to form even tighter knots of warriors.

Doridun sounded the alarm of the Warbeasts, setting them into motion a few heartbeats later. Diocletus and his Protectors formed the outer rank, their glaives projecting an impassable wall of blades and points. Around the Lord-Celestant, the axe-wielding Decimators led by Martox stood shoulder-to-shoulder. Arkas scanned his surrounds, searching for any threat, but all he could see was forbidding rock and fire.

Theuderis rode his dracoth towards the head of the column, evidently where the first alarm had been raised.

'Make way!' snapped Arkas, pushing through the Decimators to head after Theuderis. 'Dolmetis, Doridun, with me! All others hold fast.'

They broke into a run, hurrying after the lord of the Silverhands. The Knights Excelsior were like statues, every warrior facing front with unwavering attention, the Primes at the centre of each retinue ready to respond. Not a single head turned as the Celestial Vindicators raced past.

Arkas caught up with Theuderis at the edge of a ravine some three hundred paces away. The Silverhand had dismounted and was peering over the edge, a cluster of Judicators around him pointing into the depths.

They turned at the scrape of Arkas' boot on the rock, bows and crossbows raised. Seeing that it was the Warbeast who approached, the Knights Excelsior parted, moving along the lip of the chasm to give his party room.

'What is it?' Arkas stepped up beside Theuderis to look down into the ravine. The Silverhand did not need to reply.

At the bottom of the chasm a winding river of fire cut through the darkness. The smog was thick, carried on the gusty wind along the canyon. But it was not this that had unsettled the scouts. Cut neatly into the vertical wall of the chasm was a set of steps, starting somewhere off to the left and zigzagging down until they were swallowed by the fumes. At each turning was a short landing where the wall was marked by archways, although there were no visible breaks in the rock. In places there were bridges, narrow spans that curved across the chasm, their silhouettes fading into the smog.

'Duardin ruins,' said Dolmetis. 'Why such alarums?'

'Look again,' said Theuderis. 'Not ruins.'

Arkas examined the closest steps more carefully. The Silverhand was right, they showed little sign of wear. In fact, had they existed before the eruption of the volcanoes they surely would have been broken and scattered.

'They were cut after I was born,' said the Warbeast. He turned around, surveying the surface for any other sign of habitation. There was nothing, though the conditions cut visibility to a few dozen paces. The design of the solid archways was consistent with the duardin style. 'Maybe the skaven had duardin slaves?'

'What skaven could survive this heat?' said Theuderis.

'Perhaps they escaped by building this way out of the skaven tunnels,' suggested Doridun. The others looked at him.

'With dressed stone and perfectly built arches?' said Dolmetis. 'A very circumspect escape attempt.'

The Knight-Heraldor realised the ridiculousness of the statement and withdrew a few paces, embarrassed.

'There was something else,' said Trajos. The Judicator-Prime stepped into view. 'Several reports of figures seen. In the fire, in the smoke.'

'Watching?' said Dolmetis. 'That's what I thought I saw.'

Trajos nodded.

'I do not think they are related to the skaven,' Theuderis

concluded. 'It is not in the ratkin's nature to make such constructions and they cannot possibly make use of these steps themselves.'

'Something else is here,' said Arkas. 'Something that arrived after the mountain broke.'

Theuderis nodded and stepped back from the precipice. 'The question is whether they mean us harm, whether they are allies or enemies.'

'Or neither,' said Dolmetis. 'If they have been watching us they have made no effort to make contact or attack.'

'They are thinking the same about us,' said Theuderis. 'Gauging whether we are friend or foe, perhaps?'

'If they wished us ill, they have had sufficient time to plan and execute and attack,' said Trajos. 'In fact, we are not far from the end of the fire-morass. Crags and canyons lie ahead, but no more lava or volcanoes.'

Arkas turned around, standing with his back to the chasm. He thought for an instant he saw a fleeting glimpse of something in the heat haze across a lava stream a few dozen paces away. A face, flat-nosed and broad, surrounded by hair and beard of fire. The figure had been squat and solid, like a duardin... but different.

'They are watching us pass through their territory,' he said to the others. Arkas raised his voice. 'We are the Stormcasts of the God-King Sigmar. We seek only to bring justice to the minions of Chaos, we are foes only to the forces of destruction. We are passing through these lands, to wage war against the skaven. We have no intent to stay and mean no harm to any that struggle against the Dark Powers.'

It seemed as though he were talking to himself, the fiery spectre a hallucination of heat and the effort of the march.

'Over there,' whispered Trajos, nodding to the right.

A group of five duardin-like shapes stood silently amidst the fires of a lava flow, oblivious to the deadly temperature. They were all but naked, wreathed in the flames rather than clothes. The shimmer of the heat made it impossible to see where the fires stopped and the figures began. In their hands they held what looked like wands and staves, but on better inspection Arkas saw that they were the handles of axes with blades of fire.

One of the duardin-folk took a step closer, eyes like coals regarding the Stormcasts solemnly, moving along from one end of the line to the other. The figure nodded once, slowly, and raised a fire-axe towards the north-east.

Turning his head, Arkas saw the fires dimming, a path of blackness curving through the lava, flames, geysers and tar pits. He raised his hammer to return the salute, but the figures had already vanished.

'What do you suppose they are?' he asked Theuderis.

'I do not know, but it is not the last we will see of them, I think,' said the Silverhand. 'We will be upon our enemies all the sooner with their aid. Attaxes, signal the advance.'

CHAPTER
THIRTY-SEVEN

The sun had not yet risen when the Stormcasts fell upon the outer strongholds of the skaven. Coming down the mountain from the Skagoldt Ridge, the warriors of Sigmar swept towards the surface ruins of the ancient city. Theuderis' Angelos Conclave formed the spearhead, their attack concentrated to slash a path to the entrances of the underground lair. The Silverhands' Paladin Conclave would follow, forcing a breach into the undercity through which Arkas and his Warbeasts would launch their assault.

The light of celestial beacons lit up the ruins as strands of lightning wreathed the heavens. Arkas had never ventured here in his mortal life and marvelled at the extent of Kurzengor. He had seen nothing of the spectacle in his vision. The mighty city he had defended on the day Sigmar had taken him for Reforging was but a bastion of a far mightier conurbation that had once stretched across the highlands of Ursungorod.

The concentric rings of the old city walls divided cramped

streets and high towers, broken apart where those soaring edifices had collapsed to scatter immense stones, leaving foundations and lower storeys jutting like broken teeth above the skyline. Plazas opened up wider spaces where temples to forgotten gods and palaces of long-dead nobles looked upon cracked mosaics and stained tiles.

He could see where markets had once bustled, shop fronts and domiciles had been home to countless thousands of humans and duardin. Onion-domed cathedrals sat broken next to a dry riverbed crossed by stout duardin-built bridges. Centuries of subterranean perturbations had torn open large gouges in the city, exposing the duardin dwellings below. The azure celestial light was swallowed by huge shafts and sinkholes that split vast throne halls and treasure vaults.

Despite its state of ruin, the city was not empty. Wooden walkways and rope bridges criss-crossed the old streets from sagging rooftops and cracked chimneys. Ramshackle fences and walls had been erected to delineate the territories of vying warlords. Vast swathes had been levelled and replaced with corrals for monstrous beasts and Chaos-tainted steeds, while pits and scaffold-decked gorges pierced the underbelly of Kurzengor, countless slaves sleeping where they had laboured on the unforgiving planks and cable.

The ground beneath the city showed its tortured past. In several areas it rose up to high plateaus reached by rope ladders and clumsily constructed scaffolds. Neighbourhoods had been swallowed by churning tar pits that continued to bubble and gurgle. Parts of Kurzengor had been reclaimed by the landscape, tentacle vines swallowing whole districts, the remains of houses and workshops caught in the branches of gargantuan trees, granite and marble fingers pulling at stretches of curtain wall and watch towers.

The fires of the Skagoldt Ridge had also made intrusions. The craters of dead volcanoes and fissures bleeding lava marked the outer quarter closest to the Stormcast advance. Sinkholes opened into crystalline shafts that dropped into the depths, lined by seams of sapphires, emeralds and diamonds.

Entire tribes that Arkas had never seen or heard of occupied the vast city. As he looked down on the maze of roads and shattered buildings he wondered if any clan still resisted the skaven and the touch of Chaos. It was a short-lived hope. Immense sacrificial pyres and monstrous effigies to the Dark Powers dotted the cityscape, built from the ruins of churches and shrines dedicated to lesser, fallen gods.

As elsewhere, the dominion of the Horned Rat was evident in many places. On the doorstep of the undercity, penned in by the indomitable peak itself and the fires of the Skagoldt Ridge, the tribes here had no option but to succumb to the power and temptations of the Chaos Pantheon.

Death was always an option, he reminded himself. He and his united clans had been willing to die rather than submit. There could be no pity for those who sought the sanctuary of Chaos worship, no matter how dire their predicament. Their weakness simply strengthened the foes of order, exchanging personal gain at the expense of Sigmar and their fellow humans.

An undulation in the mountainside gave way to reveal even more of Kurzengor's environs. Long boulevards crept up the slope, radiating out from the more densely packed centre. Villas and manses lined these streets, their gardens long reclaimed by nature, family estates overrun by the wild once more.

Arkas recognised tombs also, some distance outside the city, but closer to the richer quarters than the mercantile inner city. They were like the cairns raised by his own people but far grander. Some were ziggurats of obsidian and marble and other exotic stone. Though distance obscured any detail, he could see plentiful statuary and small dome-roofed family shrines scattered among the larger memorials.

He stopped, taken aback by what he saw next. Angry muttering broke out from the Decimators around him until he silenced them with a barked command.

The rocks of the mountain had been carved in an age past, creating immense visages in the cleared stone. So vast were these faces that Arkas could see windows in their eyes, balconies and stairs formed by wrinkles in the skin, doorways hidden in folds of beard and hair.

The monuments had been both duardin and human, though most likely fashioned by the craft of the former. All seemed to be kings and queens, proud of expression, crowned helms on their heads.

Eight there had been, though one was almost nothing but bare rock, its remnants broken asunder by some shift in the earth in the intervening years. The others were marred by advanced age, but also by deliberate vandalism. Noses were chipped and broken, lips cracked, cheeks hollowed and ears removed.

The masonry that had been stolen had been put to a fresh purpose, built atop the central face. The design was crude, the construction showing much patching and improvisation, but the subject was all too clear. Horned and glowering, green flames burning in the gaps of its eyes, the mask of the Great Horned Rat stared down over the ruined city.

'The account will be settled soon enough,' Arkas told his incensed warriors. He raised his runeblade, the sigils etched into the weapon flickering in the light of the celestial storm.

'We head for the realmgate. No more delays, no distractions. We win or we die.'

'We win or we die!' came the return shout.

CHAPTER THIRTY-EIGHT

Sentries across the city looked up to the skies, baffled by the storm clouds swiftly gathering. They did not think to look towards the fire-lands, for what threat could possibly come from that direction? The first they knew of their coming doom was when flights of shining warriors descended from the storm on iridescent wings, accompanied by bolts of lightning hurtling down into the tumult of broken buildings and earthquake-twisted streets.

Brash war horns and warning drums sounded across the city, far too late.

The Retributors and Decimators led the advance on the ground, an armoured fist of white and blue aimed towards the heart of the city. Guided by the blazing storm of missiles overhead, they marched at speed through the deserted streets, the uniform tramp of boots ringing from the dead buildings, watched only by empty windows and doorways.

Theuderis rode with them to ensure that the breach into the skaven undercity proceeded exactly as planned. While his attack speared through Kurzengor, his officers would oversee the following sweep and occupation of the city. He glanced back to assure himself that Arkas was close behind – the turquoise plate of the Warbeasts reflecting the celestial energies roaring across the storm above.

The other conclaves were fanning out along the line of advance, moving forwards to engage any foe that threatened the flanks of the breaching force. Theuderis paid them no more mind, confident that they would acquit themselves as only Knights Excelsior could. His mind was bent towards the achievement of his own objective – attaining entry into the undercity.

As they crossed a star-shaped plaza, the wind changed, swirling from the right. A snarl from Tyrathrax warned Theuderis of something untoward.

'Namazar!' He bellowed the name of the nearest Protector-Prime. The Lord-Celestant angled his sword towards the tumbled remnants of what might have been an old trade exchange, guildhall or perhaps some kind of mint or treasury. Its colonnaded front had completely collapsed, but several statues of mercantile-looking folk could be seen amongst the debris. There were other stone figures, not on plinths, of Chaos warriors and beasts in various poses of combat or flight. Theuderis recognised the threat immediately. 'Rearguard!'

The Protectors quickly peeled away after their Prime, a phalanx of glaives directed towards the rubble-strewn steps of the building. From the shadows of the main hall prowled an enormous beast – part cat, part lizard, its mane a nest of writhing vipers that hissed and spat. Its long tongue licked the air, tasting the presence of the intruders. Snarling, it bounded into a run, heading directly for the Protectors, baring teeth as sharp as any sword. In its wake, half-naked savages poured from the ruin, their hooting calls echoed by other warbands emerging from other nearby buildings. They were heavily scarred, pierced and tattooed, barely a patch of exposed skin not ornamented in some way. Screeching, waving bone and flint weapons, the troglodytic clansmen sprinted towards the block of waiting Stormcasts.

'Keep on,' Theuderis reminded his warriors. 'Continue the advance.'

He watched as the monster leapt at the Protectors, its savage nature undaunted by the rows of points confronting it. Sigmarite blades cracked against scaled skin, piercing deep, slashing long gouges through the flesh. In turn its claws and fangs raked welts across the ivory armour of the Knights Excelsior. The beast landed, crushing a Protector beneath its bulk while its serpent-mane spat gobbets of saliva that hissed and bubbled on the plate of the Stormcast Eternal.

The Celestial Vindicators entered the plaza, breaking into a charge to sweep into the unprepared savages. Theuderis saw Arkas leading the attack, carving bloodily into the disorganised mobs with swift blows from his hammer and blade.

Soon the skirmish was out of sight, though the shouts of the Warbeasts and the screams of the Chaos-tainted followed the Lord-Celestant for some time.

The street pushed up towards a hilly outcrop ringed by broken walls, an overgrown orchard within. The road split to encircle the ground, but Theuderis ordered his men straight on. They vaulted the remnants of the wall and plunged through the thicket of undergrowth and twisted trees, snapping branches and trunks with their bulk to shoulder their way through. Surprised by the quiet of their passage, Theuderis examined his surrounds in more detail and saw that the trees grew green and brown feathers instead of leaves.

To one side, the remains of the great house whose gardens they violated leaned precariously on its footings, kept upright only by the tangled limbs and roots of immense trees bursting from one of its dilapidated wings. There were platforms and huts constructed in the upper reaches of both building and tree, but of the inhabitants there was no sign – perhaps they were sensible enough not to confront the armoured giants advancing through their domain.

The wall on the far side of the garden was still intact, until the lightning hammers of the Retributors made short work of its bricks and mortar. Bursting onto a cobbled road that swept down towards the central city, the Stormcast Paladins broke into an easy run, Tyrathrax loping alongside them, Theuderis in the saddle.

On one side, the city descended into a tangle of alleys and steps too tight for the Stormcasts to easily traverse. On the other, a succession of terraces climbed up the mountain, each level home to the decrepit remains of terraces and warehouses, stores, smithies, armouries and jewellers. The road angled away from the pits into the undercity. It was not the most direct route but it was still the swiftest.

Several times more they encountered scattered bands of Chaotic tribal warriors. Some were barely more than animals, like those they had first seen, while others were more organised, better armed and armoured. It made no difference. The Paladin Conclave cut through them all in turn, ruthless and efficient, driven on by Theuderis' demand that there be no delays.

The few that survived this onslaught were little resistance to the Celestial Vindicators following behind. Those not cut down by the white-and-blue spear of the Knights Excelsior were crushed into oblivion by the hammer blow of Arkas' force.

It was not only humans that tried to waylay them. In abandoned parks overrun by tides of beetles and spiders, and orchards with trees that grew eyeballs and bloody organs instead of fruits, beastmen and monsters had made their lairs. Theuderis did his best to avoid these, knowing that to become embroiled in an extended engagement would not only needlessly spend time, but might allow the gathering creatures to wholly surround them. The most desolate, broken areas he skirted around, staying to the wider avenues and squares where the enemy had to present themselves more openly.

Despite every effort, Theuderis was painfully aware of the growing light as the sun crept above the mountains. The skaven would have lookouts positioned, if only to guard against treachery from their subject-tribes and those clans still swearing allegiance to gods other than the Great Horned Rat.

How long would they take to muster a force?

Through a combination of evasive manoeuvres and brute strength, Theuderis' Paladins carved a path for Arkas, on occasion smashing their way through buildings to forge the best route.

When the first rays of dawn shone on the many-coloured domes ahead, they were almost at the closest slave-pit, the opening into the skaven domain just a few streets away.

The way ahead was blocked. Stretching from one side of the road to the other was a wall four times as tall as a man, raised from stone and earth and reinforced with sharpened stakes and thick timbers. The buildings to either side were similarly fortified, crude ramparts built along rooftops, windows and doors barricaded.

A storm of arrows greeted the Knights Excelsior, raining

down from the wall and surrounding heights. Theuderis led his warriors to the left, seeking a route around the obstruction. The next street was similarly blocked, and the next. Iron-tipped arrows clattered from armour and stone around him as he pulled Tyrathrax to a stop to assess the situation. For all that he could tell, the wall could stretch for a considerable distance.

He looked up and saw warriors in mail and leather scrambling over the roofs, bows and javelins in hand. On the wall armoured figures waited, waving axes and swords, their jeers echoing along the walled-off road. He had seen no sign of gate or bridge. A glance back towards the main street revealed the Celestial Vindicators approaching fast.

'Up, my lord?' suggested Elegias, the Retributor-Prime. He pointed to the closest building with his starsoul mace.

'You have the right of it, Retributor.' Theuderis stood in the saddle and pointed his blade towards the roofs. 'We go over these wretches!'

The Paladins piled into the nearby buildings, crashing through boarded windows and doors, the light of their gleaming weapons shining through shutters and cracked walls. Theuderis rode along the road a little further, ignoring the occasional missile sparking from his armour and the moss-covered flags as he sought ingress for Tyrathrax. A few dozen paces on, a building had collapsed, a slump of rubble spilling down into the street. Assorted tools and containers showed that the tribe had been in the process of rebuilding the breach.

Tyrathrax sensed his intent and broke into a run, heading for the improvised ramp. Three bounding strides and a leap took them onto the roof of the adjoining townhouse, claws sending broken clay tiles skittering to smash on the street three storeys below.

From this point Theuderis could see how close he was to his

objective. Barely a hundred paces beyond the wall, steps and wooden ramps led down into the slave pit.

The scale of the obstacle in front of him was also clear. The roofs and wall were thronged with foes, more of them spilling up from trapdoors and rope ladders like ants from an agitated nest. Warriors swelled by Chaos power, clad in thick armour plates, gathered in front of him, axes and shields held up, faceless helms staring at him in challenge.

Lifting his blade, point heavenwards, Theuderis drew down a bolt of celestial power. The lightning earthed along his weapon and crackled across his armour. Above, the storm clouds seemed to roil, swirling with their own energy.

Moments later, the Angelos Conclave burst into view. With Samat and the other Knights-Azyros at their head and Arkas' Prosecutors alongside, they plummeted groundwards at blistering speed.

The tempest of fire from their weapons lashed along the roofs ahead of Theuderis. Lightning-wreathed javelins and flaming hammer-bolts tore into the Chaos warriors, slicing through armour, scorching the flesh within. Tiles, brick and slate exploded, jagged shards ripping through the marauders scrambling up stairwells and hauling themselves across rope bridges.

On and on the torrent came, slaying everything in the way of Theuderis' charge. The blaze of celestial beacons shone in the morning gloom, the power of Sigmar's light blinding and burning the impure. Chaos worshippers staggered, holding their hands to their faces, screeching and screaming as they toppled from the roofs in panic and desperation.

'Onwards!' roared Theuderis.

Tyrathrax charged, ripping up more roof tiles with every stride. Theuderis' blade trailed purifying flame. Ahead, Prosecutors with blazing hammers descended onto the wall, the bodies of their foes smashed from the ramparts as they advanced. Behind, the Paladins of the Silverhands roared their battle cry and followed their Lord-Celestant into the fray.

'For the glory of Sigmar!'

CHAPTER
THIRTY-NINE

The Silverhands cleared the enemy with astounding speed, but Arkas knew better than to waste time admiring their bloody work.

'Straight on,' he told his warriors, heading directly along the street to the wall across it. 'Our turn will come soon enough.'

The Warbeasts surged between the fortified houses, trampling the dead and dying cast from the rooftops. Arkas threw himself the last few paces at the wall, driving the head of his hammer into the patchily mortared masonry. Dust sticking to the caked blood on his armour, he used the hammer to haul himself up, driving in his sword to form the next handhold. Around him his warriors ascended with equal speed, unchallenged now that the wall's guardians were battling the winged heralds of Theuderis' host.

In a few more heartbeats, Arkas dragged himself over the jagged crenellations and took a quick stock of the situation. To his left and right, his Prosecutors and the Knights Excelsior had sliced through the wall's guardians, opening a breach for his group. The number of Chaos followers was quickly swelling though, a wave of twisted humanity building up against the line of Stormcast Eternals like water at a dam.

There was no time to waste.

He leapt down the far side of the wall, boots cracking the flagstones further with the impact. In a heartbeat he was off and running again, heading directly for the maze of walkways, steps, ropes and scaffold ahead. Beyond, the ground dropped away like a cliff.

A stream of wasted, unwashed humanity spilled from the gash in the world, some still struggling with shackles, chains and rope bindings, their bodies covered in sores and welts. They stared in dumb wonder at the Stormcast Eternals, unsure whether they were liberators or simply new masters. All of them had the touch of Chaos about them, Arkas noted, as he watched them scrambling and sprinting past – tiny horns, patches of discoloured or scaled skin, tails, claws, jagged teeth, disjointed limbs. For all that they had endured untold misery they were still tainted.

'Leave them for our shining companions,' Arkas barked as some of his warriors moved towards the pitiful wretches with hammers and axes ready. 'We have a pressing appointment below.'

The pit was a ragged wound in the earth. It burrowed down at a steep angle, shelves of harder rock and ledges built of debris from the demolished city creating staging levels still littered with the corpses of slaves dead from exhaustion and starvation.

The rickety boards and ladders looked incapable of taking the weight of a Stormcast. Arkas chose to descend in swifter fashion, leaping towards the closest outcrop. He crashed through mould-slicked timbers onto the rock. From here he bounded to a ledge on the left, and then let himself drop down to another below.

His warriors followed, some tracing his route, some picking their own way down into the darkness. Though the opening of the pit had seemed large from the surface it soon dwindled into a pale oval above as they descended, and then disappeared to leave the only light the gleam of Azyr-forged weapons.

There were offshoot galleries and tunnels but Arkas ignored them. The scene from the vision was vivid in his memory, as deeply etched as if he had already been into the depths in person. He remembered the sound and sparkle of an underground river nearby. When they found that, they would have their route to the realmgate.

Down they went, down into the bowels of the mountain, leaving behind the scrapings and workings of the tribes above, into a nether-realm between the city of humans and the skaven undercity. Here the duardin ruins were still intact in places, giving the Celestial Vindicators bridges across the cracks in the world, straight-hewn passages and winding stairs to follow.

Unlike the ruins he had seen on the surface, neither light nor wind had scoured these underground streets. Arkas was surprised by the amount of colour and texture. There were bright murals of geometric patterns and stylised scenes of builders, smithies and miners; the pillars and archways were decorated with bands of blue, purple and deep red. It brought home that Kurzengor had once been a thriving metropolis, rivalling Sigmaron in size, home to tens of thousands of humans and duardin.

Before the Age of Chaos. Before the skaven.

He tightened his grip on his weapons, his mood souring again.

Though the city was more engineered in these lower vaults,

passage through it was still difficult. Like the City of Ice, it had been constructed by inhabitants smaller than the warriors of Sigmar. Tight passageways and sharp turns hindered them and several times the Stormcasts in the vanguard were forced to turn back, either encountering dead-ends or slender subterranean alleys that simply would not allow them access. Frequently Arkas' helm or elbow would break the plaster rendering on the walls, turning works of art that had survived centuries of neglect into shards and dust.

As he descended, Arkas could feel the weight of the mountains pressing down upon him. More than that, it was the weight of expectation, of history. He moved towards a fateful confrontation in the unfolding saga of Ursungorod. With equal awareness he could also sense the power of Ghur churning in the foundations, trapped in the bedrock below. The further he went down, the stronger grew its lure, and the greater was its power. It was a primal force – contained, but struggling to break free.

The Shadowgulf.

Just like the Skagoldt Ridge, it was uncharted territory, a yawning emptiness that he had been aware of as far back as he could remember. He thought he knew now what it was – the void beyond the realmgate, a hole in the depths of Ursungorod that led to the place between realms, the vacuum of nothingness and raw Chaos leaking into Ursungorod through the inter-realm gnaw-ways of the skaven.

It was uncharted, but not unknown, and no longer impossible to penetrate. With Stormcast Eternals at his command, there was no barrier he could not cross, no territory he could not enter. The thought of piercing the undercity of the skaven brought a visceral thrill. For so long he had been denied vengeance, and now the victory he had craved on the walls of Kurzengor was within his grasp.

His oath fulfilled, his pain salved.

'Are you all right, my lord?'

Dolmetis' question dragged him out of his thoughts.

'Yes, why?' Arkas snapped.

'I... I thought you said something.' Uncertainty wavered in the Knight-Vexillor's voice. 'Growled.'

'Dust,' Arkas said quickly. 'In my throat.'

'Of course, my lord.'

The further down they went, the warmer it became, and the air carried on it a stench that grew stronger with each level they passed. Sometimes the smell waned as they encountered shafts and airways cleverly fashioned into the old city to bring draughts of chill mountain air from the surface, while the wider duardin chambers and halls dissipated the unpleasantness for a time. Where they had to squeeze through narrower galleries and corridors, the reek added to the suffocating claustrophobia.

They came across a large hall, the ceiling held by metal pillars and vaulting, a firepit at the near end. It was a grand chamber, swallowing the echoes of metal-shod feet. The Stormcasts spread out, heading towards large archways on the opposite side, grit crunching underfoot. The far wall was lost in shadow until Arkas held up his hammer and let forth a burning blue flame of celestial power.

In the flickering shadows, giant faces danced. Angular and flat, they were stylised versions of the duardin rulers carved into the mountainside above. Steps rose to a dais on which a stone chair sat, ornately carved with knotwork and more sculpted duardin faces.

'A king's throne room,' muttered Doridun.

'Not so,' announced Martox. The Decimator-Prime stood at one of the arches with his retinue, looking into the lighter shadows of the space. 'Perhaps a prince's.'

Arkas joined him and looked into the adjoining hall, the Prime's meaning becoming clear. The cavernous space was enormous, even vaster than the hall in which they stood. The floor was covered in intricate geometric tiles, each the size of Arkas' hand, many shattered to reveal smooth rock beneath. The walls had a more natural finish, undulating and bulging in places, but polished, every strata and striation of colour catching the dismal light. Rusted sconces for hundreds of torches marked the walls, and there were similar ruddy spots on the ground where braziers had stood for many decades before being taken by looters.

The throne dais here was not only taller than the one in the antechamber, but at its summit were five thrones, all of similar size, though differing in design. Onyx, amber, marble and granite had gone into the construction, so cunningly wrought that even the skaven had not been able to prise them from their anchoring bolts.

The hall was split by a crack no wider than Arkas' outstretched arms, running from one corner to the other directly across their line of advance. Moving closer he heard a trickle of water. He looked down into the chasm and could see nothing but a vague movement far below – but the sound of the stream was definite.

'Not far,' he said. 'Listen...'

The Stormcasts stopped, statue-still. Above the faint hissing of water another sound carried through the passages and halls. A faint murmur. The tink of picks and scrape of shovels. Cracks of whips.

'This way,' said Diocletus, pointing to archways behind the thrones. 'It's coming from...'

His voice died away as the background noise changed subtly. The same sounds were there but there was another – the pattering of feet, the scratch of claws, the rustling of cloth.

A bell tolled, the nerve-jangling noise reverberating into the hall from several directions. It sounded another knell. And then there was the discordant clash of a disfigured gong. And drums. Over a few cacophonic rounds they came together, crashing out a sombre beat.

Growing louder.

A green flicker of warpfire lit the passages beyond the archways, a dull, shifting light at first, becoming a paler, greener flicker over the cut stones and weathered flags.

Arkas looked down at the ground again, lowering his hammer so that its glow illuminated the floor. The tiles were not just broken and cracked, there were dozens of scratch marks, and a faint sheen betrayed grease trails. Casting his gaze about he saw smears of droppings and small pools of urine. Only now did he register the stronger stench of filth, mould and rot.

From other directions the warp-glow strengthened. In front and behind, to the left and the right. The scraping grew louder and louder, the inharmonious drums, gongs and bells resounding closer and closer, a repetitive moaning accompanying the discordant crashes of noise.

Long shadows jumped along the walls as the Warbeasts formed a circle. Their weapons gleamed with celestial fire, lighting impassively masked faces, a knot of turquoise in the blackness. Putrid green warp-light spread into the vast hall from all around.

'They have found us,' said Arkas.

CHAPTER FORTY

The power of Skixakoth's fang was intoxicating. Filled with the blessing of the Great Horned Rat, Felk could feel the armoured giants as though they were a scab on his own flesh. They reeked of celestial magic, a sore upon the well of Ghurite energy that saturated everything from the Whiteworld Above to the undercity.

It hadn't only been his unnatural senses that had warned him of the intrusion from the scavenger city on the surface. Thriss had shadowed them unseen for some time, and when it had become clear they would head for the old throne room, Felk had set his forces into motion. The gutter runner had slipped away again after delivering this message, on some devious personal mission, most likely.

'Close-close, so very close,' Felk told Skarth. 'Not long, not long at all.'

The light coming from the unearthed realmgate was brightening all of the time, as the last few rocks and boulders were levered out of the way. The runes upon its structure added their own glimmer to the proceedings, a rhythmic oscillation of pale golden energy that sparkled up a pillar, across the keystone and down the other side.

'All is ready,' said the fangleader. He indicated the rings of spitevermin and lesser warriors around the realmgate plinth, facing outwards.

'Yes-yes!' Felk let the power of the Great Corruptor swell inside him. He could feel it burning through his veins. It empowered him but consumed him also. He knew that his time was short. It did not matter. Once the realmgate was opened he would corrupt the swirling forces that permeated the Realm of Life and stave off the call of death. Until then he would be sustained by the tooth of the verminlord piercing his heart.

With bounding strides he sped after the ranks of plague monks he had set upon the Sigmar-spawned warriors. He wanted to see the foe crushed, and then when he had proven his power once again he would break open the Realm of Life and glut himself on the swirl of released magic. Fresh forces awaited his command on the other side, Thriss had assured him. The armoured giants in the surface city would be swept away and all of the Whiteworld Above scourged or enslaved.

He reached the ancient throne room just as the most fanatical of his followers were hurtling towards the invaders. Frothing and screeching, these plague monks wielded immense censers that billowed with warp vapour, the pierced heads of their weapons spilling sickly fog that wreathed into strange shapes around them as they charged.

Behind these fanatics, the other plague monks continued their measured pacing, gathering through several arches and corridors, their shambling march starting to quicken.

The giants sprang forwards to meet the attack of the frenzied skaven hurtling across the throne hall, heedless of the heavy spiked censers crashing against their armour as they swung their gleaming weapons.

Driven mad by the fumes of their own weapons, possessed by the death-fervour of the Great Witherer, eyes bulging and teeth gnashing, the censer bearers flailed and swung without heed to their own safety. Spitting infected breath, they bit and scratched in their death throes, tearing at the unyielding plate of the giants with cracked claws. They crashed the spiked balls of their weapons against the armour of their foes even as they were spitted on glaives and pulped by glinting hammers. Though rusted and worn, the balls and chains were wreathed in warp power, and broke apart in tiny flecks and splinters that gnawed and worried at the enchanted metal.

The fog of death surrounding these manic disciples of the Great Horned Rat burned the eyes and filled the lungs of the warriors. Though superhuman, they were not wholly immune to the effects of the smog. Several doubled over retching and coughing. Others fell back with hands raised to their masks as the acidic fumes assaulted their eyes and mouths.

Incensed by the fighting, the plague monks quickened their pace, feeling the rage of the Great Horned Rat descending upon them. In Felk's chest the plague-fang burned, the sudden pain and vitality shocking him into renewed effort.

'Kill-kill!' screeched Felk, waving his horde onwards. 'Kill-kill-kill!'

The mass of plague monks broke into a run, brandishing staves, rusted daggers and jagged swords. Hoods and robes flapping, clawed feet skittering over ancient tiles, they poured towards the interlopers seeking to desecrate the holy under-city of the Withered Canker.

'Purge-purge!' shrieked the Poxmaster. 'Pray and slay and flay!'

Hissing and snarling, the skaven launched themselves towards the warriors, who were still reeling from the attacks of the censer bearers and the cloying fog left in their wake.

CHAPTER
FORTY-ONE

If the Warbeasts stayed they would be swamped by a tide of maddened ratkin. Arkas fought back the urge to simply kill without thought, focusing on the mission he had agreed with Theuderis. The Silverhand would be following, bringing down his entire army, but the Celestial Vindicators had to secure the route to the realmgate.

Amongst the throng of incoming vermin, one stood out. Taller and bulkier than the others, one of the plague priests held itself proudly, hood thrown back to show a head marked with nodules of horns and bubo clusters. This skaven was different in other ways. It tore through the pool of Ghurite energy that Arkas could sense lying dormant in the hall, and it left behind it a ragged trail of warp power greater than anything Arkas had encountered before.

Murderous instinct roared at Arkas to confront this creature, to destroy the architect of the plague and vermintide that had laid low the Ursungorans and doomed Arkas' descendants to a dwindling death.

'Enough,' growled the Lord-Celestant, tossing aside the rag-doll corpse of another censer bearer. 'Warbeasts, follow me!'

He cleaved a path not towards the rat-leader but to one of the archways from which the sounds of digging had earlier emanated. The hammer-blow charge of the Stormcasts smashed into the leading plague monks, cutting a gouge into their ranks in a burning tempest of starsoul maces, lightning hammers and thunderaxes. With Arkas at the front, the Warbeasts slew a dozen plague monks in the moments of impact, leaping over their tumbling bodies to fall upon the diseased vermin pressing behind. Another dozen fell without striking a blow in return, and as swiftly as they had been surrounded, the Warbeasts were clear.

The sudden breakout took the skaven by surprise, allowing the Stormcasts to quickly fight their way through the dregs of plague monks still arriving, reaching the relative sanctuary of the corridor beyond. Forced to press into the close confines after the Sigmar-chosen, the skaven were easy targets for a group of Decimators left as a slowly retreating rearguard.

Ahead Arkas could see a different hue merged with the ever-present shimmer of warp-light and phosphorescent fungal growths. A golden aura suffused the tunnel, coming from a vast cavern beyond.

The Stormcasts burst into the chamber of the realmgate with meteoric force, crushing and slashing the milling slaves in their path. The corridor had brought them out almost directly opposite the realmgate, the vivid picture from Arkas' vision now wrought physically before him.

The skavenslaves fled from the approach of the Stormcasts, pulling down the whip-handlers in their stampede. Like regular vermin exposed to the light of day, the pathetic creatures bolted for every nook and hole and exit they could find, swarming away from the turquoise-armoured warriors to leave their larger, more aggressive kin to protect the prize for which they had so painfully laboured.

Arkas slowed, allowing his warriors to form up on either side while he evaluated the situation. As well as pressing in along the corridor behind, the plague monks flowed back through other tunnels and passages to the left and right, seeping into the large cavern like filthy floodwater.

Several score of armoured skaven with wickedly bladed halberds stood directly in the path of the Stormcasts, guarding the realmgate. In turn, to either side of them were hundreds of lesser skaven, most with shields and simple mauls and blades, some with spears or scavenged halberds.

The realmgate itself was set back slightly, the excavation that had uncovered it leaving a short defile before it. A maze of scattered stalagmites, crevasses and pits further broke up the approach to the objective. But in Arkas' mind's eye he did not see obstacles, only defensible positions. If his force could break through the skaven's elite, the Warbeasts could seize the final approach to the realmgate and negate the mass of the rat-filth's numbers.

With this simple plan in mind, Arkas descended to the cavern floor, picking up the pace to ensure the flanking plague monks could not surround his several dozen warriors. Glancing to each side, he saw the plague monk leader entering the chamber off to the right, while several other plague priests emerged from the shadows at the edges of the great cavern, and scores more skaven followed from the gloom.

Faced with the incoming Stormcasts, the nerve of the armoured elites broke and they moved aside, seeking shelter behind their lesser companions, who were thrust cursing into the path of the vengeful Sigmar-blessed warriors. These proved little better than the slaves, fodder that bogged down the advance of Arkas' warriors but did not halt it. While the War-beasts hacked and bludgeoned their way towards the realmgate plinth, more and more plague monks filled the cavern.

The battle-heat was on Arkas and he barely had to think as he struck down foe after foe. His focus was like a fiery spark directed at the next enemy, his purpose single-minded and irresistible. Yet as he cut down yet another skaven, another sense was nagging at him, a more rational part of him trying to warn him of something amiss.

He realised two things in quick succession. Firstly, the plague monks were not throwing themselves after the Stormcasts as he had expected. They came together in several masses, cutting off any route back out of the cavern, content to allow him to clear a path to the plinth. Many of them were bowing hooded heads as though in prayer.

Secondly, as another foe fell beneath his sword, his gaze fell upon the realmgate again. The runes were not flickering as they had been before, but glowing with a steady light. Beneath the arch the air shimmered, the rock face beyond obscured in shadows cast by immense trees on the far side.

Amongst the clamour, he heard a chittering laugh echoing across the hall. He glanced back to see the skaven leader with his hands raised, arcs of power leaping between them, igniting the magic of the chamber and lancing overhead. The bolts struck the duardin-carved pillars and the runes flared like newborn stars.

The realmgate opened.

CHAPTER FORTY-TWO

The cavern trembled, bringing gravel and dust spraying down from the high ceiling. The throbbing in Felk's chest intensified in time with the tremors, every pulse sending a shock of energy through his diseased frame.

'Witness the power of Poxmaster Felk!' he crowed, lifting up a claw that danced with warp power. His words seemed to take form, noxious breath spilling from his mouth as he spoke.

The impetus of the armoured warriors was faltering. Their leader, the giant with hammer and sword that never stopped, halted on the first step to the realmgate dais. Though his weapons continued to arc left and right with blasts of power, his gaze was clearly fixed on the opening portal.

'All hail Felk!'

The Poxmaster quivered as his name issued from thousands of throats, accompanied by the din of gongs and bells. 'Power to me!'

The realmgate called to him, trying to drag him towards it.

He felt it in his chest, the fang of Skixakoth like a white-hot shard in his heart. Forks of power crawled across the stones of the portal and leapt across the gap. They rapidly grew faster and brighter. The flashes were mesmerising, each flicker drawing in Felk's consciousness, trying to snatch his mind from his brain.

He howled in triumph and pain, and threw out his hand in a spasm, involuntarily letting loose another arc of warp power that speared across the cavern and struck the keystone of the realmgate. The detonation sent a shockwave rippling out over the occupants of the hall, throwing skaven and Sigmar-warriors to the ground. The blast of energy snuffed out the warp-lamps, leaving the chamber lit only by the crawling fires engulfing the realmgate.

With a thunderous crack, the gap between worlds was breached and the cosmic bridge opened. Shimmering sun-light tinged with arboreal green crept into the cavern, bringing with it a gust of wind carrying the smell of mouldering leaves and rotted flesh.

The view through the gate was not altogether clear, but shuf-fling shapes quickly resolved into more hooded plague monks, icons of the Greater Witherer held aloft, drums and gongs banging as they marched out of the coruscating aura that filled the portal's frame.

'Beloved am I!' screeched Felk, his triumph overcoming the agonising gnaw of the fang impaled through his breastbone. 'The ranks of my disciples swell!'

The fighting abated, the warriors of Sigmar halfway up the steps, Felk's followers gratefully drawing back from their mer-ciless weapons now that reinforcements had arrived.

Another shape loomed in the translucent energy of the gate, almost blotting out the light from beyond. Felk stumbled to one knee as the pain in his chest flared to unbearable levels, a scouring agony that burned through every organ and coursed along his bones and nerves. Death seemed certain. Vile dread welled up where sweet victory had resided moments before. Squinting against the brightness, the Poxmaster watched as something monstrous and holy pushed through the veil between realms.

Its pinkish flesh was protected by rust-edged plates of warp-forged iron and its rat-like face was guarded by an angular helm fashioned to accommodate the profusion of horns that curled about its head. It wore a thick black belt from which hung a massive tome – the Liber Cankorum, in the pages of which were held the secrets of the Miasmic Flux. In its hand it held a four-tined spear that trailed tendrils of power from the realmgate.

Verminlord.

The musk of fear was strong around Felk as he watched the greater daemon of his god stride onto the realmgate dais. The monster's eyes were drawn immediately to the Poxmaster and he felt the fang in his chest throb powerfully.

'Felk.' The verminlord's voice was a sinister whisper that carried with it the weight of a booming shout. 'Poxmaster of the Withering Canker.'

'Mighty Skixakoth, Corruptor of the Pure, Sagacity Incarnate, Bearer of the Sacred Text!' The list of titles devolved into a rambling mash of syllables as Felk's nerve failed him.

The verminlord thrust a scimitar-like claw at Felk. The fang hummed with magical power, wreathing the Poxmaster in a greenish vapour. The same issued from the mouth of Skixakoth as it spoke.

'Did you think I would not miss it?' hissed the verminlord. 'Did you think I would let you freely bargain with *my* power? Steal *my* victory?'

'No-no!' wailed Felk, demeaning himself more by falling to his belly, though he could not drag his eyes from the verminlord. 'For-*for* you, greatest of the great, Skixakoth Right-Hand. Open gate, destroy Whiteworld Above, slay tree-queen for glory of Skixakoth.'

The verminlord's lips rippled with what might have been a snarl or a smile; it was impossible to tell. It turned its gaze on the armoured giants formed in a tight group on the steps before it.

'Kill them,' it snapped, casting a bolt of power from its spear.

CHAPTER
FORTY-THREE

Arkas raised his hammer just in time to catch the warp blast on its head. Corrupting magic and celestial power sprayed like sparks. At the verminlord's command the skaven were filled with renewed fervour and poured across the cavern towards the surrounded Stormcasts. Even the pitiful slaves picked up stones and wooden clubs and scampered after their betters.

The Warbeasts stood shoulder-to-shoulder in a solid ring, weapons presented to the foe. Arkas fixed his gaze on the verminlord, a terrible wrath building in his heart.

Skixakoth.

This monster had laid low Ursungorod, destroyed the resistance of Arka Bear-clad and enslaved the people of the mountains. More than that. The Lord-Celestant's eyes moved to the fell grimoire upon the daemon's belt, a spell book containing virulent curses and devastating plagues – the same that had slain his adoptive mother in her bed, and even now gnawed the life from Katiya and her kin.

The rage was almost unstoppable. Arkas barely felt the earth trembling, thinking it was his own limbs quaking with power as Ghurite magic surged up into his body from below. With it came pain, the agony of memory a physical sensation.

But it was not Arkas' pain, Arkas' memories that consumed him. He felt the torture of Ursungorod itself, the spirit of the land tormented and corrupted by the infiltration of the skaven and the lashing of Chaos power at its heart.

A single desire possessed him – to free the lands of their tyrant, to slay the verminlord.

But that was not his purpose here.

He thought of white snow and a cool breeze, birds aloft in the mountain sky, free from this turmoil, desperately trying to calm the beast that raged inside his chest as though in a cage.

He was not Arka Bear-clad, he was Arkas Warbeast. Stormcast. Lord-Celestant. Commander. Servant of Sigmar.

The Celestial Vindicator ran these thoughts over and over in his head as the noose of skaven tightened around his warriors. Through the ruddy veil that had descended on his vision he searched the surrounds, though he was not sure what he was seeking until he found it.

An island, of sorts. The base of a gigantic stalagmite that had been smashed aside as the skaven had dug for the realm-gate, blocked on three sides by cracks freshly widened by the convulsing earth.

'Reform! Withdraw on me!'

With a clash of weapons, the Stormcast ring turned into a spearpoint with Arkas at the tip. The dozens of Paladins flowed like liquid, parting to allow Arkas to pass through, heading for the stalagmite.

A mob of plague monks stood between them and their objective, their leader a plague priest with two crooked blades scratched with skaven runes that caught the light from the realmgate in strange ways.

The plague priest snapped a command, eyes full of madness and hate as Arkas and the Warbeasts plunged back down the steps in a long triangle of turquoise sigmarite and gleaming celestial energy that rippled down the levels like a flood of raw Azyrite power given form.

Arkas kicked as the skaven priest leapt at him. His boot connected with its chest. Thick, tattered robes absorbed some of the impact but still the blow sent the creature spinning back into its fellows, toppling two more. An instant later, Arkas was into the gap, sweeping his weapons left and right to carve the breach even wider.

He piled on, ignoring the blows that rang from his armour, cutting down all in front of him, trusting to his companions to do the same to any that he passed. Bone crunched underfoot and he pulled his feet free from grasping fingers and entwining rags, smashing his hammer through another handful of foes. Striding on, he angled through the small gap between two precipitous chasms, less than ten paces wide, and turned as he set foot on the stalagmite.

The Warbeasts coursed around him, spinning in turn to take up fresh positions defending the natural island while their fellows moved past.

They were just settling into these new positions when the verminlord attacked.

The greater daemon leapt across the gorge to the left, easily covering the gap, its hooves striking sparks from the stone as it landed. The miasma of decay that followed it billowed across the Stormcasts, almost blotting out the light.

Arkas reacted without thought. He threw himself between the charging verminlord and his warriors, hammer and runeblade ready. With supernatural speed, Skixakoth twisted, bringing the long haft of its spear around to block Arkas' sword, the hammer crackling through the fog where the verminlord had been a heartbeat earlier.

A massive fist crashed against the back of the Lord-Celestant's head. He moved with the blow, completing a full forward roll to negate most of the impact. A hoof caught him in the mid-riff as he turned, knocking him back.

He had his back to the crevasse. Ahead, the plague monks screamed and shrieked their dedications to the Great Horned One as they launched their attack against the Stormcasts, the first dozen ratmen cut down by hammers, maces and glaives, the following skaven throwing themselves forwards undeterred.

That was all Arkas had time to glimpse before he had to step to the right, bringing up his hammer to deflect the spearhead of Skixakoth.

'I know you...' The greater daemon's brow creased into deep furrows. 'A strangely familiar smell.'

Arkas said nothing. He launched himself at the daemon, aiming his runeblade for its midriff. Its spear deflected the attack, but not the hammer-blow that followed, smashing into the creature's shoulder. It staggered, snarling and spitting.

A spear thrust forced Arkas to retreat several steps, until he could feel the yawning precipice behind him. The verminlord leered, displaying dagger-like fangs.

'I have not killed you before, have I, little Sigmar-thing?' It splayed the talons of its free claw, warp lightning crack-ing between them. 'No, that is not it. They were iron-clad and you are not.'

Arkas dodged aside to avoid the blast of warp lightning, but in doing so moved into the range of the verminlord's spear.

It pierced the side of his chest, below the right shoulder, two rusted tines shredding sigmarite and flesh.

Arkas cried out as corrupting magic poured into the wound, splitting bones and shredding sinew. He tore himself away from the spear and stumbled, thick blood gushing from the grievous injury.

'I will see you soon in Azyr!' cackled Skixakoth, driving its fist into Arkas' masked face.

The blow hurled him back. He fell hard and scrabbled for purchase, but after an agonising moment Arkas discovered there was no ground beneath him.

He dropped into the chasm. His last sight before darkness engulfed everything was of the verminlord looking down over the edge of the precipice, a halo of warp-light surrounding its horned face.

Arkas hit an outcrop and bounced heavily, spinning laterally. He threw out a hand to grasp something, anything projecting from the side, but his fingers gripped only empty air.

He could feel waves of Ghurite energy buffeting him like updraughts of air. Arkas let the magic lap around him, soothing his troubled thoughts, comforting him like a friend. A brotherly embrace.

The light from the cavern of the realmgate was just a faint line far, far above when he hit the bottom of the ravine.

The agony was thankfully short-lived, the Stormcast's bones shattered, organs pulverised, flesh pierced and gashed by buckled sigmarite plates. He felt it for just a few heartbeats, until that heart gave out and the celestial power in the core of his being exploded. It disintegrated what was left of Arkas Warbeast and as a bolt of pure energy shot up into the heavens.

CHAPTER
FORTY-FOUR

The battle for Kurzengor had eached an impasse. Theuderis and his Paladins had reunited with the Angelos Conclave and the rest of his warriors. They held three routes down to the undercity – the slave pit they had first seized, a tunnel network beneath a crumbling temple and a sinkhole that had collapsed in one of the gardens of a sprawling palace.

Against the warriors and weapons of the Chaos tribes these positions were virtually impregnable. The three forces were arrayed in a triangle so that not one of them could be surrounded without the enemy being caught with their backs to another Stormcast enclave. Justicars and Prosecutors raked celestial missiles into any foe that approached too close, but were content to let them flee beyond range when their spirit broke. Those that dared and survived this barrage of arrows, bolts and javelins were confronted by a shield wall of Liberators, who received the brunt of the initial assaults and then peeled apart by retinue to allow the Paladins within each armoured ring to counter-attack.

Several times this strength had been tested and the streets and plazas of Kurzengor were thronged with corpses, the bloody remnants of corrupted humans waist-deep in places. The rooftops, courtyards and alleys were similarly littered with the dead. It had started to snow again and streams of crimson pooled from gutters and downpipes, staining the fresh fall.

Thousands of the Chaos-tainted had been slain but not without losses to the Knights Excelsior. Theuderis' Paladins in particular had paid heavily for their presumptuous thrust into the city, and more than a third of their number had already been returned to Sigmar.

For all their solidity, the three forces were mutually dependant. If Theuderis led one into the depths to relieve Arkas then the remaining two would be surrounded. It was this dilemma that Lord-Relictor Glavius raised with Theuderis, as the two stood on a mansion roof above the wall that girded the slave-pit. From here they could see almost the entire circumference of the defences, and across to the other forces in the neighbouring areas.

A swathe of the city was on fire, torched by the Chaos marauders in the hope that the smoke and flames would drive out the interlopers. The swirling winds had thwarted that plan and the few dozen warriors daring enough to sneak through the fume clouds had been easily picked off by Trajos and his Judicators.

'We should already be on the heels of Arkas, my lord,' said Glavius. 'We do not know how far into the depths we must descend.'

'He knew the plan and was willing to accept the risk of his part in it,' Theuderis replied. 'Without a secure base any movement into the undercity will likely splinter and fail.'

'That is true.' Glavius looked over his shoulder towards the expanse of the slave pit. 'Even so, a degree of rapidity would not go amiss. Our route is uncertain.'

'You do not have to labour the point, Glavius.' Theuderis gestured in a wide arc, encompassing the other two Storm-cast enclaves. 'I planned for two possible approaches to the next phase of the attack. The first is to launch a three-pronged assault, each battalion collapsing in behind its Redeemer Conclaves to make steady advances into the deeps. Alternatively, we can bring the entire host to a single ingress and make one concerted push for the realmgate.'

'You speak as though you have already decided which is the better,' said Glavius. 'But perhaps are not yet ready to commit.'

'I have weighed the risks and benefits of each course, and there is little to choose between them as far as chances of success or failure go,' admitted Theuderis. 'To come together risks attack and disruption on the surface but guarantees a more cohesive assault below. To make three separate invasions shares the risk, negating the dangers of attack from the tribesmen but leaving us separated against the skaven.'

'Which would be the quicker?' asked the Lord-Relictor.

'A speedy move to defeat is pointless against a more measured advance to victory.'

Theuderis could sense his companion's frustration but he would not be cajoled into a hasty decision. He had only half the force with which he had entered Ursungorod. Though he would not shirk from sacrificing the other half if it brought victory, a hurried venture into uncertain terrain against an uncounted, unknown enemy was not his idea of a sound strategy.

'Lord...'

The tone of Glavius' voice rather than the word drew Theuderis' attention straight to the slave-pit. Several retinues of his Prosecutors were hurling their missiles into the depths while

315

the Decimators and Protectors stationed at the gantries and scaffolding withdrew, moving into more defensive postures.

Samat was a streak above, flashing down towards the Lord-Celestant, but whatever warning he thought to bring was unnecessary. Moments later Theuderis saw for himself the nature of the threat emerging from below.

Towering above the Stormcasts, a verminlord burst out of the pit, spearing a Decimator on the blades of its polearm. Missiles converged on the greater daemon, sparking and splashing from its unnatural form. In its wake a wave of robed skaven boiled out of the hole like froth overrunning a cup, streaming after their god's avatar as it slashed the head from another Knight Excelsior.

Samat descended, wings trailing spirals of celestial energy that melted the falling snow.

'We hold,' Theuderis barked. 'Take word to the other battalions to unite and make fast where they can. We will delay the foe as long as possible.'

'What of you, my lord?' asked the Knight-Azyros.

'I will make my stand here.'

Samat nodded and sped away, becoming a blur against the clouds. Theuderis took a step towards the stairs down from the roof but a hand on his arm stopped him.

'Where are you going?' said Glavius.

'To fight,' Theuderis replied.

'You cannot, my lord.' The Lord-Relictor removed his hand. 'It is more important that you lead the army.'

The Lord-Celestant looked at the skaven horde spilling from the undercity, and at the line of white and blue arranged against the dark mass.

'I will lead the defence,' Glavius continued. 'But you are needed to muster what force you can with the rest of the host.'

'No,' said Theuderis, stepping past the Lord-Relictor. 'My place is here. I am a commander, but a warrior first. The others will know what to do and will await my return.'

He would listen to no further argument and ran for the steps, heading down to ground level as swiftly as possible. Tyrathrax awaited him beside a broken-down gatehouse, padding back and forth as the sounds of battle increased.

'You cheated death once, but it comes again,' he told his steed, swinging into the saddle. 'I will be reborn. Lessened, but alive. Your spirit will return to the great flux of Azyr.'

The dracoth did not seem the least perturbed by this and threw herself into a sprint, heading down the street directly for the Stormcast line. Prosecutors and Judicators did their best with volleys of fire, and had driven the verminlord back into the pit for the time being. Against the numberless horde their celestial bolts and arrows had little impact.

Over the heads of his warriors, Theuderis spied the skaven leaders – a cabal of staff-wielding priests directing the attack from the rim of the slave-pit.

'If we do nothing but slay their commanders we will have struck a vital blow,' he bellowed to his warriors as Tyrathrax bounded through a gap between two brotherhoods of Decimators. 'Attack is the surest defence!'

Skaven bodies were flung aside by the rampage of the dracoth, while bolts of celestial energy forked from her maw to strike down even more. Theuderis' blade moved constantly, every whip-fast sweep and precise thrust finding a throat, skull or heart amongst the tightly packed skaven monks.

He could see his goal less than fifty paces away. One of the plague priests was larger than the others, swollen with warp-touch, eyes gleaming green, its staff crackling with the same power. Perhaps it was coincidence or perhaps the priest sensed Theuderis' approach. It turned its eyes towards the Lord-Celestant. He thought to see concern, knowing skaven were a fearful breed in their hearts. He was met with a stare of hatred so intense he almost felt it like a blow.

Screeching, the priest pointed its staff at Theuderis, waving a fresh mob of priests towards the Knight Excelsior. Dozens more furred and robed creatures scampered into the space ahead of Theuderis.

Tyrathrax stumbled. A skaven corpse was tangled around her front leg by a frayed rope belt. It was almost nothing, and she quickly recovered, but the loss of momentum proved consequential. The plague monks pressed in harder still, swamping the dracoth and her rider, battering and hacking from every direction. No matter how quickly Theuderis struck, or how viciously Tyrathrax bit and clawed, their progress was slowed to a halt.

Skinny fingers with broken claws grasped and scraped at Theuderis and plucked at the armour of his steed. Rusted blades found the saddle-cinch and moments later the Lord-Celestant felt himself slipping sideways, dragged down by dozens of scabbed, blistered hands.

Tyrathrax howled as she too was overwhelmed, buried beneath a living, snarling avalanche of frenzied rat-beasts. Theuderis managed to twist to his feet as the dracoth pitched sideways and the saddle fell free. He could barely see anything, tatters of cloth across his face, gore and blood clotting the joints of his armour. He struck out with blade and fist, but could not fight his way free.

His mask was ripped away and he caught a glimpse of vermin faces, drooling and manic. He tasted rusted metal. It was confusing, until he realised the blade had entered his mouth from beneath his chin.

He rolled over, crushing the plague monk beneath his bulk, but half a dozen leapt onto his back, using the edges of his armour plates as handholds, hammering and stabbing with delirious intensity.

Pushing himself to one knee, the Lord-Celestant swept his sword in a broad arc, severing the legs of a handful of foes. Something pierced his cheek from behind and he reached back to pluck the offending attacker from his shoulder. With a grunt he smashed the squealing skaven into another robed foe, breaking the spines of both.

He was almost upright when his knee gave way, tendons severed by the sawing of jagged knives. A serrated sword entered his eye, not quite deep enough to pierce the brain. Roaring from the pain he punched the head from the monk trying to drag the weapon free.

And then Theuderis fell, toppled to his back by the weight of his foes. He saw a last glimpse of grey clouds, the snow falling heavily.

Through swimming vision he saw the priest, the one with the jade eyes. There was something in its chest, revealed through the tatters of its robe, smoking and bubbling in a patch of scorched fur. It raised its staff, the skull at its tip chattering wildly, though the sound was distorted, muffled, masked by the drumming of the Lord-Celestant's heart and the lessening throb of fleeing blood.

The pain stopped.

Furnace heat. Searing. Melting. Reforming.

Hammers crash. A forge, not battle. Anvils ring. Thunder rumbles.

Sparks, bright. Forks of lightning. The glow of forges. Starlight above.

Sulphur and hot steel. Charcoal. Boiling blood and charred flesh.

CHAPTER FORTY-FIVE

He heard chanting – his name – and Ermenberga waved him towards the parapet.

'Your subjects await you,' she said, eyes moist with joy. She patted her stomach meaningfully, 'and soon you will have other news to brighten their spirits further. I think it is a boy...'

Theuderic was struck dumb, his thoughts whirling. He pulled himself up onto the rampart edge. His army, led by princes and dukes and war leaders of many other castles and citadels, erupted into even greater noise, such that Theuderic almost didn't hear the rumbling of thunder above.

He looked up and saw that the darkening sky was filling with ominous clouds. Fearing some last treachery of the alter-folk, Theuderic glanced back at his family.

With his name still ringing in his ears, and the loving, upturned faces of his wife and children etched into his mind, Theuderic juddered as a bolt scythed through his body without warning.

In a moment, all that he knew, the wide plains and jagged hills *of the Glittering Breaches, dropped down beneath him. The great keeps and fortresses of his lands became specks of gold and silver before they too were lost, and in a moment the blur of the Auric Shield of Lyonaster disappeared from view.*

He thought for a moment that he had been swallowed by a star, suffused with light and heat.

Pain returned.

He retreated, letting it consume his body, protecting his mind from its ravages.

In time the agony became a dull ache.

Theuderic was consumed by the storm, reforged into the Silverhand. But he was not yet Stormcast again, merely a mote of power hanging in the firmament of the quenching chamber. An idea bound into a miniature star. Celestial energy awaiting form.

He rebuilt himself without thought. Mind, body, armour.

Re-clad, Theuderis Silverhand waited for the last of the pain to wash away. The walls of the quenching chamber fell away with a last crackle of lightning, leaving the Lord-Celestant standing upon white marble floors, the high crystal-paned vaults of Sigmaron above him.

He was not alone.

Like shades from the past, the dead Knights Excelsior stood in ranks close at hand, waiting patiently for the return of their commander. There were fewer than he had feared.

Were the rest still in Ursungorod, or yet to be remade? Was the battle already lost?

A single note rang across the chamber, resonating inside his mind. A summons he could not ignore.

With swift strides he made his way to the grand hall of the

God-King. Through great arches and windows he saw scores of other Strike Chambers from half a dozen Stormhosts gathered about their commanders, awaiting the Tempest of the God-King to send them on their missions. There was motion everywhere, columns and flights of Stormcasts ready to add their strength to the ongoing campaign to seize back the realmgates.

Entering the hall of his lord, the Silverhand found Sigmar sitting statue-like upon his throne, a giant that dwarfed even the Stormcasts of his armies. He was clad in golden armour, and his hair and beard flowed in the celestial gale that surrounded him.

The Warbeast was already present, some distance from his lord, bent to one knee, head bowed.

Theuderis tried to avert his gaze but the moment before he did so, the God-King looked directly at him. He expected anger, perhaps disappointment. He felt nothing but understanding, even admiration.

'We failed, Lord Sigmar,' Theuderis whispered, taking position next to Arkas. 'Ursungorod is lost.'

The God-King rose from his throne and approached. As he neared them he seemed to grow smaller. His presence did not diminish in any way, but his form shifted, so that when he was standing almost within reach he was just a little taller than the Lord-Celestants.

'Rise,' the God-King commanded. They obeyed. 'You have not yet failed. There is still time.'

Theuderis thought he would have been more moved by this revelation, but his mood was level, his spirit placid. Cold, even.

The Warbeast had not looked at him, but out of the corner of his eye Theuderis could see the Celestial Vindicator. His hands were fists, shoulders hunched. There was a palpable aura of anger emanating from him.

'The division of our enemies has granted us opportunity,' Sigmar continued. 'The skaven and the Chaos tribes war with each other. Lord Silverhand, half of your force survived and awaits your return not far from the city.'

Theuderis nodded, accepting this fact without comment. Sigmar turned his attention to Arkas.

'The Warbeasts were not so fortunate, but they have been reforged.' The God-King crossed his arms. 'You have one chance more to seize the realmgate. Lord-Castellant Durathos stands ready still. You will take the realmgate and summon Durathos to bring forth his Knights Excelsior.'

'I will lead the attack,' growled Arkas. Now he looked at Theuderis and there was a sullen rage behind his gaze. 'This time there will be no hesitation.'

Sigmar raised a hand to silence Theuderis' protest before it was voiced.

'The assault on the All-gates is fast-approaching. I can spare no other Strike Chambers for the attack on Ursungorod.' Sigmar looked from Arkas to Theuderis and back again. 'Arkas, return to your Strike Chamber and prepare for the Tempest. Your hour of vengeance has not yet passed.'

Arkas hurriedly raised a fist in salute and stalked away. Theuderis watched him depart, already calculating a strategy that would take into account the Warbeast's increased fury.

'I do not understand why you approve of such ill-discipline, Lord Sigmar,' he said when Arkas was out of sight. 'These Warbeasts are barely controllable. Unfit to be Stormcasts.'

Sigmar's expression soured.

'It is not your place to question my judgement.' He relented as Theuderis again sank to one knee in silent apology. 'But I will indulge you on this occasion. My Celestial Vindicators are rough gems, that is certain. They are unpredictable, often barbaric. Not every great hero of the Mortal Realms is a prince or knight, Lord Theuderis. The Warbeasts are savage, relentless and meteoric. Let them be free and they will take you to the realmgate.'

'Arkas seems possessed by an even greater wrath than before.'

'Aye,' said Sigmar. His gaze moved away, as though looking at the departed Warbeast. 'His Reforging was costly.'

'Angry commanders make poor decisions, my lord,' Theuderis said.

'But they make decisions,' Sigmar said, and Theuderis flinched at the words. 'They take risks which can achieve great reward. Not all problems can be solved before a blade has been raised. Have you ever considered that I might *want* Arkas to be angry?'

The thought had never occurred to the Silverhand and his silence was admission of the fact.

'Go,' said the God-King. 'The tempest of war calls you. Strike with the speed and fury of my wrath.'

'Your wrath, my blade,' Theuderis replied.

CHAPTER FORTY-SIX

'A sight that pleases me greatly.'

Felk shuddered as the verminlord's words scuttled into his ears, sending tiny shockwaves through his system. Whiskers and tail twitching like disturbed serpents, the Poxmaster looked out across the city. He could see everything from the vandalised faces carved from the mountain rock. The snow fell thick in places over the masses of the dead, freezing the dying. Fires raged elsewhere, their glow lighting broken buildings and ruin-cluttered streets.

Here and there bands of skaven and the human tribes still clashed. The noise of their skirmishes carried far in the quiet aftermath of the skaven attack.

'Late-late,' mused Felk, swallowing hard. 'Long time needed.'

'Yes,' said Skixakoth. 'Vermalanx throws war at the sylvaneth queen, but is blind to other routes to victory. His fall shall be my rise.'

Felk said nothing. He had known he tampered with the

schemes of beings far greater than him, but it had seemed a distant, abstract danger. Now there were warriors of Sigmar – Stormcasts they were called – bringing battle against him, and verminlord Corruptors taking an interest in his schemes.

Yet not for a heartbeat did he regret any action or decision. If not to be the greatest, if not to be seen by the eyes of the Great Corruptor, what was the point of existence? Though by nature his body was weak and cowardly, his ideals held him to a greater standard. He was driven by ambition, not courage, but would, when tested, prefer death to failure and slavery.

'We will kill-kill storm warriors and nothing will stop us,' said Felk. He could see the azure glow from the host of the giant warriors. They had taken up position on the mountainside between the city and the fire peaks.

'No.' The single word made Felk flinch. 'The Whiteworld Above is of no consequence. The realmgate is open, our forces united. Vermalanx will fail and I will rise.'

Skixakoth strode away, tail lashing back and forth. Felk hissed at his back, emboldened again by the verminlord's departure. He waited until the daemon of the Horned Rat had descended into the passages behind the duardin kings' memorial.

'I smell you,' he said quietly. 'Strong fear, yes?'

Thriss emerged from the shadows to the left.

'I am Eshin,' said the gutter runner. 'No friend to Corruptors of the Horned One.'

'But serve me?'

'For payment.' Thriss flashed fangs in the gloom. 'For *more* payment?'

Felk fought back a threat. He had little bargaining power left since the arrival of the verminlord. He sighed.

'Yes-yes. Double warpstone. Triple slaves. Yes-yes?'

Head cocked to one side, Thriss considered the offer and then nodded.

'Good-good.' Felk scratched at the open wound containing Skixakoth's fang. His eyes strayed back to the Stormcasts upon the hill. They had not fled, but were waiting for something. He had heard the verminlord taunting one of the giant's commanders, the one that had tried to seize the realmgate directly. Its words had implied that death was no barrier to Sigmar's chosen. They could return. The wheels of his mind turned and he looked at Thriss. 'Fetch Skarth. Have missions for two of you.'

CHAPTER FORTY-SEVEN

Even the storm that had heralded the arrival of the Warbeasts paled in comparison to the Tempest of Sigmar's power that boiled through the sky over Kurzengor. The stars turned blue and then were swallowed by the thunderheads of celestial energy blanketing the heavens from horizon to horizon.

In the city skaven and human alike looked up at the immense magical conflagration and knew that war was not yet finished in Ursungorod. The boom of a single thunderclap was like the bellows of the God-King himself, toppling decrepit buildings, bringing avalanches of snow and rock tumbling down the mountainside onto the outskirts of the ancient city.

The flare of lightning started an instant later. It peaked in just a few heartbeats, hundreds of strikes lashing the mountain around the perimeter of the Stormcast position. So fierce was the return of the Warbeasts and fallen Silverhands that the snow was turned to rivers of meltwater cascading down over rocks and down gullies to flood into the contested city below.

A corona of power still crackling around him, Arkas Warbeast sucked in a deep lungful of air. Almost immediately he could feel the wash of Ghurite energy, the spirit of Ursungorod welcoming him back with a feral snarl in the back of his mind.

The Reforging had awakened the spirit of the Bear-clad again, but this time it had not dissipated. Arkas and Arka existed as one and the same. There was no more doubt, no inner conflict, just a rage, pure and focused, an animal instinct to slay his foes without thought of the consequence. It felt good. He felt stronger. Stronger than he had been before.

Released. Freed.

His gaze found Theuderis, who, sitting astride his dracoth, was surrounded by a growing cadre of Silverhands officers. Knights-Heraldor and Knights-Vexillor dashed from the Stormcast encampment to greet their returned brethren and receive their commands, while the ranks of the Knights Excelsior stood silent guard.

Dolmetis and Doridun approached, several Primes a few steps behind them.

'My lord,' the Knight-Vexillor began, but Arkas cut him off with a snarl. It was hard to form words, to bring some coherent thought from the swirl of anger that embroiled his mind.

'I will speak to Lord Silverhand and then we attack,' he said, pushing past the knot of Stormcasts.

The Silverhands parted at his approach. Theuderis saw the Warbeast's mood and bade his officers to depart a short distance. His dracoth snorted and snarled as Arkas approached, nostrils flaring. The Silverhand dismounted and offered a salute.

'Your mount takes a dislike to me,' said Arkas, meeting the hostile glare of the dracoth. It backed away several steps.

The Silverhand patted the monster's shoulder. He turned his

gaze back to the Warbeast, his tone clipped and precise. 'We will attack in a single, coordinated assault.'

'We will,' replied Arkas. He reigned in his emotions, leashing the animal that was trying to break free. 'I will lead, you will follow. We kill everything we meet until there is nothing left to kill.'

'Yes, but we n–'

'We strike now.' Arkas drew in a deep breath through his nose, pushing the bestial growl from his voice. 'The skaven still fight with the tribes. They cannot both attack and defend.'

He feared what might happen if Theuderis prevaricated further and so turned away. His officers fell in beside him, silent, cowed by his demeanour.

'Warbeasts!' He raised his hammer, a signal for mustering. When the Stormcasts had assembled, he lowered the weapon to point to the city below. 'We fight. We kill. We win.'

'We fight. We kill. We win.' The chorus growled from the throats of his immortal warriors, echoed from their masked helms. 'We fight. We kill. We win. We fight. We kill. We win.'

With this martial chant filling the air, Dolmetis raised the standard of the Warbeasts high and Doridun let forth a blast from his clarion. The call became a thunderous roll from the storm and a single stroke of lightning flashed to crackle down the icon of the Knight-Vexillor.

'Sigmar commands it,' laughed Dolmetis. 'He blesses the deaths of our foes.'

'We fight!' Arkas' voice rose over the continuing tempest-clamour in the skies. 'We kill! We win!'

CHAPTER
FORTY-EIGHT

Ignoring the insult of Arkas' actions, Theuderis watched with detached interest as the Celestial Vindicators commenced their bellowing and chanting. It was quite unseemly, the display of brute emotion, but he remembered the words of Sigmar: *Let them be free and they will take you to the realmgate.* Considering the words again it seemed that they were not so much an instruction as a foretelling. Did mighty Sigmar have insight beyond the present? Could he know what would happen?

Every part of Theuderis' calculating mind railed against another impetuous, ad-hoc assault into the undercity. It made no sense that what had failed before would succeed this time, even if the skaven were currently occupied with trying to retake the city from the humans.

Yet his master had commanded, and the part of him that was the loyal knight could not refuse Sigmar's will. Oaths had been sworn, promises must be upheld.

'Follow the Warbeasts,' he told his officers. 'All brotherhoods.'

'What of a rearguard, my lord?' asked Attaxes. 'The city is filled with foes that might fall upon us as we pass.'

'My orders were clear, Knight-Heraldor. Sound the general advance.'

Progress through Kurzengor was even swifter than during the Stormcasts' first assault. Without delaying to secure their flanks or finish off the scattered bands of humans or skaven that crossed their path, the Warbeasts and Silverhands had slashed their way through to the centre of the city by the time dawn was rising, fully a day after their initial attack had begun.

Knowing that speed was more valuable than stealth, Arkas led the force not to the slave-pit where they had descended before, but to an area of the city where many of the buildings and streets had collapsed and subsided, undermined by the skaven tunnelling below. Where the duardin parts of the city had been extended by the gnawholes of the skaven, entire districts had been swallowed. In the twilight before sunrise, the unnatural gleam of fungi and warpstone lit cracks and holes from below, a dull beacon that drew Arkas on.

The army of Sigmar's chosen plunged down through the ruins by chasms and caves, bursting into the cellars of toppled mansions and the crypts of looted temples. They came upon an immense cavern dominated by the piled ruins of the buildings that had fallen from the surface.

The outer parts of the skaven city were a maze of hovels, ragged tents and reclaimed buildings patched and reinforced by a mad scattering of debris. As well as covering the brick-strewn ground, the city teetered up the bases of massive stalagmites, the towers crisscrossed with bridges and walkways, ratlines running from the roofs to the tips of hollowed stalactites. From the midst of this scavenged urban tangle, a causeway of masonry and mud cut back and forth out of the buildings until it met with the broad stones of what had formerly been the vaulting arches of a human temple.

This dismal edifice speared like a living mountain from the effluence and trash of the undercity, in places shaped by the hands of humans, in others crafted by duardin skill, all smeared and smashed together with reckless abandon by the Chaos ratmen.

The pilaster of decay was wreathed in fumes and vapours that issued from smokeholes and chimneys and rose from streams of filth and sluggish rivers that dribbled from stolen gutters and cracked sewer lines.

Its peak seemed broken, a tangle of splintered wood and split rope, collapsed gear housings and huge wheels piled atop each other. The remnants of something bronze embedded in the structure glinted in the witchlight of countless warpstone-fuelled lanterns.

Though a great many of the skaven contested the city above, their undercity was not undefended. Streams of ratmen poured forth from the filthy warren, setting upon the Stormcasts from all sides. From the depths of the central mass marched forth columns of robed plague monks, swaying in time to the bells and gongs, thirteen tendrils of matted fur and dirty cloth each led by a ranting plague priest.

Arkas and the Warbeasts speared into the heart of the skaven, driving deep through their line and across the causeway leading to their shrine. Possessed by his fury, Arkas paid no heed to defence, but such was the ferocity of his coming none survived to land a blow upon the plates of his armour. His hammer and runeblade slew everything they touched, killing with single blows, their celestial power fuelled by his rage.

Commanded by Theuderis, the Silverhands were more

deliberate but no less swift in their encroachment. Like the horns of a bull, brotherhoods of Paladins swept out around the cavern, each tipped by winged Prosecutors. The Lord-Celestant and his Redeemer Conclave formed the centre, pushing steadily through the ramshackle huts and streets, churning through skaven warriors with irrepressible force.

There was little thought to Arkas' approach. Even the simple mantra, 'We fight. We kill. We win,' had devolved into something even less specific – a primal desire to destroy. A *need* to slay. Pure animal fury, defending the nest, the attack of a predator, the battle for dominance of the herd. Unthinking and savage, it pushed Arkas further and further into the undercity, the spirit of Ghur that writhed in his gut calling him deeper and deeper into the belly of Ursungorod.

CHAPTER
FORTY-NINE

The plague monks attacked Theuderis directly, trying to break between the Knights Excelsior and the Celestial Vindicators. The Silverhand could see the crude strategy unfolding like jittering clockwork – a spasmodic mechanism that was easy to disrupt. He called to his Judicators and before the skaven had made much headway they were confronted by volley after volley of flaming missiles and celestial bolts.

Impetus was the key, and he did not allow the attack to sway him from his course – his brotherhoods had to keep pace with the haste of the Warbeasts' advance. Yet for all his endeavours, he could not prevent a separation occurring. His army was simply more unwieldy than the compact force of Arkas, and more prone to delay by the unforgiving terrain and surging assaults of the plague monks.

Arkas was almost gone from view, forging towards one of the corridors to the lower levels, when another factor further impinged upon Theuderis' evolving strategy. From upon the

walls and buttressed towers of the massive temple, catapults
hurled festering payloads of rocks and waste. Encrusted pots
and slime-covered boulders crashed into the Knights Excelsior. The impacts were severe but it was the splash of noxious,
warp-strengthened filth that proved the greater threat. Like
the fume cloud of the plague rats and censer bearers, these
missiles carried a toxic mix of infection and acidic vapour
that hissed and bubbled across the armour of the Silverhands.

Prosecutors sped up from the city, unleashing salvoes of
lightning-wreathed missiles against the crews of the machines
and falling upon them with blazing hammers. Freed from the
swooping attacks of these warriors, the plague monks below
charged down the causeway and thrust up from the catacombs,
attacking with renewed fervour.

For all that Arkas and his warriors crashed into the foe
with unmatched ferocity, these fresh attacks dragged at
the flanks and heels of the Warbeasts, slowing their impetus. Skaven forces arriving from deeper into the mountain
swarmed up the tunnels, confronting the Celestial Vindicators head-on, choking the path to the depths with a mob of
hissing Chaos vermin.

The horns of the attack had also stalled, not quite encircling
the cavern as Theuderis had intended. Glavius fought at the
head of one tip, trying to break through to Arkas' increasingly beleaguered position, but the weight of enemies before
him was still increasing. On the other flank, Theuderis could
see the icon of his Strike Chamber amongst the broken buildings where Voltaran had similarly been swamped by skaven.

The situation threatened to spiral out of Theuderis' control.
The whirring gears of his mind processed every extant aspect
of the battle, analysing and assaying possible strategies, dis-
carding them all in turn. Even as Tyrathrax spat lightning and

his blade bisected wailing skaven, he focused his thoughts on a single purpose.

The realmgate. Deliver the Warbeast to the realmgate.

Cursing his own stupidity, he realised that he did not have to be with Arkas to protect him. If the Celestial Vindicators could reach the realmgate their icon would act as a lode-star for Durathos, who was waiting with an entire Strike Chamber in Sigmaron. Theuderis just had to protect the Warbeasts' backs to allow them to get close enough.

Before he could enact his plan, the atmosphere in the cavern changed. A foetid wind blew across the burning, broken skaven slum, bringing with it the acrid taste of warpstone and an even deeper stench of decay and ruin.

The verminlord.

It was silhouetted against the dawn light at one of the gashes into the city above, towering over a sea of its verminous followers. A spark of warpfire from its spear lit the air.

At the same time, almost directly opposite Skixakoth, the chief plague priest appeared at the gate atop the causeway. Theuderis remembered the wound in its chest, and could see the gleam of warp-power from beneath the creature's robes.

It mattered not. Theuderis' disparate trains of thought came together, the pieces of the plan sliding into place like the levers of a carefully machined duardin engine. At its centre, the gear around which it all revolved, was Arkas. One piece of wisdom from the God-King shone bright in Theuderis' mind, perhaps another semi-prophetic pronouncement, masked as a question: *Have you ever considered that I might* want *Arkas to be angry?'*

'Samat!' The Silverhand's call cut through the clamour of weapons and shrieking of rat-warriors. Even as the Knight-Azyros heard his lord's command, he turned on glittering wings and sped down.

'What orders, my lord?'

'Take this to Arkas and make him listen.' Theuderis followed with his message, clearly enunciating every word. 'Say it exactly as I told you. Make sure the Warbeast hears it.'

Whether he understood the implications of the message or not, Samat flew away, shafts of dull sunlight from above catching his white form as he cruised over the battle.

Theuderis cleaved his way free of the skaven that had been pressing up around him. His gaze moved from the plague priest to the verminlord, assessing the validity of the two courses of action before him. To attack one left his forces vulnerable to the other.

'A reckoning,' he told his dracoth, turning her towards the verminlord. He raised his voice to a thunderous bellow. 'Silverhands, today the plan is simple. We fight! We kill! We win!'

CHAPTER FIFTY

Fatigue was a greater enemy than the Chaos-tainted rat-creatures that fell beneath Arkas' blade and hammer. As a fire burns its fuel, so the celestial force that powered the Warbeast – the very same essence of Sigmar from which his entire being was formed – was consumed by the rage of the Lord-Celestant. He could feel his power waning, sapped by every blow that decapitated and eviscerated.

Around him frothed waves of magic, swells of Ghurite energy trying to pierce his will as the skaven weapons tried to pierce his armour. It sought the chinks in his consciousness, flashing memories of standing upon a wall looking down upon a desolate field as the skaven poured forth on their conquest. It was a voice inside his head, saying nothing, but its panting, bestial presence was a constant temptation to free himself.

He had sworn oaths, to serve Sigmar, to be Stormcast. The God-King granted him life, an immortal existence, in exchange for his service. The celestial force that ebbed from his body was the same power that sustained him.

A shout pierced the ruddy cloud of his thoughts. A name. His name.

He stepped back, allowing his Decimators to push on around him, hacking and crushing, their axes and maces glowing with mystical force. The voice called again and he looked up to see an angelic being above, ivory and blue lit by a halo of distorted sunlight.

Something arced down towards him, catching the light. The Knight-Azyros, Samat. He hovered just above Arkas, his wings of lightning flickering with power.

'A message, Warbeast!' the Knight Excelsior called down. 'From my lord, Theuderis Silverhand. "The taint will be purged. Your people are dead".'

Shaking his head, Arkas did not grasp the importance of the words. His mind laboured over their meaning, but intellectual thought was made impossible by a rising tide of pure instinct, a subconscious understanding that swept through him.

Pain. The pain of memory. Katiya lying on the bier, plague eating her from the inside.

But not Katiya. His mother. No, his sister.

Confusion, torment, the agony of failure.

An oath. Words spoken on the deathbed of his mother-sister. A promise older than his fealty to Sigmar.

A promise unfulfilled.

Snatched away by the God-King. Friends, companions, family left to die and be enslaved.

His land abandoned.

Ursungorod betrayed.

But he would save his people. The omens...

The words came to him, crystal-clear across the vast ages.

'I did not say our people would be saved,' Radomira chided. *'You must pay attention to detail, I have told you before. I said from the events of this day our lands will be freed.'*

Failure. Again.

Arkas tore off the mask of his helm and howled, feeling the rush of Ghurite energy pounding into him like water through a broken dam. The spirit of Ursungorod filled him where the power celestial had diminished.

This time he did not fight it. He welcomed it.

He barely noticed his Stormcasts moving away, forming a defensive circle around their stricken commander. Arkas' thoughts were a vortex of pain.

The Lord-Celestant accepted the pain, took it as his own. It was a burden he had carried as Arka Bear-clad, a role he had abdicated as Arkas Warbeast.

He let the Ursungorod pit pull him down, funnelling his pain into a bright star of frustrated rage, drawing him into the heart of the mountain – into the Shadowgulf where all light and hope died.

Here the power of Ghur found its home.

Arkas touched something vast and cosmic. He felt it stretching out into the impossible gulfs between realms. A fragment, an avatar, a memory from the world-that-was. The spirit of Ursungorod, trapped and in agony for countless lifetimes, ravaged by the fires of Chaos, split and rent and broken, a body of fallen mountains, chasms and cracks. His flesh crawled as he felt the aching emptiness of skaven gnaw-ways burrowing through his immortal frame like worms and maggots, trying to corrupt him from within.

He shuddered at the pain, and the world above shuddered with him.

Arkas ascended again, sent up through the rock like a mote

lifted on a geyser, a channel, a conduit for the eternal rage of the spirit buried under the mountains. With a bestial roar that shook the cavern of the undercity, he burst back into his body, immolating himself with the power of Ghur, burning with the vengeful fire of the beast.

The mountain broke.

CHAPTER FIFTY-ONE

The power manifested itself as a monstrous bear, a churning maelstrom of erupting force that hurled half of the mountain skywards with its eruption. Thousands of skaven were drawn up by the raging beast as its slavering maw and immaterial claws swept through them, their terrified squeals and shrieks swallowed by the earth-shattering boom of the roar it shared with Arkas.

The undercity was ripped asunder, its jagged innards exposed by the rising of the beast. The incarnation of Ursungorod's spirit became a thick cloud, a creation of dust and shattered stone that roiled away into the dawn light, leaving sunbeams lancing down into the heart of the broken peak. Skaven bodies fell like hail.

Panting, snarling, infused with the beast-magic, Arkas squinted against a painful light. Something blinding and golden shone in the depths. The realmgate sat fully exposed on its dais, the cities of men, duardin and skaven scoured clear. The archway was alight with magic, flames licking from the stones in fluttering golden waves.

'Go!' he commanded his warriors, dragging the word out of the depths of his mind, language almost forgotten. He thrust a finger towards the exposed realmgate. '*Go!*'

The Celestial Vindicators hesitated, unsure of what was happening. It was Doridun who reacted first, lifting his clarion to signal the charge. Dolmetis responded, turning to lead the attack into the crater left where the Ursun-spirit had erupted.

The ivory-clad warriors of Theuderis were spearing towards the verminlord, the Silverhand leading the charge from the back of his dracoth. Arkas set his sights on another target. From the causeway spilled the plague monks, yelling and screaming their praises as they launched themselves into the flank of the Silverhands' attack. The leader stood at the gate still, surrounded by ranks of his armoured elite.

Letting the Ghurite magic flow through him, allowing the beast-power to push aside the celestial force that had created him, Arkas broke into a run. He took up his weapon two-handed as he charged, but as he leapt into the attack, hewing at the robed skaven with revitalised strength, he swung not a hammer, the symbol of Sigmar almighty, but a great axe.

The axe of his mother.

Rocks fell like meteors onto Stormcast and skaven alike, though it was the latter that suffered the greater casualties from the plummeting remnants of the mountain. Theuderis was not sure he would ever understand what had just happened. He had thought to rejuvenate Arkas' flagging assault, but the consequences of unleashing the Warbeast's full anger were far greater than anything he could have expected.

Despite the surprise manifestation of cosmic power, the

battle was not yet won. The verminlord descended into the cavern, its presence spurring the skaven into apoplectic fury. Billowing spews of noxious magic engulfed the Stormcasts as they attempted to surround the greater daemon, seeping into their armour, choking and burning them inside the moulded sigmarite.

The counter-attack from the despicable temple was dragging more of Theuderis' warriors away from the main thrust towards the greater daemon. There was nothing the Lord-Celestant could do to prevent his warriors defending themselves, but the consequence was a faltering assault, his force drawn into two battles.

For good or ill he had to remain committed to the course of action he had chosen. The Celestial Vindicators were heading for the realmgate. Arkas himself fought like fifty Stormcasts as he chopped his way into the ranks of the plague monks. The preservation of his force for its own sake was of no value. He had to destroy the verminlord or any attempt to protect the realmgate would be in jeopardy.

Felk was still stunned by the explosion of Ghurite energy that had rocked the mountain and torn the heart out of his city. His ears rang with the noise of the detonation and his vision was blurred by the unwelcome dawnlight slanting from where the peak of the mountain had once been.

The one that had summoned the beast was death given form, ripping his way into Felk's followers like a claw tearing at unprotected flesh. Though the plague priest and his closest council stood behind the lines of spitevermin, he felt far from safe. Apparently Felk's underlings did not feel the same.

'Not lost-lost,' squeaked Festik. He jabbed a claw down towards the dust cloud-swathed lower levels. Giants in turquoise armour were clambering into the ruin, obviously intent on the realmgate. 'Attack-attack, from behind!'

'Mighty Skixakoth leads us to victory,' exclaimed Chittir, redirecting the Poxmaster's attention to where the vermin-lord was slaying the Sigmar-chosen with wide sweeps and armour-piercing thrusts of its crackling spear.

'Attack-attack!' parroted Priest Kirrik. 'Snap-snap like rat ogre jaws!'

Felk looked at them with contempt. The fang of Skixakoth trembled and burned in his chest, reminding him of the plan.

'Fools,' he hissed. 'Treachery! Make peace with Skixakoth against me? Only one rules the Withering Canker. Praise Felk!' He glanced at Skarth and nodded.

The fangleader cut the head from Kirrik with a single blow from his halberd. The other two plague priests turned on their betrayer with raised blades. Festik gurgled blood as Thriss struck from behind, emerging unseen from the ranks of spite-vermin, weeping blade taking the priest across the throat. Felk deflected the attack of Chittir, his warp-infused body barely registering the pain as the rusted blade cut through his robes and caught in the flesh of his arm. He tore out the priest's throat with a slash of sparking claws.

Stepping over the bodies, Felk squealed a command to his remaining underlings and then disappeared into the Great Shrine, heading for the tunnels in the lower levels. The spitevermin followed, trampling the bodies of the dead plague priests.

Thriss remained a little longer, watching as the plague monks under the sway of Felk melted away from the fighting. The war-leader that glowed with painful fire was getting closer. Tail trembling, Thriss dashed after his employer.

CHAPTER FIFTY-TWO

The beast-possessed Arkas hewed a bloody path through the remaining plague monks. The inexplicable departure of the plague priest and many of its followers left Theuderis with no distractions. Rallying his warriors with a shout, the Silverhand pressed on towards Skixakoth.

The verminlord wreaked carnage amongst the Stormcasts, its doom-wreathed weapon crackling and steaming as bolts of celestial energy shot skywards from dismembered warriors. The chosen of Sigmar did not fall lightly. Starsoul maces and thunderaxes boomed as they struck the greater daemon's immaterial flesh. Flickers of celestial lightning trailed from warblades as they cut its unholy skin.

The skaven frothed around the periphery of the combat between Skixakoth and Theuderis' warriors, sometimes bringing down a Silverhand from behind, more often cut down themselves by a backswing or trampled underfoot by the massive warriors. The verminlord cared nothing for its followers and the wide sweeps of its four-tined spear struck down more skaven than Knights Excelsior.

Into this melee burst Theuderis' dracoth, snarling, forks of blue lightning springing from her open jaw. Skixakoth turned towards the Lord-Celestant, the shimmer of heavenly power creeping across its arcane armour.

Theuderis felt nothing when the murderous gaze of the greater daemon fell upon him. Neither fear nor triumph nor anger troubled his heart. The verminlord was just another problem to solve, another enigma to unravel. Victory depended upon finding the solution, nothing more.

Tyrathrax responded as though an extension of his body, leaping aside as the enormous spear of the verminlord lanced towards her rider. Theuderis' sword caught the weapon behind its barbed head, the star-forged blade leaving a notch in the ensorcelled metal. The force of the clash almost knocked him from the dracoth, but he clutched the saddle horn and hung on while Tyrathrax leapt at Skixakoth, claws raking across its thigh.

The skaven drew back from the duel, fearful of the white warrior that dared face their demigod. Not so the Silverhands, who leapt to the attack with jubilant shouts, hammering and slashing with renewed determination.

'For the glory of Sigmar!' they chorused.

Its barbed tail lashing limbs and heads from its attackers, the verminlord snatched up a Liberator, encasing his head in its massive claw. Plague-magic churned, turning flesh to a molten slurry that dripped from the armour before a flare of celestial power carried the warrior's spirit back to Sigmar.

Theuderis lunged with his runeblade, thrusting the tip into a gap in the daemon's armour below its outstretched arm. Snarling curses, Skixakoth spun away, the haft of its spear crashing against Theuderis' shoulder, unseating him and throwing him to the ground. The dracoth moved to put herself between her master and his foe.

Recovering, the verminlord loomed over beast and Lord-Celestant, hatred flowing from it like waves of heat. Ichor streamed from rents in its armour and its horns were cracked and broken, but in the depths of the helm, twin eyes of warp-fire pinned Theuderis in place.

On his back, the Lord-Celestant was defenceless.

Except for one manoeuvre. A sacrificial move.

The spear-points descended and Theuderis acted without hesitation, rolling underneath Tyrathrax. The tines of the daemonic weapon followed him, lancing into the head and shoulders of the dracoth, piercing armour, flesh and skull.

Theuderis continued his roll while Skixakoth tried to drag its spear free, emerging from beneath the collapsing dracoth. Using her crumpling body as a step he launched himself at the verminlord, slamming the point of his sword through the eye slit of its helm. Grabbing a stump of horn, he rode the greater daemon as it staggered back, drawing out his blade to ram it into the other eye, pushing with all of his strength until the crosspiece ground against the unearthly material of the verminlord's helm.

The greater daemon folded into itself, its grip on the Mortal Realm severed. The physical form of the verminlord fell apart, becoming hundreds of rat corpses, mangy and boil-ridden, that melted into a viscous pool beneath Theuderis as he landed on the filth-covered ground.

Still victory was not certain. The Stormcasts were surrounded, their enemies beyond counting. The gleam of celestial energy in the depths reminded Theuderis of the mission.

'Glavius!' he bellowed. 'Summon the Lord-Castellant!'

The Lord-Relictor held aloft his mortuary staff, chanting an invocation to the God-King. A stream of lightning leapt from the tip of his icon and then dissipated into the air. Nothing happened.

'The warpstone corrupts everything, the Celestial Realm is blind to us,' said the Lord-Relictor. 'I cannot summon them.'

'The realmgate, can you use its power?' asked Theuderis.

'It is too far,' replied Glavius, looking towards the distant crater. 'Unless...'

The Lord-Relictor again held up his bone-clad staff and called upon Sigmar. This time the bolt of energy did not launch skywards, but seared across the cavern, seeking the tip of the icon wielded by Arkas' Knight-Vexillor, Dolmetis. The celestial power flashed like a beacon fire lit and then leapt again, forking madly as it earthed into the pillars of the realmgate.

The sickly glowing runes dimmed, their yellow-green light replaced by the azure blaze of heavenly power. Like a hurricane unwinding, the vortex of energy surrounding the gate became a near-blinding star. In the depths, the realmgate shuddered, the stone of its structure cracking, splinters falling away from its surface.

The realmgate burst with another detonation of power. Ignited by the celestial energy of Glavius, the cosmic portal shed the stone prison the duardin had laid upon it, turning the archway to shards and dust. In its place burned a white flame, tongues of fire licking across the stones and caressing the air. A pulse of energy snapped back along the route of the beacon-power, jumping from Dolmetis' icon to the mortuary-relic of Glavius.

'Sigmar!' the Lord-Relictor bellowed, channelling the renewed power through his body, sending it as a surge of lightning that flared into the skies revealed by the collapse of the mountain.

In an instant, scores of lightning blasts flashed down in reply.

Theuderis saw a bright flash of golden light reflected against what was left of the cavern ceiling. He turned as horn blasts reverberated around the chamber of the shrine, announcing the arrival of Lord-Castellant Durathos.

Faced with the death of their god's avatar and the drum of marching boots from the depths, the skaven faltered and scattered, bolting for whatever runs and holes they could find.

Ever mindful of his duty, Theuderis called his warriors to make for the realmgate to link with the Celestial Vindicators and other Knights Excelsior. Samat led the pursuit of the fleeing ratmen, but the craven creatures soon lost themselves in the mire of the undercity.

Theuderis looked down at the remains of Tyrathrax. There would be no miracle this time. The ease, the speed with which he had been ready to let her die nagged at him, as did his lack of emotion as the blood pooled amongst the decaying remnants of the verminlord. It was known that each Reforging affected a warrior profoundly – stripped away a layer of their humanity. Mortals were not meant to live forever and there was a price to pay for becoming a celestial being. The Reforging of Arkas had left him prone to the beast within.

As he turned away from the dissipating remains of his mount, Theuderis was not sure what he had become.

EPILOGUE

They found Arkas unconscious at the shrine gate after climbing and hauling their way through a veritable mountain of skaven dead. In his hand he still held an Ursungoran-style axe. The Warbeast woke as Theuderis rolled him onto his back. He reached up and removed his mask, sitting up to look around the cavern.

Snow was falling from the broken roof and he glanced up, surprised to see the clouds. Getting his bearings, he could see that the shrine hall was devoid of enemies. The only skaven left were the thousands of dead littering the ghetto of huts and hovels. Already teams of Knights Excelsior were heaping the verminous creatures onto pyres built from their polluted homes, the smoke thick and oily.

Warriors in white and blue were everywhere, though there was a knot of turquoise-armoured figures not far away. Theuderis extended a hand and Arkas allowed the other Lord-Celestant to help him to his feet.

'Ursungorod belongs to the Knights Excelsior,' he said. 'A well-earned victory.'

'Lord-Castellant Durathos,' said the Silverhand, indicating the officer behind him. 'He will be in charge of rebuilding the city here, and the garrison for the defence of the realmgate.'

'Take good care of these lands,' said Arkas. 'Its people bled to keep a part of it free long enough for us to save it.'

'I...' Theuderis shook his head and dropped his voice, perhaps concerned to speak in front of Durathos. 'I do not understand what happened.'

'Something from the World Before,' Arkas said quietly. 'Manifested in the sea of Ghurite energy we called the Shadowgulf. A demigod, perhaps, or a god of a dead people. Trapped, tortured by Chaos. The skaven burrowed through it, enslaved part of it for their diabolical ceremonies, used it to pollute the magic. It tried to break free once before – that is what caused the eruptions on Skagoldt Ridge on the day of my birth. It found me, has been calling to me all of my life, looking to share its pain.'

'It is gone now?'

'Mostly.' Arkas looked at the axe in his hand. 'I can feel a little part of it remaining.' He tapped his breastplate. 'In here, where it's always been. I can accept it now. The beast within me. The bear's anger.'

The Silverhand accepted this with a silent nod.

'What next? We await the command for the assault on the Lifegate?' As he asked, the thought twisted in Arkas' gut. Perhaps something of his reluctance showed on his face.

'You have another plan?' asked Theuderis.

'Many skaven escaped,' Arkas admitted. 'Their chief priest amongst them. My people are dead. Others will build a new civilisation here in time. I am the last. I would hunt down the creature that destroyed the Ursungorans. But, that is not the will of Sigmar. We have a higher calling, to free not just one people but all.'

'Sigmar is wiser than that,' said Theuderis. 'Some of us are constructors. Some of us... You are a conqueror. You are his Warbeast. He did not save you to raise castles and cities for him. He raised you to fight, to kill, to win. But, you do not need my permission, Arkas. You are Lord-Celestant of your Strike Chamber, commander of the Warbeasts. Your will is Sigmar's will. The God-King means for you to rid him of these filthy skaven.'

'Then with your leave, if not your permission,' said Arkas, 'I still have vengeance in my heart and the need to spill skaven blood. We each serve Sigmar in our own way.'

Arkas started down the causeway, but a call from Theuderis drew his attention back.

'Lord Arkas! Kill them where you can, righteous is your vengeance. But heed your oaths to the God-King. We have a staging ground to seize the Lifegate, and the other routes to the Allpoints will be secured by the endeavours of other Storm-hosts. When the call of the God-King comes, when we march on the Allpoints to destroy Archaon, be ready to answer.'

'I'm always ready, Lord Theuderis!' Arkas fitted his mask. 'For the glory of Sigmar!'

ABOUT THE AUTHOR

Gav Thorpe is the author of the Horus Heresy
novels *Deliverance Lost*, *Angels of Caliban* and
Corax, as well as the novella *The Lion*, which
formed part of the *New York Times* bestselling
collection *The Primarchs* and several audio dramas.
He is particularly well-known for his Dark Angels
stories, including Space Marine Legends novel
Azrael and the *Legacy of Caliban* series. His
Warhammer 40,000 repertoire further includes the
Path of the Eldar series, The Beast Arises novels
The Emperor Expects and *The Beast Must Die*, and
a multiplicity of short stories. For Warhammer,
Gav has penned the End Times novel *The Curse of
Khaine*, the Time of Legends trilogy, *The Sundering*,
and much more besides. He lives and works in
Nottingham.

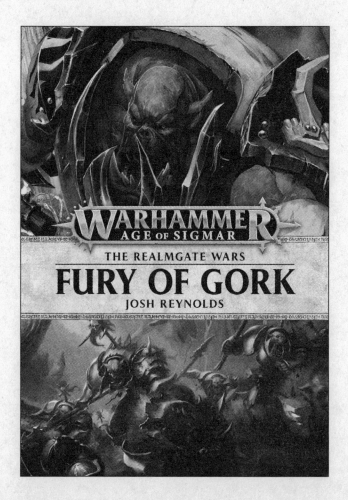

WARHAMMER

AGE OF SIGMAR

THE REALMGATE WARS

FURY OF GORK

JOSH REYNOLDS

An extract from

FURY OF GORK

By Josh Reynolds

The Black-Iron King roared hollowly and charged. The death-bringer's baroque, smoke-spewing armour creaked shrilly as he trampled over bloodreavers and the orruks they battled alike in his haste to reach his foe. The fiery maul he wielded tore flesh and crushed bone as he swept it out in a vicious arc to clear his path.

'Deliver thyself to me, beastling – I am thy doom, and the doom of all thy kind!' the Black-Iron King thundered, pulverising an orruk too slow to get out of his way. He had been shouting the same thing for hours, calling for Gordrakk. And, at last, Gordrakk, the Fist of Gork, had decided to oblige him.

After days of skirmishing, the orruks had cornered their foe in a narrow canyon made from the spread skeletal jaws of some long-dead monster. Now, the Five Fists of Gordrakk pummelled the Black-Iron Legion with a relentlessness that set even the most hardened worshippers of the Blood God back on their heels. Ardboys, led by brawling brutes, clashed with armoured reavers amid a forest of sun-bleached fangs. Their confrontation saw thick clouds of dust thrown into the air, blotting out the light of the amber suns far above.

The maw-krusha bounded forwards with a peculiar hopping gait, its scaly jaws wide. It was larger than anything else on the battlefield, save perhaps the Black-Iron King himself. The beast crashed down, flattening an unwary blood warrior beneath its bulk. Gordrakk thumped Chompa on the head with the haft of one of the axes he carried, eliciting a thunderous bellow. Those blood warriors closest to the maw-krusha died instantly, bones shattered and brains burst by the incoherent force of that furious sound. Those who survived, and made it past the maw-krusha's jaws and talons, leapt onto the creature, scrambling towards its rider.

Gordrakk laughed and stood up in his saddle. He clashed his axes together and tore them apart in a spray of sparks. Kunnin' hummed in his grip, whispering in one ear, while its twin, Smasha, bellowed in his other. Gordrakk's head was always filled with noise – just the way he liked it. Silence was boring. The axes had been silent until he had pulled them apart, making two weapons where there had once only been one. Two axes were better than one; this way he had one for each hand, and could crack twice as many skulls.

The boss-of-bosses whipped Kunnin' out in a shallow arc, cutting the legs out from under a blood warrior, even as he crumpled the chest-plate of another with Smasha. He blocked a blow from an enemy axe and gutted its wielder. He twisted, driving an armoured shoulder into an opponent's chest, and knocking him backwards off Chompa's skull. Before the warrior could rise, Chompa crushed him with a massive fist. Gordrakk thumped the beast with his foot.

'Oi, he was mine, ya greedy git. Get your own!'

Chompa roared in protest and swung its thick arms, slapping Bloodbound from their feet. Axes and heavy blades bounced off the monster's thick hide even as it smashed their wielders into paste. Gordrakk bellowed laughter and fell back into his saddle as Chompa surged instinctively forwards, carrying them towards the heart of the fray. Gordrakk had ridden many maw-krushas in his life, but only one equalled his sheer, unbridled lust for battle. He urged Chompa to greater speed, kicking its flanks.

The Black-Iron King held court at the centre of the narrow battlefield, surrounded by the broken bodies of brutes and ardboys. The Chaos-nob was tough, no two ways there. Gordrakk leaned forwards in his saddle, eager for the fight to come. At Chompa's roar, the smoke-wreathed shape of the deathbringer whirled about and extended his maul.

'Yes. Come to me, beastling. Come, Gordrakk, and meet your prophesied doom,' the Black-Iron King shouted. 'The All-slaughter has been drawn and the wings of death shadow you!'

Gordrakk blinked and glanced up, and saw carrion-birds circling overhead. He laughed. The Chaos-nobs always talked rubbish. They talked before they fought and while they fought – talk, talk, talk. Even so, Gordrakk couldn't help but feel a bit of pride. Everyone had heard of Gordrakk, the Fist of Gork. Even the iron-shod Chaos-things and the duardin in their deep-holds. It was good that they knew him and came looking for a scrap. It meant he always had a fight waiting, wherever he went, even if he didn't know where that was until he got there.

He urged Chompa forwards and roared, scattering his warriors. This was his fight and his alone; his boys knew better than to get between the Fist of Gork and his foe. For his part, the Black-Iron King seemed to welcome Gordrakk's charge.

He spread his long arms and set his feet. As Chompa drew near, the deathbringer took a two-handed grip on his maul and swung it out. The weapon slammed across Chompa's scaly jaw, staggering the beast.

Gordrakk growled and vaulted from the saddle as Chompa swayed drunkenly. He slid down the maw-krusha's snout and dropped to the ground, axes whistling out in opposite directions to drive the Black-Iron King back several steps.

'At last,' the deathbringer rumbled. 'The gods have spoken, brute, and your death shall be my stepping stone to–'

Gordrakk lunged, driving his skull against the ridged helm of his opponent. The deathbringer reeled with a metallic squawk. Gordrakk bulled into him, knocking him back.

'Talk or fight, not both,' he snarled as they broke apart.

'Ho, it speaks!' the Black-Iron King rasped. 'Good. You shall be able to beg for mercy.' He tromped forwards, joints creaking, vents hissing. The fiery maul looped out in a blow that would have removed Gordrakk's head, had he not swayed beneath it. Kunnin' whispered to him in Mork's voice, or maybe Gork's, calling his attention to his foe's armour. There – a chink in one of the joins.

Swiftly, Gordrakk whipped both axes up and around, slamming them into the weak spot as one. The Black-Iron King screamed and stiffened. Gordrakk tore Smasha free and drove it down again. Cracks formed, running along the seams of the daemon-armour. Wherever Smasha struck, even the strongest iron buckled. Foul gases and smoke spewed from the deathbringer's armour as he sank to one knee.

Weakly, desperately, he swung his maul, trying to drive Gordrakk back. 'Doom... I am your doom... It was written...' the Black-Iron King gasped in disbelief. Gordrakk laughed and hit him again. He used the edge of one axe to hook the head of his opponent's maul and tug it from his grip. The Black-Iron King lurched forwards, clawing for the weapon. 'Doom...' he wheezed.

'Shut it,' Gordrakk growled. He drove the other axe into the back of his foe's helmet. Hell-forged metal crumpled and split. Ichor spewed and a convulsion ran through the Black-Iron King's gigantic frame. Then, with a whine of abused metal, he toppled forwards and lay still. Gordrakk set his foot on the dead warrior's skull and lifted his axes. 'Gorka-MORKA!' he roared.

'GORKA-morka-GORKA-morka!' his warriors began to chant, stamping their feet and clashing their weapons, until the bones that rose up around them trembled. The remaining Chaos-things were fleeing now, scarpering back into the maze of bones. All the fight had been knocked out of them by the death of their chieftain.

Gordrakk spread his arms, soaking up the adulation of his boys. This was what it meant to be the boss-of-bosses. He was the best, the biggest, the baddest and the most blessed. Gorkamorka spoke to him, in his head, and punched him in the heart, filling him with divine fury. His fury was shared by the rest of the Ironjawz. The Big Waaagh! was coming. They could all feel it in their bones, rising up from the soles of their feet to the tops of their heads – it was like being hit by lightning all the time. Gordrakk threw back his head and roared wordlessly.

It didn't matter what their enemies did, how hard they fought or how well they hid – the Ironjawz always found them and gave them a beating. He lowered his arms, looked down at the trio of heads that dangled from his belt and gave them an affectionate thump. He knew all their names: Oleander Hume, the Knight of Silk; Poxfinger; Baron Slaughterthorn.

It was good to know the names of those you had beaten. That was the word of Gorkamorka, and it was good enough for Gordrakk.